DOUBLEDAY
CELEBRATES
100 YEARS OF
EXCELLENCE

annette meyers

doubleday

new york london toronto

sydney auckland

the groaning board

a smith and wetzon

mystery

PUBLISHED BY DOUBLEDAY
a division of Bantam Doubleday Dell Publishing Group, Inc.
1540 Broadway, New York, New York 10036

DOUBLEDAY and the portrayal of an anchor with a dolphin
are trademarks of Doubleday, a division of Bantam
Doubleday Dell Publishing Group, Inc.

book design by dana leigh treglia

Library of Congress Cataloging-in-Publication Data

Meyers, Annette.
The groaning board : a Smith and Wetzon mystery /
Annette Meyers. —1st ed.
I. Title.
PS3563.E889G76   1997
813′.54—dc20   96-29065
CIP
ISBN 0-385-47654-X
Copyright © 1997 by Annette Brafman Meyers

All Rights Reserved
Printed in the United States of America
June 1997
First Edition

1   3   5   7   9   10   8   6   4   2

My thanks to Dr. Mike Ellis, Southeast Texas Poison Control Center, to Dr. Rolando Diaz, New Jersey Poison Information and Education System, and especially to Dr. Marina Stajic, Director of Forensic Toxicology, New York City Medical Examiner's Office, and Dr. Wendy Gunther, Assistant Medical Examiner, Shelby County, Tennessee, Medical Examiner's Office, and to Dr. Michael Levy, Clinical Assistant Professor, Cardiothoracic Surgery, State University of New York at Stony Brook. Thanks as well to Judy Kern at Doubleday and Kate Miciak at Bantam, and to my agent, Chris Tomasino.

The New York Public Library and the New York Botanical Garden information services provided delicious and intriguing data.

And, as always, to Marty.

For Linda Ray,
who makes food, finance,
and friendship an art

Ye Tables groan before ye Feaste
Ye Feasters groan thereafter.

—*A True Bill Agaynst*
Christmass

The chimneys blaze, the tables groan.

—*Oxford Sausage, 1764*

I'm an entrepreneur. Without people like me there would be no technological revolution, no innovation, no strong economic growth.

—*Hemingway Barron*
President, Barron Venture
Capital

the groaning board

c h a p t e r   1

The Fourth of July

"Damnation, Smith, look at that!" Wetzon said as a bouquet of chrysanthemums exploded and streaked across the sky. "We're missing the fireworks."

"I don't know why you're always in such a rush." Smith shifted down and pulled the Jaguar into a parking place on Liberty Street. She was in her most maddening mode: running on her own personal timetable.

Whistle, pop, pop, pop, whistle. Red, white, and blue colors burst, forming a huge American flag. Held a moment, then melted into a brilliant arc.

The boat basin off the World Financial Center, with its variety of crafts, could have been a painted set, except that tonight almost every boat was a party. Glasses clinked, voices, mellow with wine and summer and holiday, rose and fell.

"Which one is it?" Smith demanded.

"Let's see, Laura Lee said the boat sleeps six and is called *Bread Pudding*. Straight down, first right, boat's on the left." Wetzon, following the directions, called, "Down here, Smith."

"Hi, there," someone cried as another and another arrangement lit up the sky. Baby's breath, on fire.

"Hi, yourself," Wetzon responded, then looked back for her lagging partner, who *would* insist on wearing high heels. As if she needed the height. "Here we are, Smith." The *Bread Pudding* was like the other boats, full of people on deck, conversation flowing like the rippling water in New York Bay.

"Well, really," Smith said suddenly, outraged. She'd come up behind Wetzon, breathing disdain.

"Now what?"

"Would *you* take a swim in the Hudson?"

"What are you talking about? I'm not interested in swimming. Let's go." Wetzon raised her voice. "Hello, *Bread Pudding!*"

"*Bread Pudding!*" A woman's voice. "Do you believe it? Why not *Crème Brûlée?*" The boats rocked gently against their moorings and the dock, with soft, sweet *chungs*.

Why indeed not, Wetzon thought, much preferring the latter to the former.

"Look at her if you don't believe me," Smith was insisting. "Get out of there! You'll get all kinds of diseases." Smith leaned over, yelling down at the water.

She's taken leave of her senses at long last, Wetzon was certain, as she peered over Smith's shoulder. What she saw made her jerk back, almost losing her balance. Good God, there really was someone in the water—a woman, in fact. She wore a long white dress and was wrapped in garlands of flowers.

"Oh, poor Ophelia," Wetzon murmured.

The woman wasn't swimming; she was floating facedown in the murky water.

And then the entire sky erupted, showering multicolored stars down on them.

chapter 2

Three Months Earlier

Micklynn Devora handled the knife deftly, perhaps a little too deftly. She slipped it into the flesh and with a small, vicious twist, removed it. That she was angry was obvious. With an inelegant hand, she reached for the glass of chardonnay from which she'd been taking steady sips. The glass was empty when she set it down and turned back to her work.

She inserted the sliver of garlic and half a pitted niçoise olive into the slit the knife had fashioned. The perfume of the room—if one thought garlic was a perfume, and Leslie Wetzon certainly did—was Garden of Sensual Delights.

"The cranberries give it a rather sour flavor," Smith said. "What do you think, sweetie pie?" Her voice wore a glaze of silkiness that didn't quite cover that characteristic edge of impatience. Small tasting plates of food were arrayed in front of her on a rustic antique table.

Think? Wetzon ground her teeth as she moved back to the table. "I think," Wetzon said, "if you don't decide on your menu in the next ten minutes, I'm going to start screaming." There was no silkiness whatever in her tone.

They'd been in the splendid kitchen of The Groaning Board, the catering and gourmet food shop of the moment, since three o'clock—well over two hours on a lovely April afternoon—sampling food while the usually decisive Smith tried to make up her mind. And it was infuriating that she seemed oblivious to the staticky tension in the room, punctuated by the constant bleating of the telephone, which rang in the kitchen but was being answered in the shop.

A. T. Barron, Micklynn Devora's partner in The Groaning Board, had set up an array of main courses for them to sample. All veal. Smith had insisted on veal. There was a chop in a lemon caper sauce, to which Wetzon had been partial although she was not particularly fond of veal. The scallops with shiitake mushrooms in a light cream sauce was too rich; besides, veal scallops bored her. And then there was the roast.

"A.T., sugar." Smith moaned dramatically, hand to brow. "Help me out here."

"Go with the roast," A.T. said. "You can't go wrong." Her hair was medium brown with sun streaks of blond. Long and frizzy, it curled like an unruly hedge around her angular face. Her eyes were set close together over an emphatic nose. When she smiled, her thin lips revealed a not unattractive overbite. When she didn't, the whole effect was rodenty. Her face was devoid of makeup, perhaps the only holdover from her undergraduate days at Bennington in the sixties. A.T. was a couple of inches taller than Wetzon, but nowhere near Smith's height. Thin and hyper, she wore loosely pleated Armani trousers, a black tee shirt, and a casually cut jacket. You couldn't miss the look. Nor could you miss that it was spotless. Wetzon wondered if A.T.'d ever actually stirred a pot or caught any remnant of food under her dark dagger fingernails. It didn't seem so. "You know," A.T. continued, "it's so simple and classic. We did it for the Perelmans, and the Weills were there and they called us . . ."

She went on and on until Smith finally said, "Well, I don't know." Smith stared hard at Wetzon, who shrugged.

It appeared that A.T.'s approach to sales was: talk your client to death. She didn't seem able to steer the pitch to a close. Ask for the fucking ticket already, Wetzon thought. A.T. would never have made it on Wall Street.

"We'll give you tiny russet potatoes in butter and chives and white asparagus. We just did—"

"We'll do a rice mold with a mix of wild mushrooms." Micklynn, terse and almost condescending, overrode her partner. She was rinsing anchovy fillets under cold water, pressing them onto paper towels. She did not look at A.T., and the stiff set of her shoulders seemed ominous, relating, it appeared, to something Smith and Wetzon had interrupted over two hours earlier.

"Mick—" The skin around A.T.'s lips crinkled white. She was furious.

"Sounds good to me," Wetzon said quickly.

A. T. Barron's "Marvelous" came after a hesitation that lasted less than a mini-second. The pause would probably have gone by unnoticed, but Leslie Wetzon's partnership with the formidable Xenia Smith was not an easy one, and Wetzon was certainly more sensitive to the nuances in similar relationships than most.

Whatever was going on, Wetzon had picked up the vibes the instant they'd entered the kitchen from the bustling storefront room with its clusters of hanging garlic heads, drying herbs, baskets of breads, and jars of richly colored preserves and sauces.

The Groaning Board occupied the ground floor of Micklynn Devora's three-story brick carriage house. At Eighty-first Street just off Second Avenue, the building was on a block of similar houses that in the early nineteenth century had garaged the trappings of the wealthy, who usually lived a street below in magnificent town houses.

The extra-wide doors had been replaced with a picture window through which could be seen the warmly inviting shop, its crowded marble countertops surrounded by old wooden cupboards. Two normal-sized doors, one opening into the shop and the other leading to the duplex above, flanked the window.

The Groaning Board was "definitely the sexiest food shop in New York," according to Gael Greene in *New York* magazine. And the *New York Times* critic, who didn't review food shops as a rule, was rumored to have spent a tasty afternoon with Devora and Barron. In a market survey the critic pronounced them, their kitchen, and what it produced "seductive" and "delightful."

Through an arrangement with one of their suppliers four years earlier, the two proprietors had begun to package, manufacture, and sell their products in supermarkets and specialty shops under The Groaning Board label to enormous success. Demand for their flavored vinegars and olive oils, the raspberry confit, the lemon curd, muffins, macaroons, and rugalach was almost overwhelming. Addicted displaced New Yorkers, particularly those who had moved to LA, had their orders FedEx'd.

Behind the center counter of the shop was a doorway meant to be concealed by a drapery, but not hidden at all because traffic through it was constant. Everyone, it seemed, wanted to make personal contact with Micklynn, whose genius was in the original preparation. A.T., who had at one time managed a food shop at Bloomingdale's, handled the business, the sales and marketing, as well as (A.T. herself often said) some of the cooking—"just a few special things."

When Xenia Smith and Leslie Wetzon arrived that afternoon, A.T. had been summoned. She'd appeared after a short delay, slightly disheveled, her hair, which obviously had started the day pinned up, standing out from her head in great kinky gobs. Flinging back the curtain, A.T. had ushered them into a huge country kitchen infused with the scents of lemon and sugar and melted butter. Impressions of chocolate hovered, beguiling, in the air while the Grateful Dead sang the subtext.

And then there was the odoriferous garlic that underscored the entire opus.

Doubles of everything lined the walls: sinks, dishwashers, food mixers and processors, stoves, refrigerators, freezers, ovens.

Micklynn, in a long, loose dress and cross-training shoes, was kneading dough on a wooden board, up to her unfettered bosom in flour and bits of dough. Her arms were fleshy and muscular, and she seemed to be handling the dough like an attack dog with an intruder's coat in his jaws.

"You know Micklynn, of course."

"Of course," Smith had replied. "This is my partner, Leslie Wetzon."

Micklynn gave a half turn and nodded.

"And this is Minnie Wu."

How odd, Wetzon thought. She hadn't noticed the other woman until Minnie moved away from the table on which rested a harvest of red, yellow, and green peppers, white and purple eggplants, and vases of deep green basil. Minnie was wearing camouflage of like colors that had made her virtually disappear.

Minnie Wu was Chinese, a short, thick-waisted woman in pants and a shapeless overshirt. She fairly oozed hostility.

"I'll be back in an hour," she'd said, not acknowledging the introduction. "My camera and sound people will be along sooner, so let's not have these . . ." She shrugged a rounded shoulder at Smith and Wetzon.

A.T.'s smile was a twitch. "Minnie, I think our clients would like—wouldn't it be nice to see us interacting . . . ?" To Smith and Wetzon she said, "We're doing some TV promotion for our cooking show."

Flicking her eyes back over Smith, then Wetzon, then back to Smith, Minnie pronounced, "Too old."

Wetzon's cough barely covered the laugh that burbled in her throat. Someone was making a choking noise. She sneaked a look at Smith. Smith's mouth was hanging open.

The choking noise came from Micklynn as she slid the veal roast into the nearest oven. She caught Wetzon's eye for a moment, then slammed the oven door.

"Minnie, really—" A.T. began.

"Maybe we should leave *now*," Smith had said, seething.

"No, no, please," A.T. pleaded. "Minnie doesn't mean—"

Minnie shifted the curtain and stepped into the shop, calling back, "I mean it. Get rid of them."

chapter 3

"Coffee? Wine?" A.T.'d begun to flutter, moving back and forth, picking up mugs, glasses. "I am so sorry. It's one of those things . . . you know how it is, I'm sure—"

"That's the rudest whi—woman I have ever met."

"Decaf," Wetzon said. A.T.'s penchant for rambling overexplanation was setting her teeth on edge. The atmosphere in the otherwise pleasant room was making her itch. And Smith had been about to say "white woman" when she realized that Minnie Wu was Chinese.

"Wine," Smith said. *"White."*

There. She'd gotten it out. "Nice, Smith." Wetzon couldn't smother her laugh and got an outraged glare from her partner.

"Open another bottle," Micklynn said.

A.T. took a bottle of Chappellet pinot blanc from one of the huge refrigerators, peeled away the jacket, and plunged a corkscrew into the cork, folding the wings back. The cork gave an infinitesimal sigh as it left the bottle. A.T. poured a glass for Smith, then replenished Micklynn's.

The bottle was empty and another opened by the time Smith made her choice of main course, picking her way through the dense descriptions A.T. attached to everything. Wetzon was beginning to contemplate a switch away from coffee, and decided not for the first time that Xenia Smith would drive a teetotaler to drink.

"Now that we've settled on the main course, the rest should be easy," A.T. said. Without Wetzon's having to ask, she brought her a glass and one for herself. Now they were all drinking wine. Smith had driven them bonkers. Take Smith, fold in A.T., salt with Minnie Wu, Wetzon thought. Recipe for hives.

A camera crew of two women in combat boots and one man with dangling earrings had arrived with a mass of cameras and equipment. They dropped everything in the middle of the room and went out for a smoke and to wait for Minnie. Minnie was late.

The sort-of country French table Smith, Wetzon, and A.T. were sitting around was as big as a bed. It was piled with platters, earthenware pots, and bell jars of every size, filled with every variety of beans, couscous, and rice, and mysterious pickled things.

Smith said, "What about a pâté for a first course?"

"I think perhaps a pumpkin risotto . . . or"—A.T. pursed her thin lips—"a chicken liver pâté with cilantro would be lovely." Detaching the pencil from her hair where she'd parked it earlier, she touched the lead point to her tongue.

"Absolutely not," Micklynn said. She'd divided her dough among three bowls and set them aside. Now she came over to the table, wiping her hands on her voluminous apron, scattering flour and dry flakes of pastry like confetti.

"Really? And what would you suggest?" A.T.'s tone would have made a polar bear shiver.

"A vegetable terrine. Several. We could use beets, white beans, black beans, and leeks. It's much lighter and will complement the veal roast."

"I'm not wild about beets. Stains everything bloody," Smith said.

"Then eggplant. It's the color more than anything. Will you be wanting a soup course?"

Smith frowned. She looked at Wetzon.

"I can just see me standing around with a cup of hot soup in my hand getting jostled by tall people," Wetzon said. "Your carpet will never be the same."

"It's going to be sit-down," Smith said.

"You'll have an unforgettable chorus of slurpers."

"No soup," Smith said.

A loud thump came from above them. They all looked upward.

"Having some work done upstairs," A.T. explained hastily. "Workmen are so careless . . . they drop things, you know. It's so hard to find a contractor—"

"Isn't Ellen out front?" Micklynn said, severing A.T.'s babble. Without waiting for an answer, she swept back the drapery separating kitchen from shop, only to be greeted by delighted shoppers. Her response was a distracted "Hello. Yes. So nice to see you. Try the quail salad. I'm sure you'll like it. Excuse me. Tom, I thought Ellen was here with you."

An exaggeratedly female/male voice responded, "She went upstairs to study. Said she'd be back."

". . . mesclun with a raspberry vinaigrette," A.T. was saying.

"Fine," Smith said. "Now for dessert."

Wetzon watched her partner for some reaction to what was happening around them unrelated to the menu for Smith's dinner party. It was amazing that Smith didn't seem to have absorbed any of it.

"She's upstairs with him," Micklynn cried in an anguished voice. She began wringing her hands obsessively, wandering one way a few steps, then another.

"Excuse me a moment." A.T. jumped to her feet. "Mickey is letting everything get to her today." She caught hold of Micklynn. "Come on now. Ellen's a good girl. You know that."

"I don't know that at all. I told her she wasn't to have him in the apartment."

Wetzon, the voyeur, was jolted from her rapt attention to the scene by a swift, sharp kick. Elaborately, Smith handed her a printed list of desserts. Wetzon had been wrong; Smith was as fascinated as she was by the combustion.

"Come on, Mickey. Ellen's an A student, she's not into grunge, she helps us out after school. Lighten up."

"You're buying into her fiction," Micklynn said hotly. She twisted from A.T.'s grasp and flung her long braid behind her, scattering flour, and disappeared up a flight of stairs Wetzon hadn't noticed because it was half hidden by lush hanging plants.

A.T. cast a worried look after her partner, then came back to the table, where Smith and Wetzon were pretending to be absorbed in the dessert menu.

"Nothing serious, I hope," Smith said.

"No. Not really. We made an important business decision today, and of course she's worried about Ellen."

"Well, I can certainly understand a parent's problems in dealing with adolescent behavior," Smith said. "My boy came through it, and while it wasn't easy, I was able to bend with all the changes. He came back to himself and now he's finishing his first year at Harvard."

Wetzon rolled her eyes. Who was Smith kidding with all that bullshit? In her dreams was she able to bend with all the changes. Smith's son, Mark, had concluded his otherwise uneventful adolescence by coming out, revealing he was gay. The resulting trauma had been Smith's.

"Ellen is a wonderful girl," A.T. said. "You might have seen her when you came in. She's lovely, smart, and quite mature for her age."

"Which is—?" Wetzon asked.

"Sixteen."

"I would have liked to have a daughter," Smith said with an ostentatious sigh.

Sure, Wetzon thought. The competition would have made semipro.

"So would I," A.T. said. "But Ellen's not Mickey's daughter. She's a relative of Mickey's first husband. Mickey took Ellen in two years ago after Ellen's mother died in an accident."

A volcano of sound erupted above them.

A.T. raised her voice over the commotion. "I'd suggest a hazelnut torte with a lemon cream filling. We're talking forty people?"

"Yes."

"Four tortes will be more than enough. And two big bowls of strawberries and a bowl of crème fraîche."

"What do you think, Wetzon?"

"Personally, I prefer rice pudding."

"Oh, hush. You and your rice pudding. We'll go with the hazelnut tortes, A.T. And I'd like Eli Zabar's skinny bread, if you don't mind. Um . . . have we left anything out?" Now they were all talking louder to be heard over the shouting.

"I don't think so, but we have plenty of time in case there's anything you want to add." A.T. rose and took a large white envelope from a drawer in one of the buffets. "Our press kit includes a copy of our standard contract. I'll have one drawn up with the menu we discussed."

The noise above them stopped abruptly. Footsteps thundered down the stairs; a door slammed. No one came through the kitchen, Wetzon observed regretfully.

Envelope in hand, Smith contemplated her tiny bag, as if willing the envelope smaller. Finally, seeing magic was not forthcoming, she thrust the envelope at Wetzon. "Here," she said, "you can put this in your briefcase and give it to me tomorrow."

"Thanks a lot." Wetzon stuffed the envelope into her briefcase.

"Do you want to stop somewhere for a drink?" Smith asked halfheartedly.

"No, I've had enough. I'm going to walk it off through the park."

Minnie Wu was coming in with her crew as Wetzon followed Smith through the shop—where end-of-the-day shoppers were lined up out to the street. Outside the carriage house, a young girl with straight blond hair, parted in the middle, was sitting on a fat, old-fashioned leather valise. Her pretty face was stoic as tears streamed down her cheeks.

"Oh, my," Smith said. "You poor child."

"Do you need help?" Wetzon asked.

The girl turned exquisite green eyes from Smith to Wetzon, but before she could speak, A. T. Barron rushed out of the shop and clutched the girl to her bosom. "Now don't you worry about anything," she said. "You'll always have a home with me."

"She hates me," the girl said. "She'll make you suffer if you take me in to live with you."

"No one," A.T. said in a voice that gave Wetzon the creeps, "no one makes me suffer."

chapter 4

It had started, inauspiciously enough, with a veal roast. And most of the cast of characters had made their appearance by the time Smith and Wetzon left The Groaning Board late that April afternoon and parted on Second Avenue. But neither of them knew this.

And neither had any inkling that one—Micklynn, A.T., Minnie, or Ellen—would end up doing the dead man's float in the section of the Hudson River known as New York Bay.

When they arrived at Smith's apartment building on Seventy-seventh Street between Second and Third, Smith said, "What route are you taking home, sweetie pie?"

"Why do you want to know? Oh, my, be still my heart. You're thinking of putting on your running shoes and joining me." That'll be the day, Wetzon thought. Smith didn't believe in exercise, ate whatever she liked, and still maintained her slim, svelte figure. It was loathsome.

"Are you mad?" Smith said.

"Oh, totally."

"So how are you walking?"

Wetzon sighed. "I don't know. Probably past the Shakespeare theater. Why?"

"Why? I can't believe you're asking me that. The Park is so dangerous. What if you disappeared on your way to the West Side?"

"Oh, pu-leeze," Wetzon said.

It was still light and the air along Fifth Avenue emanating from the depths of the Park was fragrant with the scent of dogwood. The magnolia buds were swelling; clumps of forsythia streaked the landscape with gold and the lilacs were just starting to bloom. In the spring Central Park dressed to kill.

All of which in a few short days would lead to itchy, runny eyes and sneezing. But match allergies against spring in New York . . . no contest.

On the splendid steps of the Metropolitan Museum, crowds of young—and not so young—people sat, ate, talked, read, waited for dates, friends, or just basked in the warm sunlight.

Taking the path behind the museum, Wetzon turned into the Park and headed downslope, veering to the left and then circling the ball fields. Amateur teams from assorted leagues were playing, and the smack of bat hitting ball seemed the perfect invitation to spring in the City.

Babes were all sitting in their high chairs by this time and those ubiquitous foldaway strollers were conspicuously absent; the Park belonged to the joggers, cyclists, and roller-bladers, and those like Wetzon who walked through Central Park on the way home, pretending it was exercise when it was really balm for the soul.

New York women were exercise-obsessed. Thin wasn't enough; thin and muscular was it. Which is why fitness shoes over white socks over panty hose was de rigueur. Olive Oyl feet all over town. Oh, yes.

Wetzon wasn't in her Reeboks today, and although she wore only one-inch heels, her feet began to protest. It was a legacy from her years as a dancer. Dancers, present and past, ex and otherwise, always had a host of foot problems.

When she came to the Delacorte Theater, where free Shakespeare was performed all summer, every summer, thanks to the late Joe Papp's obstinate lobbying, she sat on a park bench. Slipping off her shoes to massage her feet, she thought about the afternoon.

What was there about Smith that attracted her to crazy people—and vice versa? Like those bacteria that are scattered over an oil spill. Wetzon had felt it the minute they'd walked into The Groaning Board. Gregory, who seemed to be in charge of the shop, was flyaway gay, with his touch of pink lipstick, blue eye shadow, and false eyelashes. He had "the voice-gene," as her friend Carlos would say. The other person behind the counter when she and Smith had arrived had been pretty little Ellen, the girl on the suitcase.

"Crazies," Wetzon said aloud, slipping her feet into her shoes, letting a man in an automated wheelchair whir past her before she got up.

He was talking on a cellular phone. "The Pacific Rim," he said. "Emerging . . . there are several that meet my criteria." From a wheelchair, no less, and in the middle of Central Park.

As she walked westward again, Wetzon's mind moved to the search she and Smith were doing for Bernard's Bank. A multilingual individual with a private banking background as well as some retail sales from the brokerage side to cover Latin America. Specifically Brazil and Argentina. The bank wanted the person to work from New York. She actually had found four people who fit the specs, but all were in Miami and refused to come back to New York. Getting to Latin America from Miami made for an easier lifestyle.

Dusk was settling over the Park now. Wetzon switched her heavy bag to her other shoulder and began to fast-walk. It was then she noticed that someone was keeping pace with her.

Don't make eye contact, she warned herself, wishing her heels would sprout wings.

Still, there were plenty of people about—the dog walkers and joggers—so not to worry. Then the person spoke.

"Leslie Wetzon," he said.

She stopped and looked at him. He wore running shoes, shorts, and a clean white V-necked tee, from which white chest hairs protruded.

"I thought it was you," he said.

"Have you been following me?"

Bill Veeder laughed, and the lines around his eyes creased and multiplied. That might have made him ugly, or even frightening, but it did not. In laughter, his features softened, became more youthful. Yet every-thing about him was cold. Blue eyes like a winter sky. Hair almost white. Tall, with the lean, hard body of a runner. "I suppose you might say that," he said. "I'd just done my six miles when I spotted you near the Delacorte and backtracked. I've been meaning to call you."

"Me? Why?"

Bill Veeder had been Richard Hartmann's law partner. Hartmann, the Mafia lawyer and Smith's late great lover, had been assassinated by the very people he represented when it became known he was naming names. Whether Veeder was dirty too, Wetzon didn't know and didn't much care, though there was no denying he was a very attractive man.

"I thought we'd have dinner one night and discuss it," he said.

"Discuss what?"

"A business proposition. I understand the Wall Street headhunting business has slowed down considerably."

A little warning bell pinged in Wetzon's brain. Now who could possi-bly have told him that? Smith, of course. She had undoubtedly kept in touch after Hartmann's murder.

"Oh? A business proposition, huh?" Wetzon dug into her briefcase for her card, found it, and held it out to him.

"No need." Veeder didn't take the card. "I know where to find you." He gave her a meaningful look, the essence of which she didn't under-stand, then turned and jogged off.

Wetzon watched him for a minute, trying to shake off his presence, before she continued her walk. She hated the way he made her feel. Her sometime lover, NYPD Detective Silvestri, was full-time these days, and she was happy.

Then why was she attracted to Bill Veeder?

Because he was dangerous, she told herself. No question about it. Could she have a flirtation with him and emerge unscathed? Never.

She left the Park near the Museum of Natural History and walked uptown. What was she thinking of? It was a perfectly innocent encoun-ter, at the end of—what had he said? A six-mile run. He wanted to talk business.

Right.

Right, a little snide voice nudged her. An innocent encounter, nothing else, after a six-mile run. And not a drop of sweat on him.

chapter 5

Carlos was pissed. He was pacing Wetzon's living room, seething, while Izz, Wetzon's Maltese, sat on the sofa turning her head back and forth, watching him as if he were a tennis match.

"Birdie," Carlos said, "I swear to God I will kill Mort Hornberg before I check out." Anger made the skin around his dark eyes taut. Even the diamond stud in his left earlobe glowered.

"Oh, were you thinking of leaving any time soon?" Wetzon asked. She handed him a beer. He had burst in on her ten minutes earlier and had yet to tell her why he was so upset.

"Yeah, well, foolish me, I thought I was doing the movie of *Hotshot,* but our friend Mort aced me out."

"The shit. I'm sorry. Didn't you have doing the movie in your contract?"

"If you remember, Mort and I shared the same agent at the time. Joel said he couldn't get it in writing for me, but Mort agreed to give me first refusal."

"On Wall Street these days verbal agreements aren't worth the breath it takes to make a promise. It's everybody out for himself and protecting his ass. Oops, that sounds just like Broadway."

Carlos shook his finger at Wetzon. "Now, Birdie, there are still some of us around the theatre who keep our word."

"And then there's Mort Hornberg."

"Didn't want to share billing. That's what it's about. My reviews were too good. They hired someone named Orson Tree."

"Orson Tree? Never heard of him. Are you sure he's a choreographer?"

"The only thing I'm sure about is that this Tree person has become Poppy Hornberg's new best friend."

"Ah. Explains all."

"Yeah." Carlos plopped down on the sofa next to Izz, who climbed into his lap and smothered him with kisses. "I really wanted this, Birdie."

"I know. It's despicable of Mort. You will never work with him again."

"Birdie . . ." He slitted his eyes at her and cocked his head.

"But you will."

"Birdie!"

"Because all you theatre people are such whores."

"Ouch," Carlos groaned. "But for the love of the work, Dear Heart, for stardom. Not for money, like you Wall Street types. Cheers." He raised the beer bottle to her and she raised hers to him. They both drank. "Where's your copper tonight?" Carlos asked.

"On a case."

"We have tickets for the Joyce. Mark Morris. I can try to get another seat."

Wetzon shook her head. "I've been up since six, had a breakfast at seven, a meeting at eight, then spent the afternoon with Smith at The Groaning Board. I'd konk out the minute they lowered the houselights."

"The Groaning Board? The Barracuda is having a catered affair?" Carlos said, using the name he'd bestowed on Smith from the day he'd first met her.

"She is indeed."

"What did you think of the Tempest and the Teapot, as Devora and

Barron are known in the trade? Tell the truth now." He shook a slim finger at her.

"You know them," she accused.

"Birdie, darling, everybody in New York knows everybody else. Besides, there are only seven people in the whole world. It's John Guare's six degrees of separation," he added smugly. "I know Mickey Devora because she used to live down the hall from Arthur. We were her unofficial tasters. I lost five pounds after she bought that carriage house and moved out. And . . ." He paused dramatically.

"And what?"

"And I went to Bennington with the Teapot, the impossible Alice."

"Alice? Is that what the A stands for? What about the T?"

Carlos grinned. "Toklas."

"You're kidding. No wonder she calls herself A.T."

"Well, if she called herself A.B.T., she'd have to share it with the American Ballet Theatre." He'd come out of his funk. "The formidable Barron *père* met Gertrude and Alice in Paris after the Liberation. Have you met Hem?"

"No. Who's Hem?"

"Hemingway Barron, the brother."

"The financier?"

"The very one."

"Well, now that's interesting. So *père* and *mère* Barron were bohemian expatriates."

"Actually, *père* was the original authoritarian personality, convinced most women were weak-brained, except for the lesbians. He did admire those girls. But the Barrons were money, honey. When the old folks died, they left a ton of it. Half was split between Hem and Alice, a quarter went to a family foundation, and the other quarter is in trust for their heirs."

"Of which there are?"

"None. Minnie and Hem have been trying for years. In vitro and all that."

"Minnie? Wait a minute. Don't tell me that Minnie Wu is married to Hem Barron!"

"I won't tell you, then."

"Christ, Carlos, that Minnie is a nasty bitch."

"I see you've met our Min."

"Met everyone except Hem."

"You're in for a treat."

"No way, José, am I ever going to have any more to do with that repulsive group," Wetzon declared.

Which goes to show that nothing is certain in this world and which immediately cleared the way for the gods to meddle in her life, for Wetzon of all people should have known that one should never say *never*.

After Carlos left, Wetzon fed Izz, then lounged in her tub for a half hour. Then, in her sweats, her hair unbound, she reveled in being alone.

She wasn't really hungry, but she had the nibbles, a chronic condition that could only be soothed by chocolate. She brewed Starbucks decaf roast and broke off a chunk of dark chocolate from a larger brick. With mug and chocolate, she curled up on the sofa next to the drowsing dog.

Damn. She hadn't unloaded her briefcase. She got up and brought the case back to the sofa. That effort called for a large bite of chocolate.

She went through her papers. Nothing major to deal with. It could all wait till the morrow.

Everything went back into the briefcase except the white envelope with the press kit and sample contract that A.T. had given Smith. It was awfully thick. She turned it over in her hand. Was there any reason she shouldn't look at it? No, of course not. But why would she want to bother?

"Idle nosiness, that's all," she told Izz, who gave her a magnificent yawn. Wetzon opened the clasp and removed the papers.

What she found was not p.r. material, nor was it a contract for a catered affair. She read the first page. She had seen these things often enough. The pages were a preliminary prospectus for an IPO, an initial public offering for a company in the process of going public. The left border of its cover was printed in red ink, which gave an offering of this kind its name in Wall Street jargon: a red herring. The red ink served as a warning to would-be investors that the prospectus did not contain all the pertinent information about the offering and some information contained within might change when the final prospectus was ready. CONFIDENTIAL was stamped in red across the cover.

The company was The Groaning Board.

She turned the page. Under a paper clip marking the second page was a folded sheet of notes. The writing was in a hand she recognized. When she unfolded the notes, the notepaper bore the name of a money manager: Wetzon's friend Laura Lee Day.

chapter 6

"Did you hear the news?" Darlene said, for the second time. The mask over her nose and mouth and the screeching of an electric drill made it hard to understand her.

The skeletal slats of the new staircase led up to nowhere, it seemed at the moment. Eventually it would lead to the parlor floor of their brownstone on East Forty-ninth Street. Wetzon stood on the third slat and surveyed the rubble. Her black patent Ferragamos wore a bridal veil of plaster dust.

Smith had gotten her wish. Adding Darlene Ford to their staff had proven a windfall of monumental proportions. An architect had arrived while Wetzon was still saying, "Don't you think we ought to wait and see what the climate on the Street will be?"

"Really, sweetie pie," Smith had said as if she were talking to a simpleton. "It doesn't matter what the climate on the Street is. We can write off expanding the office, and we'll have added value to our property."

She was probably right. Immediately after they'd formed their company, they'd rented the ground floor of the brownstone. When the original owner put the building on the market during the recession three years before, they'd bought it at a bargain price. At the time, real estate in the City was at its lowest. And not long after, as it always did, it had come roaring back.

Ruth Abramson, their accountant, had agreed with Smith. So here they were in the throes of a massive renovation.

Wetzon had insisted on using her friend Louise Armstrong to do the construction, only to find that Louie, an artist who supported herself through contracting jobs, was in the midst of preparing for her first gallery exhibition. Smith had found Noonan Brothers, and Noonan Brothers, three of them, had filed renovation plans with the City, come in and broken through the floor with only minor damage to a riser, built the frame of the staircase, then departed to do another job. At least that's what Wetzon thought, because they only returned every three or four days to do one day's work. Undoubtedly somewhere else in the City another client of Noonan Brothers was grinding his teeth as Wetzon was.

Wetzon looked down at their associate with mixed feelings. In addition to the surgical mask, Darlene wore a green surgeon's scrub over her dress and a clear plastic shower cap over thick blond hair. The look, whatever she'd intended, was not Darlene Ford, surgeon, but Darlene Ford, bag lady.

Darlene's arrival last fall had been serendipitous. Smith had stolen her away from Tom Keegen, their major and most virulent competitor in headhunting stockbrokers on Wall Street.

Business had been in the doldrums, as client after client merged themselves out of existence. There was no question, odd as she was, that Darlene had a gift. She could talk the most reluctant broker into meeting with another firm. And a first meeting was like kicking the tires; once you kicked the tires, you were halfway to buying the car, or in this case, making a move to another firm. "Our chubby little diamond mine," Smith called her, but never to her face. Smith had been jubilant, but

Wetzon had rather liked the intimacy of their neat little firm. Darlene had changed the vibes, that was for sure.

"I said, did you hear the news?" Darlene said again, a soupçon of irritation in her tone.

"What news?" Attitude was always just below the surface with Darlene. Nothing you could put your finger on, just a scent of something else, which Darlene—so far—was sensational at covering up.

"Watch it! Watch it!" The whine of the drill ceased; a thundering crash followed, then the brutal sound of metal meeting metal. Plaster dust showered down on them.

Wetzon looked at her suit. It had been a medium gray pinstripe when she'd put in on that morning. Cupping her hand around her mouth, she called, "Everyone all right up there?"

"Shit!" someone said. "Whaddayacrazy or somethin', Herbie?"

Wetzon came back down the stairs, dusting herself off. "Somebody is crazy or something," she muttered. She picked her way across the plastic-drop-cloths toward her desk, then lifted the dusty plastic that covered her datebook and suspect sheets. Debris slid to the floor, only to be lost among other debris already there. She should have played hooky today, like Smith. But she had the not so ridiculous feeling that if she didn't show, neither would the workmen. Perhaps by showing up every day and letting them see her, she could make it happen faster. Sure, Wetzon, think again.

"Are you ready for this?" Darlene asked.

"Shoot it to me, Darlene," Wetzon said.

"Loeb Dawkins took Abe Gershman off the hoot and holler because he sounded too Jewish."

Abe Gershman was the national sales manager of Loeb Dawkins. It was Gershman's job to conduct the sales meetings from New York that were piped across the country into every branch office on what was affectionately known as "the hoot and holler."

The national sales manager at a brokerage firm played the role of super-coach, telling brokers what the firm wanted them to push, to buy and sell.

"Too Jewish?" Wetzon said. "Too New York, obviously."

"He sounded like a garmento," Darlene said. "I guess it doesn't play well in Dubuque."

"I guess it doesn't play well with all those Waspy types in the offices of

Mather & Company that Loeb Dawkins bought last year. They'll likely get some lukewarm cup of tea to do it."

"Dwight Whitcomb."

"Perfect." Dwight Whitcomb was as bland as you could get on the Street. He'd been carried along because his father still owned an obscene amount of Loeb Dawkins stock. "Maybe I'll give Abe a call," Wetzon said.

"I've already talked with him." Darlene's eyes blinked rapidly over her mask. "He sends you his best."

"How nice." Wetzon had to work on being as bland as Dwight Whitcomb.

"I knew you'd understand," Darlene said.

Oh, I do, I do, Wetzon thought. "And does Abe want to do anything?"

"Not yet. I suggested he meet us for a drink—"

"He'll be hard to place, Darlene. No book. He'd have to be a branch office manager and that's a real comedown from where he is now. We can think about it." Brokers who became managers with the big wire houses gave up their books. A dangerous thing to do in this climate. A broker's lists of clients and their accounts were kept in black looseleaf books. They were the most valuable asset a broker had. Managers were fungible. A book gave you clout. Without a book you were nothing.

The phone rang and Darlene quickly adjourned to her tiny office to answer it.

Max, Smith and Wetzon's receptionist and part-time cold caller, wouldn't be in before eleven. A retired accountant in gum-soled shoes, Max was a thorough, if anal, worker. He never got pulled into Smith's— or Darlene's—magnetic field of lunacy.

Wetzon glanced around at the wreckage of their office, the room she and Smith had shared now for over ten years. Eventually, Darlene would have a portion of this room, and Smith and Wetzon would be upstairs in a brand-new office on the parlor floor. The space their ex-tenant, the rare-book dealer, had occupied until January.

Wetzon would miss this room with its windows that looked out on their garden. Of course, it would still be their garden, but Smith was having a deck built overlooking it. An outside staircase would travel down. Smith and Wetzon was becoming Smith's longtime dream: a duplex. The peons would work below, as they should.

Removing the plastic draped over her chair, Wetzon saw that the plaster dust had penetrated everything. Suspect sheets containing the biographical data from interviews of stockbrokers were coated with a fine white film. With a tissue, she dusted off her chair and sneezed. A mini dust storm took flight over her telephone.

When Smith had called her that morning to say she was going up to her house in Westport, leaving Wetzon to cope with the mess in the office, Wetzon hadn't mentioned The Groaning Board IPO. Smith loved inside information, particularly if she thought she could make some money on it. Wetzon should probably have called A. T. Barron and exchanged envelopes, but she was curious. She could torture Smith with it later, after she talked to Laura Lee Day.

The IPO market certainly had heated up this year. Even old, privately held companies like Estée Lauder were making the move into some portion of public ownership. The move was attractive to owners as they entered middle age because they could cash out.

"Hi, darlin', what's cookin'?" Laura Lee's soft, upbeat Southern tones spilled from the phone.

"What's cookin', darlin'? Why, The Groaning Board, sweetheart," Wetzon said.

Silence followed, growing pregnant along the cables between them.

Wetzon smiled, not giving an inch. Silence made people anxious, got them to fill the void, usually with information they weren't ready to share.

"Well," Laura Lee said finally, "are there no secrets left on Wall Street?"

"None whatever."

More silence. Wetzon pressed her lips together and waited Laura Lee out.

"I'm goin' to be havin' a drink at the bar at Oceana at five o'clock this afternoon. Why don't you come and whisper in my ear how you found out, Ms. Leslie Wetzon, darlin'?"

"Let me look at my schedule." Wetzon counted to fifteen. "I could do that."

"You know, you have just told me in an obscure way that you know somethin' almost no one on the Street knows. I am dyin' to hear all about it."

"I'll see you at five."

"Wetzon, wait a minute. I want you to promise me you won't say a word to *anyone* else about this. That means you-know-who with whom you share your office. For this kind of inside information, darlin', some people would kill."

chapter 7

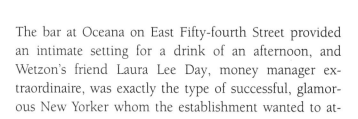

The bar at Oceana on East Fifty-fourth Street provided an intimate setting for a drink of an afternoon, and Wetzon's friend Laura Lee Day, money manager extraordinaire, was exactly the type of successful, glamorous New Yorker whom the establishment wanted to attract.

Of course, when Laura Lee made an appearance anywhere, she attracted attention. Waiters stumbled over one another to serve her, and men of all ages wanted to make her acquaintance. It wasn't that she was beautiful, because she wasn't. What she had was an inner glow, a *joie* and an intelligence filled with humor. The combination set her apart from other women. Unlike most on the

Street, Laura Lee read books other than Tom Clancy's, partook of the theatre, opera, ballet, concerts, and museums, all the cultural events her adopted city offered. Because of her lively curiosity and imagination, Laura Lee was always interesting.

She'd come to New York from Mississippi to be a concert violinist and ended up at Merrill Lynch because her daddy had refused to pay for any more music lessons. Not long after Wetzon had become a headhunter, she'd met Laura Lee and placed her at Oppenheimer, and they'd become friends. Laura Lee was still studying the violin, but now she was paying for her own lessons.

At the top of the stairs near the entrance to the bar, Fabio sat at a table by himself. He looked utterly out of place with his long hair, oversized features, and his open shirt—the better to see the pecs, my dear. His body language gave away his need to be recognized. Wetzon thought: Fabio, your Warhol fifteen minutes of fame is over.

The bar was elegant and understated. Quiet and dark. Wine racks rose to a soaring ceiling, at the pinnacle of which was a huge metal fish.

"Ah, there you are, darlin'." Laura Lee waved at Wetzon. She was surrounded by waiters and a couple of attractive men in the pinstripe-and-white-shirt uniform of the financial world. The heads all swiveled. Wetzon was on display for a brief moment before the heads all swiveled back to Laura Lee.

"Sit yourself down right here." Laura Lee patted the banquette she sat on and slid over.

The crowd parted for Leslie Wetzon, the thin blonde with the long neck and topknot, ex-Broadway chorus dancer in costume of Wall Street headhunter. Everyone dispersed except for, luckily, one waiter, who looked expectant.

"Amstel Light," Wetzon said. She twitched her nose and pointed two fingers at him. The waiter disappeared.

Laura Lee rolled her eyes. "Practicin' witchcraft?"

"I find it's good to keep trying new things after the age of forty. Helps one stay young and full of beans."

"I can attest to that," Laura Lee said. She took a sip of white wine. "How's the renovation comin'?"

"Don't ask. They knock things down, break through walls, then go away for days—to work another job, I'm sure. I just wish Louie had been able to handle it."

"Why couldn't she?"

"A SoHo gallery offered her a show. She needed the time to put it together."

"But a show, my, that's grand. Are you lendin' your paintin'?"

"If she wants it."

"And how is your dear partner?" She pronounced it *dee-ah.*

Wetzon look askance at her friend. Why wasn't she coming directly to the point? Laura Lee didn't care a hoot about Smith. "In her prime, thank you. She's—would you believe—talking with Mort Hornberg about producing TV specials."

"Give me a break," Laura Lee said.

"The one on *Combinations* was a blockbuster . . ."

"Is the grand Xenia givin' up huntin' heads?"

"No way. We've got Darlene Ford, the Sammy Glick of headhunters, practically running the business out from under us."

The waiter set the beer, foaming in a tall glass, in front of Wetzon.

"Do you mind?" Laura Lee asked Wetzon. "About Darlene and the business?"

"Sometimes. But I'd rather have her working for us than for Tom Keegen. I'm just waiting for her to lock horns with the mighty Smith. It'll be bloody, mind you."

"Why, Wetzon darlin', if I didn't know better I'd think you were looking forward to it."

"*Moi?*" Wetzon grinned at her and took a swallow of beer. "Truth is, I wouldn't mind making a few waves. Recruiting is dull right now. The whole business has changed. Clients merged with nonclients. Happy hunting ground go bye-bye. And all these new pension plans the firms have instituted are nothing but golden handcuffs. No one is moving."

"I hear that the big upfront deals are dryin' up," Laura Lee said.

"It's a real drought. A manager actually told me he was happy about it because now brokers would join his firm for its quality without the bribe of money."

"You're joking. He actually said that?"

"I swear, Laura Lee. Any fool knows that no one would consider going anywhere without a deal. He thinks his firm is so special, wait till he sees he can't recruit."

"Tsk, tsk. Your account is up thirty-five percent so far this year. You can always rest on your laurels."

"What and leave show business?"

They laughed, clicked their glasses, then studied each other. Wetzon was unwilling to ask the first question.

"Did you see Fabio when you came up the stairs?" Laura Lee ran her tongue around her full lips.

"Yes. He's so weird-looking."

"It's the bod, darlin', the bod."

Wetzon shook her head. "Not my type."

"Speaking of your type . . ."

"He's fine, though I haven't seen him since yesterday morning. He's working on some special case."

"So . . ." Laura Lee said. She looked past Wetzon in the direction of Fabio.

She's stalling, Wetzon realized. Then she thought, no, she's waiting for someone. Wetzon took another sip of beer and rose. "Well, it's been fun, but I have to run along now."

Laura Lee jumped up. "Oh, no. You can't go—"

"What is all this about, Laura Lee? If you don't tell me right now, I'm going home."

"Ah, there he is." Again she was looking over Wetzon's shoulder.

Wetzon turned. A slim, bearded man in a gray Armani suit with a black tee and no tie was shaking Fabio's hand, patting his shoulder. Leaving Fabio, he came toward Wetzon and Laura Lee, a smile on his face. He was carrying a yellow leather backpack.

A wide expanse of scalp cut a path back from his forehead to the top of his head.

Wetzon knew him from somewhere. Where had she seen him before? She looked at Laura Lee, puzzled. Laura Lee pointed to the banquette from which Wetzon had risen. Wetzon sat down and waited for the arrival of the mystery guest. His progress was slow because he was meeting and greeting everyone in the room as if he were some kind of celebrity.

When he finally reached their table, he cheek-kissed Laura Lee, straightened, and offered Wetzon his hand. "Leslie Wetzon, I presume?" He had a small hand with plump fingers. On his wrist was a watch that told the time in every world capital.

Wetzon waited for the introduction.

Laura Lee smiled. "Wetzon, darlin', this is Hem Barron."

c h a p t e r   8

"It's exploratory," Hem Barron said. His smile was so intimate that Wetzon could barely keep from crossing her hands over her breasts.

Twirling her empty beer glass, she noted that Laura Lee was assiduously avoiding eye contact. "Of course, a red herring."

Hem fished the olive out of his martini and ate it. "We're just in the proposal stage, you understand. Not for public consumption."

"Oh, I see." Wetzon nodded. "Not for public consumption. Isn't that an oxymoron?"

"Your friend is very funny," Hem told Laura Lee. He focused sincere brown eyes on Wetzon's bosom.

"My friend is very smart, Hem," Laura Lee retorted, "so let's cut the *schlag*."

Hem's composure never even wavered. "It was my idea," he said. "I gave the girls their start-up money and kept an interest in The Groaning Board. No need to say I stand to make a killing on the transaction."

"I'm sure the *girls* are just filled to overflowing with gratitude," Wetzon said, staring hard at her friend.

"They should be, but it's very disappointing," Hem said. "A.T. is more grateful than Micklynn, I'm sorry to say. Micklynn doesn't want to go forward with it."

"That's why we didn't want this to get out." Laura Lee sighed and gave Wetzon a pleading look.

"Actually," Hem said, leaning close to Wetzon, "Micklynn hasn't even seen the prospectus. When it's polished up and we have a chance to convince her, I'm sure she'll go along."

Hem was wearing some kind of exotic cologne that was making Wetzon's nose itch. He was oleaginously sure of himself. She couldn't resist asking, "What if she doesn't?"

"That'll never happen, believe me." Hem tilted his head to Laura Lee. Her turn to pick up the ball?

"Wetzon, what we're askin' is how you found out. Even Micklynn doesn't know—"

"Excuse me? Micklynn doesn't know? About her own company going public? How did you manage that? Isn't she a partner?"

"Of course, Micklynn knows," Laura Lee said. "It's just that she's always been the hands-on person with the catering, and A.T. has handled all the business arrangements."

"A.T. is my sister," Hem said. "It's in the family, you might say. Bringing The Groaning Board public will allow the girls to expand the business with the demand. Hire more support—"

Now where had Wetzon heard that before? "Expanding is not always the best thing for either the firm or the owners." She reached into her briefcase, pulled out the white envelope A.T. had mistakenly given Smith, and handed it across the table to Laura Lee. "Smith is having a catered affair."

"Smith is Wetzon's business partner," Laura Lee explained to Hem. She opened the clasp and slipped the prospectus out an inch, then slid it back and closed the envelope.

"You don't mean *Xenia* Smith?" Hem practically had an orgasm. He beamed an extra-huge smile at Wetzon.

She shaded her eyes. Shit, hell, and corruption, she thought. Another one of Smith's conquests. But why was she surprised? Smith made it her business to know everybody important. "You've met, I see."

"At one of Bill Veeder's parties last year. She's gorgeous. We really hit it off."

You would, Wetzon thought bitchily. Especially as you both agree on the most important thing in life—money.

"But how did you get hold of this, darlin'?" The white envelope had disappeared into Laura Lee's attaché.

"A.T. gave Smith what we all thought was p.r. material and a sample contract yesterday."

"Smith *saw* this?" Horror mottled Laura Lee's smooth complexion.

"She couldn't fit it in her purse, so she gave it to me to hold for her. I looked at it last night. Smith hasn't seen it because she's in Connecticut till Monday. And no, Laura Lee, she knows nothing about it." Wetzon got to her feet.

"I'll have A.T. messenger over the right envelope," Hem said, also rising.

"Wetzon, darlin', please give me your word that what you know will go no further." Laura Lee's words and manner were all super-professional, but her eyes gave her away. They carried a plea.

"You have my word, Laura Lee, along with a few extra words of advice from a not so impartial observer: Don't stampede this over Micklynn."

"Oh, she'll come around. She has to," Hem said. Wetzon's immediate thought was: Your picture is sure to be next to *smarmy* in the dictionary. "It'll make her life so much easier. Once the offering goes through she'll never have to cook another day of her life."

"You think that's what she wants?" Instinct told her that cooking was Micklynn's life. Wetzon touched her finger to her brow in a salute. "See ya," she said.

Hem changed his seat so that he was facing Laura Lee directly. As Wetzon walked away, she heard him say, "Laura Lee, you have the most beautiful breasts."

She turned back to Laura Lee and made a gagging gesture. Laura Lee's lips twitched, but that was as much as she gave.

Wetzon was out of sight before Hem Barron looked over his shoulder. On the street, Wetzon breathed in the honest fumes of automotive pollution. A vendor was selling honey-roasted peanuts and she stopped to buy a bag, hoping they would mitigate the bad taste in her mouth. She knew that Laura Lee would call her later to try to explain that this was a business relationship, which Wetzon could see it was. But was it worth it?

As she headed uptown toward the Upper West Side and home, it was Smith's comment about stockbrokers that came to Wetzon's mind: "Lie down with stockbrokers, get up with fleas." Anyone who lay down with the likes of Hemingway Barron would be lucky to get up with only fleas.

chapter 9

"Metzger's sister-in-law. Sheila," Silvestri said. He divided the mofongo—an amalgamation of mashed plantains and pork rind shaped into a cone, surrounded by a garlicky gravy—between them unevenly.

"Hey, you took more for yourself."

"I'm a growing boy." He grinned at her, daring her to say more. The scant shadow of dark beard lay half buried in the cleft of his chin.

"I won't comment," she said.

"That's a comment." His voice was muffled as he wolfed down his oversized share.

Once at Café Con Leche, their favorite neighborhood restaurant, a woman at the table next to theirs had been eating mofongo. When Wetzon asked about it, the woman told her it was a Puerto Rican peasant dish and gave them their first taste. They were sold.

"We have to drive out to West Hempstead tonight," Silvestri said.

"Oh? How come?"

"Metzger's sister-in-law."

"What about her?" Artie Metzger was Silvestri's old partner at the Seventeenth Precinct.

"She died."

"Oh, I'm so sorry. Was she sick for a long time?"

"No." He signaled the waiter for another beer.

"It must have been a shock, then. Was she much older?"

"Younger. Forty-four."

"Was it breast cancer?"

"No."

Silvestri was answering her in monosyllables. Not that that was unusual. It was just that this time she felt she was missing the subtext. "What did she die of?" She forked the last of the mofongo into her mouth.

"Good question." Something in his voice drew her attention away from the platter of roast pork, black beans, and yellow rice in the middle of the table.

She set down her fork. "God, Silvestri, Metzger's sister-in-law is a *homicide?*"

"We don't know yet."

"That's what you've been working on."

He nodded. "We're waiting for the autopsy results."

"Jesus, how awful. Was she mugged?"

"No. Judy Metzger found her."

"God. A break-in?"

"Not so you'd notice. Only one thing seems to be missing."

"What?"

"Her briefcase."

"Was she a lawyer?"

"No. A schoolteacher." He shrugged, dispatched the beer. "Judy talked to her Saturday afternoon. Sheila was complaining about stomach flu. When Judy couldn't get her on the phone Sunday, she went in, found her, and called Artie."

"She lived in Manhattan?"

"In one of those classy tenements all the way east on Seventy-second

Street. They found her on the floor of the bathroom. Either she fell and cracked her head or someone did it and made it look like a fall."

"When you get one of those stomach viruses, you feel faint and—"

"She was a nice girl," Silvestri said. He pushed his plate away. It was still full of food.

"Was she married?"

"No. You still hungry?"

"No." The news about Metzger's sister-in-law had put a damper on everything.

Silvestri waved the waiter over. "Pack it up," he told him. "We'll take it home." To Wetzon he said, "They're sitting shivah at Metzger's house."

"I'm glad we're going. Shouldn't we bring food or something? I can go over to Zabar's right now—"

"I'll take this stuff home, get the car, and pick you up in front of Zabar's."

Early morning was the best time to shop at Zabar's; second best was near closing. True, a few people were still waiting at the cheese counter, and more than a few stood in front of the deli counter clutching their numbers, but there were no long lines and you could get in and out in minutes.

Wetzon decided that the rugalach were the safest choice. She picked out a box and got on the cash-only line. An attractive young couple in front of her were discussing whether they had enough food as they unloaded their shopping cart. It was enough for an army. Her mind wandered over her day as she watched the clerk check them out.

That's when she realized that she hadn't asked Silvestri the most important question. Maybe she didn't want to know and had in some Freudian way avoided asking it.

Silvestri's black Toyota sat in a line of double-parked beauties, mostly BMWs and Mercedeses, in front of Zabar's.

After Wetzon got in and fastened her seat belt, she asked the question.

"Was there something between you and Sheila, Silvestri?"

He didn't answer right away, so she knew there had been. Of course there had been. Metzger's wife's single sister. They would have fixed Silvestri up with her.

"It was a long time ago, Les," Silvestri said, not taking his eyes off the road.

"Long before I met you," Wetzon sang softly.

"Long before I met you," he repeated. A damp fog made the city lights fuzz around them. Beads of moisture formed on the car windows. They were heading for the Triborough Bridge to Long Island.

"Was she pretty, Silvestri?"

"Yes. Sheila was pretty and smart, and a good guy. You would have liked her, Les."

"Were you in love with her?"

"I don't remember."

"You don't remember?" His response upset her. What if she—Wetzon—had died and Silvestri was driving with another woman and she asked him the same question? Would he say, "Leslie Wetzon? Was I in love with her? I don't remember"? Or was she upset for Sheila, the poor woman who'd died? That Silvestri couldn't remember if he'd loved her. She watched him drop the three-dollar-and-fifty-cent toll into the Exact Change bin.

So far inward had she turned that when his hand touched her thigh, she jumped. She placed her hand over his, feeling the blood rush from thigh to hand to hand. "Silvestri—" she began. "I—"

"Chill out, Les," he said. "What was then, was then. What's now is now."

c h a p t e r 1 0

"They always warn you about accidents in the home, but considering what it's like on the streets in the City, you never think something terrible will happen to you or your children in your own home."

Artie Metzger's mother-in-law was a buxomly attractive woman, even with sad, red-rimmed eyes. Her hair was a little too golden and her nails a little too long and too red. She was wearing a black dress with pearls. On her feet were baby-blue house slippers. Behind her, a white bedsheet was draped over a mirror. Both the slippers and the mirror, Wetzon knew, were a Jewish mourning custom.

The woman hugged Silvestri as if he were family; he kissed her cheek and called her Bea.

"This is Leslie," Silvestri said.

"Thank you for coming, dear," Bea said, pressing Wetzon's hand. Beside her stood a gawky boy rapidly approaching adolescence. It was disconcerting to see he already had his father's eye pouches and hangdog look. "This is Aaron, my handsome grandson."

"Aaron and I know each other, don't we, buddy?" Silvestri shook hands with Aaron solemnly. "Meet Leslie."

Wetzon held out her hand. Blushing deeply, the boy gave her a limp, damp handshake. He didn't meet her eyes.

Metzger's Cape Cod on its corner lot had been lit like a beacon as they drove up. Cars were parked bumper to bumper on the driveway and on neighboring driveways, as well as on the street. Cops—you couldn't mistake them—sat smoking on the front steps, talking shop. Although the rules had changed some and cops no longer had to carry their guns when off-duty, Wetzon observed these guys were all carrying.

"Sheila was such a wonderful girl," an elderly woman told Wetzon over the coffee urn. "Are you a friend from school?"

"I didn't know her," Wetzon replied, wondering if the coffee was decaf.

"Oh, what a shame. She was such a fine person. Everybody loved her."

Everybody except Silvestri, Wetzon thought. He can't remember. "So I understand. Is any of this decaf, do you know?"

"It's all decaf, dear, for us old ones, you know."

Wetzon helped herself to a cup. She was obviously one of "us old ones."

Moving away from the coffee urn, she was confronted by a slim girl of about ten. The girl started to say something but couldn't seem to get the words out.

"Hi," Wetzon said. "I'm Leslie. What's your name?"

The child had her hair pulled back in a tight knot on top of her head. "Jessica Metzger. My daddy said I should talk to you because you're a dancer." Braces contributed to a soft sibilance and tiny dimples on both sides of her mouth. In her stance was that awkward grace of the young dancer in imitation of the ideal.

"I can tell you're a dancer," Wetzon said, catching Artie Metzger's eye where he stood head and shoulders over the glut of women in the small living room. Artie had sent his little girl over to talk to her.

"You can?" Jessica's plain little face was transformed as if some inner light had been turned on, giving her translucent skin a golden glow.

Wetzon knew the feeling, saw a very young Leslie Wetzon in Metzger's Jessica. "Let's see if we can find a place to talk," she told the girl, wondering herself where in the crowded-to-bursting house that could be.

"My room," Jessica said eagerly. She led Wetzon around the edge of the crowded room and up a short flight of stairs.

The second floor held three bedrooms, a large master and two smaller ones, and at least one bath that Wetzon could see. Jessica's room was small and tidy, with pale yellow walls and a yellow floral print quilt, ruffled pillowcase and matching curtains. A desk, a chest of drawers, and a night table all in nicely waxed country pine gave the room a lovely, warm feeling.

On the walls were framed posters of Darci Kistler, a principal with the New York City Ballet, flying through the air, and Wetzon's favorite, Natalia Makarova, in a classic pose. From a hook on the wall behind the bed hung a pair of porcelain ballet slippers, exactly the same as the pair Leslie Wetzon had hung on the wall behind her bed thirty years ago. For an instant, she felt as if she'd stepped backward in time and her eyes teared.

"What a nice room," she said.

They sat on the bed, Wetzon sipping coffee while Jessica told her about her audition coming up for *The Nutcracker*. Then Jessica said, "Will you tell me about Broadway?"

"Do you tap?"

"A little."

"You must study tap, and jazz. They're different movements entirely and it's important to be expert at each if you want to cross over and do theatre."

On the night table was a framed color photograph of Jessica in a tutu, in a deep curtsy, and another of two women and Jessica in front of the fountain at Lincoln Center. One of the women was Judy Metzger. The photograph was obviously recent, because Jessica looked as she did this evening.

Wetzon picked up the second photograph. "I recognize your mother. Is that your Aunt Sheila?"

The child stared at the photograph as if seeing it for the first time, and without warning began to cry. Wetzon dropped the photograph on the bed and took Jessica in her arms as the girl's body was racked with misery. Between sobs, she gasped, "She took me to the ballet and to *Damn Yankees* and *Crazy for You.*"

"And you loved your Aunt Sheila very much and will miss her terribly," Wetzon whispered, stroking Jessica's slender back. "And what you make of your life will be part of a tribute to your Aunt Sheila."

Jessica's head nodded against Wetzon's dampening bosom.

Wetzon looked down at the photograph on the bed. Sheila smiled up at her with heartbreaking bravura, no thought whatever that she was soon to die.

"It's not fair," Jessica said, her voice muffled, the sobs diminishing.

"No, it's not fair," Wetzon agreed. "But accidents happen. Good people get hurt. And good people die. And we must go on. Your aunt will always be as she was; she'll never get older because you will never forget her." Wetzon dried the child's tears with a tissue.

Tears still shimmering in her eyes, Jessica pulled away from Wetzon, folding her arms across her narrow chest. "It wasn't an accident."

"What do you mean?"

"Someone did it on purpose."

"Did what on purpose?"

"Killed my Aunt Sheila." She shook her head in denial. "It wasn't an accident."

"How do you know that, Jessica?" Surely, Wetzon thought, it was a child's imagination running wild.

"The phone calls."

"What phone calls? Does your father know about this?"

"Aunt Sheila made me promise not to tell. She was getting these really weird phone calls."

c h a p t e r   1 1

"Sheila was getting weird phone calls, Silvestri," Wetzon said. He hadn't said a word since they got into the car, much as she'd tried to draw him out. It had been an exhausting evening. Emotionally exhausting.

"Now how would you know that, Les? You didn't even know Sheila." There was enough irritation in his voice to make her defensive . . . as if Sheila were his property and she was trespassing.

"I listen when people talk, Silvestri. You're emotionally involved, so you're going to miss things."

Silvestri braked sharply to avoid being sideswiped by a yellow cab. The dark was slashed with headlights. "I am not emotionally involved. What Sheila and I had was over a long time ago. I haven't seen her in years." His reply came through clenched teeth.

Wetzon sighed. Not emotionally involved, huh? "Jessica told me about the phone calls. She was there once when Sheila checked her answering machine. It was on the tape."

"Metzger didn't say anything about it."

"Metzger didn't know. Sheila made Jessica promise not to tell. He probably knows now because I told Jessica she had to tell him right away."

"I'll call him when we get home." Silvestri rolled down his window and paid the bridge toll.

He'd become a stranger again, closing her out. In the middle of the East River, the brightly lit apartment houses on Roosevelt Island floated like a multicandled wedding cake. What made her think about weddings just now, when their relationship seemed to be unraveling?

Traffic on the Triborough Bridge came to a dead stop. Somewhere ahead there'd been an accident, for the swirling lights of the EMS wagon and the whine of police sirens took charge of the night.

"Fuck," Silvestri said, hammering on the wheel.

His beeper went off. After checking the number, he took his cellular phone from under the dash and punched in some numbers, waited, then spoke. "I'm on the cell because we're stuck on the Triborough, so keep it clean." He listened for a moment, glanced at Wetzon. "Yeah, I just heard." Listened again. "Okay. Let me drop Les, and I'll meet you there. Take the Fifty-ninth Street Bridge. We're backed up here till kingdom come." He disconnected and replaced the phone.

Traffic began to creep, then move.

"You and Artie are going to Sheila's place?"

"Yeah. First I'm taking you home."

"You don't have to."

"You want me to put you in a cab?"

"No. I want to go with you."

"That's crap, Les." They came off the bridge and onto the FDR Drive.

"You said the Crime Scene Unit went over the place with a fine-tooth comb, so I wouldn't be interfering with anything."

"Forget it."

In the glancing light from other cars, she saw his jaw was set against her. Infuriated, she said, "Isn't it odd? Only a few months ago you actually asked for my help with Terri Matthews' murder, Silvestri. How quickly we forget."

"This is different."

"How is it different? Because you happen to have been involved with Sheila? You don't even know that she was murdered. The CSU has gone over the place; I won't touch anything. And maybe I'll spot something you guys'll miss. I did find out about the phone calls, didn't I? Why didn't the CSU find the answering machine tape?"

"I don't know. There was no sign of a break-in, no sign that anyone else had been in the apartment. Accidental death pending autopsy results." His tone was stiff and cold.

They didn't speak again until Silvestri found a parking place on First Avenue and Seventy-third Street. When they got out of the car, Silvestri took a small sack from the trunk.

"What's that?"

"Gloves and booties." He slammed the trunk closed, made sure the car was locked, then walked off quickly, leaving her to race after him.

Seventy-second Street was a cul-de-sac this far east. On both sides of the street, cars were parked bumper to bumper.

"Metzger's here already," Silvestri said. Metzger's car was on a slant in front of a fire hydrant, a flashing gumball on its roof. Silvestri looked up at the building. A light went on in the fourth-floor window. The blinds were down. "Come on," he told Wetzon.

The building was one of four whitewashed tenements with new white-rimmed thermal windows. Fire escapes climbed the fronts like geometric ivy. Two cement steps led up to a small square vestibule with a flooring of tiny black and white tiles in a mosaic pattern. Built into the wall was a cluster of mailboxes next to a list of tenants, a buzzer beside each name.

Silvestri pressed the buzzer for 4F. *S. Gelber.* A loud buzz released the lock and let them into the building.

The fourth floor really meant eight flights of stairs, but the building was clean and the stairs well lit. Sounds of life drifted past them: a too loud TV with the Channel 5 evening news. Music. The throb of rock that made your heart beat faster. Here and there a whiff of fried onions. Cabbage. Cigarettes. People sneaking puffs behind closed doors since the City had gone smoke-free almost everywhere.

When they reached the fourth floor, Wetzon got wicked pleasure in seeing that Silvestri was breathing harder than she was. He handed her a pair of latex gloves, then crouched. She put one foot and then the other into the booties he held for her. He tied them around her ankles. A glancing caress of her knee let her know he wasn't angry anymore.

She reached out to touch him, but he was pulling on his own booties. When he straightened, all he said was "Gloves."

The door still wore the tattered remnants of the police seal, which presumably Metzger had broken.

A gloved and bootied Metzger opened the door. He glanced at Wetzon. "I thought you were taking her home."

"Her refused," Wetzon said. "I won't touch anything."

Metzger held the door for them without a word. He had powder dust—some white, some black—on his trousers.

The apartment was a railroad flat, so called because one room opened into another. The overlay of Lysol couldn't quite cover the sour odor of vomit. And something else, more powerful. Something feral. Something evil.

Wetzon stood in the middle of the living room watching Silvestri and Metzger methodically go over every square inch, starting with the kitchen on the right. When they finished the living room they moved on to the bedroom, leaving Wetzon still standing in the same place. She studied the cozy room and then began to move around, getting acquainted. White powder covered every surface indiscriminately.

The apartment had a used, though loved quality to it. Even the background sound: the *plop, plop, plop* of a dripping faucet.

The furnishings were worn except for the sofa, which looked fairly new and was inset on a bookcase wall. The books looked read. In a corner near the doorless kitchen, a small oak dining-room table and four chairs were positioned under an opaque white globe. The table held a box of tea bags and a mug, bills: a doctor, a dentist, Macy's, Con Edison, and NYNEX, as well as an empty clasp envelope. A nice, somewhat worn kilim covered the floor.

On a glass-topped table in front of the sofa was an open manila folder which held what looked liked exams. Sheila must have gotten sick early on and quickly, because her red pencil was still sharp and it lay on top of a large stack of uncorrected papers, alongside a smaller stack of those that had been corrected. Wetzon leafed through them. The Romantic Poets. Shelley, Byron, and Keats. There was a yellowish stain on the carpet near the coffee table and a denser smell of Lysol.

Either someone had been in to clean up or maybe Sheila herself had tried to when she first got sick.

Wetzon wandered into the kitchen. The odor here was gross, sour, putrid. Black powder on refrigerator door and countertops.

"Who unplugged the answering machine?" she heard Silvestri say.

"That's the way it was. No tape. You think Sheila unplugged it?" Metzger sounded weary.

"Maybe. If the messages were being left on the machine . . . She didn't say anything to you or Judy about it?"

An old Waring blender, a toaster oven, and a bread machine crowded the narrow counter. In the stainless-steel sink, under a dripping faucet, was a small plate washed clean, except for a few crumbs, of whatever it had contained. Wetzon tried to tighten the faucet. It was already tight. And she'd broken her promise; she'd begun to touch things.

"No," Metzger told Silvestri. "Jess was here when Sheila played back one of them. That's how she knew. Sheila told her the calls were just an annoyance that would stop if no one responded to them."

"Okay, Sheila unplugged the goddam machine," Silvestri said. "Where would she have put the tape?"

Wetzon thought, where would you have put a tape if you wanted to hold on to it, but *not* have to see it every day? Put it on ice, so to speak?

The refrigerator was like Wetzon's in that its freezing compartment was on top. She opened the door and a soft white fog floated out at her. Everything inside was neatly layered and labeled. Two shell steaks, three chicken breasts, a foil package marked "4 muffins," but by the look of it Sheila'd eaten one of them. A plastic sandwich box, unlabeled. Wetzon shook it. What was inside rattled.

"Silvestri."

"What?"

"Here. In the kitchen." She propped the plastic container against her hip and pried it open.

The object was wrapped in a napkin, the napkin taped closed. Wetzon didn't need to remove its protective coat to know what it was.

chapter 12

"Hi, Sheil, it's six o'clock. Give me a call when you get home."

Metzger flinched. "Judy," he said.

Beep.

"Ms. Gelber. This is Dr. Fochios' office calling to remind you about your five o'clock appointment today."

Beep.

They were standing in Sheila Gelber's bedroom. Metzger had plugged in the answering machine and it was now playing the cassette. Sheila's pink fleece bathrobe lay across the foot of her bed as if she would be back soon. What if she came home and found them in her bedroom? Wetzon shivered. Sheila wasn't ever coming home.

"Sheila?" A deep male voice. *"It's me again, cunt. I know you're up there on the fourth floor thinking about how I'm going to do you."* After the initial not unpleasant salutation, the voice had become raspy, breathy, and distorted, as if the sound had been mechanically slowed. *"It's getting closer now. Any day . . . any day . . ."*

Beep.

At first, no one spoke.

"Oh, God," Wetzon said, hugging herself. "Oh, God." Silvestri wrapped her in his arms.

"Jesus." Metzger had turned pasty-faced. "Why didn't she say something?" He let the tape play out. There were no other messages. He turned the cassette over, letting it play out on the other side. Nothing further. Removing the cassette, he dropped it into his pocket.

"When will the autopsy results come in?" Wetzon asked, thinking: Can we leave now? Please, please, can we leave—

"They're backed up because of that fire at that Dominican social club in the Heights. Sheila didn't look like a homicide. There was no urgency. . . ." Metzger's voice trailed off. His swallow was audible.

"There is now," Silvestri said. "I'll go over in the morning and put a little pressure on." He stepped away from Wetzon with a suddenness that jolted her, leaving her feeling exposed, or worse, invisible. He looked ill.

Wetzon reached her hand out to him, but he ignored it. His eyes took in the room, the robe across the bed, the fuzzy slippers peeping out from under the bed, the photos on the bureau. The tray of makeup—Clinique—and the perfume. He opened the blinds and looked down at the street, closed them.

Wetzon left the room, walking into the living room and on to the kitchen. She opened the cabinets—there weren't many—and saw glassware, china. Silverware was in an under-the-counter drawer. A tall, shallow metal cabinet, painted white like the rest, was a pantry of sorts. Cans of tomatoes, boxes of pasta with an unfamiliar logo. She looked closer. Spinach stone-ground rice pasta. The shelf above the pasta held a bag of brown rice flour, a bag of tapioca flour, cornmeal, polenta, potato starch flour, and powdered whole milk.

"What are you doing, Les?" Silvestri stood in the doorway holding the clasp envelope from the dining table. By the shape of it, it was no longer empty. He sounded annoyed.

"You know, you can tell a lot about a person by looking in their cupboards and refrigerators."

"Oh, yeah? And what did you learn, Sherlock?"

"Let's go," Metzger called.

She closed the doors of the cabinet. "Forget it, Silvestri."

"Not on your life. I'm all ears. I'd love to hear all about it."

She hated him when he got like this, but she said, "All right, then. Your Sheila was a health-food freak."

"She was not." He seemed to resent her involvement, as if Sheila Gelber still belonged to him. And she wondered if he meant she was not a health-food freak or not *my* Sheila.

"Oh?" Wetzon said with an edge. "Then you've seen her recently?" When he turned away and headed for the door, she followed him. "People change, you know."

"Come on, children." Metzger was obviously distressed. "This is no time to fight. Just be happy you have each other. Right, Leslie?" He patted her shoulder, looking over her head at Silvestri.

The night had a particular chill to it, or so it seemed to Wetzon. Or maybe it was Silvestri's icy introspection keeping her at arm's length. Whatever it was, she felt hurt and angry. They rode through the Park in stony silence.

Silvestri drove around the block twice, then backed the Toyota into a parking place near the corner of Amsterdam and turned off the engine. He made no move to get out.

"Are you coming up?" Wetzon asked. He'd held on to his Chelsea apartment because it was rent-controlled, or so he said. But Wetzon figured it to be his escape hatch, so he'd have somewhere to go if they split up. These days he used it for his poker games.

"Why wouldn't I?" he said abruptly, giving her an uncompromising stare.

"Jesus, Silvestri, don't do that. I haven't committed a crime . . . yet. I only thought you're so upset about Sheila, maybe you want to be alone."

"It's not what you think, Les."

"How do you know what I think? You make no effort to try to understand. Everything I say seems to bug you—"

"You think," he said quietly, "that what was between me and Sheila was deep."

"Wasn't it?"

"No, it wasn't. It was just something that Judy and Metzger wanted to happen but wasn't right for either of us. I haven't seen or talked to her in years."

"Then why are you . . ." The tortured look in his eyes prevented her from going on. She'd never seen him so upset.

"Come on," he said. He got out of the car and came around for her, still carrying the manila envelope.

He's taken Sheila's bills, she thought.

The night was blustery; swift-moving clouds scudded black-edged against the moonless sky. It matched the emotions of the moment.

In the elevator he put his arm on her shoulders. "This is how it is," he said. "It has nothing to do with you and me. This time you can't help. It's something I have to work out for myself."

chapter 13

She'd fallen asleep sitting up, her book in her lap, and woke when he closed her book and turned out the light. Izz whined when he set her in her dog bed on the floor.

For the first time in a long time Wetzon had been afraid of the dark, not wanting to remember the sound of that terrible voice on Sheila's answering machine.

When he got into bed beside her, she folded herself against him. They made love, but it was different this time; his need was so intense, it threatened to crush her.

Sometime during the night she heard him get up, heard him moving around; he didn't come back.

It was after nine when she woke again. Izz was nestling in the small of Wetzon's back. Silvestri was gone. And so was the manila envelope.

The farmers' market was meager. Wetzon was cold in her trench coat. She pulled her beret over her ears. A halfhearted drizzle misted over everything. She bought apples and one green and one yellow zucchini squash. The woman behind her kept pushing at her. Furious, she spun around.

"How about a cup of hot cider, darlin'?" Laura Lee grinned at her.

"You owe me. I accept. I mean, what else can I say to someone with such beautiful breasts?"

"Ouch," Laura Lee said. "He is a dreadful man, isn't he?"

"I've known worse, but I didn't go into business with them."

"Darlin', you have to understand that it's the deal that's important. It's goin' to make everyone a ton of mon, especially Micklynn. And may I remind you that you are in business with one of the worst . . . so get down off your high horse."

"Forget the hot cider, Laura Lee. I feel a weak hungry coming on fast. Let's go to the Columbus Bakery, get a cappuccino, and gorge." Laura Lee was right, of course. Smith was probably no better than Hem Barron. And Wetzon could readily see Smith working behind her back to sell out their company exactly as Hem and A.T. were doing to Micklynn.

At the Columbus Bakery, they made their choices, then took their plates to a small table.

"Come on, darlin', it's time to lift yourself out of this funk you're in." Laura Lee swathed butter on her cranberry corn muffin.

"Business is lousy, Laura Lee, and Smith just keeps spending more money on expansion and saying it's a business deduction."

"But that's not it, is it?" Her friend gave her a knowing look.

"You're right. That's not it. An old girlfriend of Silvestri's died under mysterious circumstances."

"Ah," Laura Lee said.

"He says it was over a long time ago, but—"

"Did somebody kill her?"

"They don't know yet. He's all wrapped up in the case and not talking very much."

"Uh-oh, and he's not loquacious on his good days."

"I hope the autopsy says it was an accident; otherwise, he's going to obsess about finding her murderer." Wetzon cut her sticky bun in four pieces and scarfed one wedge down.

"You know, it's always nice to have another man hangin' around worshippin' you, takin' you out for nice lunches and dinners."

"Laura Lee!"

"I'm not sayin' have two lovers, Wetzon. Though for some that could be very interestin'." Her eyes were filled with mirth. "I'm just sayin' that there are some men who would love to hang out in your radius."

"Your radius, Laura Lee, not mine." Then she smiled.

"You've thought of someone," Laura Lee said gleefully.

"I ran into him in the Park the other day, and I got the strangest feeling that he was hitting on me."

"Tell me who, darlin'. Isn't this delicious?" She wasn't talking about the food.

"Bill Veeder."

"Bill Veeder. Now there's an interestin' man. He and his wife have a salon at their palacial apartment every couple of months."

"His wife?"

"Well, that's another story. She's had a stroke or somethin' and sits in a wheelchair in front of the fireplace like the ice queen, not even flickerin' an eye, while her nurse sees to her and Bill keeps bringin' people over to meet her. She can't talk, can't walk, and I'm not sure that she understands anythin' goin' on around her."

"Then I'm wrong. He seems like the perfect husband."

"*Seems* is the operative word here, darlin'." Laura Lee patted Wetzon's hand with buttery fingers. "There is no such thing as the perfect husband," she said.

Max handed Wetzon a suspect sheet. "His name is Carl Grant. He has his own TV show on CNN, and he's got a radio call-in show. He wants a million dollars upfront. He kept saying I should know who he is. He wants someone to get back to him who does."

"And I suppose," Smith said, "that he does two million in gross."

Stockbrokers worked on commission based on their gross production. Their earnings ran according to the firm's payout—that is, the percentage of the gross commissions paid to the broker. The percentage varied slightly from firm to firm, with Merrill Lynch near the lowest and boutique firms like Bear Stearns and DLJ near the top. A broker doing a million dollars annual gross would carry home about thirty-nine percent at Merrill and fifty percent at Bear Stearns. Because of this disparity, the Bear offered few enticing incentives, other than payout, to come on board.

"What is his gross, Max?" Wetzon asked, scanning the suspect sheet. "You haven't written anything down."

"He said he'd tell me *after* I find out who he is."

"Oh, pu-leeze," Smith said.

"I'll call him. Thanks, Max. This is good work." Wetzon frowned at Smith.

Smith tossed her head. "You're just wonderful, dearest Max. Now go on out there and dial for dollars."

"Darlene had another start today," Wetzon told Smith after Max closed the door behind him. "The big producer in Allentown."

"Didn't I tell you? Our little gold mine is going to take care of us in our dotage."

"I wouldn't count on it. Nor would I count on her." Wetzon picked out Carl Grant's phone number. "It's a good thing we have her on contract."

"Mr. Grant's office," a cheery female voice said.

"Hi, is he there?"

"He's on his other line. Who's calling, please?"

"Mrs. Wallingford."

"Can you hold, Mrs. Wallingford?"

"Where is she today, anyway?" Smith demanded.

"Yes, I'll hold. She had to take Pinky to the vet."

"Wouldn't you just know she'd be a cat person," Smith said.

"She's not. She's a Vietnamese potbellied pig person."

Smith let out a shriek.

"Carl Grant here."

Wetzon shook her head at Smith. "Hi, Carl. Leslie Wetzon, your friendly neighborhood headhunter. I understand you spoke to Max in our office and I must tell you, I'm really impressed. I want to hear all about your TV show. I'm amazed that Loeb Dawkins lets you do it."

"Well, I don't really have my own show. I've been a guest on several shows."

"Oh, I see. You've been a guest on several shows," she repeated for Smith's benefit.

"Humpf," Smith said, throwing up her hands.

Carl Grant continued: "I was asked to be on Oprah when she did that

57

show about investment clubs, but the firm was afraid I'd get asked questions about the legal problems here."

"Oh, yes, legal problems." Loeb Dawkins had been hit with class-action lawsuits regarding the risky limited partnerships the firm pushed brokers to sell in the eighties to inappropriate investors, like the elderly, the widowed, and the orphaned. "I would think the firm's bad publicity makes it difficult to hold on to clients," she said.

"You know it's that guy in the *Times* who keeps picking away at us just because he wants a book deal."

"So, tell me, Carl, what are your numbers?"

"I'm annualizing at $800,000."

"And you're looking for a mil upfront?"

"That's my asking price."

"Forget it. If you were doing two mil, we could talk, but these days most of the upfront deals have dried up. On $800,000, you might be able to get $250,000 or $300,000."

"No way. They pay me a mil and get a TV personality too. Otherwise, I stay put."

"You're absolutely right to stay put, Carl. You're probably locked in with proprietary products that are not portable. You'd leave half your book on the table."

"But—"

"It was nice talking with you. I'll watch for your TV appearances." Wetzon hung up.

"See what scum they are," Smith said. "This is a perfect example of how they lie all the time."

"Not all of them."

"Oh, I know you always have your favorites, but you're so gullible, sweetie pie. What am I going to do with you? You believe whatever anyone tells you." She took her Tarot cards from her handbag and began to shuffle them.

"Smith—"

"And it's such an endearing quality, sugar," Smith continued, shuffling languidly. "By the way, I want you to be nice . . ." She lingered on the word *nice,* ". . . to Bill Veeder. He's such a lovely man."

"Excuse me? Bill Veeder?" A thought hit her. "Dammit, Smith, is that why you were so insistent on knowing my route home last week? You were setting me up."

Smith smiled her Cheshire cat smile; she held the deck to her breast for a moment and closed her eyes. When she opened them, she began to lay out the cards across her desk, all the while carrying on an indistinguishable murmuring.

"Grrrr," Wetzon said. This was so typically Smith. Condemn, flatter, manipulate, change the subject. Still, Smith did have a sixth sense. It had been over a week now since Sheila Gelber's shivah and Silvestri was hardly around, physically as well as emotionally. Wetzon looked down at the next suspect sheet, picked up the phone, and called Benny Flaxman at Loeb Dawkins in Ashland, Oregon. Max had cold-called him last year and Wetzon had stepped in because it appeared Benny was unhappy. Yet he sat there like a body at rest. The only positive was that he'd gone to talk to Rivington Ellis and it had been a good first meeting and a better second meeting.

"I hate it here, Wetzon," Benny told her now. "I didn't do any of those frigging limited partnerships and I get tarred with the same brush as the worst of them here."

"Benny, you've been complaining to me for months. Now Rivington Ellis wants to write you a check to come to New York and kick the tires. Do it."

"I'll think about it. I had a call from this guy—another headhunter. I asked him about Rivington Ellis, said I was being set up by someone else, and he told me they're on the block."

Wetzon gnashed her teeth. Why did brokers have to listen to everyone with a story? "Not true, Benny. They just turned down a German bank who wanted to buy a piece. They want to stay independent. Who was the other headhunter?"

"I don't know. Tom something or other."

That damn Tom Keegen was out there poisoning the well, Wetzon thought. She said, "Oh, yes, I know him. He's a bad guy. You don't want to listen to him."

"Okay, Wetzon, you know I trust you," Benny said. He hung up.

An infinitesimal tapping came from above. The flooring was being laid. Incredible progress had been made, or so it seemed, because they were no longer inundated with dust, grit, and noise. In a couple of weeks they'd have their new office. The problem was, Wetzon didn't care one way or the other. She'd lost her enthusiasm for the business. It wasn't fun anymore.

The upfront deals had virtually disappeared, the firms bowing to the pressure from the SEC. Many of the firms had instituted attractive pension plans, and two of Smith and Wetzon's best clients had stopped working with headhunters.

"You're too expensive for us," Chip Constantine, the head of retail for Marley Straus, had told Wetzon. "Our managers will have to do their own recruiting."

"Chip," Wetzon had said, "I wish you good luck." Most managers had neither the time nor the talent to recruit. They tripped over their own egos.

Chip. Why did so many of these men in finance carry their little-boy names into adulthood with them? She knew four Buzzes, two Chips, five Chucks, two Spikes, one Buck, four Buddys, four Sonnys, one Fuzzy, three Skips.

Skip to m'lou, m'darlin'.

Smith's hiss yanked Wetzon out of her reverie. "What's the matter?"

"Everything. Nothing is working out right," Smith muttered. She was staring down at her cards.

Max knocked, then stuck his head in the door. "Phone call for you, Wetzon."

"Who is it, Max?"

"The King of Cups is reversed," Smith said.

Max squinted at Smith, utterly confused.

"What does that mean?" Wetzon asked Smith. "Who did you say it was, Max?"

"He said it was confidential," Max said. "He has a funny voice. Wheezy."

"Confidential, what else?" Wetzon picked up the phone. "Leslie Wetzon." No one responded, but the line was open. Someone was there. She could hear him breathing. She slammed the phone down.

"It means," Smith said, "that someone is not what he seems to be."

"Oh, sure."

Smith turned on her, very upset. "You may make a joke of this, but I wouldn't. I never joke about the Tarot. He's dangerous."

"And the Tarot never lies."

"That's right."

"And this King of Cups . . . reversed . . . is coming into our lives?"

Smith sighed. "He's already here."

chapter 15

May

"Birdie, you are coming tomorrow?" Carlos had to shout over musical underscoring. As if he were in a rehearsal studio.

"Where?" Wetzon bit down on a carrot stick, her late-afternoon snack.

"Wait a minute. Guys, can you keep it down for a minute?" The music receded somewhat. "What did you say?"

"I said, where am I coming tomorrow?"

"The backers' audition. Don't tell me you need a special invitation."

"I think it might help."

"The Barracuda . . . I'll be right there," he called. "Give me a second."

"I can hear you're very busy. Tomorrow, you say? I think I can make time for you in my busy schedule. Can I have the specifics, please?"

"Excuse me, Miss Priss. The Dramatists Guild penthouse in the Sardi Building. Five."

Wetzon laughed and cradled the receiver. What had he started to say about Smith? Well, never mind. Her brush with the breather slipped back into her consciousness, but only for a moment. He had not called again. Whatever it was, she would have none of it. It was nonsense, didn't mean anything.

Yet when the phone rang, she was distinctly aware that she was alone. Smith had left in midafternoon for a facial. Max had completed his hours. And Darlene was at home playing nursie to her Vietnamese potbellied pig.

The phone rang again. She answered, "Smith and Wetzon."

"Wetzon! I'm glad I got you and not that snooty partner of yours."

"Roy Weissberg!" She'd recognized his voice and the tinny delivery, along with the sounds of ongoing traffic. Roy was the only manager who consistently called her from his car. "What can I do for you?"

"Well, we're getting a little pressure here from Division to find qualified women to stick into management development."

Oh, sure, Wetzon thought. Irwin Thornton, head of training, was a holdover from the sixties. "Roy, do you honestly think Irwin can work with women?"

"Irwin can't work with anybody."

"So what are we doing?"

"You gotta find me some broads, Wetzon. It's coming down from Division."

"Broads, Roy?"

"Come on, Wetzon. You know I'm kidding."

"Yeah, I know," she said. "The *women* I can show you are probably more qualified than half the men in Division."

"That'll get them off my back."

That probably also means, Wetzon thought as she hung up, that Irwin Thornton is history. "That's it," she said out loud. "We're outa here."

She put on her coat and switched the answering machine to "answer," then cleared the tape of messages. When the phone rang, she let the machine get it.

"Leslie, I'm sorry I missed you, but I've been in court all day—"

She picked up the phone as if she'd been waiting for the call. What the hell was the matter with her? "Hello, Bill, I was just leaving the office."

"Good. I presume you're heading west anyway, so why not join me for a drink?"

"I don't think—"

"The Rainbow Promenade? In half an hour?"

"It's been a long day, Bill. Maybe another—"

"I won't take no from you, Leslie. Come on. Where's your spirit of adventure?"

Yes, where, she asked herself. Laura Lee would say yes. "Okay," she said. "In a half hour."

But she regretted it immediately. Bill Veeder's voice, his inflection, everything about him was seductive. So why had she agreed? She'd agreed because Silvestri had withdrawn from her and she was confused. She could understand his upset about Sheila Gelber's death, but he was a cop, a homicide cop at that. Didn't cops detach themselves from death? Usually. But this time Silvestri's involvement was personal, no matter his protests to the contrary.

So she'd let Bill Veeder intrigue her. What was wrong with a mild flirtation with a man who wore the mystique of power casually? She felt the sweet tremor of danger, and she liked the feeling.

Yes, she would meet Veeder for a drink. And the Rainbow Promenade was a stunning place for . . . just that.

chapter 16

The Rainbow Promenade, on the top floor of 30 Rockefeller Plaza, although elegant, even glamorous, attracted
tourists, squares, and seniors with nostalgia. It was not
one of those inside places with cachet, like the Mark Bar
or the bar at Oceana, that fast-track New Yorkers fre-
quented.

It was also the perfect place to meet a lover because it
was a given that you'd never run into anyone you knew.
Lover? Is that where her mind was? What on earth was
she thinking of?

Unsettled by her train of thought, Wetzon folded her
trench coat over her arm and took the express elevator
up to the sixty-fifth floor with five Japanese tourists
loaded down with cameras and blue Tiffany shopping

bags. The other passengers were two German-speaking men in casual clothes, and a couple dressed for a night out . . . in Savannah. The man wore black tie and the woman was in aqua Southern-belle chiffon, her hair a lacquered bubble about a fading pretty face.

The headhunter, Leslie Wetzon, carrying a black briefcase and the trench coat, wore, of course, New York black: a wool crepe suit, black-and-white silk blouse, and at her throat a long silk scarf in a pin-drop pattern, white on black.

The Promenade was dimly lit, the better to show off one of the most spectacular views of Manhattan. Or hide one's companion? There it was again.

Regardless, the experience of a drink here at sunset might be old-fashioned corn for jaded New Yorkers, but Wetzon had never quite lost her awe for her city—her land of Oz—and its magic was immediately apparent from the windows of the Rainbow Promenade.

Responding to the maître d', Wetzon said, "I'm meeting William Veeder."

"Ms. Wetzon?"

She nodded.

"Mr. Veeder just called. He'll be a few minutes late. He asked that you be seated at his table."

She thought, his table? For drinks? Give me a break.

"He has a favorite table," the maître d' said, as if she'd commented aloud.

On second thought, maybe he always said that to Bill Veeder's girls.

"May we bring you a cocktail while you're waiting?"

"An Amstel Light, thank you."

The favorite table looked out over Manhattan as the sun was setting. Wetzon's heart caught in her throat. How lucky she was to live here! Her anguish over Silvestri began to recede, her restlessness calmed. She wanted to put her arms around her city, clasp it to her. Tears pooled in her eyes.

"Well, I see I chose the perfect place for our rendezvous." An immaculate Bill Veeder tucked his tall frame down in the chair opposite hers. With long, slim fingers, he adjusted his French cuffs. You couldn't miss the gold wedding band.

"Rendezvous? What an odd choice of words," Wetzon said, brushing her tears back with her fingertip. "I thought this was to be a business drink."

"More of a get-acquainted drink." His eyes inhaled her; she caught herself leaning across the table toward him and jerked back. "I understand you call it in your . . . business . . . exploring the possibilities . . ." A waiter set a martini in front of Veeder and poured Wetzon's beer foaming into a large glass.

When Veeder raised a dark eyebrow, she was glad she'd ordered the beer. His passing resemblance to Paul Newman—his craggy face, close-cropped white hair with those dark brows, and sharp blue eyes—was disturbing. His eyes caught hers again and held for a long instant, until Wetzon pulled away, unsettled. She'd felt the caress although he'd never moved his hands. Jesus, she thought, I'm over my head here.

"Do you like olives?" His voice was husky with innuendo.

"What?" She felt her cheeks go hot.

"Olives," he said, offering her one from his martini.

"Oh." She shook her head. "I love olives, but not the ginned ones." He was freshly shaven, she saw, close and clean. No shadows, like Silvestri. She wondered how old he was. Early to mid-fifties perhaps. Senior partner. He wore a spicy scent that made her dizzy. Or was it the beer? She pushed away her half-empty glass.

"It's funny what a small world it is," Veeder said.

"What do you mean?" Could he see the thumping pulse in her throat? She tugged at her scarf. It was choking her.

"One of my clients mentioned you the other day."

"Really? Who?"

"Hem Barron."

Hem Barron, she thought. Wouldn't you know? She said, "I met him briefly a couple of weeks ago, with a friend." She caught herself frowning and realized all at once she was taking this too seriously; she'd forgotten how to flirt. Or maybe she'd never ever known. *Lighten up, Leslie,* she told herself. She took a swallow of beer and smiled at Veeder. *You have the upper hand here, lady. Keep it that way.*

"Yes, Hem was a little concerned that you might say something premature about the offering—"

"Oh," she said, not hiding her disappointment, "is that what this mysterious drink is all about?" She looked out at the City. The vanishing rays of sunlight were yellow arrows on the glass and steel buildings.

"No," Veeder said. "Not at all. Just coincidence, really. It's something I've wanted to do since . . ." He watched her with a terrifying self-assurance as Wetzon flashed automatically back to the Christmas party not six months earlier. Smith had dragged her to his law firm—to see the annual tree-lighting ceremony at Rockefeller Plaza.

When Veeder had observed she didn't drink champagne, he'd taken her to his office for a special single-malt scotch. They'd watched the tree lighting from his window. Disarmed by the moment, Wetzon's defenses were almost breached by the sexuality of the man as he stood so close to her they might have been lovers. That word again.

She shook her head to block the memory. Outside, shimmery lights in all the surrounding buildings made the City seem surreal. She looked at Bill Veeder. "No," she said, making the leap.

"Why not?" The blue eyes didn't blink. He knew exactly what she was referring to.

"I'm in a relationship . . ." The words came out so lukewarm, it staggered her. She looked down at her fingers worrying the paper napkin to shreds.

"I have a wife." His hand reached across the table suddenly, fingers touching her breast. "Your button is open," he said. He buttoned the blouse for her while she held her breath.

"Bill, how nice to see you again." A woman's voice, behind Wetzon.

Veeder rose to his feet to shake hands with the woman and her companion, whom he greeted with "How's it going, Rog? We really have to get together on that Garelick-Weisman merger."

"I'll call you," Rog said. He looked down at Wetzon with what seemed a knowing grin. "Aren't you going to introduce us?"

Wetzon felt herself shrinking into her seat. What she wanted most was to be out of there, never to have been there at all.

"Forgive me," Veeder said smoothly. "Of course—"

He doesn't want to introduce me, Wetzon thought, choking back a nervous giggle.

"I'd like you to meet two of my colleagues, Leslie. Roger Asher and—" A wave of nausea hit Wetzon.

"Leslie and I already know each other, don't we?" Rita Silvestri said.

chapter 17

"How do you know Rita Silvestri?" Veeder demanded after Rita and Rog had left—what seemed like hours but was only moments later.

Wetzon, in an aura of gloom, hadn't even seen them depart. "My relationship . . . is with her son."

Veeder was unfazed. "Ah, I should have connected it. The detective."

Wetzon was up, ready for flight.

"Sit down, please, Leslie. Let's talk this over. Think of it as a business arrangement between two consenting adults."

She shook her head, slipped on her coat. "We don't have any business to conduct," she said. If she didn't get out of there, she was going to be sick.

"Loose ends must be tied off; otherwise, everything unravels, my dear." He was standing now too. "Sit down and let me tell you how it is."

She stared at him. Silvestri had used a similar phrase. "I don't think we have anything to talk about, Bill." She forced the words through her teeth.

On the run now, she was oblivious to the startled expressions. Only peripherally was she aware she had satisfied the delighted curiosity of the strangers visiting her City, who, having been alerted by their travel agents and the media to the unpredictable eccentricities of New Yorkers, were looking forward to just such a performance from one of the natives.

A short time later in Central Park, shoulder resting on an ancient oak, she threw up, ridding herself of the poisons she'd allowed to creep into her being. It was Silvestri she loved, and she would hold on to this. They would work through their problems. If he let her help. Sheila Gelber was dead. There was no escaping that.

She wiped her mouth with a tissue, embarrassed by the mess. But then, Central Park was well over a century old. Surely other people had been sick to their stomachs here. She patted the crusty bark of the old oak, readjusted her scarf, and was on her way toward Central Park West and home.

The last few hours had been an aberration, and she could blot out most of it . . . temporarily at least. It would all come surging back at her the moment she settled her head on her pillow and turned out the light. She could not remove Rita Silvestri from her thoughts. Would she tell? No, Wetzon didn't think so. But Wetzon had seen something in Rita's eyes—not *understanding,* exactly—but was it *acknowledgment?*

Damn Smith and her "be nice to Bill Veeder"!

Hold on there, Leslie Wetzon, she told herself. This is your doing entirely. She couldn't blame Smith for anything but the power of suggestion.

Clutching an armload of mail, she let herself into her apartment while Izz danced around and made guttural sounds. Hardly the hysterical greeting the little dog saved for Silvestri. "No doubt a female-to-male thing, right, Izz?" she said. "I do understand."

Wetzon switched on the light and the globes of her art-glass chandelier glowed with oranges and blues. Izz yelped at her impatiently. "Yes, yes, I'll bet you're hungry. Let me just drop this stuff and take off my coat."

Except for the chandelier, the apartment was dark. She raced around turning on all the lights, Izz on her heels, then dropped her coat on a chair and shook as much dried dog food as the little dog would let her into the empty dish. Leaning against the counter, she watched Izz gobble for a few minutes, then filled the water bowl and left the kitchen, trying to ignore the answering machine blinking that there were four messages waiting.

In the bathroom Wetzon rinsed her mouth again and again. She wiped off her makeup, then stood in a steaming shower for a long time until she felt clean again.

The apartment was cold. That damp cold that builds up after management turned off the heat and yet outside it wasn't warm enough to extend inside. She pulled on sweats, put Mozart on the CD, and worked at her barre until she felt her mind begin to dissolve into her body.

She made a pot of coffee, toasted a bagel and slathered it with cream cheese, took it and a mug of coffee into the living room. Her answering machine was still blinking. Five messages. Damnation. One must have come in while she was in the shower. She hit the playback button. Couldn't everyone leave her alone?

"Silvestri? Call me." Metzger.

Beep.

"Les, I'll be home around seven." Silvestri.

Beep.

"Silvestri? Where the hell are you?" Metzger again.

Beep.

"Sweetie pie, we have to talk. Call me the minute you get home." Who else but Smith?

"I will not call you, bitch." Wetzon wrinkled her nose at Izz, who was sniffing at the bagel. It was seven-thirty and no sign of Silvestri. Why was Metzger so anxious to talk to him? Had something come in from forensics on Sheila?

Beep.

The line was open. No one spoke, but she could hear the breathing. She was meant to hear the breathing. The disconnect came abruptly. She sat absolutely still, foot curled under her, until she became aware it had fallen asleep. As she flexed it to get the pins and needles out, she said aloud, "It was a wrong number." It had to be. But she hated it. Hated the way it made her feel. Vulnerable.

Izz shrieked and literally flew over the coffee table, arriving at the door just as Silvestri opened it. She then leaped and cavorted until he picked her up and let her bathe his face with wet kisses.

"Metzger's been trying to reach you," Wetzon said, leaving her half-eaten bagel and limping into the foyer. "Foot's asleep." Silvestri hadn't moved.

"He found me." Still he didn't move. Just kept looking at her as if he weren't really seeing her. He set Izz down.

She thought: Rita told him. "What is it?" She touched his face, felt the bristles of his beard. He gave her back her hand, but not before he kissed her palm. "What?" she said again.

"Sheila is officially a homicide." Silvestri turned away from her and hung his jacket over the back of a chair, then slipped out of the shoulder holster, rolled it around his gun. "I'm beat," he said. His voice was hoarse. He rubbed his eyes. Grim lines had settled in around his mouth.

"You look terrible." She followed him into the kitchen and watched him take a beer from the fridge. "How did she die?"

He took a hefty swallow. His eyes were bloodshot. "In agony," he said.

"Sheila was poisoned." Silvestri popped the cap and tilted his head back, drinking a long swallow.

"How?" Wetzon took four eggs, goat cheese, and some leftover roasted zucchini from the fridge. She filled the kettle with cold water.

"They don't know. Something she ate. It took about six hours to kill her." He was staring at Wetzon as if it was something she'd done. "She went through hell."

"She didn't call anyone—?" Wetzon dropped a chunk of butter into the pan, lit the gas, then with a wire whisk she whipped the eggs into a froth.

Silvestri flinched. He took another long swallow. "By the time she knew it was more than stomach flu, she may not have been able to think, let alone move."

"There was a plate sitting in the sink." With the butter sizzling, Wetzon poured the eggs into the hot pan and began rocking it. "The faucet was dripping. I guess it washed the crumbs away."

"Cornmeal."

"Cornmeal?" She nudged the omelet gently with a spatula to cook the center.

"She had half-digested cornmeal in her—"

"My God, the muffins."

"What muffins?"

"In her freezer, Silvestri. There was a foil package of muffins." She sliced two bagels and put them in the toaster oven.

"The M.E. sent someone over this morning and cleaned out everything from the freezer, the fridge, and the cupboards. They'll find whatever it was."

"It's in the corn muffins." She sprinkled the goat cheese over the omelet, folded it in half, and divided it between two plates.

"So you're a toxicologist now, are you?" A trace of a smile flickered across his eyes. He picked up the plates and brought them to the dining table.

Wetzon buttered the bagels, carried them and the coffee to the table. "I know I can help, Silvestri, if you let me." She went back to the kitchen for the mugs.

He dug into his omelet. "This is good, Les. Didn't know you could cook."

"There's a lot you don't know about me," she said with more sharpness than she meant. She concentrated on her omelet.

"Oh?" He stopped eating. "Like what?"

She thought of Bill Veeder. Her aborted flirtation. "I ran into Rita today."

"Oh, yeah? Where?" He began eating again.

"I was having a drink with a potential client," she said glibly. Liar, liar, liar. "Rita was with a colleague. . . ." Silvestri was staring down at his plate. He'd tuned her out.

They finished eating without speaking, and she took the empty plates and put them in the sink.

When she came back, he was ranging around the room oblivious of Izz's dancing attendance.

"Goddammit, Silvestri, I've had it. You have to tell me what the hell is going on with you."

He stopped pacing to stare at her. A chill like a ghostly prescience settled over her. In his eyes she saw she was a stranger. Finally, he said, "Sit down, Les. There're some things I have to talk to you about."

"Sounds ominous." She gave him a nervous smile. Filling the mugs with coffee, she handed him one.

He took the mug but didn't return her smile. "You're going to take this personally, but it's something I have to do. I can't do it here."

Trying to follow him, she lost her way. What was he saying to her? "Let me get this straight," she said, hating her small voice. "By *here,* you mean with me." She felt herself shattering. This was worse than she'd expected.

"I knew you would take it personally. It's not personal, goddammit. I have to work this out myself."

Don't be so selfish, she told herself. It's about him, not you. "But I can help you, Silvestri. Aren't we supposed to be friends? Talk to me."

His eyes were granite. "See what you're doing? You stand over me, nag at me. I don't need that now. I can't think clearly and you don't leave me any space."

Nag? That was the only word that penetrated. It went deep. "I don't nag. I want us to communicate. We should be sharing the pain if we're going to—" She stopped, swallowed the lump in her throat. "You're leaving."

He was looking everywhere but at her. "I'm just clearing out until I get my head straight."

"Straight," she repeated bitterly. "You haven't been straight with me since Sheila Gelber was . . . murdered. I told you I understood—"

"See?" He was shouting at her. "That's what I mean. You won't leave it alone." He stamped off down the hall. Tears stung her eyes. She refused to let them out. From the bedroom, then the bathroom, came the sound of slamming doors, drawers. He was packing.

Izz, who had wandered along after him, her tail drooping, returned and nestled against her ankles; she knew they were in trouble.

Silvestri had called her a nag. Hardly a term of affection.

"Les," he said, his voice cracking. He was standing across the room from her. "I don't mean to hurt you. I need time to sort this out and I've got to do that alone."

"I seem to remember a time when you were there for me. Let me be there for you."

"This is different. I have to put what we have aside for a while. There's no reason for you to know anything or be involved."

"There's every reason. We either go on or we don't. What do we really have, Silvestri? We pass each other: good morning, good night, see ya later. You won't give, you won't take. So tell me, what *do* we have?"

He turned away from her. "I don't have time for this."

Her fury was cold and deadly. "Silvestri, if you leave now, like this, don't come back."

The ring of the phone sliced through the anger and hurt. She answered it.

"Leslie," Metzger said. "Is Silvestri there?"

"Hold on." Wordlessly, she handed Silvestri the phone.

"Yeah?" He laid his garment bag over the back of a chair. A beat later, he said, "Christalmighty." He looked at Wetzon, looked away. "When will they know?" Eyes on Wetzon again. "Not here. I'm going back to Chelsea for a while." He hung up the phone quickly, but not quick enough for Wetzon to miss Metzger's exclamation.

She folded her arms. "For a while? Why didn't you tell him the truth?"

"What is the truth, Les?" He bent and kissed her on the lips. "This is the truth."

But she refused to let her lips respond. "Whatever that means."

He fastened his shoulder holster, put on his jacket, and picked up the garment bag. When he opened the door, Izz scurried out into the hallway.

"Come back here," Wetzon cried, grabbing the squirming furry creature. "Not you, Silvestri. You're history."

"I'll be back."

"Don't count on it. I'm not about to sit around and wait for you."

"Do what you have to do." He laughed suddenly, as if this were all a joke. "I love you when you're angry."

"Fuck you, Silvestri. Get the hell out of here. This is not a romance novel."

He pressed the elevator button. "You're also one smart babe."

"Smart babe!" Outraged, she slammed the door, shutting him out. What the hell was he trying to do? Make up? Too late. It was over. Over. She paused. What did he really mean when he said she was one smart babe? She opened the door. Izz tried to wriggle out of her arms to get to Silvestri, who was on the elevator but holding the door, waiting for her.

He knew her too well. He'd known she would act on her curiosity.

He let go of the door, and as it slid shut, he called, "The poison *was* in the corn muffins."

chapter 19

A wild uncomprehending anger gripped her well into the night. She was hot, cold, hot again. She got up, lay down, got up, walked through the apartment. Izz, who'd followed her every move, finally curled up on Silvestri's pillow and went to sleep.

In the early hours of the morning, anger was replaced by an overwhelming hurt. He didn't trust her. He'd closed her out. He wouldn't share his feelings about Sheila Gelber's death.

If it were Wetzon having the crisis and needing him, he would be there. She knew he would. He'd been there for her when she was going through post-traumatic shock. But he wouldn't let her do the same for him.

The center had not held.

Silvestri was intent on hiding something from her. What was it? That he'd loved this woman and had a mad, passionate affair with her years ago? What was there to hide? What was there about the relationship between Sheila and Silvestri that was so private he couldn't talk about it? And yet he'd told Wetzon that he couldn't remember if he'd loved Sheila or not.

Then there was the other thing gnawing at her. He'd called her a nag. Is that what he really thought of her? How could that be? All she wanted was for them to have a life together. It was a two-way street.

Her alarm was a foghorn blasting her from her stupor. She staggered out of bed and into the shower.

By the time she got to the office, it was well after ten, and now relief was the only sensation she was aware of. The relief came from the realization that she wouldn't have to keep up the maintenance on their relationship. It was over. She could be alone, which right now seemed not half bad.

Wasn't it difficult enough trying to deal with Smith . . . ?

Instinctively, Wetzon knew it was not this dead woman who'd come between them. It was Silvestri himself. He was not a sharer. He did his own thing. Well, okay, that was fine. Let him fly solo.

Darlene brought her a mug of coffee. "You look very pale," she said. "Is anything wrong?"

So solicitous was she that Wetzon's level of paranoia, normally low, rose. Darlene was neither sensitive nor caring—that is, unless you happened to be a Vietnamese potbellied pig. Darlene's motivating forces were money and power, rather like Smith's. But at this moment Darlene's face wore a tell-me-all-about-it Sally Jessy Raphaël mask of pseudo-kindness.

"Thanks, Darlene," Wetzon said. "Where's Smith?"

"She was here when I came in, but said she'd be out the rest of the day. She said to tell you she'd see you later."

"Okay, thanks, Darlene. Max'll be in any minute, so you'll be relieved of phone duty."

"Oh, that's all right, really. I don't mind at all. In fact, I rather enjoy the change. Open or closed?"

"Closed, please."

Darlene smiled and left, closing the door.

With the back of her pencil, Wetzon tapped in Sonny Torcelli's number. Sonny was the Atlanta manager for Larson McKenzie, a small wire house about the size of the old Smith Barney before the advent of Sandy

Weill and Smith Barney's merger with Shearson. Wetzon had arranged for him to meet with two very big, very unhappy Pru brokers.

"Wetzon!" Sonny screamed into the phone. "I really goofed. Me and my big mout. You gotta help get me outa dis."

Sonny had the kind of Brooklyn accent and manner that didn't go over really well outside of New York. It was so colloquial, he almost needed an interpreter.

"What happened, Sonny? They were really psyched."

"Listen, Wetzon, I'm from New Yawk."

Gedowdaheah, Wetzon thought.

"I get all excited about tings, so I said someting like 'goddam fucking' . . . You know, da way I always tawk, and you don't take offense. Whyn't you tell me dey were born-again Christians?"

Wetzon pressed her lips together so her laughter couldn't escape.

"Did you know?" Sonny demanded.

"No, honestly, I didn't," she admitted. "It never came up in our talks."

"Get on da phone and tawk to dem. Get me outa dis mess. I gotta have dem in the office. It'll look good on my record when I'm up for review."

"Are you sure? You'll have to watch your language."

"Oh, dat don't bodder me. Once dey're here, dey'll get used ta me. Everybody does."

It turned out to be easier than Wetzon had first thought. The two born-agains wanted money as much as the next broker and Larson Mc-Kenzie was offering the biggest upfront deals on the Street now. These guys did two mil together. Their signing package would be for one mil, plus perks like expense accounts, computers, sales assistants, and a fifty percent payout for two years. At another major firm, they'd be lucky to get forty percent payout for one year. And they certainly wouldn't get a check for one mil.

"Sonny has such a passion for the business, he gets carried away," Wetzon explained to them. "And don't forget, he's from New York." Traitor, she thought, as she dialed up Sonny and scheduled the two brokers for a second meeting.

"You're a wonder, Wetzon," Sonny said.

"Thanks, Sonny." She hung up and sighed. "And a nag too."

Max knocked. "Good morning, dear," he said. "Isn't it a beautiful morning?" He was wearing his bull-and-bear braces under his shiny brown suit. "Darlene went out to get a sandwich. She'll be right back."

"Fine. The phones are quiet. Smith won't be back, and I have to leave around four. Can you work until five today?"

"Of course. Do you want me to call into any particular firms?"

"Take a look at today's *Journal,* Max. I think we should be calling Smith Barney brokers. There've been rumors for the last few weeks that Sandy Weill is shopping again. He's supposed to have his eye on Pru. He wants to be bigger than Merrill. Let's see what his brokers have to say. My guess is they're not going to be happy campers, because they're already complaining they don't have support and can't get answers. Being one of eight thousand brokers is bad enough; one in fifteen thousand will be horrendous."

The phones began ringing, two lines at once. Max rushed to his desk. "Smith and Wetzon, good morning. She's at a meeting . . ."

"Smith and Wetzon," Wetzon said.

There was no response . . . except for the breathing, along with some muffled background noise that Wetzon couldn't make out.

"Who is this?" she demanded. "What do you want?"

The line went dead.

She didn't need this right now. On her desk was a stack of her updates. She flipped through the suspect sheets but couldn't focus on any of them. Where was Smith? She would have liked to talk this over with Smith. Had they alienated someone in the industry? Maybe Smith was getting these calls too. Rising, she walked over to Smith's desk and looked at her appointment book. Smith had blocked out the whole day with a big scribble.

The outside door slammed. Wetzon went back to her desk and looked at her pink messages. William Veeder had called. And Rita Silvestri. Shit. She dropped the messages on her desk. She'd have to think about this. Call Rita back at some point. Don't call Veeder. Why not call Veeder? No. Definitely not call Veeder.

"Wetzon?"

"Darlene?" How long had Darlene been standing in the doorway?

Darlene smiled. "You looked as though you wouldn't take time for lunch, so I brought you a snack." She held out a brown paper bag.

"That's very nice of you, Darlene." Be gracious, Wetzon ordered herself. She didn't feel gracious. "Actually, I have half a bagel that'll get me through, so long as there's coffee." She took the bag with the Mangia logo from Darlene and looked inside, then removed a big crunchy macaroon. "I love these, Darlene. How did you know?"

"Heard you mention them once. You seem so down today I thought you could use some comfort food."

"Down? Do I seem down?" Dammit, she thought, I won't have it. "I am not down. I'm just distracted. But thank you so much."

The phones began their syncopated jangle again. Darlene waved at Wetzon and left the room.

"Laura Lee Day for you, Wetzon," Max called.

She picked up the phone. She was Wetzon, curmudgeon. "What?"

"Uh-oh," Laura Lee said. "You sound down—"

"Damnation, Laura Lee, why can't everyone leave me alone?"

"There you are. I'll say no more."

Wetzon sighed. "Silvestri and I have split up."

"Good heavens! You poor dear. No wonder. Tell Mama Laura Lee all about it."

"I can't now. The phones are going crazy and Smith—"

"Is not there."

"Right."

"Why am I not surprised?"

"Can we talk later?"

"Yes, of course. But don't hang up. I have a story to tell you that will make you laugh. At least I think it will. Take a minute."

"Okay. Talk fast."

"True story, Wetzon. A major firm has a regional managers' meetin' on insurance in Tahoe. The meetin' is being conducted around the pool, of course."

"Of course."

"Now this one head of an entire region—and he shall be nameless—finishes his report, turns, and pisses in the pool—"

"You're kidding."

"I am not kiddin'. Do you believe it?"

"Is this a male thing, Laura Lee?"

"The penis fixation? For sure, darlin'. They're so enchanted with it, they don't know what to do with it."

The laughter started slowly, then became gales, until Wetzon, gasping, dried her eyes. "Thanks a heap, Laura Lee. I needed that. I'll call you later."

"No, wait," Laura Lee said, catching her breath and giggling again. "Hem and Minnie are giving a huge party in their loft the week after Memorial Day. You're invited."

"Me?"

"Hem actually said, and I quote: 'Don't come without your friend Leslie Wetzon.' Unquote. And I do want to be there, Wetzon darlin'. They're supposed to have the most amazin' place with a roof terrace, and they've just bought the rest of the floor. And they know everyone . . ."

"Oh, please, Laura Lee, it'll be chock-full of New York's beautiful, but exceedingly boring, people."

"Except for thee and me. Truth is, and I'm breakin' a confidence here, there's this guy—an incredibly successful attorney, if you must know— who has a thing for you. I won't mention names, but Bill Veeder made a special request for your presence."

"Not on your life, Laura Lee," Wetzon snapped. "I am tired of the emotional wrenching that comes with relationships."

"I couldn't agree with you more, darlin'. That's why it's so much fun to play with fire. If you are really careful and contain it, you won't get burned."

c h a p t e r 2 0

Maybe, Wetzon thought, that's really what all of this is about. Men enchanted with their penises.

It had started to rain, soft warm drops like tears on your cheeks. She opened her umbrella and, heading westward, jaywalked across Second Avenue in a traffic lull. Forty-ninth Street between Second and Third was a well-kept enclave of privately owned brownstones, home to, among others, Katharine Hepburn and Stephen Sondheim, Wetzon's favorites.

Wetzon paused in front of Sondheim's house and made her usual obeisance. Closing the umbrella, she set down her briefcase and bowed deeply. Rain dribbled down her nose, frizzled her hair in its topknot. Sorry, Steve, you get short shrift today. She pressed the button on her furled umbrella; it snapped open, she righted it, and went on her way. She would look a total wreck by the time she arrived at the backers' audition.

Unless . . . She could stop at the Chanel counter at Saks and get someone to make her up.

Which is exactly what she did.

It was that time in the afternoon when the shop-till-you-drop crowd were wending their way home, and the after-work contingent had not yet arrived. Wetzon perched on a high chair in a private alcove and let the cosmetologist clean off her streaked makeup, fill in her tiny lines, and erase the dark circles under her eyes. She was quickly dabbed and brushed with the latest eye shadows and liners, moving her away from subtle browns to purples and wines, a touch of white on her lids. The palest of lip color completed the transformation.

Handed a mirror with a sly smile, Wetzon was stunned by her reflection. She looked like a different person. Sultry, somehow. The flare of her eyebrow let the world know how assured she was. Yes. Unattached. Yes. Her hair, loosened by the rain, blurred the sharpness of her nose, chin, and cheekbones. On the make, Leslie Wetzon? Why the hell not? Silvestri had walked out on her, expecting her to be patient and understand that he preferred not to include her in this portion of his life.

So she was free.

By the time she left Saks, the rain had stopped, and the sky was a mellow blue streaked with pink. May would have it no other way.

On the corner of Fifth Avenue and Forty-fourth Street, where she again turned west, a snack cart operator, his knees resting on a piece of cardboard, was praying to his God. New Yorkers passed him by; tourists stopped to stare.

The penthouse office of the Dramatists Guild—its opulence still visible in the carved-plaster and gold-leafed ceiling of the huge room—had once been the home of J. J. Shubert, the oldest of the legendary three Shubert brothers. The empire the trio left still operated most of the theaters on Broadway.

A coatrack fat and dripping with wet raincoats and slickers stood near the entrance. Rows of folding chairs, almost all occupied, were lined up in front of a grand piano. A man in his thirties stood, leaning against the piano, while a very stout woman perhaps a little younger, took up most of the piano bench.

"Well, look at you, Birdie mine!" Carlos grabbed her waist and twirled her around; his face was flushed with excitement. He kissed her lightly on the lips. "I saved a seat for you, right up front."

When she turned to talk to him, he was gone. Wetzon spread her coat loosely over the back of the chair and sat down.

"We have met, I think," the woman beside her said.

It was Micklynn Devora, her substantial figure draped in what looked like layers of woven and fringed shawls. A thick braid hung down her back. She wore no makeup whatever, so her eyelashes and brows seemed to disappear entirely. Her lips glistened without color.

"Leslie Wetzon." Wetzon held out her hand. "We met last month when my partner brought me to The Groaning Board to taste some food for her party."

"Yes. I remember now. Xenia Smith." She rolled Smith's name on her tongue as if she were tasting it.

Wetzon smiled. This was a different Micklynn Devora from the one she'd met previously. "Carlos and I have been friends for almost twenty years. He told me that when you lived next door you kept him and Arthur from starving."

This seemed to amuse Micklynn. "I doubt that, really." She looked past Wetzon. "Oh, there's your partner now."

"My partner? Excuse me?" Wetzon turned in her seat. Smith was coming down the aisle toward her, but she sailed right by Wetzon with a casual wave. She went directly to the couple at the piano as if she knew them, then faced the audience and smiled.

"Ladies and gentlemen," Smith began, radiating charm, "I am your host, Xenia Smith. I want to introduce you to a new musical. I am certain that after you've heard this wonderful score, you will be eager to make an investment."

Host? Wetzon was so floored she missed the next few lines of Smith's introduction.

". . . for *Softly*. I'd like you to meet two wonderfully talented people: Marian Lesser at the piano and Ez Carpenter, standing. The next Kander and Ebb."

Did Smith realize that John Kander and Fred Ebb were *men?*

"Before we start," Smith continued, "we have an open bar set up and a snack table. Why don't you help yourselves to drinks and food, and while you're doing that, take a look at some of our literature."

"Are you all right, Leslie?" Micklynn whispered. She didn't have to, for people were noisy about getting up. En masse they moved toward the back of the room for the free booze and Cheez Doodles.

"Yes. No. Why?"

"You're whimpering."

"Godalmighty," Wetzon said. "Excuse me a minute." Smith was totally surrounded, so Wetzon made a beeline for Carlos, who was talking warmly—would you believe—to Mort Hornberg.

"Birdie!" Carlos cried, giving her the no-no sign behind Mort.

Wetzon ignored him. "Mort, darling, I thought you were in California making *Hotshot* without Carlos." Carlos was now doing a St. Vitus dance in an effort to shut her up.

"Delighted to see you too, Leslie darling," Mort said. He took out a small dispenser from his inside pocket and sprayed his mouth.

"What is Smith doing here, Carlos?" Wetzon gave up on Mort and zeroed in on Carlos.

"Representing your clients," Carlos said.

"My clients? What clients? You'd better tell me slowly, Carlos. Very slowly."

"You represent Lesser and Carpenter and *Softly,* Dear Heart. I thought you knew that. It's a Smith and Wetzon extravaganza."

"Shit, Carlos. We're not agents."

"You're managers, I was told. Don't tell me you don't know. I thought you knew all about it."

"Goddam," Wetzon said. I will kill her for sure now, she swore to herself. In some terribly painful, terribly slow manner.

"Sweetie pie!" Smith greeted her with an oversized, perfumed hug. "I'm so glad you got here. Isn't this perfectly thrilling?"

"Oh, I'm thrilled all right. Why didn't you tell me about this?"

Smith summoned up a truly hurt expression. "I did tell you," she said with supreme patience.

"No, you didn't."

"Of course I did. You poor thing, you've been so distracted lately, sweetie pie. I just don't know what to do with you. Oh, there's Twoey!" She kissed her fingertips and touched them to Wetzon's cheek, then went off after her former lover Goldman Barnes II, known as Twoey. Twoey had bored Smith when he was an investment banker and intrigued her when he walked away from Wall Street to become a Broadway producer.

"Done it again to you, has she?" Carlos said, at Wetzon's shoulder. He waved to Arthur Margolies, Esquire, his lover, who had just arrived.

Wetzon gave Arthur a quick kiss, then scooped up a handful of Cheez Doodles and a glass of Perrier. She returned to her seat next to Micklynn, who was sipping a glass of wine.

"Sorry about that," she told Micklynn.

"Please, don't be. I find I'm an expert in partnership relationships. Been there, done that, so to speak." Micklynn finished her wine and set the empty glass on the floor near her feet. She was wearing Birkenstock sandals; her feet were bare. "I have often prepared the most lethal of poisons in the most succulent of offerings . . . figuratively, of course."

chapter 2 1

After Wetzon was able to squirrel away her anger and listen, she was charmed by the music, by the lyrics, by the whole performance. For the most part, Lesser played and Carpenter sang and did brief, delicious riffs of book material in between numbers.

How had Smith found them?

"They found me—us, sugar," Smith told Wetzon when the performance concluded. She had her arms around each. "Marian, Ezra, I want you to meet Leslie Wetzon."

"Ah," Carpenter said, "the silent partner. We wondered about you."

"Really, Ezra, sweetie, you could have asked me,"

Smith said peevishly. "I thought I told you how busy Wetzon was seeing to the renovation of our office."

"That's me," Wetzon said, "office slave, chained to the desk. So busy that I guess I just didn't hear Smith tell me all about you two. Happy to meet you . . . finally." Had Wetzon's eyes been blowguns, Smith would have been a pincushion of poisoned darts.

Lesser, who had short dark hair and a humorous mouth, raised an eyebrow. "Ez, we only have the sitter till seven."

"Wonderful, guys," Carlos said, shaking hands all around. "I love the material. We'll talk."

"Call *me*," Smith said pointedly.

"Why, Xenia, darling, would you think I wouldn't?" Carlos' delivery was so arch that Wetzon laughed. "Come on, Birdie, Arthur and I are taking you to dinner." Arm draped over her shoulder, he drew her aside. "You look a mite peak-ed."

"*Pissed* is a much better word. My partner is sneaking around behind my back and my lover has moved out."

"Oy." He nuzzled her cheek. "Come have dinner and tell us all about it."

"Can't talk yet. Too raw."

"About the Barracuda, Dear Heart, I wouldn't let it concern you. She has no taste."

"Then how did she find Lesser and Carpenter?"

"God gave Mark Smith all the taste in that family. Lesser's kid brother is at Harvard with Mark."

"Why is Mort Hornberg here?"

Carlos studied the ceiling. He was so intent that Wetzon took his shoulders and shook him gently. "You're not."

"I am." He couldn't look her in the eye.

"But after what he did to you on the *Hotshot* movie? Oh, Carlos."

"Arthur's doing the contract. It'll be rock-solid this time."

"Oh, sure." She turned Carlos and gave him a push. "Go on, Arthur's waiting."

Wetzon wandered back to Smith, who was walking around like a goddam producer, thanking everyone for coming. Lesser and Carpenter had disappeared.

When Smith got to Wetzon, she was on such a roll, she almost thanked Wetzon for coming too. Instead, she snapped her fingers and said, "Fifteen thou."

"For what?"

"That's what they paid us. Lesser and Carpenter. It's a retainer. We represent them."

"We're not agents, Smith."

"We're managers, babycakes. Agents only get ten to fifteen percent. Managers can ask for as much as they want. We get twenty-five percent of any income related to this score. How do you like that?"

"It sounds a little exorbitant, but it's fine, I guess, if we do the work. The real question is, do we want to babysit talent? I'm not so sure. In any event, I would like to be consulted on any decision pertaining to our partnership. Is that asking too much? This is not something new. You know how I feel about it."

Smith rolled her eyes. "Oh, for pity sakes. We must carpus dee-us."

"By all means. Seize everyone's day, Smith."

"What is the matter with you, sweetie pie? You might as well tell me. You know I can read you like a book—"

"No, you can't, goddammit." It made Wetzon crazy when anyone said that, especially Smith. "When will you next deign to grace our office with your presence?"

"Tomorrow, of course. Don't you remember? The new furniture is coming." She gave Wetzon a sharp look. "I told you last week to keep tomorrow clear. What's wrong with your memory?"

"Gosh, I seem to have lost it somewhere." Had she? Or was she just tuning out? She had no memory of Smith having told her the furniture was being delivered tomorrow. "I'm beat. I'm going home."

"Tell Dick Tracy to give you a massage," Smith said.

"Dick Tracy and Tess Trueheart have split."

Smith practically exploded with joy. "So that's it! Well, sweetie pie, congratulations. You are well rid of him. I am absolutely thrilled for you . . . and for me. We must celebrate. It used to be so much fun when we were both detached at the same time."

"Detached?"

"Xenia, darling, coming?" Mort's voice. He had a slim young man, who had gathered up all the printed material on *Softly*, in tow.

"Just a minute, sugar," Smith called. "I have to powder my nose."

Wetzon went down in the elevator suddenly sorry she hadn't gone to dinner with Carlos and Arthur and sobbed on their loyal shoulders. After all, she'd arranged with Albert, the handyman, to feed Izz before he went home. There was nothing calling her home.

What to do? Maybe a slice and a movie. She stood on the street in front of Sardi's looking for a cab.

"You look as if you could use a drink." Micklynn Devora's breath was warm and boozy.

"After I've eaten something. On the other hand, maybe a whole lot sooner." Wetzon peered into Sardi's. The bar was too crowded.

"I have a suggestion, then. What are you doing this evening?"

"Going home?"

"I don't think so. You are coming up to my place. I have a lovely wine. Think of it as a favor to me. I can use the company. I'll make us dinner. Come— Oh, there's a cab!" Micklynn was halfway down the block holding the yellow door for two people just stepping out. "Come on, Leslie," she called.

Wetzon thought, why not? Why the hell not? She had nothing to do but brood, and she would get a splendid dinner out of it. She got into the cab after Micklynn.

"Nice score," Micklynn said. She told the driver her address and sat back, giving Wetzon her full attention.

"Yes, it is."

"Your partner is a piece of work."

"Yes, she is."

"So is mine." The cab squeezed onto Eighth Avenue and immediately got caught in rush-hour traffic. "We have something in common, then."

"Do we?"

Micklynn sighed, changed directions. "I saw you in the *Hotshot* revival. Carlos got me tickets. You were wonderful."

"Thank you."

"Carlos tells me you're on Wall Street. Maybe you can help me understand something."

So that's what this is all about. "What?"

"Why in the world would I want to take my company public?"

"To cash in, then cash out."

"But I don't want to cash out. It's my life. I don't want investors telling me how they think I should make a sweet potato casserole, or that the balsamic vinegar I use is too expensive."

"If you go public with The Groaning Board, it won't be yours anymore, but you'll be rich."

"Rich? That's a laugh." A vein pulsed in Micklynn's forehead. "I'd rather be dead."

chapter 2 2

Micklynn's duplex above The Groaning Board was loft-like on its first floor. The kitchen was modern and efficient looking with a lot of stainless steel, a room made warm by clutter. A cook's kitchen, it opened to a huge, equally cluttered dining-living room. Between the kitchen and the dining area was a broad counter, topped with black granite. Four high stools were placed in front of the counter, backs to the dining area.

The jumble consisted primarily of collections of antique cooking utensils. They hung from walls, lay on tables, sat on the floor. Paintings and etchings of food and feasting, both antique and contemporary, filled every available wall space.

Wetzon paused in front of an Andy Warhol Campbell

soup can. The painting was personally inscribed to Micklynn from the artist himself.

"We have a Warhol in our office, on a subject slightly more suitable to us," Wetzon said. "Ours is a thick roll of dollar bills."

"It was a joke," Micklynn said. "Andy knew I would die before I used Campbell soup." She took Wetzon's raincoat and hung it from a bent-wood wall rack. "Make yourself comfortable while I see what I can put together. Red, I hope." She held up a bottle of cabernet sauvignon.

"Red."

While Wetzon sat on one of the barstools, Micklynn uncorked the wine bottle, then shook nicoise olives from a plastic container into a small plate. Slivers of garlic and lemon rind speckled the deep purple of the olives. Next came little balls of goat cheese, steeped in olive oil and herbs, a waste plate and napkins, and two fat wineglasses.

"Finger food," Micklynn said.

Wetzon eyed the wine bottle. Come on and breathe, baby, she thought. She was suddenly ravenous. She took an olive, let it splay on her tongue. Heaven. She removed the pit and reached for the goat cheese.

"Allergic to anything?" Micklynn's voice came from inside her fridge—Sub-Zero, of course.

"Only men." Wetzon's shoes fell to the floor with a thud. She flexed her toes and wrapped her legs around the stool.

Micklynn turned and gave her a slow smile. "Pour the wine," she said. She began unloading small plastic-wrapped bundles and containers from the fridge and tossing things into a colander. One hand held the colander under the cold water, the other took one of the wineglasses. "No men on the menu tonight." She raised her glass to Wetzon, who responded in kind. "Funny how prevalent that allergy is. It gets worse if you marry them. Are you—?"

"No." The wine was a deep, rich ruby. Woodsy fruit.

Sipping the wine, Micklynn set the colander in the sink, and turned off the water. "Smart girl. I married three of them. One died and two I divorced. And then there are those loose ends, the ones you dally with but wouldn't marry." She tossed mushrooms into a colander, passed over them with a little brush, and moved on to dicing the zucchini. Everything went into a sauté pan that was already sizzling with mashed garlic in hot butter.

The aroma from the stove swept over Wetzon like an herbal bath. It was sensual. She tasted the wine and sensed herself begin to unwind. "God, it's been . . . weeks, no, months . . ."

Micklynn's only comment was "Vegetarian?"

"Hell, no."

"Good. Dieting?"

"Never."

"Double good." Like a conjurer, Micklynn presided over her pots, snipping herbs with her scissors, tossing the contents of the sauté pan, pouring boiling chicken stock into a pot of arborio rice.

"Shall I set the table?" Wetzon asked. The wine had gone to her head, faster than usual. She needed to move around.

"Place mats and china in the armoire. Silver, same place. You'll see."

Wetzon got off the stool. She was a little unsteady. The armoire, an old French country piece and easily over eight feet tall, stood between two windows. It had been stripped and waxed, which may have reduced its value as an antique, but probably enhanced its value as a decorative piece.

The inside had been redone, fitted with shelves stacked high with plates, platters, and serving pieces, as well as linens. A flat silver chest rested on the bottom shelf.

She took what she could reach, setting the stripped and waxed table with woven natural linen place mats. She selected plates of heavy pottery in beautiful designs and muted colors.

"Ah, you've chosen well," Micklynn said. She was uncorking a second bottle of wine. "Do you know the potter?"

"No. Should I?" Wetzon refilled her wineglass, more goat cheese, more olives. Divine.

"His name is Lanzrein. He's a former dancer—like you—but ballet. He sits upstate in High Falls and creates these wonderful pieces and sells them to Tiffany and to people who make the trek up to his studio."

"It's this psychic streak I have." Wetzon grinned. "I am drawn to the gypsies in this world. Salad bowls?"

"Of course."

Wetzon went back to the armoire for the bowls. After she set them on the table, she finished her wine.

Her face moist and flushed from the heat of the stove, Micklynn said, "Fill the glasses, Leslie."

"Yes, ma'am." Wetzon refilled both glasses. The room was warm. She took off her jacket and loosened the neck of her shirt. "Okay to open a window?"

"Sure." Micklynn poured the last of the broth into the pot of risotto and stirred.

The sills of both windows were lined with plants and herbs, as was the floor beneath them. Some of the plants were flowering, pink and white, giving off a spicy fragrance. Careful not to knock anything over, Wetzon raised the window a couple of inches. The cool evening air had the damp, earthy smell of spring after a shower.

She was out of herself, in a strange place with a woman she hardly knew who was cooking up a gourmet feast just for her. What could be bad? She leaned over to smell a funnel-shaped flower. Something was lying on the floor between two stone pots. A toy of some sort. She picked it up and it tinkled.

Micklynn gave a startled cry, spinning around. "Jimmy?" When she saw what Wetzon held, she said, "I'm sorry. I thought it was Jimmy."

"I didn't mean to frighten you. Who's Jimmy?"

"My cat. He's dead." She said it so flatly that Wetzon, who had started to offer consolation, kept her mouth shut. "I thought I put all of his things away. I guess I missed one. Drop it on the counter for me, will you? I'm about to serve dinner."

They dined sumptuously on arugula salad with a raspberry vinaigrette dressing tossed with tiny bits of peeled and seeded tomatoes. Dinner was a zucchini-and-mushroom risotto laced with prosciutto and topped with thin ribbons of parmigiano reggiano.

"I love you, Micklynn Devora," Wetzon said. "No one has ever cooked for me like this. How do you do it? You made a feast out of what looked like odds and ends."

"Thanks." In her element, Micklynn, whom Wetzon had thought rather a plain woman, had become beautiful. "I have this passion for food, but really, anyone who loves food can be a great cook."

After dinner, they sat over their wine smiling at each other. Purring.

"How did you get into this?" Wetzon asked.

"I grew up in New York, went to Barnard, married Simon—my first— the one who died. I got an entry-level job at *Gourmet* as a secretary. I used to cook for the fun. It was great. I could actually make people happy. Coffee?"

"Decaf."

Micklynn filled the kettle and measured coffee into the filter. "Then Simon died suddenly and I was this young widow with his life insurance—one hundred thousand dollars." She took a bowl from the fridge and set it on the table. Apricot halves sprinkled with sugar, then stewed and topped with toasted slivered almonds. "I took myself to Paris and studied at La Varenne. Then came home and did a stint at every cooking school in the area, including the CIA. Hyde Park, not Langley."

"The Culinary Institute of America," Wetzon said.

"Right." Micklynn spooned the apricot mixture onto two cut-glass compotes. When the kettle began to hiss, she turned off the gas and waited until the boil stopped, then poured water into the filter.

"And The Groaning Board?"

"I started a little catering service in my building. I lived in the Apthorp at the time. I used to supply all the yuppies with great dinners they could claim as their own. That's how I met A.T." She filled mugs with coffee and brought them to the table. "What about you, Leslie?"

"Grew up on a farm, went off to Douglass—colleges for women are the best, aren't they?—then came to the big city to dance on Broadway. That's how I met Carlos." She smiled. Carlos always made her smile. His friendship was like having a lucky penny in your pocket. He was always and forever her best friend.

"You stopped dancing."

"I just didn't want to be an aging gypsy with sporadic jobs—if I was lucky—arthritic joints, and no life. I got out before it could happen to me."

"Try these," Micklynn said. She opened a tin, folded back the waxed paper.

"I love biscotti." Wetzon took a wedge from the tin and tasted it. "This is terrific. What's different about it?"

"It's made with cornmeal."

"Cornmeal? Really?"

"Can you keep a secret?"

"I can."

"I'm a chef with a food allergy. I'm allergic to gluten. If I eat anything with wheat, oats, rye, or barley in it, I get sick."

"That's horrible. You mean you can't eat sourdough bread or bagels or pasta? I'd die."

"Among other things. And you wouldn't die. You'd make the adjustment if it meant you felt good again. It's been about a year now since I've had the diagnosis, and I'm adjusting. I've been experimenting with different flours, like rice flours, tapioca flour, potato starch flour, bean flours."

Rice flour, tapioca flour . . . where had Wetzon seen these on a shelf recently? She'd had too much wine. Suddenly she knew, but what did it mean? "If someone has all those things in her cupboard, does that mean she has this gluten allergy?"

"Probably. It's actually called celiac disease," Micklynn said. She emptied the rest of the wine into each glass.

"If someone sneaked gluten into your food, could you die?"

"Oh, hardly. My gastro system might be knocked out of whack for a while. . . . Why?"

"Sheila . . . a woman I know . . . the sister-in-law of a friend. She had all that stuff in her cupboard. She was poisoned."

"Sheila Gelber was poisoned?"

Wetzon stared at Micklynn. Micklynn's face was an ashy gray. Tears were coursing down her cheeks. "You knew her?"

"She was my friend."

chapter 23

"I can't believe you knew her." At first, Wetzon was dumbfounded, then, "But this is New York. It happens all the time."

Devora had opened another bottle of wine and steered them into the living room. It was a large open space with beamed ceilings and three overstuffed sofas around a fireplace. The sofas held loose papers, folders, and notebooks. Micklynn cleared off one of the sofas by moving everything to the floor. All except the cat hair. "How do you know Sheila was poisoned?" She poured wine into the glasses Wetzon had carried from the dining table.

Should Wetzon say, *My ex-lover was her ex-lover?* It

was getting too complicated. Keep it simple. No need to mention Silvestri. "I know Artie Metzger, Sheila's brother-in-law."

"Right. The cop. This is really strange, talking to you about Sheila. How was she poisoned?"

"I guess I shouldn't have said anything. I don't really know anything more than that."

"She wouldn't have done it. She couldn't have—"

Wetzon's glass shivered in her hand. "Do what? You know someone who had a motive?"

"Motive? No. I mean Sheila. She never would have committed suicide."

"Suicide!" Had anyone even considered that, Wetzon wondered. Aloud she said, "Was she depressed?"

"Depressed? The way we all get sometimes, I guess. But suicidal? No way. Not Sheila."

"What was she depressed about?"

"I don't know. She sort of backed away from me, from everyone. Except the kids, of course. She loved the kids. I guess you know she was a schoolteacher."

"Yes. When was the last time you spoke to her?"

"About a week before it . . . happened. She called me and told me if I didn't stop she would report me to the police. 'Stop what?' I said. 'Let's talk about this.' She hung up on me. I was pretty upset. You didn't know Sheila. It was so crazy. But she must have taken her phone off the hook, because I kept getting a busy when I called back."

"You never spoke to her again?"

"I had two really big affairs to cater. . . . Then a few days later I heard she fell in her bathroom and hit her head and—oh, God. What did she think I was doing to her?"

"She was getting threatening phone calls." Damn, Wetzon thought, too much wine was making her indiscreet. Yet she liked Micklynn. What was the harm?

"And she thought I was making them? Oh, no, she couldn't have—it's too crazy."

"I heard one of them on her answering tape. It was pretty scary. The voice was too distorted to be recognizable."

"Jesus God, I failed her. I fail everybody." Micklynn filled her glass again. "Simon . . . I thought Simon was a hypochondriac, always complaining. Then they said he had pancreatic cancer and he was gone so fast we hardly had time to say goodbye." She was slurring her words now.

"Did you meet Sheila in college?" Wetzon's lips were numb; they felt swollen. Was she turning into an aging, disappointed-in-love alcoholic? The thought was sobering.

"Uh-uh." Micklynn was focused on some distant object. "Met her a couple of years ago. She was Ellen's English teacher at Colton. Ellen is Simon's cousin's kid. I took her in after her parents died."

"She's at Colton? That used to be one of the most aggressive academic private schools in the city."

"Still is. When Ellen came to live with me, we visited a few of the private schools. What do I know about schools, or kids, for that matter? She liked Colton, so that's where she went."

"She's a very pretty girl."

"She's . . . not living with me anymore."

"Oh."

"When Simon's cousin died, Ellen was eight or nine. Simon was gone by that time. The Moore side of his family all lived in Oregon. I didn't know them at all. Then Ellen's mother died in an accident and she lived for a year with an elderly neighbor. That's who called me about her. There were no other relatives. I'm not good with kids, but I was the good guy—I took her in."

"So you dropped everything and went out there to get her. That was very nice."

"To be honest, I didn't have the time. I told the elderly neighbor to pack her up and put her on a plane, which she did. Medford is a small town. Before Ellen got here, I was worried about her adapting to city life. I needn't have. It was as if she'd always lived here."

"But you didn't get along?" Micklynn fixed Wetzon with an *et tu* stare, and Wetzon held up her hands. "Sorry. It's what I do. Slip right into it, unaware." She set her empty glass down and tried to get up. "It's late. I'd better go." The already busy room spun with flying objects; the floor dipped.

"Don't go." Micklynn reached out and held her arm. "This has been great. I miss Sheila a lot and you—"

"Remind you of her?" The question fell just short of bitter.

Micklynn looked quizzical for a moment. "Not at all, Leslie. You're nothing at all like Sheila, except that you're both good people."

Standing now, Wetzon said, "Thanks, Micklynn." She looked around for her purse and briefcase. At least the room had stopped tilting.

Micklynn struggled to her feet and gathered up the two empty wine bottles. Good Lord, how much had they drunk? A third bottle stood half empty on the busy coffee table.

Two unhappy people . . . no, Leslie Wetzon was not going to deal with her ruptured relationship by becoming a wino. I am not unhappy, she told herself. It was time to move on.

"It's a cross to live with someone everyone thinks is perfect, don't you think?" Micklynn stood in her kitchen holding the empty bottles.

"It's not easy living with anybody—" Wetzon hooked her bag over her shoulder. "But Ellen is just a young girl with no family except you. Maybe counseling . . ." What in hell was she talking about? How had she gotten to this point, doing social work without a license?

"No, you don't understand. Nobody does. Everyone said: Such a lovely child. So pretty, so blond, so brilliant. Perfect in every way. Except . . . they had no idea." Micklynn smiled a sly smile as if they—she and Wetzon—had become co-conspirators.

Wetzon felt a sense of dread. *Get out of here. Something horrible is going to happen.* It came like a premonition. "Thanks for the wonderful dinner," she said. "And the good company."

"I'm sorry, Leslie." Tears gushed down Micklynn's cheeks. Her wet eyes looked dazed. "Don't desert me too. Please be my friend." She was holding on to the wine bottles for dear life. "I need a friend, now, especially."

"I *am* your friend, Micklynn."

"Everyone thinks I'm the bad one because I threw her out. And no one understands . . ." Micklynn stopped, horrified, as if she'd suddenly remembered something.

Wetzon thrust her briefcase under her arm. "What is it, Micklynn?"

Micklynn sank to the floor, legs akimbo. The bottles slipped from her arms and rolled around her. "Soon enough," she mumbled. Her head lolled.

Kneeling, Wetzon lifted Micklynn's head and looked into her eyes. She was all right, only drunk and drooling slightly.

Micklynn gave her a bleary, self-satisfied smile, and said clearly, "A.T. will rue the day."

chapter 24

"Didn't I tell you Micklynn Devora is strange?" Smith said after Wetzon described her evening. Smith flipped through her messages, actually rested on one, then reverted to her old self and tossed them all into her wastebasket. Which one had made her pause, Wetzon wondered, eyeing the wastebasket. "A.T. is the talent in that partnership. And furthermore, anyone could see that pretty child was being abused."

"Things aren't always what they seem, Smith," Wetzon said sharply. She was feeling she'd betrayed Micklynn somehow. And she had a splitting vino headache.

"Ellen is at the top of her class at Colton and she's not a nerd. She's also on the tennis team. She's perfect—"

"I suppose the Tarot revealed all of this?"

"Humpf," Smith said. "A.T. and I have had a few têtes-à-têtes. We are really on the same wavelength. The Groaning Board is going public, by the way."

"Is it really? Who told you?"

"A.T., of course, and she swore me to secrecy."

"Which is why you're telling me."

"Oh, you don't count, babycakes. I'm thinking of introducing her to Mark."

"A.T.?"

"No. Ellen."

Wetzon groaned. "Mark is gay, Smith."

"Oh, it's just a little adolescent fad he's going through. He'll get over it. Now about tomorrow night—"

"Look, I'm sorry about the empty seat." Tomorrow was Smith's sit-down dinner party, catered by The Groaning Board, and Wetzon was coming alone.

Smith removed a wooden folding measure from her handbag. "There was no empty seat, sweetie pie. Let's face it, Dick Tracy never fit into our world. He has no respect for what we do. Besides, I knew he wouldn't come. The Tarot told me that you and he were finished."

"Oh, it did, did it? It would have been nice if you'd told me. I might have been able to prevent it." And then again, maybe she would have let the fates take it . . .

"Exactly." Smith was so absolutely delighted with herself that Wetzon threw up her hands.

"I give up. You win. Just tell me one thing. Did the fabulous Tarot seer mention that I'm getting phone calls from a breather?"

The folding measure in Smith's hands creaked from the pressure of her squeeze. "What kind of breather?"

"A breather. Are there different kinds?"

"A threatening breather?" *Creak.*

"Oh, please, don't all breathers come with an implied threat?"

"At home or in the office?" *Creak.*

"Both."

"Well, I'm not surprised." *Creak.*

"What do you mean you're not surprised?"

"What you deal with every day. Pond scum. And you're always giving them your home number. It's a wonder it hasn't happened before."

"You think they're from a broker?"

"What else?" *Creak, creak.*

"After all these years? I don't think that's likely." But maybe Smith was right. A disgruntled broker. Someone Wetzon or Darlene had turned away. Yet Wetzon turned no one away if she could help it. "I take it you're not getting any strange phone calls?"

"I'm not. Did you tell Dick Tracy?"

"No." Why hadn't she told Silvestri? She'd meant to, but he'd been so wrapped up in his old girlfriend's death that there was no room for her.

"What does he do besides breathe?" *Creak.*

"God, Smith, will you stop that?"

"Stop what?"

"Creaking that measure. It's making me crazy."

"Oh, for pity sakes!" She set the measure on her desk. "You haven't answered my question."

"What was your question?"

"Does he do anything besides breathe?" She picked the measure up again.

"Isn't that enough? Forget it. I'll talk to Artie Metzger. I have to speak to him about something else anyway."

Darlene knocked on the door, then opened it. "The furniture is here, Smith. And, Wetzon, Keith Pullman is on the phone for you."

"Take the call, then come up," Smith commanded. She was already sprinting up the stairs.

Damn her! She was forty-two, didn't diet, was tall, slim, and moved like a gazelle.

Wetzon pressed the blinking button and picked up the receiver. "Keith? How are you?"

"Wetzon, I have heard from every other headhunter I know, and even some I never heard of. Why haven't you called me?"

"Now, Keith, we've been talking for years. Tell me honestly, are you ever going to make a move? How many years have you been there?"

"It was E. F. Hutton when I sat down. Then it was Shearson Lehman Hutton, then it was Shearson American Express, then it was Shearson Lehman Brothers, and now it's Smith Barney."

"And in all that time you haven't even changed your seat. So why now?"

"The CRAP Plan."

"I don't think that's what Smith Barney calls it."

Keith was talking about the Capital Appreciation Plan—the CAP plan. It had come out of the merger of Shearson and Smith Barney and had been instituted by Smith Barney in order to reward top brokers and tie them to the firm by paying bonuses in stock instead of cash. The stock is purchased at a twenty-five percent discount and restricted for a three-year period, meaning it cannot be sold within that time. Disgruntled Shearson brokers had immediately dubbed it the CRAP Plan, and so it remained.

"It's crap all the same, Wetzon. If I leave before three years or if they throw me out for any reason at all, I get nothing and any stock I've bought with my money they get to keep. A nice scam, don't you think?"

"So who do you want to talk to? Merrill Lynch?"

"Are you nuts, Wetzon? Go from the frying pan into the fire? Merrill makes you sign a noncompete paper that says all your accounts belong to Merrill, and if you leave, they hit you with a restraining order and sue your *cojones* off."

"How about a really nice regional firm with some class, a decent payout, and good investment banking?"

"Call me next Wednesday at five."

Wetzon hung up and made a note to call Keith on next week's calendar. He would either put her off, blow her off, or actually commit to an appointment.

Wetzon climbed the stairs. Her head ached. Her life was "Call me next week" . . . "I can't talk now" . . . "I don't want to talk about it . . ."

"No! No! That goes *there*." She heard Smith say in the voice Smith saved for those she called the drones. Smith was, after all, the Queen. "No! Don't do *that!*"

Wetzon made a U-turn and went back down the stairs. She couldn't deal with Smith at this level. She opened the door to the reception area. Max had arrived and was fielding a call. He pointed to the phone with an unspoken question.

Who? she mouthed.

He wrote on his pink pad of message slips: *Rita Silvestri*.

She shook her head vigorously. Take a message, she told him silently. When she closed the door and was back in the office she and Smith shared, she could hear arguing voices above. Cringing, she took a deep breath and climbed the stairs. Doors slammed and Smith said, "Well, really." Then there was quiet.

It was an awestruck Wetzon who stood at the top of the stairs. At the beginning of the renovation, Smith had banned her from the second floor "because of your negative aura." Now, for the first time, she saw the plastered and painted finale: Everything was open except for the conference room in the back and the elegant black marble bathroom, which Smith made a point of taking Wetzon through first.

"You changed your mind about private offices, I see," Wetzon said after the grand tour.

"You said you didn't care, and I realized how much I'd miss you, sugar bun."

"That's not the real reason, my darling partner. Admit it, you're just so nosy you want to know everything I'm doing."

"*Moi?*" Smith rounded her eyes in an attempt to look innocent.

The furniture was high-tech from Knoll, very attractive, black and steel, very functional.

Wetzon sat in her chair. It hugged her back, made her feel comfortable. "I like this." The walls were white, the other themes deep wine and black. A funny sound like a lamb's bleat erupted from under the desk. "What's that?"

"That's your private line. I have one too. NYNEX installed it yesterday, so you're the only one who has the number. And you're the only one who answers it."

When the bleat sounded again, Smith said, "Go ahead." She had a pleased smirk on her face.

The phone was attached to the side panel under her desk. Wetzon picked up the receiver. "Hello?" She expected a friendly voice, set up perhaps by Smith herself.

She got, instead, the breather.

chapter 2 5

She was a vision in black when she stepped out of her building. The dress was a scoop-neck, sleeveless shell that stopped well above her knees. It came with a sheer black coat, the same length.

"Cab, Ms. Wetzon?" Tony, the doorman, asked.

"No, thanks, Tony. I think I'll walk. It's such a nice night."

And it was. The days were lengthening, the air was softening. She walked toward Columbus. Soon enough it would be dark.

Her thoughts roiled. This wasn't like the last time she and Silvestri separated. That time she'd been devastated. Now . . . ? What did she really feel after all the anger and hurt burned away? Relief. Maybe their relationship had run itself out.

"Leslie—" A car going in the opposite direction had pulled up and double-parked a few paces ahead of her. "Leslie?"

Metzger reached across the seat and opened the car door.

"Artie?" She came to the door and peered in at him. He looked exhausted, more somber than usual.

"Where are you off to this time of night?"

"Smith's giving a dinner party."

"Come on, I'll ride you over. East Side, right?"

She climbed in and closed the door. "East Seventy-seventh, off Second."

"Put on your seat belt." He hadn't moved the car. "You and Silvestri have split up?"

"Seems we have. He wanted out, and maybe he was right. It has something to do with Sheila."

"Sheila?" Metzger seemed surprised. "That has nothing to do with you and him."

"Can we go, Artie?"

He edged the car forward. "You're good together. Don't let this happen. Life is too short."

"He left *me*, Artie, not the other way around. Anyway, there's nothing to do for it."

"I'm dealing with two hardheads," Metzger muttered. He turned up Amsterdam and circled back to the Eighty-sixth Street Transverse through Central Park to the East Side.

"Can we just change the subject? I was going to call you."

"What about?"

"Sheila. Have you talked to her friends?"

"Some of them. We've been going through her address book. Some have already contacted us."

"One of her closest friends was Micklynn Devora."

"Devora? Should I know her?"

"She's half of two caterers who own The Groaning Board."

"I think I remember her name from the book. I've got two rookies working on it."

"I thought Silvestri was the detective on the case."

"If he was, it wasn't for the Department. Silvestri's taken a leave of absence."

She stared at Metzger, openmouthed. "A leave of absence? Never. He wouldn't if he was dying. Silvestri loves the Job, loves his work. You know that, Artie."

"Believe me, he did."

"God, Artie, did he tell you why?"

"He told me nothing. I found out when I called him at the House."

"He would never do this, Artie. Something is terribly wrong." Was Silvestri having some kind of breakdown? If he was, she certainly hadn't been very sympathetic.

"Whaddayasay we take a ride down to Chelsea?" They were coming out of the Park.

"I'll be late," she said feebly.

"What's it gonna hurt?" He zipped across Fifth, made a left on Madison, and came back through the Park on Eighty-fifth.

She didn't reply. She stared down at her thighs, wondering if her skirt was too short.

Metzger drove straight down Columbus. "How did you connect Micklynn Devora to Sheila?"

"Micklynn told me. It was accidental. When Micklynn said she had this allergy to gluten and was experimenting with alternate flours, I remembered seeing all those weird flours in Sheila's cupboard. I made the connection and Micklynn filled it in." It was warm in the car; she rolled the window down farther. "She said Sheila had been acting strangely for a while."

"What did she mean strangely?"

"Paranoid, or something. You'd better ask her. Sheila even accused Micklynn of making those calls."

"She did?" Artie said thoughtfully. He didn't seem surprised. "I'll talk to her."

"Artie . . . about those phone calls . . ."

"Yes?"

"Well, not those. Others."

"What others?" He inched through the dense traffic around Macy's.

"The ones I'm getting," Wetzon said in a low voice.

"Jesus H. Christ!" Metzger pulled over in front of a fire hydrant. "You'd better tell me about it."

"They started about two weeks ago. He doesn't say anything, Artie, he just breathes. He has my office number and my home number, and he also has my new private number at the office. I feel as if he's watching me. It's creepy. What should I do?"

"To trace it, hang up, then pick up and press star fifty-seven. The info will go to the Annoyance Call Bureau. I'll let them know I'm working on it. If it's out of the area, we can't get the number, and if he's using a pay phone, there may not be much we can do. Maybe it's a pissed-off stock-broker and he'll stop when he burns himself out." Metzger pulled away from the curb and continued down to Chelsea, a once dumpy section of the City from about Fifteenth Street, just above the Village, to Twenty-third Street, from Fifth Avenue to the old piers along the Hudson. Now the piers were being refurbished into tennis clubs and moderately mid-dle-class entertainment. Chelsea was going through a renaissance.

Silvestri had a rent-controlled one-bedroom apartment in an old brownstone on Nineteenth Street. Wetzon had never been there; she'd never been invited. He had always made it seem like his sacred ground.

Metzger backed into a parking spot and slapped his bubble on the roof of the car. "Come on." He opened the door.

"You go, Artie. I'll stay here." She searched the front of the building. "Which one is his?"

"You've never been there?"

She shook her head. Metzger looked as if he didn't believe her.

"He's in the back, second floor." He took her hand. "Come on, Leslie. You belong together. Don't let this happen. Put up a fight."

She pulled her hand away. "You know something, Artie? I'm tired of fighting for this relationship. And I don't know why I'm here. He hurt me, Artie, so don't butt in. Just go on up there and tell me he's all right, then take me to Smith's."

"You're—"

"I know. I'm a really terrific person, and he needs his head examined."

"Okay, okay." Metzer stepped out of the car and lit a cigarette. It was getting dark and the tiny light of his cigarette was easier to see than he was, even with the bubble rolling light. "Two goddam hardheads," he said. He looked up and down the street, inhaling deeply, breathing out through his nostrils. "I'll be right down."

"Do we need the bubble? It's so conspicuous."

Without a word, Metzger took the light off the roof, closed it down, and tossed it on the backseat. He admonished her to lock the doors again, then went into the brownstone.

An elderly woman went by, walking two ancient pugs wearing bandannas around their necks. The woman looked at Wetzon with curiosity, but didn't stop except to let her dogs lift their legs on Metzger's tires.

Wetzon eyed Silvestri's building. It was one of a number of wide brownstones that lined both sides of the street. In daylight the window boxes under the front windows, if they were planted with flowers, probably gave the tired building some color. Under the streetlamps, a magnolia tree in the yard across the street wore fat buds.

Silvestri was coming down the block talking intently to a pretty woman with a wild profusion of long, dark hair. He was carrying a big bag of groceries and she was carrying a supermarket shopping bag. Instinctively, Wetzon slid down, slipping from seat to floor. Any minute now he would notice Metzger's car.

She edged open the street-side door and crept out, crouching down. He mustn't see her. She tapped the door shut. You idiot, she thought. Have you no shame?

On the sidewalk, the footsteps stopped for a moment. "Anything wrong?" the woman asked. She had a deep, smoky voice.

"My partner's car. Maybe he's waiting inside."

Wetzon flattened herself against the fender and was rewarded by the familiar little ping, and then the tickle as her panty hose laddered up her thigh. Damnation. Brand-new panty hose. She flattened her palms on the door and scoped through the car windows. Silvestri and his lady friend were climbing the front steps of the brownstone. Then Metzger appeared in the doorway.

Wetzon crept along the outside of the parked cars, careful not to get hit by passing vehicles.

A cab came to a stop near her. "You looking for a ride, lady?" the driver asked, not in the least curious about what she was doing there, crouched in the street in her evening finery.

She opened the door and crawled into the taxi, only subliminally aware that someone was shouting her name.

c h a p t e r   2 6

"Sweetie pie! I was beginning to worry about you." Smith greeted Wetzon with a tight smile and a cheek brush. "Where have you been?" Her lips did not move through her painted smile. She smoothed her slip over her hips. At least that's what the thing she was wearing looked like: a long, black satin slip with spaghetti straps. And she obviously had nothing on underneath.

"I got a run on my way over and had to go home and change. You wouldn't want me to grace your lovely party with a ladder up the front of one thigh, now would you?" Wetzon stepped into the foyer. "Of course, if I'm too late, I'll just turn around and go home. . . ."

"Oh, for pity sakes! Ellen, sugar, get my grouchy partner a glass of wine. We were just about to sit down," Smith added, to Wetzon.

I give you the beautiful, controversial, ubiquitous Ellen Moore, Wetzon said to herself. Was she surprised to find Ellen there? Not at all. It was probably part of her job, working at The Groaning Board shop, working on the job. So what if she was living with A.T. and not Micklynn.

"Red or white?" The perfect Ellen was wearing black silk trousers, a black silk turtleneck, and a black tuxedo jacket. A sheer complexion was not marred by a smattering of pale freckles. Her champagne-blond hair was straight, parted in the middle and slightly below shoulder length. She wore no makeup; her whitish eyebrows and lashes were undefined, further adding to a wide-eyed innocence.

"Red." All the furniture in Smith's living room had been removed and four round tables were set with elegant crystal and china. Each table sat six.

Wetzon took the glass from Ellen. She was still agitated by the sight of Silvestri and the woman, the domestic scene she'd witnessed. Her heart palpitated unevenly as if she were on a caffeine overload.

"How are you, kiddo?" Twoey Barnes gave her shoulders a squeeze. "What's the good word?"

"Business is lousy, and I'm unattached again. How are you doing?"

Twoey had legitimate freckles that went with his red hair. "Weeeeell," he said, drawing out the word the same way Smith did, which was enough to give Wetzon an ominous twinge. "I'm going to co-produce *Softly* with you and—"

"Huh? What do you mean, *with me?*"

He looked down at her, his eyes blinking behind his metal-rimmed glasses. "Xeni, you, and Mort. Mort and I will be general partners. You and Xeni will be associate producers. But you know that."

"Xeni and me? No, I don't know that. *Xeni's* been full of surprises lately." She growled under her breath.

"I'm sure. Now what's this about being unattached?"

"It's over between Silvestri and me." Sure, go ahead, tell the world, Leslie Wetzon. Telling it will make it so.

Twoey was easing her into an empty patch. The room seemed full of people all talking at once.

"You know, Alton still asks about you—"

She shook her head. "Can't go down that road." Alton Pinkus had come into Wetzon's life the last time she and Silvestri had split up. Successful, solid, wealthy, Alton was a widower with grown children. She'd come close to making a terrible mistake by marrying him. "He was the wrong man for me, Twoey."

"Is there a right man for you, Leslie?" The voice came from behind her.

"Bill—" Twoey gave Wetzon a curious leer and reached around her to shake Bill Veeder's hand. "How's Evelyn?"

"Fine, fine. She's been overdoing it; otherwise, she'd be here tonight."

Uh-oh, Wetzon thought. He's alone. I'm alone. It's just the kind of thing Smith would . . . "Is Sunny here?" she asked Twoey. He'd been seeing sometime producer Sunny Browning for the past two years.

"Sunny and I have split up too, Wetzon."

"Oh, I'm really sorry, so I must be your dinner partner tonight then?" What a relief.

"Well, now, Wetzon." Twoey beamed at her. "Xeni and I—"

Veeder interrupted. "I'm afraid you and I will have to suffer each other as dinner partners, Leslie." He seemed to be enjoying her discomfort, playing with her head.

At this moment, Smith suggested that dinner was about to be served and that everyone should look for place cards.

Veeder clamped his hand on Wetzon's elbow; she wiggled it away. "Stop trying to control me," she told his tiepin. She didn't trust herself to meet his eyes. The attraction was there, and he was a married man.

He laughed. "We're over here."

Their tablemates were Mort and Poppy Hornberg and Hem Barron and Minnie Wu. Poppy flounced into her seat with an aura of pure disgust; Mort kept a nervous smile glued to his face. As perhaps one would when handling a time bomb. True, Poppy could go off at any moment. She wore a tight green dress with metallic glitter. Her bosom was flaked with cracker crumbs. Her lipstick still outlined her lips but she'd eaten away the inside. "I don't know why we have to be here," she said, ignoring everyone at the table. She twisted off the crunchy end of Eli's Bread and slathered it with butter, then pushed the whole thing into her mouth.

Minnie Wu, another winning personality, whom Wetzon had found rude and unpleasant at their first meeting, was still rude and unpleasant. She glared at Hem, and picked at the fringe on her red dress, hardly the ideal choice for her lumpy figure.

"The table from hell," Wetzon murmured. *Get me outa here.*

"As soon as we can do it comfortably," Veeder said, answering her thought.

She sneaked a look up at him now. He was very attractive and he was reading her mind. He was married.

Ellen and the very mincy young man from the shop, who also wore black silk, served the vegetable terrine with a small ball of grapefruit ice. The terrine was strongly defined by spinach.

Was Micklynn in the kitchen, Wetzon wondered. "Has anyone seen Micklynn or A.T.?" She directed her question to Hem. As A.T.'s brother, he ought to know.

He did. "A.T.'s in the kitchen. I think Micklynn left a while ago. What is everyone drinking here?" He began passing the wine.

"Leslie, darling, it's wonderful to be working with you again," Mort said with false heartiness. He made kissy-poo across the table at her.

A disparaging noise came from Poppy, and Mort turned crimson.

"Thank you, Mort dear," Wetzon said sweetly.

"So you're coming to Min's and my anniversary party, Wetzon," Hem said. "Laura Lee told you?"

The glare Minnie Wu fixed on Wetzon was raw with hatred.

Jesus, Wetzon thought, what did I ever do to you?

A hand touched her thigh, then moved off.

"Oh, he likes the ladies, my husband does. Don't you, Hem?"

"I like interesting people, Min. So do you. Admit it."

"But you favor the women, don't you?"

"Excuse me." Hem rose. He mumbled something about a phone call and left the room, threading around guests and tables.

The veal roast arrived looking superb next to the mushroom-rice mold. Mort poured the wine.

"What's the new project, Min?" Bill Veeder asked.

"Project?" Minnie seemed distracted. "Oh, yes. Cooking show. The Groaning Board. We just sold twelve episodes to PBS."

"That ought to be fun," Mort said. "Let's do it as a musical. Ha, ha."

"I want to go home," Poppy said. *"Now."*

Wetzon had had enough. "Excuse me a minute." She got up, began to make her way around the tables. She stopped at Smith's; Smith's bosoms were roller coasters as she cut into the veal. Every man at the table seemed transfixed. "Lovely cleavage, dear," Wetzon whispered in Smith's ear, then moved on.

Hem must be on one long phone call, she thought, because there was no sign of him. She stuck her head into Smith's bedroom. No one. Used the bathroom and touched up her lipstick. Came out of the bedroom and bumped into a harried A.T. Her hair was kinking out of its pins.

"It's going very well, A.T."

"I guess, I guess." A.T. dried her hands on the towel tucked into her belt and ducked past Wetzon, heading for the bathroom. "Don't go into the kitchen, it's a mess. If you need anything, I'll send Ellen to your table."

Now that was silly. Wetzon pushed open the kitchen door. The kitchen was steamy and chaotic. A man whose back was toward her was making incautious love to the bare breasts of a woman whose head was pitched back on the counter. The woman's hands were inside Hem's pants.

"Jesus!" Wetzon said.

Hem jumped back.

Wetzon made to get out of there, but someone had come in behind her, then pushed her aside roughly.

"Bitch!" Minnie Wu shouted.

Ellen righted herself. Slowly, almost defiantly, she pulled her silk turtleneck over her perfect breasts.

Which is when Minnie lunged for her, taking her by surprise, hands closing on her throat. "Die, bitch!" Minnie screeched. "Die! Die! Die!"

chapter 27

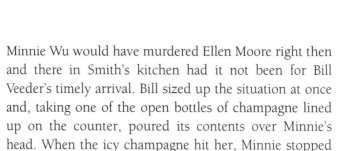

Minnie Wu would have murdered Ellen Moore right then and there in Smith's kitchen had it not been for Bill Veeder's timely arrival. Bill sized up the situation at once and, taking one of the open bottles of champagne lined up on the counter, poured its contents over Minnie's head. When the icy champagne hit her, Minnie stopped in mid-shriek. She began to sob. Dreadful, dry sobs.

Hem zipped up his fly as if it was all in a day's work. He gathered the red-fringed, wet, wasted figure of his wife, and as Bill ran defense, rushed her out of the apartment before anyone really got wind of it.

The party was in full toot. Sixties music covered the near-calamity. "I Heard It Through the Grapevine"

and Marvin Gaye rocked into the kitchen through the opening and closing door.

Wetzon hurried to Ellen. The girl was hunched over, quivering like a
terrified animal. Her hair was soaked, as was the turtleneck. She arched
away from Wetzon, nipples thrusting through the wet silk.

"Don't touch me!" Ellen's upper lip curled over her teeth like Izz's
when Izz got hold of a fresh bone.

"I just want to help."

"Keep your help to yourself."

The kettle whistled. Ellen turned her back to Wetzon, shut down the
gas. With trembling hands, she measured coffee into two oversized Krups
coffeemakers, then poured the water through.

A.T. appeared, charging through the swinging door as if she'd sensed
trouble. "What's happened here?" she demanded.

"Long story," Wetzon said. She tried to edge around A.T.

"Ellen?" A.T.'s face was drawn; her clothes were disheveled as if it was
she who'd fought with Minnie. Ellen didn't respond, her back a firm
holdout against all kindness.

"Your brother and your houseguest got too friendly and Minnie was a
little upset," Wetzon said. She could feel the faint throb begin over her
right eye. Migraine on the way.

"She tried to kill me!" Ellen cried, getting her voice back.

A.T. rushed to the girl and held her close, stroking her wet hair,
cooing to her. "Baby, baby, don't worry. . . . I'll make it all right. . . ."

"Come with me, Leslie." Wetzon hadn't heard Bill return, but there he
was. He led her out of the kitchen and out the door to the elevator. "I
told Xenia you had a migraine."

"Thank you." How did he know she got migraines? Or was it just a
lucky guess? "So that leaves only Mort and Poppy at the table from hell."

They got on the elevator.

"No, it leaves an empty table. The estimable Poppy felt one of her
viruses coming on, so Mort had to take her home. He said he'd be back."

"He probably will. He likes the social . . . intercourse."

Veeder smiled. "Just for the record, Hem's a philanderer."

"Philanderer? Are we in a Restoration play? No, never mind. *Philanderer*'s just another synonym for *man,* wouldn't you say?"

He studied her with an intensity that made her uncomfortable. "Some
women play on a man's weakness," he said.

They came out of the building. The sky was aglitter with stars. And Silvestri had a girlfriend. "Weakness? Really? It doesn't strike me that you suffer from that, Bill."

"Don't endow me with qualities I don't have, Leslie. I'm a man; I'm human."

There were plenty of cabs cruising up Third Avenue with their center lights on. "Thanks for getting me out of there." She held out her hand. "Good night."

"I didn't break you out so you could run off, Leslie." He took her hand and gave a gentle tug.

She resisted. "Excuse me, what were we saying about philanderers?"

"Please, Ms. Wetzon, won't you come with me? I want you to meet someone." He began walking her away from Smith's building.

At least they were walking west. And she had to admit she liked the way her hand felt in his. He was a man who had evolved. Or seemed to be. "Where are we going?"

"To Park Avenue. I want you to meet Evelyn."

"You want me to meet your wife?"

"Yes. All charter members of the Philanderers Club bring the philanderees to meet their wives." He was laughing at her.

"You're not kidding?"

"No, I'm not kidding."

They crossed Lexington and she faltered. "I don't think this is such a good idea."

"Are you afraid to meet Evelyn?" he asked. "Guilty thoughts perhaps?"

"Not at all. Why should I be afraid?" But she was. He was right too. Something was germinating between Bill Veeder and Leslie Wetzon. She wondered if he would kiss her breasts as Hem had Ellen's, then shook the thought away. What was the matter with her?

"Good evening, Mr. Veeder." Park Avenue and Seventy-seventh Street. The doorman spoke with a slight burr.

"Good evening, Scotty." Veeder bent and whispered in her ear. "You're holding my hand awfully tight, Ms. Leslie."

His breath made her shiver.

A doorman and an elevator man. A first-class building. Another "Good evening, Mr. Veeder," and up to the fifteenth floor.

As Veeder nudged her out of the elevator, she began, "I don't think—" But he was unlocking the door, holding it open for her.

The apartment was very formal. The gallery floor was marble and it went on and on. Big stiff pieces of French furniture with lots of ormolu. An old tapestry on the wall. More old tapestries. A very serious apartment.

"Oh, Mr. Veeder. I thought it was you." A light-skinned black woman in a black uniform came toward them.

"Elsie, this is Ms. Wetzon. Is my wife still up?"

"Yes. She's in the sitting room." Elsie was about fifty, hair streaked with gray, very muscular in build. She wore black oxfords with chunky heels.

As they moved through the gallery, the strains of a Mozart piano concerto came toward them.

The sitting room needed a gardener. It was overgrown with blossoms. Yellow-blossomed chintz blanketed the windows and both sofa and easy chair. A needlepoint rug of fat cabbage roses covered the floor. On a sofa table was a huge glass bowl of fresh flowers. The floral arrangement almost obliterated the sofa and the woman who sat there.

"Evelyn," Veeder said softly. "I've brought someone to meet you." The woman didn't respond. He put his palm in the center of Wetzon's resisting back and moved her around to the front of the sofa. "Evelyn," he said again. "This is Leslie." He bent and kissed the woman on her pale forehead, stroked a lock of streaked blond hair back from her expressionless face. The huge Siamese cat on her lap didn't move, didn't purr.

Evelyn wore a silk floral robe. She stared out at them with unblinking blue eyes. The same color as the cat's.

"Say hello to Evelyn, Leslie." His hand remained on Wetzon's back. He had to have felt her shudder. She shrank back. Evelyn's eyes did not move or show any recognition that anyone was in the room with her.

Wetzon said, "Hello, Evelyn."

Again, the figure on the sofa didn't respond. The cat meowed twice.

"Leslie is a headhunter on Wall Street," Veeder said, as if the mute, unseeing woman on the sofa understood everything. "You would enjoy talking to her, I know."

And Leslie Wetzon would have enjoyed nothing more than to have the earth open up and swallow her. What could he have been thinking? Why had he brought her here? She could never get involved with him.

Elsie returned with a wheelchair. "Time for bed, Mrs. V.," she said cheerfully. "No need for you to stay, Mr. Veeder. We have it all down to a science, don't we, dear?"

Because Bill Veeder was lifting his wife and placing her in the wheelchair, Wetzon's escape from the room was smooth. Her head spinning, she sank into one of the chairs at the end of the long gallery. She heard the timbre of Veeder's voice, but not what he said.

"Excuse me?"

"Come on, Leslie, let's get you home." He pulled her to her feet and out of his apartment.

She didn't know what to say. "I'm sorry—"

"I wanted you to meet her. Evelyn was a wonderful, vibrant woman." His voice was husky. "I loved her very much. I still love her."

"How long has she been . . . ?"

"Eight years. It's a form of Alzheimer's. She has no idea who I am or where she is."

The elevator came and took them to the lobby, where Veeder asked Scotty to get them a cab.

On the street, Wetzon said, "I'm so sorry." Why was she crying? She brushed the tears away with her fingertips. It was so sad.

"Oh, my dear." He put his arms around her. "I didn't mean for you to take it like this."

"What did you mean, then?" she mumbled into the lapel of his blue pinstripe.

"I simply meant for you to see that my wife is living, but she's not *there*. Do you understand?"

A cab came around the corner and, in response to Scotty's signal, stopped in front of the building.

"Bill, look—" Wetzon released herself. "I know what you're saying, but—"

"Get in, Leslie."

"Good night." She got in the cab and all of a sudden he was climbing in after her. He gave the driver her address.

"Hey," she protested. "I'm a big girl. I don't need an escort."

"I know that." He was looking at her legs, where her skirt had crept up her thighs.

So he was a leg man. She sighed and tugged at her skirt, getting nowhere. What a night. She felt as if she'd lived three lifetimes in the space of a few hours.

"Why aren't you married, Leslie?" Veeder asked out of the blue.

"Excuse me, did you say married?"

"Yes. Why aren't you?"

"I like being free. Besides . . . I see no happy heterosexual marriages

120

around me. Only my gay friends seem to have"—she smiled at him—"found happiness."

"Evelyn and I were happy," he said. "It's not impossible."

"Isn't it funny? Here you are, a number one philanderer and you're making a brief for marriage. Look at Poppy and Mort. Look at Minnie and Hem. He was raping a sixteen-year-old girl, for godsakes, probably not for the first time. Am I right?"

He put his hand on her thigh as if it was the most natural thing for him to do. "Leslie, I have an attorney-client relationship with Hem Barron. So let's just say appearances aren't everything."

chapter 28

"Nothing is going to happen," Wetzon told her escort as they got off the elevator on twelve, her floor. Bill Veeder was like glue on the back of an address label. Attractive, sexy glue.

"Don't worry. I just want to see where you live." His fingers glided over her topknot, down the outer rim of her ear to the nape of her neck.

She was mesmerized, keys in hand, afraid to move and lose the thrill. "God," she said, closing her eyes.

Then he said, "Shall I do the door?"

"No!" She willed herself out of the sexual languor, aware now of Izz's yelping on the other side of the door. "Beware of the vicious dog," she said as she opened the door. A whirling ball of yiping white fur leaped into her arms. "Mmm, mmm, yes, I know." Then the wriggling and licking stopped while Izz inspected the newcomer.

Veeder put his palm under her nose and let her sniff him. "I much prefer dogs to cats," he said. Izz covered his hand with kisses.

Wetzon set her on the carpet. "Bill, meet Izz."

He knelt and rubbed Izz's ears; she rolled over on her back, giving him everything she had. Great, Wetzon thought.

"Isadora?"

"Isabella."

"A grand name for a lady." He reached his hand out toward Wetzon's knee, but she moved faster. "Sorry," he said, as if it was an accident.

"No, you're not."

In the kitchen she rinsed Izz's water dish and refilled it. "Can I get you anything?" she asked Veeder, who had followed her into the kitchen. Izz was right at his heels.

"Coffee."

"It's decaf."

"My brand."

He left her to the grinding-measuring-pouring process, and she could hear him wandering through her apartment. Thank God, it was clean. What the hell was he doing?

"It's very nice," he said, startling her as she poured hot water into the filter.

"What did you think it would be?"

"I don't know what I thought. You can tell a lot about a person by seeing how he—or she—lives, don't you think? The Arts and Crafts Movement is a very strong, masculine choice for the home of a—"

"Strong, masculine woman?"

"Strong, yes. Masculine, hardly. Still, it's curious. Unless the design reflects what's-his-name . . . Silvestri?"

"No, it doesn't reflect him at all. I redid the apartment four years ago when I was flooded out. We were not together then." She poured coffee into mugs. "How do you take it?"

"Black." He picked up both mugs, carried them into the living room, and set them on the coffee table. "Now this is interesting," he said, inspecting the table.

"It's a rope bed, probably nineteenth century, used by hired hands. It still has the original rope and some of the red paint. I had the glass top made to fit over it." She was proud of her creation.

He sat on the sofa, making a space for her, but she chose the love seat. Izz scampered into the room and skidded to a halt, having to choose one surface, either sofa or love seat. "See that little brain clicking," Wetzon said. "Come here, Izz."

Izz, the little whore, chose the sofa, settling in next to Veeder, who laughed and patted his lap. "There's room for you too here, miss." Izz took it for an invitation and climbed in.

They looked at each other and laughed. Their eyes held and it was like a blood oath and they both knew it.

Wetzon groped for something innocuous to say. "I—uh—speaking of partners . . . Smith . . . A.T. told her about the IPO of The Groaning Board."

"A.T. talks too much. Everyone talks too much."

"Not you, Bill."

"Even me."

"Micklynn is not happy about going public."

"She'll come around. Once the TV show begins airing in the fall, there'll be book offers. She and A.T. are going to be too busy to run the catering business and the shop. This is the right timing for an initial public offering, believe me, Leslie."

It wasn't what he said, it was how he was saying it. It was his voice, as if he was making love to her. "The right timing, Bill," she gave it right back to him. Was this what flirting was?

"With the twelve million we raise, Leslie, the company can open Groaning Board shops around the country. It's a cash cow. Everyone will cash in, including the stockholders. Micklynn will be very rich. She's unhappy in the partnership."

"That's hardly a surprise. Micklynn and A.T. seem really mismatched."

"That doesn't mean the partnership doesn't work."

"You don't have to tell me that. Smith and I are the great mismatch of all time. Incidentally, Smith wants to be a big stockholder."

"What about you?" He was scratching Izz behind her ears.

Do me, do me, Wetzon thought, but she said, "I'm not greedy. I have enough money. I decided long ago that I'm never going to get infected by the Wall Street virus—money for money's sake. It all came crashing down in '87 and it will again. Look at this explosion in IPOs. It's insane."

"It's capitalism. Without IPOs, you have no start-up companies. The creative forces driving all these young industries need the bucks to go forward. It also goes for old-line companies who want to restructure. It's vital to our economy."

"I guess I still have glitter dust from the theatre under my feet. Still, I understand Micklynn's reluctance. I don't think I'd be too happy if Smith were intent on taking us public."

Veeder was stone quiet. His hands stopped working Izz's ears.

"She's already broached the subject with you?" Wetzon waited for a response. She didn't get one. "Goddammit, Bill Veeder!" She stood up. "And don't give me any of that client-attorney privilege shit. This is my life too. Smith and I are partners."

He set Izz aside and stood. "It was a social consult, Leslie. I told her it wouldn't work. It's the high-tech, biotech, and food services that are flying now. Xenia told me you knew all about it."

"Oh, please—"

"I'm very fond of Xenia."

"Oh, I admit I have my moments. This does not happen to be one of them." She walked to the door and waited for him, arms folded. Izz jumped off the sofa and followed.

"Well, now, don't kill the messenger."

"I wouldn't. Because I might need a criminal defense attorney after I kill my partner."

"Then I'm afraid I'd be the wrong man for you, Leslie."

"Why?"

He caught her elbows before she could unfold her arms and pulled her to him. She felt his breath on her face, the thumping of his heart, or was it hers?

Something familiar nudged her cheek, reminding her instantly of Silvestri.

Bill Veeder was carrying.

chapter 29

In spite of her anger at Smith, at Silvestri, and her confusion about Bill Veeder, Wetzon slept late on Sunday. The sleep of the righteous, or something like that. She did her barre work, walked Izz, and went back to bed with the *Times,* trying not to think about Silvestri, the breather, or Veeder. She went to bed early that night and would have made it to eight hours had not Rita Silvestri called her at 6 A.M.

"Breakfast, eight o'clock, Barney Greengrass," Rita said. Before Wetzon could respond, Rita disconnected.

"Be there." Wetzon finished the sentence and got into the shower.

She'd completed less than ten minutes of barre work when her downstairs buzzer sounded. Damn, Rita was pushy. The least she could do was let Wetzon have a couple of hours to herself before . . . She had half a mind not to respond. But she did.

"Yes?"

"Miss Mickey coming up," the doorman said.

"Damnation," she told Izz, who was already dancing attendance at the door, "it's like I'm giving therapy by the hour here." She opened the door. Micklynn was getting off the elevator. She was decked out in her embroidered shmattes, her hair in its long braid. Her face looked ravaged.

"I'm sorry, I'm really sorry, but at least I didn't wake you." She glanced at Izz without really seeing the dog. "I've been up all night going over and over everything."

"Come in and sit down, Micklynn." Wetzon led her inside. She reeked of gin. "Can I get you some orange juice?"

"The kitchen," Micklynn said. "Let's go to the kitchen. I'm more comfortable in kitchens."

Wetzon settled Micklynn on one of the high stools and gave her a glass of orange juice. "How about a bagel or coffee?"

"How about some gin?"

Wetzon shrugged and opened the fridge. "I only have vodka." She put the bottle of Absolut on the counter, and Micklynn unscrewed the cap and gave her orange juice a hefty dollop. "Maybe . . ."

"Don't say it, Leslie."

"I have an appointment at eight, Micklynn."

"I'll make it quick. I've been thinking about this since we had dinner together. Carlos told me you sometimes do consulting, and I want to hire you. I *have* to hire you." She drank the orange juice as if it were water.

"I don't understand, Micklynn." Wetzon looked at the vodka. Maybe she should take a shot. Maybe then she would understand all the insane things that were going on around her.

"I want to hire you to find out how Sheila died."

"But you know all that."

"I want you to find who killed her."

"The police will do that."

"Oh, I doubt that very much."

"Why do you say that?"

"Help me, Leslie. Say you'll look into it. I'll pay you a thousand dollars as a retainer." Micklynn took a crumpled piece of paper from some hidden pocket and tried to smooth it out, gave it up, and pushed it toward Wetzon. "Here's the check. My own personal check, not the company's. Say you'll do it. You're involved too. You said you know her brother-in-law."

"Artie'd kill me if he knew I was investigating Sheila's death."

"He doesn't have to know."

Wetzon thought, it might clear the air between Silvestri and . . . No. There was no air to clear. They were finished. Now if only she could let it go.

"He'll find out." She leaned back against the counter, thinking. "I am not licensed to do investigations of homicides, Micklynn."

"Consider this management consulting. I'm hiring you to help me with how I manage the death of a friend."

"Then you should be hiring a therapist."

"I already have a therapist, Leslie. I want to know who killed my friend. I have to know."

"Okay, Micklynn, but I have a partner and we have an agreement. We don't work alone."

She shook her head. "I don't want to work with your partner. I want to work with you. I'm in trouble. I need help from someone I can trust. Just see what you can find out. People trust you, Leslie. They'll talk to you."

Wetzon groaned.

"You'll do it?"

"Make the check payable to Smith and Wetzon and I'll see what I can come up with."

Micklynn jumped off the stool and crushed Wetzon in a bear hug. "I'll love you forever, and you'll always have a caterer for any party you throw . . . gratis." She crossed out *Leslie* on her check and wrote in *Smith and,* then drained what little remained of her vodka and orange juice. "You'll call me?"

She left Wetzon just enough time to get dressed and put on her makeup. Good thing Barney Greengrass was just around the corner on Amsterdam.

"I don't mean to interfere." Rita Silvestri gestured with her half bagel and the nova slid off the cream cheese onto the plate. She replaced it with her fingers.

"Then don't," Wetzon said cheerfully, smearing whitefish salad over her toasted bagel.

Rita Silvestri was wearing a snappy black suit, a long green print scarf that set off her red hair, and a black straw hat. She looked smart and a good deal younger than her sixty-five years. "You're the only one he ever brought to meet me," Rita said, "so I knew it was serious. What happened? Why is he back in that dump in Chelsea?"

"Ask him."

"I did. He's just like his father. The wall goes up and that's all, folks."

"What did he say?"

"He said, 'Butt out, I'm working on a case.' "

"Sheila Gelber's murder."

Rita frowned as if trying to place a vaguely familiar name. "Should I know who Sheila Gelber is?"

"She was Artie Metzger's sister-in-law. I gather she and Silvestri were an item at one point." Wetzon bit into the bagel and the salty fish was sweet on her tongue.

"Well, I never met her. So much for the item business."

"Look, Rita, I really don't know what's going on. He was very upset. I wanted to help, but he called me a nag and said he was moving out."

"Just like that?"

"Just like that. And oh yes, he said he'd be back. I told him not to bother."

"You didn't mean it."

"Oh, I meant it. I'm tired of the monosyllables, the moods. He closes up for no reason at all. I've had it, Rita."

"His father—"

"I don't care if he's just like his father. I didn't have a relationship with his father. I had one with him, or so I thought. You wouldn't understand. He's your son."

"I understand all too well, Les." Rita sighed. "I thought it would be different for him."

"How did you handle his father?"

"He died."

"Rita, listen. I'm truly sorry. I would have liked you for a mother-in-law. You'd be my friend. But don't try to fix this."

"I'll still be your friend, Les, if you'll let me."

"Okay, you're on." Wetzon held out her hand and Rita took it. "Now

I've got to get to the office." She looked down at her bagel. She'd only taken one bite. "Can you wrap this up?" she asked the waiter.

"Mine too," Rita said. She gave the waiter a twenty-dollar bill.

"If you're going to your office," Wetzon said, "I can drop you."

"Fine." But Rita looked distracted. As their cab whizzed down Central Park West, she said, "Billy Veeder . . ."

Wetzon looked out at the blooming park. "A business drink."

"He's an attractive man."

"Is he?" They were talking female shorthand, the meaning clear to each of them.

"You hadn't noticed?"

"I noticed he carries a gun."

"They never get over their thing about guns."

"What do you mean *they?*"

"Didn't you know?" Rita gave her a long, sympathetic look. "Before he went to law school and became rich and glamorous, Billy was a cop."

chapter 30

The Andy Warhol pencil drawing of the wad of dollar bills that Wetzon and Smith had bought with their first placement check at the beginning of their partnership was leaning against the wall waiting to be hung. Wetzon straightened the wire and hung the drawing on the only available wall space.

"Partnership, sure," Wetzon said to Smith's desk. "A partnership should be based on trust."

The desks were L-shaped, each facing a huge expanse of window overlooking Forty-ninth Street. In fact, there were windows everywhere, letting in fabulous light. In the back of the room, windows looked out on a deck. Stairs led down from the deck to the garden, where tulips and daffodils were in full bloom. The view was so compelling that Wetzon didn't hear footsteps on the stairs.

"Well, I never expected to see you this early." Smith set a vase of flowers on her L, arranged them, stepped back, tilted her head, then rearranged them.

"Why not?"

Smith gave her a knowing smile. "Migraine, for pity sakes. I wasn't born yesterday, sweetie pie."

Wetzon ignored her. "It was a nice dinner party." She watched the lights begin to flare on her telephone, accompanied by a tremorous ring.

"Yes, it was, wasn't it? The minute Micklynn left and A.T. took over it was perfect."

"But Micklynn is the chef. A.T. doesn't know anything about cooking. She knows marketing."

"Not true, sugar. Not true at all." Smith began to pull items from a box on the floor and set them on her desk, starting with a datebook. "You missed an incident between that dreadful Minnie Wang and little Ellen."

"Wu."

"Wu?" Smith raised her head, annoyed.

"Minnie Wu, that's her name. Not Wang."

"Whatever. Dreadful is dreadful. She tried to kill that poor child. She would have ruined my party."

"It was Hem's fault."

"Why would it be Hem's fault? He's a brilliant investment banker."

"Brilliant he may be, but he thinks with his dick. He was trying to rape Ellen."

"Sweetie pie, I don't know how you can say that. You weren't even there."

"But I was—"

"A.T. told me she and Ellen were working in the kitchen when Minnie what's-her-face broke in and tried to strangle the child. That woman is psychotic; she imagines that Hem is doing it with other women, *any* woman. Hem. Can you believe it? He's such a caring, lovely man."

"Hard to believe. Truly." Smith missed her sarcasm entirely. Hem was neither caring nor lovely, and Smith, true to form, could only see his power and his money and judge him accordingly. She designed her life and lived it by her own skewed perception of what was real. There was no point in arguing with her.

"But, sweetie pie," Smith continued in full wheedle, that knowing smile on her face again, "this is not what I want to talk about. I'm sure you have so much to tell me. I can't wait to hear." She looked around her desk as if she'd just noticed something was missing. "Do we have coffee?"

"Yes, sitting ready and waiting in our private kitchen."

"Well, hurry up and get us some, sugar," Smith ordered. "Then I want to hear all about it." This last came with a stylized shoulder roll.

Wetzon took her time pouring coffee into the mugs. She wiped down the granite counter. When she strolled back she found no sign of Smith, until she looked out on the deck. Smith had unpacked the canvas pillows and set them onto two deck chairs. She motioned Wetzon out. "Isn't it lovely?" she said. Huge sunglasses covered her eyes.

"Truly," Wetzon agreed. She'd be damned if she'd use Smith's new favorite word. She handed Smith one of the mugs.

"So tell me about it." Smith settled into the chair and put her feet up.

"About what?"

"Why are you being so coy? Read my lips. How was he?"

It was too tiresome playing the game with Smith, so Wetzon said, "Bill Veeder's an attractive man."

Smith's feet hit the deck. "You are impossible. Do you think I brought the two of you together so you could close me out? That's not fair. You had two days together. You know what I'm asking. Sex. Orgasm. I insist you share. What is Billy like in bed? I hear—"

"Insist, Dolly Levi? Oh, come now." Wetzon sat on the other chair and took a sip of coffee. "Obviously you know more about it than I do, because I haven't slept with him. And we did not have two days together."

"You haven't slept with him?" Smith's inflection indicated that Wetzon had betrayed her by doing something completely stupid. "What a dumb move. He'll never call you again. It's not his style. I set this up for you and now look what you've done. You're still carrying a torch for Dick Tracy." She sighed loudly. "What did you tell Bill?"

"Christ, Smith, give me a break, will you? Don't jump to any conclusions. I didn't tell Bill anything. He took me to meet Evelyn."

"He didn't!" Aghast, Smith raised her dark glasses to stare at Wetzon.

"He did."

"What a fool. That zombie could turn off a nymphomaniac. Why on earth did he do that? I'll have to have a little talk with him."

That did it. Wetzon stood up and boiled over. "No, you won't, Smith. You'll kindly stay out of it."

"Aaaah." Smith let go of her glasses and they dropped back on her nose. She raised her face to the sun. "I know you so well, sweetie pie. You like him. I knew it. He's been after me to get you two together since the tree lighting last year."

"Smith, goddammit, promise me—" Wetzon was suddenly conscious that the decibel level of her voice had risen precariously. "Please, please, butt out." God, that's what Silvestri had said to his mother. She dropped into the deck chair, set the mug on the floor.

"Okay, okay, babycakes. No need to get so upset." Smith sat beside Wetzon and patted her shoulder. "I never interfere when I'm not wanted. My only wish is for you to be happy. I'd never do anything you wouldn't approve of. You know that."

Wetzon said, "You wouldn't? Well, you've got us representing talent without my okay, you've got us as associate producers of *Softly,* and you want to take Smith and Wetzon public. I never approved of any of it."

Smith went back to her deck chair and sipped her coffee, hiding behind her dark glasses. Wetzon kept quiet, not giving her any help. Finally, Smith said, "You are absolutely right, sweetie pie."

Wetzon rolled off the chair. "She's admitted she's been wrong. I'm shocked, do you hear? Shocked."

"Humpf," Smith said. "Actually, I've come to the conclusion that we can't do everything, so I've found an agent for Lesser and Carpenter." She beamed at Wetzon. "I negotiated a finder's fee of two percent on all earnings. It'll be a nice bit of change for the firm."

Wetzon got back on the chair and reached down for her mug. "You're amazing." She had Micklynn's check in her purse. How would she tell Smith about it? Maybe she should just deposit it into the Smith and Wetzon account and explain later.

"As for going public, I was just testing the waters, sweetie pie. It was a theoretical question I put to Billy—friend to friend. I'm not ready to have investors peeking over our shoulders, are you?"

"No. I'd rather sell the firm outright."

"Well, of course, that will never happen. We are partners. I love you. I trust you. Whatever we do, Smith and Wetzon will be our base of operations. We can launch all of our projects from here."

"By *projects* you mean like associate producing?"

"Yes. I don't want to give that up." She took off her glasses again. "You'll be pleased to hear that Twoey and I are back together."

Wetzon was pleased, but not surprised. "I got that message the other night."

"He's such a sweetheart. I just couldn't let him settle for that awful Puerto Rican girl."

Groaning, Wetzon said, "So you saved him. You're so noble. And by the way, Sunny Browning is not Puerto Rican. Why do you keep saying she's Puerto Rican?"

"Because who else would name a child Sunny? I'm right. Admit it."

Wetzon threw up her hands. "Oh, please."

"I can't believe Billy took you to meet that lump."

"Drop it, Smith."

"Tell me honestly, you and Dick Tracy are finished?"

Wetzon nodded.

Smith gave an audible sigh. "I was afraid you'd make a terrible mistake and marry him. What did it?"

"An old girlfriend."

Smith snapped into a sitting position. "Oh, poor, poor sweetie pie, he had someone on the side?" She walked back inside and Wetzon followed her.

"No, Smith." It was disconcerting how Smith always went for the worst scenario. "This old girlfriend, Sheila—he knew her years before me—died mysteriously."

"So?"

"He couldn't handle it. I asked a lot of questions, offered help. He wanted out. That's all she wrote."

"You are a very lucky woman. I have to tell you."

"There's more, Smith."

"About him?"

"No. It turns out that Micklynn Devora was a good friend of Sheila's. And she would like me . . . us . . . me to do some checking into the murder." There, she'd said it.

"An investigation." Smith clapped her hands gleefully, then picked up her Tarot deck and began to shuffle the cards. "Yes! Yes!"

"Management consulting."

Holding the deck out to Wetzon, she said, "Cut."

Wetzon sighed and cut the cards. "What are you doing?"

"You know what I'm doing. Breathe on the cards."

"Do I have to?"

"Yes."

After Wetzon breathed on the cards and handed them back to Smith, Smith began to lay out the Celtic Cross.

A buzzer sounded and then Darlene's voice filled the room. "Twoey Barnes on line two for you, Smith. And on line three, Bill Veeder for you, Wetzon."

Smith lifted her eyes from the cards. "What do you think?" She gave Wetzon a solemn wink.

"Tell them we're in a meeting and we'll call back," Wetzon said.

"Now we're talking!" Smith held out her hand and Wetzon shook it. The intercom clicked off. They gave each other a slow bow.

"Where were we?" Wetzon said.

Smith was studying the cards and didn't respond.

"Smith?"

"How did this Sheila person die?"

"She was poisoned by some corn muffins."

"Oh, dear, oh, dear, I hope you got us paid upfront."

"I did, but what do you mean?"

"Because, trust me on this, sweetie pie, our client is the murderer."

c h a p t e r   3 1

Metzger called just before lunch. "Any more weird calls?"

"No." She was angry with him. Why? She couldn't really say. Maybe because he was connected to Silvestri, who was the true cause of her anger.

"I alerted the Annoyance Call Bureau. They'll get the trace to me directly. Remember, you've got to hang up, pick up again, and press star fifty-seven to make it work."

"Fine."

"You're mad at me."

"No."

"Then whydja run away?"

"I didn't run away. You were taking forever at

Silvestri's and I was going to be late for a sit-down dinner. I knew you'd understand," she added sweetly.

"You're mad as hell because of Sil—"

"If you say another word about him, Artie, I *will* be mad as hell. I won't discuss it with you or Rita or anybody. It's over."

"Aw, come on, Leslie. You know that's not for real."

She thought about that. Wasn't it? "What's not for real? I've met someone else, Artie." Chew on that for a while. "That's for real. He laughs, he cries, he communicates."

"Come on, Leslie, you know it's hard for us. We see so much . . ."

Goddam, she thought. He was going to give her all the usual bullshit about cops. She blurted out, "I hate to disappoint you, Artie, but this guy's a cop too."

After a palpable silence, Metzger said, "Do I know him?"

"Maybe. Maybe not. Would you mind asking your friend to drop off my keys?"

"Ask him yourself. I'm not getting in the middle of this. You both beat the shit out of me."

Wetzon laughed. The phones were too quiet. Only the second line was engaged and the third, which she was on. Smith had gone to Saks and Darlene was back at the dentist. When the first button lit up, she said, "Artie, hold on. I want to ask you about something else." She put him on hold and pressed the first button. "Smith and Wetzon."

She knew who it was even before she heard the breathing. And the breathing itself was heavier than before, as if he'd been running. "Get a life, you son of a bitch!" she screamed into the phone, hung up, picked up again, pressed star fifty-seven. She came back to Metzger. "Guess who it was," she said. Fury had seared away her fear, for the time being.

"Good. Did you do the star fifty-seven thing?"

"Yes."

"I'll check it out. I gotta go. Whatdja want to ask me?"

"Did you talk to Micklynn Devora?"

"Yes."

"That's all you're going to say?"

"It's a murder investigation."

"Artie, I might as well tell you, Micklynn hired Smith and Wetzon as consultants."

"Consultants? Consulting on what?"

"Sheila's murder."

"Oh no you're not."

"Micklynn was Sheila's friend. She feels responsible."

"Every-fucking-body feels responsible—Silvestri, me, my kid, my wife, Devora. For chrissakes, I'm going to tell you only once, Leslie, stay out of this. You're not a professional."

"Micklynn is devastated by Sheila's death. She asked for help. I want to help."

"Help, nothing. You're only going to muddy the waters."

"What does that mean?"

"It means, stay away from Micklynn Devora. There's a murderer out there who's been successful once already and may be only too willing to kill again. I'll check out that number and get back to you."

"Think of it, truffle mayonnaise," Laura Lee said. "Joanne brought it to me from Tuscany. It makes the most divine egg salad."

"Laura Lee, screw truffle mayonnaise. Your client Hem Barron is depraved. He sexually assaulted a sixteen-year-old girl at Smith's dinner party Saturday night." Phone to her ear, Wetzon sat back in her chair and put her feet on her desk.

"Darlin', you must be mistaken. Why would he do it? Hem can have any woman he wants."

"I saw it with my own eyes. It wasn't pretty. And Minnie didn't find anything to admire about it either."

"Minnie saw it too? Lord, why can't these men just keep it in their pants?"

"Maybe Hem keeps it in his pants with Minnie. Have you considered that? Maybe that's why there are no children. Maybe sixteen-year-old girls turn Hem on. Minnie doesn't qualify."

"Lordy, lordy, I wish I could have seen it."

"It was horrible, Laura Lee. She has these melon-sized breasts. He had his face in them and she had her hands in his pants . . . oh, shit."

"Doesn't sound like rape to me, darlin'."

"It would still be statutory, wouldn't it? Maybe that's what Bill meant when he said things aren't always what they seem. . . ."

"By Bill, I take it you mean the smashin' Billy Veeder?"

"Yes."

"Well, tell me." Laura Lee's Southern tones oozed across the phone lines, honey from a spoon. "What was it like? I hear he's spectacular—"

"Laura Lee! I can't believe you. That's exactly what Smith said."

"Wetzon, you really know how to hurt a girl."

"If you must know, nothing happened, Laura Lee. He brought me to meet his wife."

"Oh, the unfortunate Evelyn. Poor soul. What's his problem, I wonder, that he has to parade her at affairs?"

"She's his shield. He never has to say, 'I will never divorce my wife.' Only a heartless, avaricious bitch would demand that he leave her."

"Well, you wouldn't, darlin', that's for sure. Still, who cares about marriage these days anyway? Not me, not you. Right? The important thing is good sex . . . don't you agree?"

"Don't try to sweet-talk anything out of me, Laura Lee. Did you know that Bill was once a cop?"

"No."

"Do you think I have this thing for cops? Be honest with me."

Laura Lee giggled. "I'll have to mull that over and give you my answer at a future date."

"Oh, you just think all of this is funny. You're not taking me seriously, so forget it. What I really called to say is that after what happened the other night I don't think Hem and Minnie will be having their anniversary party—"

"*Au contraire,* darlin'. I just spoke to Hem and he reminded me about you."

"I'm not going. They're crazy, scummy people. I don't want them in my life. I hate all those chic, status-conscious East Siders and their friends."

"What about me?"

"I love you, Laura Lee, but you have terrible taste in clients."

"It's about money, darlin'. Money buys tickets for the Philharmonic, the theatre, and the opera. That's my reason for attendin' their little anniversary soiree. Your reason is Bill Veeder."

"Oh, fuck it, Laura Lee."

"There you go."

Wetzon hung up and wandered downstairs. Darlene was talking to a manager, taking lengthy notes. She was set up in half of the old office Wetzon and Smith had shared. In the other half, Max sat looking out on an extended reception area.

"Will you take a call from one of our principals, Leslie Wetzon?" Max said into the phone as she came around to his side. "Good. What's the best time for you?"

God, he was good, Wetzon thought. And to think Smith had not wanted to hire him.

When Smith reappeared with three bulging shopping bags, Wetzon was eating the leftover bagel and whitefish salad, watching the garden grow. She picked up her lunch and came back inside. "What did you buy?"

"Couple of linen dresses, silk pants, a blazer, lingerie. I opened my closet this morning and saw I had absolutely nothing to wear for the summer. Oh, and I bought you a little something because it's nothing you would buy for yourself." She rummaged through two of the bags, scattering smaller bags over the floor, finally finding what she was looking for in the third. "Here." She thrust it at Wetzon.

"For me? Really? What is it?"

"Open it. I know you can use the pick-me-up, babycakes." She grinned at Wetzon.

Wetzon opened the package and took out the item. "What the hell is this? It looks like a torture contraption. Probably designed by a man."

"It's the Wonderbra. They even make it in your size. It'll do wonders for your bosoms. Bill likes bosoms."

"I don't think so."

"Oh, what do you know? You're in your own world all the time. You are so naive. Just try it next time and you'll see his reaction."

Wetzon waved the bra at Smith. "Don't you think this is a little ludicrous? We are coming to the end of the twentieth century and bright successful women are still pushing their tits in men's faces."

"Some things never change, sweetie pie, and you might as well live with it," Smith said pityingly.

"Phone for you, Wetzon," Max announced on the intercom. "Detective Metzger."

She picked up the phone. "Artie?"

Metzger said, "The call came from a bank of phones at Saks."

chapter 32

The call came in on her private line. It rang four times before Wetzon answered with a cautious "Yes?"

"Is this Leslie Wetzon?" A tight voice, a hand-over-the-mouthpiece voice. Certainly not Smith, who had left a good half hour ago.

"Who's calling, please?" She'd give nothing away.

"A. T. Barron."

"Oh, A.T., I didn't recognize your voice." Relief flooded over her, such relief that she could have kissed A.T. had she been there. And A.T. was the most un-kissable of women.

"Leslie, can you see your way clear to coming up here right now? Micklynn insists she must see you. She won't come downstairs and we're taping the first show in two hours. I can't have this."

Promising A.T. she'd come, Wetzon packed up her briefcase, hooked her purse over her shoulder. As she started down the stairs, she thought she heard a file drawer roll shut. But Darlene was talking on the phone.

"You'd be making a terrible mistake if you went there, Charley," Darlene said. She fluttered her fingers at Wetzon.

Wetzon, the phony, fluttered fingers back. Just like Mort Hornberg's kissy-poo with his lips. At first, she'd thought she would come to like Darlene, but now she knew it wasn't going to happen. "I have an appointment," Wetzon mouthed.

"Really?" Darlene put her hand over the mouthpiece. "Have a good time. Don't worry about anything here."

That sounded ominous. Wetzon went around the partition to Max. He was writing down the names of stockbrokers someone on the other end of the line was giving him. He gave Wetzon the thumbs-up sign. He'd been the cold caller on ten placements since January; he'd make the first call, do the first interview, then Wetzon would set up the appointments, do the follow-ups, and close them.

Darlene had made only four in the same amount of time, but all were substantial; all had grosses of between three-quarters of a mil and one point five mil, billing out a nice piece of change for both Darlene and Smith and Wetzon.

In the cab up to The Groaning Board, Wetzon gave herself permission to think about what Metzger had said. That the breather had called her from a pay phone at Saks.

Smith had been at Saks. Did that mean Smith was making the phone calls? What could be her purpose? Money? Smith's purpose was always money. To make Wetzon more pliable about taking the company public? No. If it turned out it was Smith who was making the calls, their partnership would be over. That's all there was to it.

But wait. Hadn't Smith been in the room when that first call had come in on Wetzon's newly installed private line? She couldn't remember. Of course she was. It wasn't Smith making those calls. A pay phone, for godsakes. Anyone can use a pay phone.

Don't think about it anymore. Think about Micklynn. It was bad enough for Smith to believe, with no proof whatever, that Micklynn was a murderer. What had happened that Micklynn needed Wetzon so desperately she'd given A.T. the private number to call? Micklynn was the only one thus far to whom Wetzon had given her private number.

The woman behind the counter was calmly spooning parmesan chicken salad into a plastic container bearing The Groaning Board logo. A young woman with a swaddled infant in a sling hanging from her shoulders was inspecting the array of prepared foods in the display case. The peaceful expression on the sleeping child's face as it nestled on its mother's breast evoked strange emotions in Wetzon. Awe, envy, horror. She caught herself staring. Child, she thought, make the most of this last zone of peace in your life; it's the only nonresponsible time you'll ever have.

"May I help you?" the counterwoman asked.

"I'm Leslie Wetzon. A.T. and Micklynn are expecting me."

"Go on back. Just watch your step," she added apologetically. "There are cables everywhere."

She wasn't kidding. The huge kitchen area was in total chaos. Cameras and crew, mostly men, cables strewn everywhere, blinding lights on tall stalks. And in the center of it, pudgy little Minnie Wu, totally recovered from the debacle at Smith's dinner party, waving her arms around, giving orders. "No! Over there. Higher. That whole grid of lights. I want them hotter. Hot. Hot. Hot. Can't anyone do any fucking thing right?"

A working counter had been set up in front of a stove, a refrigerator, and a sink, all of which looked new and unused. It was obvious that this was where the show would be taped.

"Leslie!" Wetzon could barely hear over the hubbub. She looked around. A.T. was waving to her from the staircase. "Over here."

Wetzon picked her way across the room, concentrating on not bumping cameras or tripping over cables, so she was unprepared for the blow. It came with such force, slamming into her upper arm and spinning her around. She tottered wildly but didn't fall.

"Hey," she gasped, the wind knocked out of her.

"Sorry," Minnie said. "Didn't see you. Reuben, I need you."

Rubbing her arm where she could already feel the bruise begin to swell, Wetzon said, "Like hell you didn't see me." She could feel Minnie's eyes scalding her as she began to move toward the staircase again. "Sure, hit me, burn me, snow me," Wetzon muttered. "I'll still deliver."

A.T. came back down the stairs. "Where've you been?" she demanded querulously. "I thought you were right behind me."

"Ask your sister-in-law," Wetzon snapped. "Where's Micklynn?" Micklynn was truly a saint to put up with all these awful people.

"Upstairs. She won't come down and do the show."

"Why don't you get everything ready, and I'll talk to her." Wetzon nodded toward the maelstrom below.

"Okay, if you think you can handle her." A.T.'s reluctance was all surface. She took off.

Wetzon opened the door to Micklynn's apartment. No one was in the kitchen. "Micklynn? It's Leslie. What's happened? Where are you?"

"Oh, Leslie," Micklynn wailed.

Wetzon followed the wail. No sign of Micklynn in either dining or living room. The wail drew her upstairs to the bedroom.

Micklynn was lying on her back on the bed in a long white tee shirt, a bottle of wine pressed to her breast. A pair of blue denim overalls, clean and pressed, hung from a hanger hooked to the top of a closet door.

"They're all waiting for you downstairs."

"Let them wait." Micklynn sat up and took a swig of wine. "I knew you'd come." Another swig. "This is so awful." Another swig. "The police—oh, God, I can't . . ."

"I'm working for you, Micklynn. Tell me." Wetzon sat down on the edge of the bed.

Micklynn inhaled with a gasping gulp, then wiped her face on the sleeve of her tee shirt. "Two detectives came to see me a couple hours ago. Did you know?" She tilted the bottle into her mouth. There was very little left. "Did you know? Sheila was killed by something that was in a corn muffin she ate. They found three others in the freezer with the same poison."

"I'd heard from someone downtown."

"Why didn't you tell me?"

"It was a guess and not verified. What difference does it make whether it was the corn muffins?"

"It makes a big difference. I didn't tell them, but they knew. Oh, God." She threw back her head and finished the wine. Who knew if she could even stand up?

Wetzon said, gently, "Knew what, Micklynn?"

"That I made the corn muffins," she wailed.

c h a p t e r   3 3

Towel around his neck, Carlos dangled simian from the
barre, a midair slouch. "Dear Heart, I've been meaning to
tell you that's an ugly thing you're wearing." He nodded
to the gross-colored welt that ran upward from her upper
arm, disappearing beneath the V-necked tee. "Walked
into a door?"

"No." She lay on her mat pondering her life.

"Made someone mad?"

"Maybe." She rolled herself into a shoulder stand.
"Minnie Wu." Scissored her legs back and forth. They
were good legs.

"She beats up anyone she thinks Hem looks at. You
should have seen what she did to Mickey."

"Jesus, Micklynn had an affair with Hem?"

"She did. Min never forgives. She's a jealous creature."

"Oh, please. I am no one for anyone to be jealous of." Good legs or not. Legs together, she arched her back and came down one leg at a time into a backbend, then took a walk, a quadruped with arched back.

"It's charmed I am by your creative position. Now if the new beau could see you—"

"New beau?" She dropped to the floor and lay flat. "There is no new beau, darling." Izz climbed up on her stomach, circled, and nested.

"Oh, really?" Carlos said, raising one eyebrow and lowering one eyelid. He sank down beside her, tailor fashion. "Don't tell me the old one's back."

"The old one's gone for good, my man, and I celebrate my celibacy."

"Bullshit. Look me in the eye and say that, Birdie."

She laughed, dumping Izz on the floor as she rolled over. "There's no one, I swear." She covered her head with her hands.

"You lie," he snarled in a mock Gestapo accent and snapped his towel at her. "Vee know how to deal viz liars. Talk." He snapped the towel at her again.

"No, no, stop. I'll talk."

"Who is it? I vant a name."

Giggling, she said, "I cannot lie to you. It's Hem Barron."

"An obvious lie." He snapped his fingers at her. "Didn't I varn you? Otto, take her to the—"

Propping herself up on her elbows, she said, "One, Mr. Smartass, how do you know there's someone else, and two, how do you know it's not Hem?" She sat up and faced him tailor fashion too, their knees touching.

"Because, my dear, sweet Birdie, Carlos knows you so well. He can read you like a book. And it ain't Hem Barron."

"Bullshit."

"He's not your type, darling."

"Why not?"

"Too rich, too obvious, too shallow."

"Too true."

He leaned across two sets of knees and placed his hands on her shoulders. "Tell your best friend. *He* would tell you."

Sighing, Wetzon placed her hands on Carlos' shoulders. "You won't be judgmental?"

"Judgmental? *Moi?* Who am I to be judgmental?" He gave her a lascivious grin. "Who is it?"

"Bill Veeder."

"Oy."

"See. I knew you'd be judgmental."

"No, no, Birdie. I love you unconditionally. I just worry for you. I read Liz Smith. You never pick the easy ones."

"Okay, let me get this over with. He's married, his wife has advanced Alzheimer's, he's an ex-cop."

"Have a thing for cops, have we?" Carlos grinned at her. "I have to admit he's a looker, long lean bod. I could go for him myself." He kissed her forehead. "How's the sex?"

She pushed him over. "You're just like everybody else. You read those trashy gossip columns. Smith asked me, Laura Lee asked me."

He lay on the floor and laughed. "Too funny, Birdie, darling. I bet you didn't tell them."

"I didn't."

"Bet you'll tell me, girlfriend."

"Well, you bet wrong, sister."

"La, I guess that means you two haven't climbed into the sack yet." He was howling with laughter, rolling on the floor.

Wetzon rose straight up to her full height and uncrossed her legs. "Swine." She tickled his chest with the toe of her ballet slipper. "Get up and say that as a man."

He was laughing so hard she lost her balance and came down on top of him. "Oof," he said. "You've put on weight, little darling."

"You'd better be good and not say another word about this or I'll crush you like the flea you are."

"Birdie, darling." His wicked eyes glinted. "Whenever the spirits move you, I think you're in for a treat."

She sat up. Izz was eyeing her reproachfully; why didn't she play with Izz instead of Carlos? "Man who used to be best friend, what are you talking about?"

"Bill Veeder, my little hayseed. And I'm *not* talking about his performance in court."

When the tub was three-quarters full, Wetzon lowered herself into the steamy water. She'd turned down dinner with Carlos and Arthur. She'd turned down dinner with Bill Veeder, keeping him at arm's length, drawing out the sweetness of desire. Call it what it is, she told herself. Well, all right. Lust.

Izz stood on her hind legs leaning on the rim of the tub. Her nose twitched and she licked Wetzon's shoulder, then stuck her nose in the hot water, pulled out, sneezed.

Wetzon added more hot water, rested her hand on the edge of the tub, luxuriating in the warmth, the peace, the . . .

She woke out of a doze to Izz barking, the phone ringing. Let the answering machine get it. But she couldn't. She'd been soaking long enough anyway. She got out of the tub and wrapped herself in a towel, then padded to the bedroom phone, leaving a trail of wet footprints.

"Hello?" She was greeted by the now familiar heavy silence that preceded the breather. Then the breathing started. "We are not amused," she said, and hung up. "No, we're uneasy and growing uneasier." Picking up the phone again, she pressed star fifty-seven.

Next she called Metzger at the Seventeenth Precinct, not really expecting to find him still there. But he was.

"I'll check it out for you," he said.

"Anything new on the poison in the muffins?"

"You're taking my advice to stay out of this?"

She crossed her fingers. "Oh, absolutely," she lied.

"We know who made the muffins."

"You do?"

"Micklynn Devora. Thanks for the tip."

"Tip? I didn't give you a tip."

"Yes, you did. You said caterer, friend, odd flours. The corn muffins were made with cornmeal and rice flour. Trail led right to Micklynn Devora."

"God. Did she admit it?"

"She didn't have to. We're keeping an eye on her, checking out any unnatural deaths of people she knew."

Guilt washed over Wetzon. Pure, painful guilt. She'd gotten Micklynn in trouble and she was lying to Metzger. What should she do? Oh, hell, keep moving.

"What was the poison?" she asked.

"The chef, it appears, has a thing for flowers."

"She's got this disease that makes her allergic to gluten, just like Sheila."

"That's not what I'm talking about. I'm talking f-l-o-w-e-r-s. Not the kind you bake with usually. Except this one time."

"I'm sorry. I don't get it. How can a flower kill?"

"According to the M.E.'s toxicologist, some flowers, seeds, stems, and leaves are highly poisonous. Someone ground up the flowers and mixed them into the batter of the muffins. Sheila ate one and it killed her. It was meant to."

"Good God. What flowers are that toxic?"

"More of them than you would think. In this case," Metzger said, "azaleas."

chapter 34

She woke up angry, with a kind of manic energy, and took Izz out for a quick walk over to Central Park West and back. The day yawned before her with a cluttered New York smorgasbord of choices, any number of museums, movies, theaters, antique shows, street fairs. And for Wetzon this day had no choice at all. She waited, antsy, while Izz watered the gutter and played sniffy with all the other dogs on the block.

"Nice doggie," a child screamed from his stroller, trying to grab a piece of Izz. The mom, who, like Wetzon, wore biker shorts, was chatting on a cellular phone, her attention compromised.

Wetzon steered Izz away from the tiny grasping hand, but the child managed to snag a bit of fur and pulled. Izz shrieked.

"No!" Wetzon yelled at the child. She knelt to try to remove Izz from the tight-fisted little hand. Izz whimpered.

"Get that dog away from my baby!" the mother screamed, jerking the stroller and adding to Izz's pain.

"Get your *baby* away from my *dog*," Wetzon countered.

"Let go of the doggie, Anthony. Do you hear me, Anthony? Mommy says—"

Anthony finally let go, and Wetzon gathered Izz in her arms. "Thank you," she said quickly.

"I hate you!" Anthony screamed at his mother. "I wish you were dead!"

The mother returned to her phone. "I'm sorry, Claudia, but some people around here think dogs are more important than children."

"Some dogs," Wetzon countered, raising her voice, "have better manners than some children. Children who torture animals grow up to be serial murderers."

"Here, here!" Madge Alter, a retired schoolteacher and one of Wetzon's elderly neighbors, caught up with Wetzon. Madge was carrying a bag of groceries and another bag, from which protruded the leaves of a flowering plant. "I don't know what's happened to parents these days. They don't teach their children manners and never reprimand them when they misbehave."

Wetzon set Izz down on the sidewalk and fell into step beside Madge, who was heading back home.

"They have wonderful plants at the farmers' market, Leslie."

"What did you buy?" Wetzon peered into the bag. A spicy fragrance wafted up from the plant.

"A perfectly beautiful azalea," Madge said. Her face was deeply etched, but her cheeks were plump and pink and her eyes were bright and kind. She'd often invited Wetzon to fast-walk with her around the reservoir early in the morning. Wetzon had demurred. She liked to walk solo. "I love azaleas. They have such a nice clovey perfume, don't you think?"

"They do. I read somewhere that they're poisonous, though."

Madge said, "I shouldn't think so, but, of course, I don't eat them." She waved Wetzon onto the elevator first. "After you, dear."

Madge got off on four, leaving Wetzon, in the welcome silence, free to wonder about azaleas. This whole business was so bizarre. When she got back to the apartment, she unleashed Izz, gave her fresh water, then called Micklynn. It was just after ten.

"I was just going to call you," Micklynn said, breathing heavily into the phone. She sounded sloshed. If she'd started drinking early, which she probably had, she'd be falling-down drunk by noon.

"How has the taping been going?"

"Oh, fine. Really. I don't know." More heavy breathing.

"I think we ought to get together."

"I've just started to work on Hem and Min's party. A.T. will be here at twelve."

"Get in a cab and meet me at the Starbucks in the Barnes & Noble on Eighty-third Street. It won't take long."

"Half hour," Micklynn mumbled.

Wetzon slipped her wallet into a fanny pack along with tissues, lipstick, and a comb, and raced out to do her fast walk down Columbus from Eighty-sixth to Sixty-sixth, then over to Broadway and up to Eighty-third Street. The whole world was out on this beautiful May morning. If she didn't run into anyone she knew, she could do the walk in a half hour.

Luck was with her. Thirty minutes later, she was stretching her muscles against B & N's facade.

After checking the coffee shop and not seeing Micklynn, Wetzon went into the book stacks. The store wasn't that busy on an almost summer Sunday. Everybody who was anybody was beginning to make the trek out to the Hamptons or Westport, where Smith had her weekend house.

In the science section she found what she was looking for: a concise encyclopedia of plants. The book on poisons she found in the medical section. She took both books back with her to the coffee shop, where she spotted Micklynn sitting at a table in the rear, hunched over a latte. The coffee-tinted milk was running over the sides of the mug.

Wetzon waved to her and stopped at the counter for a decaf. There were only four other people in the coffee shop, three women, old friends, happily planning some kind of trip. The other individual was a girl with beads in her nose and lower lip, gold hoops lining the outside of both ears. She sat alone reading *The Celestine Prophecy*.

Wetzon set the books on the table, sat opposite Micklynn, and took the agreement she'd prepared from her handbag. "You said you were going to call me?"

"I was going to call you?" Micklynn looked blank, depressed and ill. "Did I say that?"

"Yes. If you still want to work with me, I've brought a letter agreement for you to sign."

"I don't remember," Micklynn said, frowning. "Here, I'll sign it." She scrawled her signature on the agreement without reading it and slid it back toward Wetzon. "I guess if it was important it'll come back to me. What do you have there?" She picked up one of the books. *"Poisons in Everyday Life."*

"Look up azaleas." Wetzon took a sip of coffee. It was scalding and strong enough to wake the dead.

"What's this about?" Her eyes were bloodshot and the skin around them puffy. Micklynn leafed through the book. "Azaleas?"

"Yes."

"Azaleas are azaleas." She stopped, began to read. Her eyes blinked rapidly. "Jesus!"

"Right."

Micklynn checked out the other book. "I see you have come prepared."

"I haven't had a chance to look at it. What does yours say?"

"It says it's part of the rhododendron family, that all parts of the plant are poisonous. Rhododendrons! Do you believe it? They're so beautiful."

"Go on."

She shook her head in disbelief, her finger searching for the place where she'd paused. "Oh, here. *Grayanotoxin. Andromedotoxin. Glycocide.* Look at this: The whole plant is poisonous. *Honey made from rhododendron flowers is highly toxic. Reaction time after ingestion is six hours. Symptoms are nausea, vomiting, paralysis, slowing pulse, lowering blood pressure, diarrhea, seizure, coma . . . death."*

"This is what killed Sheila."

"No!" Micklynn slammed the poison book shut. "It would have had to be in my batter. That isn't possible."

Wetzon watched her carefully. Had Micklynn poisoned Sheila and hoped to get away with it?

"You're looking at me as if I did it." Micklynn's voice rose and people began glancing their way.

"Why would you do it, Micklynn? I don't see a motive."

"Okay, okay. They can't arrest a person if that person doesn't have a motive. Can they?" The lopsided smile on her face was unsettling.

"They can if they have a witness."

"There was no witness," Micklynn insisted, agitated, swinging her arm for emphasis. Hand touched mug and knocked over her latte.

Wetzon grabbed the poison book, but the plant encyclopedia got doused and became an expense of the investigation. "Easy does it, Micklynn. You're saying no one was with you when you made those muffins?"

"I don't remember," she said, after Wetzon had about given up getting an answer from her. "Just find who did it, Leslie, before it's too late." Micklynn rose like a queen, though a bit unsteady on her feet, and swept down the stairs, a spectacle even for the Upper West Side.

After she wiped the book down with her napkin, Wetzon lingered over her coffee. There was no witness, Micklynn had said. Had she meant that she hadn't done it, therefore there were no witnesses? Or that no one had *seen* her do it? And she'd seemed almost smug about not having a motive to murder Sheila. And if she didn't remember, how could she be so sure?

Death by azaleas. Too horrible. No accident. Premeditated murder. Wait. What had Micklynn said? *Find who did it—before it's too late.* Before it's too late?

Wetzon returned the poison book to the shelf, then went downstairs to pay for the book on plants. A line of ten people had formed in front of the registers. She opened the concise encyclopedia of plants, looked up *azalea* in the index, and found the page. It was a beautiful plant. The flowers were funnel-shaped and somewhat two-lipped, pink.

She'd seen them before. Yes, once in Madge's bag, and once before that . . . in Micklynn's apartment.

c h a p t e r   3 5

J u n e

SoHo at night was honky-tonk, made sleazy by dirty
sidewalks clogged with vendors, tourists, and drifters.
Refuse was strewn in the gutters of its narrow streets.

Hem and Minnie owned the top floor and roof of a
converted, iron-faced warehouse, typical of the district.
Also typical was the ground-floor gallery known for its
avant-garde artists.

Getting out of the cab on Prince Street, Wetzon and
Laura Lee were confronted by an enormous naked foot
sculpture, cut off at mid-calf, in the huge well-lit window
of the gallery. A penis rose from the calf cavity, throb-

bing with translucent light. Inside the gallery several well-dressed people were admiring the piece.

"This must be the place," Laura Lee drawled.

"*Quelle surprise.* How nice of Hem to put his logo right in the front window so no one can miss it."

Although they shared the same address, the loft apartments above the gallery were separated by a small foyer with mailboxes and buzzers. Laura Lee pressed BARRON-WU.

Wetzon said, "Sounds like something from ancient China. Barron Wu, the cunning minister of an evil empire."

"Shshsh," Laura Lee cautioned. "The line is open." She spoke into the speaker, announcing their arrival. A buzzer released the door, and another released the elevator a short way down a hall.

The elevator was ancient, open grillwork and a domed, grilled ceiling; it traveled extra slowly. They rode up to the fifth floor surrounded by music.

"It's live," Laura Lee said. "Hem hired a band and he's got Tony Bennett singing."

"Let me guess. Tony is an old friend and he's doing it as a favor?"

"No, Hem's a corporate raider. He can afford to hire the likes of Tony Bennett. Don't be so nervous."

"I'm not nervous."

"Well, don't be."

"All right, I'm nervous. It's like an assignation. Bill Veeder wants me here, so I'm here. In my Wonderbra too," she added. "The damn thing is so uncomfortable. It itches and pinches and I feel as if I'm strangling, but here I am all pushed up, with cleavage, no less."

Laura Lee laughed. "I dreamed I was investigatin' a murder in my uplift bra."

"Go ahead, laugh, but I'm going to have to take it off. It's driving me nuts. This isn't me. I'm a leotard person, for godsakes." Still, Wetzon thought as she stepped off the elevator behind Laura Lee, it was no pretense that she was looking into the murder of Sheila Gelber.

Two pumped-up security guards stood on either side of the elevator like palace guards.

A sea of humanity made the room seem to undulate. "I hate crowds," Wetzon grumbled, knowing her space was about to be violated.

"Look who's here, Min." Hem could be heard but not seen. A moment later, he came rushing through the maze to bestow a big kiss on Laura Lee's lips. "You girls look absolutely gorgeous. Don't they, Min?" He didn't even wait for an answer, because he was too busy zeroing in on Wetzon.

Wetzon turned away sharply and tucked her hand into the arm of the nearest man, a rotund individual with an ill-fitting toop. "So nice to see you again," she gushed, avoiding the beady eyes of Minnie Wu.

"Wait'll you see who we have as a bartender," Wetzon heard Hem tell Laura Lee. "Bruce Willis' brother. I swear."

"What are you drinking, my dear?" the rotund man said, totally charmed by Wetzon's cleavage.

"Amstel Light." She looked around and didn't see anyone she knew. Smoke floated high up under the lights.

"Oh, I like this girl." The man spoke to a sycophantic buddy, whose claim to fame appeared to be a wax-tipped handlebar mustache. "Get the doll a drink, will you, Hy? I don't want to lose her." He'd imprisoned Wetzon's hand in the crook of his arm and was petting it.

But the doll lost herself as soon as the next surge of guests pushed through. Wetzon saw Hy carrying her Amstel and snatched it from him. "Thanks ever so," she said.

Hy's "Where's Sheldon?" disappeared behind her. She took a swig of beer. Where was the food? Waiters were cruising around with vast trays. She followed one.

Wetzon hated comments on her height: "you're so petite," was her most unfavorite, then "you're a cute little thing," then "little package." And there was the politically correct "vertically challenged." Being short could be a damn nuisance. On Wall Street it meant she got stepped on in elevators. Bob Fosse, the late choreographer, had preferred his dancers tall. Alas.

But short came in handy right now. No one noticed her amid the svelte, pathetically thin women talking to men of varying heights, all taller than Wetzon. She was a high-speed bike among Buicks. She reached a hand up and slipped something off a tray as the waiter went by. Chicken liver, wrapped in bacon. Very good. Another tray held steamed shrimp; another, small slices of pizza with a chewy crust. Could a short person commit a murder in this crowd and get away with it?

"Darling," someone yelled, but not at her. It was like being invisible. Invisible Leslie Wetzon. Now there was something to conjure with.

The music was pop and soft rock. People shifted from foot to foot, spilled drinks on the hardwood floor, oops, dropped an hors d'oeuvre. Well, never mind, grind it into the floor. Moving through the crowd, Wetzon caught sight now and then of A.T. At some point Wetzon knew she'd have to speak to her, but not yet.

She could just catch a glimpse of Micklynn working in the big open kitchen.

No sign of Bill Veeder.

But Mort Hornberg was there, *sans* Poppy, his arm draped intimately over the shoulders of an attractive man-boy with a peach-shaped dancer's derriere. And Smith in something white and beaded had just arrived with Twoey. Oh, goody, more tall people.

A metal staircase led to the roof and the beautiful people were going up and down in a steady stream.

Snatches of conversations surrounded her. "Candy . . . in the green-house . . ."

The greenhouse? She made her way up the stairs.

"You shouldn't have come. If she sees you—" A.T. stood with her back to the staircase talking to Ellen and a grungy young man with crucifix earrings and long, greasy black hair.

They were talking about Minnie.

"She won't see us. She's busy cooking," Ellen said.

Not Minnie, Micklynn.

"Are you going up or down, little girl? And can I do it with you?" The man was sliding his hand up Wetzon's leg. She stepped back and ground her heel into his shoe.

He yelled, "Ow!"

"Oh, excuse me," she said. But she'd lost her anonymity.

"How nice you look, Wetzon," A.T. said. "You know Ellen, don't you? And this is her school friend Todd Cameron."

"Is there really a greenhouse up here?" Wetzon asked, after the obligatory handshakes. Todd shook hands like a limp puppy.

"Yes," A.T. said. "Ellen dear, why don't you show Wetzon around? Ellen works here with Hem's gardener. She loves it, don't you, dear?"

"I love it," Ellen repeated, with a polite smile. "I have a green thumb." She looked bored.

"Just as well," A.T. said cheerfully. "I kill anything I try to grow."

"You don't have to be my guide, Ellen," Wetzon said. "I'll look around myself."

"No, I insist," A.T. said. She telegraphed a meaningful look to Ellen.

The roof, surrounded by a four-foot parapet, was spacious. Finished as a terrace, it had a slate floor and stylish outdoor furniture. All around were the roofs of similar warehouse buildings, about the same height.

Bill Veeder was a no-show.

Four men came out of the greenhouse, their voices boisterous. "It's on the table in the back," one told Wetzon.

"This way," Ellen said. She entered the greenhouse and held the door for Wetzon and Todd, who had as yet not spoken a word. Within the greenhouse the scents were legion—spicy, cloying, musty, earthy.

"I see a lot of herbs," Wetzon said. "Are they for The Groaning Board?"

"No, not these. They're Min's. They're for her Chinese banquets."

Todd had the jiggles and they were getting more pronounced. "Let's get a toot," he said.

Ellen smiled and steered Wetzon over to the roses. "He's just kidding. Is there anything else you'd like to see?"

"I understand you knew Sheila Gelber." Ellen started. "I wanted to ask you about her."

A thud, then a thump interrupted them. It didn't take a genius to see Todd had kicked over a pot of flowering plants.

"Oh, Todd," Ellen said. "You're such a klutz." She picked up a trowel, crouched, and deftly replaced the dislodged plant.

"Sheila Gelber," Wetzon prompted.

"Miss Gelber was a wonderful teacher," Ellen said. "I'm sorry she's dead." She rose and dusted off her hands. "Do you still need me?"

"You know she was poisoned."

"Come on," Todd said, a strain of urgency in his voice.

Ellen stiffened. "No, I didn't know. Who would do such a terrible thing?"

"I thought you might have an idea. Micklynn made the muffins that killed Sheila."

Ellen looked shocked. She took a step backward as if Wetzon had threatened her. "Oh, God, the fight."

"Fight?"

"I shouldn't . . . Micklynn's been good to me. She took me in . . . I . . . uh . . ."

Wetzon waited. She knew the rest would come.

"Miss Gelber and Micklynn were testing recipes for a book they were talking about writing together. It was Miss Gelber's idea and I think Micklynn was going to do it without her."

"I'm outa here." Todd left the greenhouse, practically on the run. Ellen gave a little shrug, a little smile, then followed.

Wetzon watched Ellen and Todd until they disappeared down the stairs. Someone was making a speech, and people were laughing. She walked down an aisle of ferns; overhead were hanging pots, spilling ivy over their sides.

A man and two women sauntered past her and out of the greenhouse. She was alone. A potting table stood at the end of the aisle. She saw clay pots piled one on the other, more herbs in small plastic pots on trays, and a plastic bag of coke, a box of gold-colored straws, a large mirror lying flat, and a razor.

No one else had entered the greenhouse. Downstairs, Tony Bennett was finally singing . . . "I left my . . ." She picked up the bag of coke. Put it down. Picked it up again.

Shelves jutted out like stadium steps, flowering plants in pots everywhere. Her eye roved over them. She had no idea what they were. Plants had never been her thing.

The subtle fragrance registered before she saw them. And there they were: azaleas in pots, dozens of them, in pinks, in whites. Dozens of them. She was tired. Bill Veeder hadn't shown. Well, okay.

Where had she put her can of beer?

She left the greenhouse and walked over to the parapet. The sky was a poor player compared with all the lights of lower Manhattan. She leaned over the parapet, turned the bag over, and emptied it into the night air. It snowed coke on Prince Street. She let the bag float away.

All the lights went out on the roof just as she finished emptying the bag. The shove caught her by surprise. She twisted away, fell on her knees, then began swinging. No one was going to throw her off a roof.

She screamed, smacked, and clawed, making contact with bone and soft flesh. Heard "Cunt!"

"Hey," someone yelled. "What happened to the lights?"

"Leslie, wait a minute. Hold on. Did he hurt you?"

"No, no!" She was still punching.

"Which way did he go?" Another voice.

"Over the roof. Leslie, I'm here."

She stopped struggling. The lights came on, and Bill Veeder was holding her and people were coming from everywhere, up the stairs, the greenhouse.

"Don't worry," Hem said. "Bruce Willis' brother went after him. He took off over the roof."

"Damn, tore my hose," Wetzon mumbled. Her knees looked raw through broken threads, stung.

"Oh, shit!" Hem came out of his greenhouse. "The candy's gone. He stole the coke."

"I'm sorry I was so late," Bill Veeder said. "This would never have happened— Jesus, there's blood in your hair." He looked at her closely. "I don't see any wound; it's just on the surface."

"Can we get out of here?" Wetzon said. She was feeling uncool, as if she were breaking apart.

They were on the stairs. She saw Laura Lee and Smith and everybody looking up at her.

Tony Bennett announced he was dedicating a song to the little lady on the roof and began singing.

The thump of feet hitting the roof came from behind them. Bill stopped on the stairs and turned. "Any luck?"

"No, he got away."

The voice . . . Wetzon looked up, over Bill's shoulder. A Bruce Willis look-alike stood at the top of the stairs. His eyes bore down at her through his small round dark glasses. He had a porkpie hat on top of his head. The day's growth of beard didn't cover the cleft in his chin.

She'd recognize him in any disguise.

It was Silvestri.

chapter 36

"About the coke," Wetzon said. "Ouch." She had her skirt hiked up and was cutting off her panty hose at mid-thigh.

"I'd be happy to do that for you." Bill sat next to her on his sofa holding a first-aid kit at the ready, watching her progress. Or maybe it was her legs that interested him.

"I'll bet you would." She finished cutting the hose into bicycle shorts and handed him back his scissors. "Now comes the hard part." She began to roll the hose down. "Ouch." Threads of torn nylon were caught in the red scrapes that marked both knees, stubbornly clinging to her flesh. "Damn."

"Let me do that," he said. He pointed to his lap. "Put 'em here, pal."

Wetzon swung her legs up and settled her back against the arm of the sofa. She watched him pick out the threads with a tweezer from the first-aid kit. Then he peeled off her hose. "Done this often, I take it?" she said.

"I'm not a bit sorry this is going to hurt," he said, dousing a cotton square with peroxide.

"Ow!" The burning brought tears. "I hate you," she said, trying to jerk her legs away, failing.

"No, you don't." He patted her knees dry with another square, following up with bacitracin, then gauze and adhesive.

She sighed and reached for the single-malt he'd poured and she'd diminished by half when they first arrived. "Where are we?" He'd brought her to an apartment in the tower over the Museum of Modern Art.

It had been "Good evening, Mr. Veeder," just like on Park Avenue.

Closing the first-aid kit and setting it aside, Veeder said, "This is my apartment."

"The other one . . . ?"

"That's Evelyn's." He was massaging her feet and she didn't want him to stop. Dancer's feet, bunions, and crooked toes. Good thing she'd had a pedicure the day before.

She leaned her cheek on the back of the sofa. "I thought you weren't coming."

"I almost didn't." He looked tired suddenly. "Evelyn had a seizure."

"Oh, God, I'm so sorry." She tried to pull her feet away. Why am I here, she thought.

"She was sleeping peacefully when I left, Leslie. That's how it is."

"Bill, I don't think . . ." His hands on her feet were making her inarticulate.

"Don't think, Leslie. Let whatever happens happen."

"God," she breathed.

"What did you start to say about the coke?"

"I took it."

He gave her a sharp look as if she'd done something totally out of character, out of the character he'd assumed she was. "Where is it?"

"I poured it out over Prince Street."

Veeder began to laugh. "You are a funny lady, Leslie Wetzon."

"Doesn't it strike you as odd that we're sitting here talking as if we've known each other for years?"

"No. Sometimes people connect immediately. It's the chemistry."

"I know all about chemistry." She singsonged, "The chemistry has to be right between you and the manager, blah, blah, blah . . ." Keeping it light wasn't going to work.

"I wanted you from the first time we met, when Xenia brought you to my office to watch the Christmas tree lighting."

"In the biblical sense, of course."

"That goes without saying. After I saw you dance—"

"You saw me dance?"

"Twice, actually. I saw you in *Combinations* when it first opened."

"You did? What did you think?" She was fishing and she couldn't help it.

He had such nice even teeth. He knew what she was doing. "You were having fun and everyone was having fun with you. You were a vivacious little package."

She rolled her eyes at *little package.* "I was very young."

"We all were."

"Nineteen years later and look what happened to the vivacious little package."

"You are so right." He was laughing. "The benefit was different. Xenia knew how I felt about you and arranged for the tickets. Now it was more than fun. Maturity brought a depth, a sensuousness . . . I wanted you in my life."

This time when she pulled her feet away, he let her. She felt overheated. The air conditioning made her shiver. Or maybe it wasn't the air conditioning. "I'm cold," she said, trying to curl her feet under her. Her knees protested. She put her feet on the floor.

Veeder got up and left the room. What the hell am I doing here, she thought again. But she didn't move.

He returned a few minutes later with a pair of white athletic socks. He'd removed his jacket, and his gun. She could see the creases in his white shirt where his shoulder holster had been.

"Figured it was safe to put away your weapon, huh?"

Veeder crouched and was slipping his socks on her feet. His hair was white, cut like a marine's. He looked up at her and grinned. Her hands began to move of their own accord, it seemed, for they smoothed his high cheekbones, ran their fingers over his thin lips, the soft bristle of his hair. An inferno burned under her skin. The hands finally got the signal from her brain and froze. She pulled them back and, moving quickly, stood. The socks bagged around her ankles.

He went back to his place on the sofa as if nothing had happened, took off his shoes, and put his feet up on the coffee table. "You knew I used to be a cop?"

"I knew you carried—"

"You know cops?"

"A few. I knew one well."

"Silvestri."

"Yes. He was there tonight. Did you know? In disguise."

"Out of the bag? What did he look like?"

"You saw him. He's the one Hem kept calling Bruce Willis' brother." She stretched one leg against the other, wincing as she bent her knee. "Not undercover, though. I heard he took a leave of absence."

"Now that's interesting. Did you know he was going to be there?"

"No. I told you we split up. I haven't seen or spoken to him in over a month."

He held his hand out to her and pulled her gently down beside him. "That's better. Hate craning my neck." He put his arm around her, his hand settled on her waist. "Tell me about the party. Start with when you got there."

Her head lowered itself to his shoulder. "Is this a deposition?"

"No, I'm curious."

"Okay. Came with Laura Lee. Do you know her?"

"Yes."

"Wait." She pulled herself upright. "I'm thinking I shouldn't have told you Silvestri was there. If he was in disguise, maybe he is undercover. I don't want him to get hurt, Bill. Bill?"

"Sounds as if you still care."

"Of course I care. I'll always care. He and I may not be together, but he's a good guy. I want you to promise me . . . Bill, please."

It was as if he was weighing and measuring, studying her minutely. He said, "I still have friends downtown. I won't get in his way. Okay?"

"Okay." He hadn't said, "Trust me." That was a plus.

"Go on with your story."

"Hem attacked us when we got off the elevator."

"Attacked?"

"You know, touchy-kissy-feely. He got Laura Lee on the mouth, but I ducked him. Minnie looked ready to kill and I'd already had one run-in with her. I don't need another."

"What kind of run-in?"

She sat up, slipped her jacket off her shoulders. Her dress was a sleeveless square-necked jumper. The bruise was now a dull purple with yellowing edges.

He ran his hand gently along the bruise. "Min's a loose cannon. I'm afraid I'm going to have to defend her in court one day." He set the jacket back over her shoulders. "Go on."

"I cozied up to a smarmy fireplug in a bad toop by the name of Sheldon. I dumped him as soon as I could—"

Veeder hugged her to him, laughing. "That could only be Sheldon Marshack. He's a media mogul, owns a slew of cable companies from here to Hawaii. He's one of the most powerful men in the country. And one of the richest."

"Pooh. That just makes him a rich and powerful fireplug with a bad toop." A yawn took over. "Don't you think you should take me home?"

"Finish the story and we'll talk about it."

Her feet were on the coffee table next to his, thigh against thigh. She rested her head on his shoulder; his shirt, a starchy essence, was crisp against her cheek.

"Overheard A.T. talking to Ellen and her grungy friend Todd something or other."

"Todd Cameron. His father's a surrogate court judge. He's a piece of work. Son, not father."

"Ellen showed me around the greenhouse. Do you know Minnie does exotic cooking?"

"Min is the worst cook in the world. She makes elaborate Chinese banquets and the food is inedible."

"But everyone comes and makes mushy on the plate because of Hem."

"Right."

"Did you ever see *All About Eve?*"

"Yes."

"Ellen is Eve Harrington, I think. She let me know that Micklynn had some problem with Sheila Gelber."

His hand roamed her waist, his lips were in her hair. "Sheila Gelber. I know that name."

She was having trouble concentrating again. "Micklynn . . . Jesus,

Bill . . ." She held his hand still for a moment. "Micklynn has a condition called celiac disease. An allergy to gluten. Sheila did also. Sheila was murdered, poisoned by corn muffins that Micklynn made. Sheila and Silvestri were lovers before I knew him."

"Silvestri again?"

"Ellen said Sheila and Micklynn were doing a book together and something went wrong."

"Ah, now I know. It was a business. Micklynn talked to me about putting together a business, mail order for specific diets. I told her she couldn't do it with this Sheila Gelber."

"Why not?"

"Because her partnership agreement with A. T. Barron precludes any other business related to food. It's ironclad. A.T. would have had to get half interest."

"Even though it wasn't her idea and she didn't work on it? That's not right, Bill."

"That's the agreement."

"Isn't there any way a contract like that can be broken?"

"Only one, Leslie. One of the partners would have to die."

chapter 37

"I'll let your doorman put me in a cab." She bent over, groping for her shoes; the socks lay on the floor. "Thanks for the socks."

"Nice."

What was he talking about? She looked up at him. He was looking at her cleavage. She straightened, stuck her feet into her shoes. "No, not nice. Not me. Wonderbra. I kept meaning to take it off."

"I could help you." He was just sitting there on the sofa with his feet on the coffee table, having her amuse him.

Pas de basque.

She recognized it as a mating dance. She wanted to say, *I want you to help me. I want you as much as you want me.* She couldn't. She said, "Oh, sure. Now you're going to join the crowd and tell me what a great lover you are."

A delicate flush tinted his cheeks. "Tell you? I wouldn't dream of it, Leslie."

He was just sitting there, not moving, watching her. She wanted to feel his hand on her waist again, his thigh tight against hers. It was a dull ache like a hunger. "Bill . . ." Her voice came out in a croak. She tried again. "Bill, I've been with only two men in the last seven years. How many women have you been with?"

"I have condoms."

"Condoms are for one-night stands."

"You want me to take a blood test." He was very solemn. She'd offended him.

"I will too."

Battement tendu.

He got up. "Don't go away." He left the room.

Leave now, she told herself. There's still time. But he was back, taking a folded piece of paper from his billfold. He handed it to her. Dropping her eyes to read it, she saw with horror, her pushed-up bosom trembling. "You're very sure of yourself, Bill Veeder." She returned the paper to him. "You did this two weeks ago? Do you think you know me? Everyone else I know does."

"Leslie, I don't think I know you at all." She stood very still as he removed her jacket, dropped it on the sofa. He took her face in his hands and kissed her forehead, her eyelids, the sides of her mouth, her throat. Soft, gentle lips for such a tough person. Someone moaned. She wrapped her arms around him, hooking her thumbs in his belt. When his lips found her mouth, she was clinging to him.

Arabesque.

He stopped and held her away from him, dislodging her thumbs, a look of astonishment on his face. "I love you, Leslie Wetzon," he said. He knew just where to find the catch on the Wonderbra.

"Oh, God," she said, reaching for him. She wanted to feel the skin beneath his shirt. It was torture not to touch.

He was smiling at her, keeping her at a distance. "Leslie, I don't want a passive partner. Are we together here? Say it."

"Yes. Yes."

Pas de bourrée.

"I've wanted to do this since the first time I met you." He turned her around and pulled her to him, kissed the nape of her neck, behind her ears. His fingers touched her topknot. He began taking the hairpins out one at a time.

Her topknot paused for a brief pristine moment, stirred, then coursed down to meet him.

Grand jeté.

Sunlight woke her, slats making stripes across the bedding, across her arms and shoulders. Sunlight and the sound of voices. One voice. The radio? She stretched and rolled over; her body felt rich, as if she'd danced all night, hair loosened, wild in her face. The sheets were silky on her bare skin. Izz? She patted the bed.

Holy shit! Her eyes flew open. Where was she? The bruised patches on her knees twinged. She snapped up like a rubber band released. My God, she'd slept with Bill Veeder. And . . .

He was talking on the phone. She eased out of bed and listened at the door. He said, "Yeah, Silvestri . . ." Then: "Thought so . . ." Was Bill going back on his promise? She had to believe he wouldn't—

She flew back to bed and pulled the sheet over her head. The door opened, but his footsteps were muffled by the carpet. The side of the bed dipped under his weight.

"I know you're awake," he said. "Let's have a look at you the morning after."

She rolled back the sheet so that just her eyes and nose appeared. He wore running shorts and a tee shirt. Lean body. Strong arms. She knew all that. Runner's legs, scant of hair. Her arm moved out from under the sheet. She ran her hand down his thigh. "Encore," she said.

The shower had a massaging head. It was just what she needed. She could smell the sex all over her . . . like a musk. She washed her hair. He'd have a hair dryer, but she had very little makeup with her. Some eye shadow, powder, and mascara. No foundation. No moisturizer. Well, then, she thought, warts and all. Warts and all. Smelling musky.

And no clean underwear.

After he left for his run in the park, she'd called her super and asked if his son could feed and walk Izz. No problem. Poor Izz. No Wetzon. No Silvestri.

The bathroom was elegant, Hollywood quality, this side of flashy. Marble floors and washstand. A Jacuzzi. A bidet. Well, of course. She opened the medicine cabinet. Well stocked. Opened a closet. Well, well, well. Moisturizers and everything one would need for body and face, oils and scented soaps. Plush towels. A hedonist's closet.

She wrapped herself in one of the plush towels and dried her hair. What had he done with her hairpins? Then again, why bother putting it up? She wandered around the apartment. It was done in browns and beiges and very spare. Like Bill Veeder. Except for the piano. A baby grand. Who played?

She felt sluggish.

No wonder. No coffee. How could she start her morning without it? The coffeepot on the counter looked as if it had never been used. She found Oren's coffee beans in the otherwise empty freezer of his fridge, a coffee grinder on a shelf along with paper filters. Coffee was soon dripping into the carafe. He'd said he'd bring back breakfast and the *Times*.

There was no food in the apartment. Maybe he didn't like to eat. That would be enough to abort the relationship. For a relationship it was, unless she had misjudged everything.

Misjudged. Micklynn. She looked up the number and dialed her. The phone rang a long time before someone picked up.

"Hello? Micklynn?"

Mumbling, but no answer.

"Micklynn?"

"Who is this? What time is it?"

"It's after ten, Micklynn. This is Leslie. Are you awake?"

"Barely."

"Why didn't you tell me that you planned to go into business with Sheila?"

"It didn't have anything to do with her murder."

"But she was shut out because of your agreement with A.T. Why didn't you tell me *that*?"

"Leslie, you seem to have it in your head that I might have poisoned Sheila. I would have more of a motive to kill A.T., not Sheila. Think about it."

Micklynn was angry and she was right. "I agree," Wetzon said, "but you've got to tell me everything; otherwise, I'm doing this blind and I might as well give you your money back."

"No, please, stay with it. Now you know everything. Leslie . . . something really odd happened last night."

"At Hem's party?"

"Yeah, some guy came on to me while I was cooking. . . . I can't tell you when the last time that happened. I'm not exactly a sexual object these days. I don't know . . . it was really strange."

"Who was he?"

"I don't know, but he was hanging around asking a lot of questions."

"Didn't you ask what he was doing there?"

"Oh, I knew what he was doing there. He was the bartender."

c h a p t e r   3 8

The Colton School made its home in three intercon-
nected town houses on Ninety-second Street. It was a
four-year private high school favored and generously en-
dowed for their progeny by performers and others in the
arts. It offered a diverse program in music, art, and com-
munications. A diploma from Colton's practically guar-
anteed acceptance in top colleges and universities, particularly the Ivy League.

It was here that Sheila Gelber had taught English for
fifteen years.

Wetzon had made an appointment to see Colton's
headmaster, Dr. Orson R. Furgason, and was even
now being delivered to his office by a slender girl in

jeans and a Princeton tee shirt, who had introduced herself as Stacy Morgenstern.

"I thought the academic year was finished," Wetzon said.

"It is. I'm just helping out till the end of the month." Stacy had tiny gold studs in each of four piercings up the side of one ear and one streaming dangle in the other. For the moment there was no jewel or hoop in her nose.

"Then camp?" The place was spotless—gleaming floors, highly polished woodwork—yet it had that indefinable, rather unpleasant smell that all schools seemed to possess.

"No. Then I'm going to Johns Hopkins. They have a summer program for high school students that starts in July."

Stacy led Wetzon through the empty hallways; they passed vacant classrooms, and others with teachers in casual clothing working at their desks.

"Johns Hopkins. That sounds wonderful. You chose to go to summer school?"

"They chose me," Stacy said with some pride.

"Very nice."

"Well, it was between me and another girl."

"And you won."

Stacy nodded.

"That's great, Stacy."

"Are you a teacher, Miss Wetzon?"

"No. I'm here," Wetzon said, "to talk to Dr. Furgason about Miss Gelber."

"Oh." The breathy response from Stacy carried with it a wisp of sorrow. Her eyes filled with tears. "Miss Gelber was the one who recommended me for Johns Hopkins." They climbed a flight of stairs.

"She was your English teacher?"

"Yes. She was wonderful."

"So I hear."

"She was very popular. Everyone wanted her for junior English. I can't believe she's dead. It's down here at the end of the hall. Dr. Furgason's office, I mean."

Wetzon hesitated. A detective would just say it to see what reaction it got. So she said, "Someone murdered Sheila Gelber."

The reaction she got was one she hadn't bargained for. Stacy stopped, then looked furtively around the empty halls. "I know," she said. "It really scares me."

"Scares you? What does Miss Gelber's murder have to do with you?"

Stacy lowered her voice to a whisper. "Please don't tell anyone. I'd die if anyone . . . I mean . . . I don't want anyone . . ."

Wetzon took the girl's hand. It was ice cold, and it wasn't from the air conditioning. "Stacy, if you know something about Miss Gelber's murder, you must tell the police."

"Are you from the police?"

"No. I'm looking into Miss Gelber's death for a client."

The girl gnawed her lip, then blurted, "It was like that thing that happened in Texas. You know, when the mother hired someone to kill her daughter's competition. The—"

"Stacy? What are you doing down there? Where's Ms. Wetzon?"

Stacy and Wetzon moved apart quickly. A horsey-faced woman in a lemon linen suit and a ponytail of streaked hair stood braced like a guard dog in the doorway at the end of the hall.

"I—" Stacy looked as if she'd gotten caught raiding the cookie jar.

"She was showing me around," Wetzon called.

"Dr. Furgason is waiting to see you, Ms. Wetzon," the guard dog reproved.

Wetzon slipped Stacy her card. "What's your phone number?"

"We're in the book. My father's name is Stuart."

"Thank you for the mini tour, Stacy," Wetzon said, raising her voice. "And good luck at Johns Hopkins."

Dr. Orson R. Furgason's hair was long on one side, parted behind one ear, and combed over the top of his head to cover his baldness. The face beneath was jowly and self-righteous, the chin weak. His suit was a well-cut summer-weight wool in a faint herringbone pattern. He couldn't have been much older than Wetzon, but he maintained an aura of ponderous academic gravity just short of pomposity. However, he rose when she was shown into his office, offered her a dry, firm handshake, and waited until she was seated before he sat. His nails were manicured.

A window air conditioner of not recent vintage maintained a persistent groan. Wetzon handed him her card. "We're looking into the death of Sheila Gelber," she told him, deciding to get straight to the point.

"I told the police everything I know," the headmaster said, a trifle too quickly. "A tragic event. Particularly so for our faculty and students. She was a very pleasant woman and an excellent teacher. What is your interest, Ms. Wetzon?"

"I'm a management consultant. My firm looks into potentially damaging situations for our clients."

"Your clients?" Furgason picked up a medallion of some sort and shifted it from one hand to the other, again and again.

"Financial institutions, insurance . . . with generous funds for donation . . ."

"Well, of course, we want to cooperate." Little beads of sweat appeared on his upper lip.

"Was there perhaps a potentially embarrassing incident or event involving Sheila Gelber at Colton before her death?" She was on to something: Furgason's eyes had shifted away from her.

"Oh," he said. "Really . . . it was nothing. Nothing at all. A misunderstanding, is all."

"I think you'd better explain, Dr. Furgason. After all, we want to be prepared in case of a lawsuit . . . the family . . ."

The headmaster blanched and jumped up, drew the blinds of his windows as if he was afraid someone would read their lips. "A lawsuit? We can't have that. No, it wasn't anything, really."

"Why not tell me what happened and let us decide?"

He sighed, sat down heavily. With the medallion in his hands again, he said, "The Johns Hopkins summer fellowship. It goes to the third-year student with the most outstanding record in English. This year we had two girls who qualified. It was up to Ms. Gelber to make the final decision. She chose Stacy Morgenstern. The other girl was extremely upset."

"That's understandable. What was the unpleasant incident?"

"Anti-Semitic accusations were made that had no validity, and there was an ugly scene. And the instigator wasn't even the other girl's mother. You see, Stacy Morgenstern and Sheila Gelber are both Jewish." He put down the medallion and removed a white linen handkerchief—tiny initials ORF embroidered in gray—from his breast pocket and blotted the perspiration from his upper lip.

"Dr. Furgason, who was the other girl?"

"I am very concerned about confidentiality, Ms. Wetzon."

"My business is based on confidentiality, Dr. Furgason. However, everything must be carefully scrutinized, as I am sure you understand. Sheila Gelber was murdered. Anything kept hidden, then later discovered, will be blown out of proportion and the school will suffer."

"But this had nothing to do with Ms. Gelber's death."

"How do you know that for certain?"

"It is inconceivable."

"What was the name of the other girl?"

With a great sigh, Furgason picked up the medallion again and stared at it, then at Wetzon. "Ellen Moore," he said.

chapter 39

Wetzon leafed through the latest issue of *Business Week,* one of several magazines on the coffee table at Veeder and Kalin, PC.

The receptionist, an attractive fiftyish woman in a formal shirtwaist dress that was unsuccessful in suppressing her full bosom, was transferring Rolodex card information to a computer. A small nameplate on the desk said: MRS. COPELAND. She looked up, catching Wetzon's eye, and assuming perhaps that Wetzon was becoming impatient, murmured, "I'm sure he won't be too long now." Her vocal tone and attitude were so neutral, Wetzon couldn't help wondering how many of Bill Veeder's women had sat where Wetzon now did.

When the phone rang, Mrs. Copeland answered,

"Law offices." Then: "Mr. Veeder is in conference. No, Mr. Kalin is out of town. Mr. Josephson is here. I'll connect you."

Actually, although it was after six, Wetzon wasn't at all impatient. They hadn't intended to eat before the ballet. The ballet. Bill Veeder wasn't letting her keep the different areas of her life in separate little compartments. Unlike Silvestri, who'd shown only a casual interest in either of her lives, Wall Street or Broadway.

In a way Bill's determination was flattering, but it made demands, flicked at her veil of passivity, drove her out in the open. Made her a target.

When they didn't see each other, he called her late in the evening, sometimes early in the morning. He wanted to know what she was thinking, what she had read, what she had done that day. She told him broker stories, made him laugh. He shared his day with her, asked for her opinions, and took what she said seriously. His telephone voice had a husky intimacy that was like a loving embrace.

A soft buzzer sounded and Mrs. Copeland picked up her phone. "Yes, sir." She cradled the phone and smiled her neutrality at Wetzon. "Mr. Veeder would like you to wait in his office. Through that door, turn right, end of the hall. Shall I show you?"

"No, thank you. I remember where it is." Wetzon remembered it well. Taupe and brown. Lots of wood and brown leather. Stickley desk. They had that in common.

On her way she passed a young Hispanic man carrying a tray of soft drinks and bottled water. He knocked on a door, then opened it. Inside, an argument was in progress and it didn't cease with the open door. Wetzon caught a glimpse of the conference room. Laura Lee was there. And Hem and A.T. She couldn't see Bill, or Micklynn, for that matter, but she heard all of them.

As the young man came out of the room with the empty tray, Wetzon walked swiftly toward Veeder's office, opened the door, and went in. She counted to twenty, then peeked out. The hallway was empty. She retraced her steps and stopped outside the door to the conference room in time to hear Micklynn's sharp, "Never!"

"You're not competent to make that decision." A.T.'s voice was cold steel. "You're drunk. It's *my* business too, don't forget."

Micklynn gave a vulgar laugh. "How could I? You're always reminding me."

Bill's voice, firm tones: "Micklynn, A.T., let's stop this infighting. May

I remind you both you're paying me $450 an hour and Jonathon $200? You're obviously not ready to commit at this time. Hem, get back to me when you're serious."

When Big Daddy speaks, Wetzon thought, the whole world listens.

"We will *not* go forward with this, and that's *final!*" Micklynn matched each word with a bang on the table.

"Thanks, Bill," Laura Lee said, opening the door. She stepped out, catching a glimpse of Wetzon, her finger to her lips. She closed the door. "Good God, darlin', you almost scared the pants off me. What are you doin' here?"

"Bill and I have tickets for the ballet. What's going on in there? And who's Jonathon?"

"Micklynn's dug her Birkenstocks in. She won't go along with the IPO. Jonathon is Bill's associate. Just out of Harvard and is he ever cute."

"What will A.T. and Hem do?" Wetzon took Laura Lee's arm and they moved down the hallway together. "And you, dirty old lady, ought to be ashamed."

"I'll have you know, Wetzon, I'm forty years old and in my prime. As for Micklynn, they'll work her over, I guess. The TV show begins airin' this fall. That might give her the push."

"And if you were predicting the future of the partnership itself?"

"Darlin', I've lived through Beatrice, Apple, RJR Nabisco, and Time Warner, among a host of other similar situations."

"And?"

"Some come to terms with each other for the sake of the business. Or one faction buys the other out. Or one finds a way to give the other a quick shove. Look what happened to Apple and Steve Jobs, and didn't he show them? Or some just dissolve the business."

"And The Groaning Board partnership? What's your sense of it?"

Laura Lee narrowed her eyes for a moment before she said, "Dead in the water, darlin'."

c h a p t e r   4 0

J u l y

"Damnation, Smith, look at that!" Wetzon said as a bouquet of chrysanthemums exploded and streaked across the sky. "We're missing the fireworks."

"I don't know why you're always in such a rush." Smith shifted down and pulled the Jaguar into a parking place on Liberty Street. She was in her most maddening mode: running on her own personal timetable. Then she smiled brilliantly at Wetzon. "Oh, my, I think it just might be you're anxious to see your lover. And to think you fought me on this as if I didn't have your best interests at heart."

Whistle, pop, pop, pop, whistle. Red, white, and blue

colors burst, forming a huge American flag. Held a moment, then melted into a brilliant arc.

Wetzon chose not to respond. She hated to admit Smith had been right. Still, it was the timing. If Silvestri hadn't . . . Oh, forget Silvestri, please, she told herself. She got out of the car and waited for Smith to lock up. Since it was a holiday, there wasn't the thick pedestrian rush of traffic in the area. All the tourists would be down around South Ferry at the tip of Manhattan watching the fireworks firsthand.

Coming toward them, however, was a solitary woman, tall, very thin, in black jeans and a vest, her hair streaming from under a peaked cap. She seemed very out of place, somehow, and as if she realized that, she suddenly veered away in another direction.

Smith dropped her keys into her minuscule bag. "So, sweetie pie, anything new on our management consulting assignment for Micklynn?"

"Not much. I went to see the headmaster at the Colton School, where Sheila Gelber taught. You know Ellen goes to Colton?"

"Yes. I hope this isn't going to be one of your long stories."

"Do you want to hear it or not?" Wetzon didn't add "bitch," although she thought it.

"Oh, for pity sakes, go on."

"Well, Micklynn made a terrible scene when Ellen was not chosen for a summer program at Johns Hopkins for outstanding students. Sheila Gelber made the choice."

"See, I told you Micklynn's the one who did it. She's nothing but a crazy drunk."

"Yes, she's a drunk, but . . . I don't know. Why would she hire me to find out who did it?"

"Camoufuge and subterflage."

"I suppose . . . But isn't it odd that she would make a scene like that when she and Ellen were not getting along? Micklynn threw Ellen out. We saw it."

"She's back now."

"What do you mean? Who's back?"

"Ellen and Micklynn. They've kissed and made up. Or something like that."

"Now I'm really confused."

The boat basin, with its variety of crafts, could have been a painted set, except that tonight almost every boat was a party. Glasses clinked, voices, mellow with wine and summer and holiday, rose and fell. Streamers fluttered halfheartedly in a breeze that was like hot breath.

"Which one is it?" Smith demanded.

"Let's see, Laura Lee said the boat sleeps six and is called *Bread Pudding*. Straight down, first right, boat's on the left." Wetzon, following the directions, called, "Down here, Smith."

"Hi, there," someone cried as another and another arrangement lit up the sky. Baby's breath, on fire.

"Hi, yourself," Wetzon responded, then looked back for her lagging partner, who, as usual, had insisted on wearing high heels. As if she needed the height. And those heels would certainly destroy a deck, so who would let her on board?

"Here we are, Smith." The *Bread Pudding* was like the other boats, full of people on deck, conversation flowing like the rippling water in New York Bay.

"Well, really," Smith said suddenly, outraged. She'd come up behind Wetzon, arms akimbo.

"Now what?"

"Would *you* take a swim in the Hudson?"

"What are you talking about? I'm not interested in swimming. Let's go." Wetzon raised her voice. "Hello, *Bread Pudding!*"

"*Bread Pudding!*" A woman's voice. "Do you believe it? Why not *Crème Brûlée?*" The boats rocked gently against their moorings and the dock, with soft, sweet *chungs*.

Why indeed not, Wetzon thought, much preferring the latter to the former.

"Look at her if you don't believe me," Smith was insisting. "Get out of there! You'll get all kinds of diseases." Smith leaned over, yelling down at the water.

She's taken leave of her senses at long last, Wetzon was certain, as she peered over Smith's shoulder. What she saw made her jerk back, almost losing her balance. Good God, there really was someone in the water—a woman, in fact. She wore a long white dress and wrapped in garlands of flowers.

"Oh, poor Ophelia," Wetzon murmured.

And then the entire sky erupted, showering multicolored stars down on them.

The woman in the water wasn't swimming. She was floating. Face down.

chapter 41

"Ohmygod, ohmygod, ohmygod!" Smith's howl rose into the night and was swallowed whole by the shriek and whistle of fireworks.

Holding tight to each other, they were like some totem of grief, shock, horror, one atop the other. Wetzon wanted to scream, *Help! Call 911,* but nothing whatever came out of her mouth.

An immense magenta poinsettia exploded in the sky. When the spray died, only the laughter and the clink of glasses could be heard. Their eyes drawn to the water below, Smith and Wetzon saw that what they'd hoped they'd imagined was real: the body spread like a float, butting and butting gently against the pilings.

And nearby the *Bread Pudding* rocked at its mooring, making hazy the silhouettes of the people on her deck.

"Leslie?" A silhouette digitized. Bill Veeder stood on the bow, or whatever it was called. Someone came up behind him.

"Bill," Wetzon croaked, arms waving. "Bill, quick, in the water. Call 911. In the water. Please. Someone's floating in the water. Down there." She knew she wasn't making any sense.

"She's drowned herself," Smith shrieked. "Do something."

Obviously puzzled, Veeder bounded to the dock, peered down into the black water. He snapped back, dropped his jacket, kicked off his Dock-Siders. His shoulder holster with gun somehow found its way into Wetzon's hand.

He was in midair when the person behind him thrust his gun and harness at Wetzon too and followed Veeder into the Bay, porkpie hat flying. "Call 911, Les."

"Help! Somebody call 911," Smith screamed. "We're drowning!"

What happened next would surely have been fodder for farces, were it not for the sodden body that Silvestri and Bill Veeder hauled up on the pier. Micklynn, a water goddess, lay huge and regal entwined in a water-soaked flowered shawl which Wetzon had mistaken for vines. And all the while a glorious, vibrant accompaniment of blossoms and diadems bloomed and collapsed overhead. Hummers spun and screamed in the sky. Mourning Micklynn.

Soon enough came the wailing of sirens. Wetzon in her Laura Ashley sundress dropped a gun into each of the deep patch pockets, more fodder for farces.

She picked up Bill's jacket and shoes and eased her way around the rubberneckers spilling out of surrounding boats and crowding onto the dock.

She knelt near the water goddess. Micklynn's hand was cold and lifeless. Blue. Wetzon floated above herself, out of body. It was the shock, definitely the shock. She heard herself plead, "Don't die, Micklynn. Please don't die."

"Stand back, people, give her some air." Bill Veeder took charge of crowd control while Silvestri began artificial respiration. Some water dribbled from Micklynn's blue lips.

"Get outa here, Les," Silvestri growled, between pushes.

"Anything?" Veeder asked him.

"Nothing. She's gone." Still, Silvestri rolled Micklynn over and began the kiss of life, just as the two EMS people came running, pounding on the dock so hard she could feel the vibrations in the soles of her feet. Wetzon clasped Micklynn's icy hand.

"We'll take it from here," one EMS worker said.

"She's gone," Bill said. He lifted Wetzon to her feet. "She's gone," he said again, this time to Wetzon.

Behind them A.T. let out a horrific groan. "Why?" she cried. "We could have worked it out."

"No!" Ellen pushed through the crowd and tried to kneel beside Micklynn, but Hem pulled her away, murmuring into her hair. "You can't," the girl cried. "Not yet." She looked up with limpid eyes. "Please."

Only Minnie Wu was missing, but not for long. Standing in the boat, she took one look at Hem and Ellen and began gathering steam. Screaming, "Bitch!" she jumped to the dock, then without warning she was flying right off the dock into the Bay as the fireworks in the sky formed themselves into a sparkling, red, white, and blue American flag.

While Minnie Wu thrashed around in the murky water, Smith stood wide-eyed on the pier, her hand rubbing her elegant ankle. Someone threw Minnie a life preserver tied to a pole and pulled her onto the dock.

"That was naughty," Wetzon said, drifting back to her partner.

"Someone had to do it."

Silvestri came toward them, a towel around his neck, fine wisps of dark hair across his brow.

"Micklynn?" Wetzon asked. She couldn't remember whose gun was in which pocket. She fished one out.

"Dead. It's the other one." He pulled on his sneakers, leaving them untied, then took his weapon.

"I don't understand how it could have happened with everybody, including you, on the boat," Wetzon said.

He ignored her, moving back toward the entrance to the pier, where Micklynn lay surrounded by cops and medical personnel. Crime Scene Unit at work. Wetzon followed him slowly, paying no attention to the people standing on the other boats, staring, shouting questions. She still had Bill's gun in her pocket.

An ambulance now stood where the EMS wagon had been. A couple of uniforms had come onstage. She saw Bill Veeder shaking hands with a gray-haired man in a rumpled suit.

When she got to Veeder, he and Silvestri were in the handshaking process. They both turned and looked at her. "I'm sorry," she said, not knowing what she was sorry for or about. *I'm sorry Micklynn's dead. I'm sorry about us, Silvestri. I'm sorry you're together.* She gave Veeder his gun. His shirt clung to his pecs; his khakis were soaked.

"I've got a change in my car," he said to Silvestri. "I'll be right back." He offered Wetzon his hand and Silvestri stepped between them.

"She's not going with you," he said. "Get back on the boat, Les."

"Don't tell me what to do, Silvestri."

"Do as he says, Leslie," Veeder said. "It's his case. I'll be right back."

"Silvestri," the rumpled suit said, beckoning. "A minute, if you please—"

"But I wasn't even here when it happened," Wetzon protested. "He knows that. He's just—"

Bill gave the back of her neck a brief caress. "It's okay. Let him do his thing. Go on back to the boat."

But she was curious, so she took her time. In fact, she bent to tie the lace of her white sneaker, which was already tied. She was close enough to hear what was being said.

The M.E. was kneeling beside Micklynn. "What are you saying, Silvestri?"

". . . I want directed testing. Toxicology compared to the Gelber case . . ."

The M.E. looked up, cleared his throat, jerked his head at Wetzon.

"Get the hell out of here, Les," Silvestri said.

Straightening, spinning around, Wetzon ran down the pier toward the *Bread Pudding,* where everyone now waited. The rest of what Silvestri had said kept repeating and repeating in her mind like a loop of tape:

"She was probably dead before she hit the water."

chapter 42

So there they all were, in the aftermath, sitting like a tableau on the deck of the *Bread Pudding,* with the sky exploding overhead and glasses clinking and conversation going on on other boats. All as if nothing untoward had happened. No corpse in the water below. No death for Micklynn.

Wetzon took inventory.

A. T. Barron, her face immobile, eyes blank, no tears in evidence: "What are we going to do?" she said for the third time, her lipless mouth barely moving.

Ellen Moore, the ingenue, in her cut-down, extra-short jeans and tight white tee shirt: her breast was stained with water and God knew what else, where she'd clung to Micklynn's body. She sat cross-legged on the deck, sobbing. Crocodile tears?

Hem Barron, who'd made several whispered calls on his cell phone, now nervously picked lint from his immaculate white ducks. He kept sneaking looks at Ellen. Or was it her bosom?

Minnie Wu Barron, her hair hanging limp, wore a fresh pair of purple drawstring pants and a sleeveless blouse. She was frowning, her thick-lidded eyes half closed. "Ten shows are in the can. If we're renewed, A.T. will do it." She seemed singularly unaffected by Micklynn's death.

A.T. stared at Min. "Are you out of your mind? I don't care about the show. What about the business?"

"You can run the business," Hem said. "There's nothing to it. The recipes are set; the products are already being manufactured. Nothing's standing in our way for an IPO now."

"Oh, Hem, shut up," Laura Lee snapped, not even trying to hide her exasperation. "The woman has just died, for godsakes."

"Go for it, Laura Lee," Wetzon said.

"Oh, please!" Smith was barefoot, having been told that one didn't hit the deck with heels. "Micklynn was a drunk and she probably toppled over the side and drowned."

"Smith," Wetzon said, "you have no charity."

"I am not a charitable institution," was her tart response.

Near the entrance to the pier Wetzon could see the lights and the men moving around and around, with Micklynn's body probably still lying on the ground. And in the sky above them, the shower of the fireworks continued, hearts and weeping willows in amber. Happy Fourth of July.

"Micklynn's been depressed," A.T. said. "She's been drinking steadily all day."

"Every day," Smith said.

"Good thing the cooking was finished," Minnie said.

"Oh, great." Hem smacked his head. "We've got all that food sitting in the galley. Let's get cracking. A.T.?"

"We probably shouldn't touch anything," Wetzon offered.

"Why the hell not?" Hem got up, heading for the galley. "Come on, Ellen. Let's get some food out here. I'm starved."

"Because it's all related to her death," Wetzon said. "Was anyone else working on the food with her?"

"I tried to help but she wouldn't let me," Ellen said. "Then I saw her throwing up over the side this afternoon. I went to get her some club soda." A look of anguish passed over her face. "Todd was on the dock. I stopped to talk to him. Micklynn wouldn't let him on the boat."

"Why? What did she have against him?" Wetzon asked.

"Micklynn had arbitrary fixations," A.T. said. "Todd happened to be one of them."

"Is Todd here now?" Wetzon hadn't seen him. Or had she? Unless . . . unless . . . Could he have been the tall, thin woman with the long hair she'd seen leaving the area when she and Smith arrived? At a distance could she have mistaken Todd for a woman?

"He left just before Xenia screamed. Didn't you see him?"

Wetzon shook her head. "No. Did you, Smith?"

"No. Is he the one with the long hair and the earrings that I saw you with at Hem's party?"

"Yes," Ellen said. "Micklynn was gone when I came back with the club soda, so I figured she was feeling better."

"You didn't check?"

"No. It's all my fault." She started to cry again.

"Found it!" Hem held up a bottle of Chivas. "Anyone want something stronger than wine?" He found some plastic cups and filled one after another with a finger of scotch, passing each on without asking if anyone wanted any.

Laura Lee said, "I'm starving. I hope this won't take long."

"It won't." Silvestri, followed by a red-haired woman in khakis and a chocolate linen jacket, came onto the deck. "I'm Lieutenant Silvestri, this is Detective Mulcahy. We'll want to talk to each of you separately for a short time, then we'll let you go. We'll probably call you back again. Let's get the timeline straight for starters, and the names." He nodded to Detective Mulcahy. He seemed to be taking a mental count of the faces, letting his eyes rest for a moment on each. "Where's Veeder?"

"He isn't on the boat, sugar," Smith said, using her most seductive voice.

Wetzon crossed her eyes at Laura Lee.

"What a piece of work," Laura Lee said, louder than necessary.

"Mulcahy," Silvestri said, "go see where—"

"There he is." Smith gave Wetzon a poke and said sotto voce, "Wasn't Bill just wonderful when he jumped into that filthy water to save Mick-lynn?"

"Silvestri too."

"Well, that's his job, sweetie pie."

Hem Barron decided to get indignant. "Why were you snooping around, Silvestri, or whatever your name is? It's insulting that you've been my bartender under false pretenses in my home and on my boat and all the while you were spying on me. I'm going to see that the Commissioner hears about this."

"Chill out, Hem," Bill Veeder said. He vaulted onto the deck. He wore jeans and a white tennis shirt under his jacket. "Let's let the PD do their job. We'll all get out of here faster."

"Thank you, Mr. Veeder," Silvestri said, overly polite.

Veeder crossed to where Wetzon sat and positioned himself beside her, his hand lightly on her shoulder.

"Can we eat?" Minnie Wu said. "There's all that food in the galley."

"Has anyone touched it or eaten anything?" Silvestri demanded.

"No . . . Has anyone?" A.T. looked around. Heads shook and nos were murmured.

"Only the wine . . . and the scotch. You ought to know. You were pretending to bartend." Hem's words had a nasty edge.

"Micklynn drank a lot of wine," Ellen said.

"She always did." A.T. looked battered.

"Look, she was upset and depressed," Wetzon said.

"How do you know so much about it?" Minnie Wu demanded.

Silvestri beckoned to Detective Mulcahy. "Sandy, you take Ms. Barron and I'll start with Xenia. Everyone else move to the other end of the boat, please." Silvestri nodded at Smith while the boat rocked with the sudden shift of weight. "And, Mulcahy, tell the CSU I want them to bag all the food here when they're finished out there. I mean everything."

"All that food?" Minnie sounded shocked. "You can't. We have guests."

Smith looked at Bill. "Any instructions before my interrogation, sweetie pie?"

"Tell the truth, Xenia," Bill said. "Don't embellish."

"Embellish? Really, Bill."

"You might mention that the Tarot lied," Wetzon said.

"The Tarot never lies, sugar," Smith snapped, raising her eyes heavenward, as if only God could help her deal with the philistines.

"Doesn't it? Didn't it say that Micklynn was a murderer?"

"What it said was that Micklynn was not going to be able to pay us any more money. I merely interpreted it wrong. I thought she was the murderer. It turned out that she committed suicide. So you see, the Tarot didn't lie. She can't pay us any more, now can she?"

"Suicide, Smith? You think her death was suicide?"

"What else? What do you think it was?" She looked at Silvestri, who had come up behind them.

Bill said, "I'd appreciate it, Silvestri, if you would talk to Leslie, and me, earlier rather than later. I'd like to get her home."

"Hey—" Wetzon began.

"Oh?" Silvestri shot an amused look at Veeder. "Are you in trouble here, Les? A little case of murder never seemed to bother you before."

She felt Veeder's muscles tighten. All eyes suddenly seemed on her and Silvestri. She forced herself to keep her tone even. "I'd like to go home. I'm sure everyone here would." What she wanted to say was: *Go fuck yourself, Silvestri.*

"Well, we'll talk after Xenia. That's a promise," he said, with more exaggerated courtesy.

"Murder? Did he say murder?" A.T. sat down hard.

"Excuse me, sir—" Ellen said faintly, only to be drowned out by Minnie Wu.

"How utterly ridiculous! She was drunk and fell in."

Too eager, Hem agreed. "Of course that's what happened. Poor Micklynn. Nothing really went right for her."

Wetzon was fascinated by the avalanche of opinion. She didn't believe any one of them.

"She really was a drunk, dear Silvestri," Smith said, batting her lashes at Wetzon's ex, who was letting them all blather.

"Silvestri," Bill said. "Most of the people here are my clients. Why don't we get this over with?"

"Was Micklynn Devora your client?"

"Her company is my client."

"Was there a will?"

Wetzon caught a silent comment exchanged between Hem and A.T. Had anyone else?

"I'm sure there is a will." Veeder chose his words carefully. "Perhaps we should talk about it another time."

"Excuse me, sir," Ellen said to Silvestri, raising her voice.

"Yes?"

Everyone stopped in mid-speech.

"Micklynn . . ." Ellen became flustered, breathy. "Micklynn . . . she didn't fall in."

"How do you know?"

"She . . ."

"Then she really was murdered," A.T. gasped. "Did you see it, Ellen? Detective, I want this child protected."

"No!" Ellen said.

"Let her speak," Silvestri said.

"I'm not sure about this, Ellen," Bill Veeder said.

"Give Bill a dollar, kiddo," Hem said. When Ellen looked utterly confused, Hem dug into the pocket of his ducks. "Here, here's a dollar. Take it and give it to Bill."

Silvestri watched the process, a politely bored expression on his face. After Bill accepted the dollar from Ellen, Bill told her, "I don't want you to say anything."

"No," Ellen said firmly. "This is crazy. It's not about me. Micklynn wasn't murdered."

"Why do you say that, Ms. Moore?" Silvestri asked, prompting her.

Bill glared at him. "Ellen, I urge you to say nothing."

"But I didn't do anything. Listen to me, please. Micklynn was really drunk and really upset last night. She kept talking around in circles and finally admitted she killed Miss Gelber."

"My God!" A.T. said.

"What did I tell you?" Smith said.

Wetzon watched Silvestri. He was trying to keep his cool and maybe the others thought he was doing it, but Wetzon knew him, and it wasn't working. His eyes met hers for a moment, then went back to Ellen.

"She was so depressed I was scared for her, but then this morning she seemed all right, even kind of happy. She said she'd found a way to fix everything."

chapter 43

"Do you want to get something to eat?" Bill asked. Since at this juncture he represented everyone involved, he'd felt an obligation to be present at the preliminary questioning.

"I want to go home," Wetzon said. It was late; she was tired, not hungry. And the reality of Micklynn's death had just begun to register. "My place."

"Uh-oh, sounds serious." He looked over at her, but she knew he couldn't see much beyond what the street-lights revealed.

"It is."

"Want to be alone?"

"No. Weren't we going to spend tomorrow together?"

"Okay, why don't we stop at my place so I can get a change . . . I can send out for—"

"I'll wait for you in the car."

"My place is not enemy territory," he said.

"Isn't it?"

So she waited in the car in front of his building, confused, on a rolling boil like a pot of popover batter, cleaning down the sides of the pot with each new thought. . . . Micklynn had had plenty of sorrow prior to all this. Why take her own life now when she was on the brink of international fame, not to mention fortune? It didn't make sense. Unless Ellen was telling the truth: that Micklynn had poisoned Sheila. Micklynn had said she felt responsible for Sheila's death. Ellen could have misinterpreted. . . .

Bill tossed his duffel in the back of the Mercedes, got in, and fastened his seat belt. "Everything okay?"

She nodded.

"I'm going to stop at the Carnegie and pick up a couple of sandwiches. Corned beef on rye okay?"

"Pastrami. Extra-sour pickles."

He grinned at her. "Welcome back, Leslie Wetzon." He'd showered and changed. And shaved. She touched the smoothness of his cheek and he caught her hand and kissed her palm.

"I want you to take me seriously," she said.

"I do."

"I don't need to be protected. I can take care of myself. You asked me once why I wasn't married. That's why. If I'd wanted someone to take care of me, I would have married—"

"Alton Pinkus."

"You know about him? Goddammit, Smith told you. I have no privacy."

"Don't blame Xenia. I know that Pinkus and Silvestri are the two men in your past."

"My *past*. Sounds as if I'm a scarlet lady."

"Hardly."

"If Smith didn't tell you, how do you know so much about me?"

"After Hartmann was killed, I cleaned out his desk and files myself."

"No telling what you'd find."

"Quite right. Anyway, when I cleaned out his desk, I found a rather detailed investigative report on you."

"That gives me the creeps."

"It shouldn't. I destroyed it."

"But not before reading it."

"But not before reading it." He gave her what could only be described as an impish grin.

"Shit," she said.

He drove up to Fifty-fourth Street and parked near the Carnegie.

She said, "I don't want you to say things like 'I want to get Leslie home.'"

"Why not?"

"It's patronizing. Hey, I'm Leslie. I can make those decisions for myself. You never even asked me if I *wanted* to go home. And it's proprietary. I felt you were telling Silvestri I belong to you now. Which isn't true."

"I'll be right back," he said. He got out and locked the door. Seventh Avenue was bright with lights. People strolled, tourists and New Yorkers, all foot traffic, few cars.

She was taking a risk that he would think a relationship with her was too complicated, but she refused to commit to anything ever again that was not totally honest.

When Veeder came back with the big bag of deli, which he set on the floor in the back, he said, "You're right. I apologize."

"I'm not scaring you off?"

"Lady, it would take more than a streak of feminism to scare me off."

"Oh, please," she said, laughing.

"Of course, you'll have to watch me carefully so that I don't slip again."

"I don't mind that."

They left the Mercedes in the garage on Eighty-seventh Street and walked to Wetzon's apartment. Someone in the neighborhood was setting off fireworks, sending strobes whistling into the sky over the Upper West Side. The air was hot and dry and when they stopped to watch the shower of silvery light, Bill held her hand.

The sandwiches were so huge, Wetzon wrapped up half of hers and put it in the fridge, returning with two more beers, and a dog biscuit for Izz, who was reclining on Bill's lap.

"So are we okay?" he asked, scratching Izz's belly. He'd hung his jacket on the back of a chair and parked his gun on the kitchen counter.

"Yes. You said you didn't want a passive partner in bed. You're not going to get one out of bed either."

"That's fine with me." He saluted her with his bottle.

"What's that on your arm?"

"This?" He twisted his arm to look at the red pinpricks. "Tetanus. Hepatitis. Gamma globulin. Defense against anything the Hudson might offer."

"Did . . . Forget it."

"Did Silvestri get the same?"

She nodded.

"He got them too. There's still something between you, isn't there?" Rather than disappointment, the idea seemed to energize him, as if he would do battle for her hand.

"He and I have a history, Bill. The relationship is over, but I care about him. Wouldn't I be a shit if I could just turn it on and off? So forget it. You are not going to duel him for me."

He laughed, then thrust out two fingers. "Fins," he said.

"What's that?"

"Put your first two fingers on top of mine. Say fins."

"Fins."

"That's Brooklyn for truce."

Now she laughed.

He got up and rummaged through his jacket. "Have something for you." He handed her a small pale blue box. "Don't look so horrified. It isn't anything like that."

Like what, she thought, bewildered. She knew a Tiffany box when she saw it. She opened the little box hesitantly. On a bed of soft cotton lay a gold cross on a fine chain. "I—God—excuse me." She was shocked and . . . disappointed. Here was evidence of how he'd misjudged her.

"What's the matter?" He was clearly as disappointed as she. "It took me a while to find the right chain."

"Why would you have even wanted to?"

"Because yours broke during our first night together."

"Mine? You think this cross is *mine*?"

"Isn't it?"

"No. I've never seen—" She stopped. "It must belong to one of your other . . . friends."

He shook his head. "It couldn't, Leslie. My maid found it on the living-room carpet when she came in on Monday. I wondered why you never said anything, then decided you might have been embarrassed."

"I wouldn't have been embarrassed if it was mine." She looked down at the little gold cross, then lifted it out of its box, letting it dangle in the air. Where had she seen a cross dangling like this? Up close too. "That night, after Hem and Min's party?"

"Yes," he said. "Someone tried to pitch you over the parapet. You put up some fight."

"Scraped my knees. . . ." She smiled at him.

"I like the direction this is going," Bill said. He took the cross from her and laid it back in the box, set the box on the table. He pulled her to her feet.

"No . . . wait, Bill. When I struggled I must have caught the cross and jerked it. Remember there was blood on my hair, but no wound? I think the cross came from an earring and must have lodged in that damned Wonderbra. So when you unhooked it . . ."

"We can play it back exactly as it happened," he said, giving her forehead, her cheeks, her eyelids, whispery kisses, saving her mouth for last. She put her fingers over his mouth for a moment.

"He was wearing cross earrings, Bill. I saw them."

Veeder stared down at her. "Who, Leslie?"

"Ellen's boyfriend. Todd. He's the one who tried to throw me off Hem's roof."

chapter   4 4

"How soon do you think they'll know for sure if Micklynn was murdered?" Up on one elbow, Wetzon watched
Izz stretch the leash as far as it would go in order to stalk
a grasshopper.

"Depends on whether there was water in her lungs,
contusions, toxicology . . ." Bill yawned. His eyes were
closed. "They probably know already."

"And if there was no water in her lungs . . ." With
her forefinger she traced a line from his throat to his
waistband. Sunday in the Park with Bill. "Hey," she said,
"don't you fall asleep on me."

They were in semi-shade, lying on a cotton blanket
on a hill overlooking the lake. A white picnic hamper

with the '21' Club logo lay on its side near a virtually empty bottle of an Oregon pinot noir. Mariachi music just faint enough to be pleasant came from distant boom boxes. The air had a summer sweetness to it, which strangers never associated with New York.

"'The isle is full of noises, Sounds and sweet airs, that give delight, and hurt not . . . ,'" she murmured.

Opening one eye, Bill gave the elbow she was leaning on a push. He grabbed her in a bear hug when she came down, then parked her on top of him. "What did you say?"

"You were asleep. Great. I must be scintillating company. I said, what if Micklynn had no water in her lungs?"

"Madam, there is no other company I'd rather be with. No water in lungs usually means she was dead before she went in. But not necessarily."

"Silvestri thinks it was murder," Wetzon said.

"Oh, he does, does he? And how would you know that?"

"I overheard him say something to the M.E."

"Wanna come work for me? I can always use a good snoop."

"Speaking of that, I guess with Micklynn dead, I can tell you that she hired me to see what I could find out about Sheila Gelber's murder."

"Let's neck," Bill said.

"Aren't you going to say I'm not a detective and it's too dangerous to muck in police business?"

"I wouldn't dare. Didn't you tell me in no uncertain terms that you can take care of yourself?" He undid her ponytail, slipping the band over his wrist.

Nuzzling his chin, she said, "I did indeed."

"So you want to tell me what you found out?"

He was laughing at her, but she answered anyway. "The only two people in The Groaning Board group who knew Sheila Gelber were Micklynn and Ellen. Micklynn was going to go into business with Sheila until you told her the contract with A.T. was airtight and she couldn't break it to include Sheila."

"And Ellen?"

"Sheila was Ellen's English teacher at Colton. Micklynn accused Sheila of favoritism when Sheila chose a Jewish student over Ellen for a university summer program. Hardly a motive for murder."

"On the surface. But murderers don't always have rational motives."

"May I quote you?"

He rolled them over so that he was on top of her. "You have no respect."

"Oh, yeah, do you see the great criminal attorney William Veeder himself, a middle-aged, married man, rolling on the grass in Central Park with that Twinkie Wall Street headhunter, what's-her-face?"

Izz gave a fierce tug on her leash as she chased a tiny bird that teased by squawking at her, then flying off. "Hey, you, come back here," Wetzon said.

"Everyone's out of town for the long weekend." Bill kissed her mouth, making love to her lower lip.

"Mmmmm . . . it only takes one person to spot us." She closed her eyes. "You know, if Micklynn was murdered, it would have to have been done by one of your clients."

"Fuck my clients. They are getting in the way of my love life."

"Hem was furious because she was holding up the IPO. A.T. for the same reason and because A.T. felt she wasn't treating Ellen fairly. Also the partnership was obviously curdling. Minnie Wu hates everybody, but in this case I think she really hated Micklynn because Micklynn and Hem were once lovers."

Bill propped himself up on his elbows. "Now how would you know that?"

"My best friend, Carlos, the choreographer, whom you haven't met yet. Micklynn lived next door to Carlos and Arthur Margolies some years ago. Carlos said Minnie beat Micklynn up because of her relationship with Hem."

"Arthur Margolies the lawyer?"

"Yup."

"I know him."

"Thought you might."

"Beat up? Explain."

"Punched out, physically abused. Know what I mean, mouthpiece?"

His laughter rocked both of them. "Hem never told me any of this."

"And then there's pretty little Ellen. Except for that punky, grungy boyfriend, she's almost *too* perfect. If anyone killed anyone else in the group I would have thought it would be Minnie who killed Ellen."

"She wouldn't do that."

"How can you be so sure?"

"Attorney-client privilege, and that's telling you too much. By the way,

I spoke with Doug Cameron, Todd's father. I asked for a meeting with Tilghman, Doug, and Todd."

"Excuse me, which one's the mother? Or is it a same-sex marriage?"

"Tilghman. Family name. Eastern shore of Maryland."

"Do they know what the meeting's about?"

"Not yet. Doug's a good man. I think I told you—he's a judge in the surrogate court. I want to make them aware there's a problem. We have no real proof—" They were speaking in whispers, intimately, although there was no need.

"The cross—"

"Circumstantial. Did you by any chance talk with Todd earlier in the evening? Before you were attacked?"

"Yes, I did. But not up close and personal. He followed Ellen and me when she showed me around the greenhouse." Wetzon shook her head. "Todd'll never admit he tried to throw me off that roof. Certainly not in front of his parents. And I want to be there when you confront him."

"I don't think that's such a good idea."

"You don't think he's going to throw me out of your office window, do you? I'd like to know why he tried to kill me. Don't I have a right to know?" Her body moved in sync with his. She was holding on by a thread.

"Yes, but I would say he's unlikely to admit it; however, we may be able to scare the shit out of him."

"Oh, goody. I'd like that." She kissed him on the mouth. Her hand crept under his shirt. "Now let's neck."

His beeper went off like an alarm, making Izz bark.

"Shit," he said, peeling himself from her. He reached into his duffel and took out the beeper. "It's Evelyn," he said. He stood up, looking suddenly torn.

"Go," Wetzon said quickly. She got to her feet. "You'll make it faster through the Park. I'll take everything home."

He cupped her face in his hands, started to say something, then didn't. He picked up his duffel and sprinted toward the path and Fifth Avenue, Izz following to the end of the leash. Wetzon and the dog watched until he disappeared from sight.

He might never come back, she knew. This is the way it was going to be. *If you don't like it,* a little voice urged, *get out now.* But Wetzon wasn't sure how she felt about any of it. Except him. And she was willing to accept what was . . . for the time being.

She folded the blanket over her arm and gathered up the picnic things, the bottle of wine, the hamper. Loosening the laces, she slipped on her Keds and walked down the grassy incline. The heat felt good on her bare legs. She held Izz's leash under her heel while she tried to pull her hair back, but Bill had gone off with her hair band on his wrist. When, she wondered, would he discover his odd bracelet? Or would someone else discover it? When she laughed, her face felt the tight flush of a sunburn.

Families and lovers were scattered all over the bucolic landscape of the Park, sleeping, eating, laughing, kissing. And all around, the buzz of insects and human voices and music, the sound of sun and heat, the dull splash of the oars against the water on the lake, the fresh, clean smell of summer grass, the soft doughy sound of bicycle tires on dirt paths. No vehicle traffic permitted: Central Park on a lazy, hot summer day.

Maybe another time we can take a row on the lake, Wetzon thought. If there was another time. She knew rowboats were for rent at the Loeb Boathouse. She'd always wanted to do it. Never the right time, never the right company.

Some years back a restaurant had emerged on the upper section of Bethesda Terrace that led to the twenty-acre lake, known only as the Lake. The steps were scattered with people, but Wetzon found a place to sit and watch the activity on the water. Izz crawled onto her lap. On the lake an adolescent boy with little experience in oarsmanship was rowing a woman in a large flowered hat. The boat was making circles on the crowded lake. The woman held on to her hat.

"Get that idiot off the lake," someone yelled from one of the other boats.

The sharp voice flitted over the water and smacked into Wetzon's consciousness. All of a sudden, with the rumble of a bowling bowl as it lurches down the alley, boats began to collide. Everyone was yelling, oars thumped as the rowers fought their way out of the tangle. They began slipping away like petals on a daisy, he loves me, he loves me not.

Two women were in the last boat to slide away. One of them had shouted the first warning.

Wetzon set Izz down and stood. She descended the steps to the edge of the lake waiting for her eyes to focus behind her dark glasses.

The voice belonged to Minnie Wu, and the woman she was with—Wetzon couldn't quite believe it—was Ellen Moore.

chapter 4 5

"Where are you?"

Wetzon held the receiver away from her ear. She slipped her feet into her patent-leather Ferragamos. "Hello. Earth to Smith. Where do you think I am? Where did you call me?"

"Oh, for pity sakes."

"What is your problem? I was just leaving."

"Don't stop anywhere, promise me. There's something you have to hear." Smith's abrupt disconnect slammed in Wetzon's ear.

"It's I who should say, 'Oh, for pity sakes,' Izz, don't you think?" Wetzon kissed the little dog's snout and set her down. Izz scrambled off and returned with her leash in her mouth, cute as you please. "Anyone would think you didn't have your walk, but you and I know better."

The night had been endless, one of those where she'd wake every hour. She had not heard from Bill. Finally, at five, she crawled out of bed, exhausted, and took Izz for a walk.

It was a hot, humid Monday. The first workday after the Fourth. Everyone's eyes looked a little glazed from the four-day weekend. No one really wanted to go back to work. Including Leslie Wetzon. Well, not really, she thought. Perspective was definitely needed as quickly as possible, before Bill Veeder became too important. Her fingers played with the gold chain around her neck. Bill had taken Todd Cameron's cross away with him.

She let a couple of cabs with open windows go by; on a day like today air conditioning was a must. In fact, it seemed that no taxis had air conditioning anymore.

Giving up, she settled for what was available. "How come no air conditioning?" she asked.

The driver was Asian. He showed her his teeth, as if she'd made some uproarious joke. "Where you want go?"

"Forty-ninth and Second." One day, she thought, before I die, I may get in a cab in New York and get a driver who speaks and understands English.

She unfolded her *Times* and reread Micklynn's obituary. It had been a slow-news weekend, so coverage of her death in print and television was extensive. "Mysterious death," it was called in the *Times*. Television's *Entertainment Tonight* called it a "fearsome tragedy" and reported that Micklynn's unique name was a combination of her father's, Mickey Bassinger, and her mother's, Lynda. *Extra Edition* hinted at foul play. The photographs of Micklynn were all of a slim young woman in sixties shmatte garb. Obviously, Micklynn hadn't changed her costume, just her body shape.

Wetzon folded the newspaper and stuffed it in her briefcase, wondering when the media would tell everyone how Micklynn really died.

When she got out of the taxi on Second and Forty-ninth, the newsstand featured the *Post*'s blaring headlines: CHEF'S STEW: ACCIDENT OR SUICIDE??

Four days without air conditioning left the office stuffy. Darlene, inappropriately dressed in a vivid fuchsia sundress with spaghetti straps that kept slipping from her plump shoulders, was taking down the messages that had piled up on the answering machine over the holiday.

She looked up when Wetzon came in. "Good morning. I'm sorry about your friend. Smith told me all about it. It must have been awful. If I can do anything—"

"Thanks, Darlene." The woman really grated on her nerves. It was all she could do not to tell her to shut up. God, she thought, I am definitely turning into a curmudgeon. "I appreciate the offer. Anything important?"

"I have to sort through them—"

"Is that you?" Smith screamed from upstairs. "Get right up here!"

"Okay, okay." Wetzon looked quizzically at Darlene, who shrugged.

"I don't know," Darlene whispered. "She was here when I came in and she's been like that—"

The doorbell buzzed.

"Wetzon!"

"I'm coming!" She started up the stairs.

At the door Darlene signed for two white florist boxes. "They're for you, Wetzon," she called.

Wetzon came back down. Flowers. She undid the bow on the first box. Elegant long-stemmed red roses. God. The smaller box held a vase full of violets.

"They're beautiful," Darlene said. "Do you want me to put the roses in water?"

"Would you?"

"Wetzon!"

"There's no card," Darlene said.

"I know who sent them." Wetzon climbed the stairs and stepped into the grand new Smith and Wetzon private office.

"I can't believe you dillydallied all this time," Smith said.

"For godsakes, Smith, it's not even nine o'clock. What's with you? What's the crisis?"

"When did I say it was a crisis? It's not a crisis." Smith became eerily calm. "So to speak. You've got to hear . . . this . . ." She paused for dramatic effect, then strolled over to Wetzon's desk and picked up Wetzon's private line. "Listen to this. It's on your voice mail, along with another call from your perverted breather friend."

"My voice mail? Let me get this straight. You were eavesdropping on my private—"

"Oh, for pity sakes, will you shut up and listen." She held the phone to Wetzon's ear.

With an angry thump, Wetzon set her briefcase and handbag on the floor. She grabbed the phone, pissed that Smith had invaded her privacy once more. Heavy breathing came across the line. "Smith—dammit—" Wetzon shook the receiver at Smith. "You have no business—"

"Leslie, where are you?" Wetzon almost dropped the phone. It was Micklynn's voice, smudged and dull with booze.

Aghast, Wetzon looked at Smith, who stood with her arms folded, smug. "What did I tell you?"

"Thoughtyou'dbehome." Micklynn's words ran into each other. She broke off into a fit of coughing. *". . . Knowexactlywhathappened . . . why. Wantyata help me set up . . ."*

The line went dead.

chapter 46

"Good God, Smith, Micklynn must have called me here instead of home last Thursday."

"Set what up? She knew something. Yes, she did."

"And what she knew got her murdered . . . and none of this means a damn thing."

"How can you say that? You heard her."

"We don't know what it was she found out, do we?"

Smith frowned. "It obviously had to do with that Sheila person's murder we were investigating for her."

"We? Oh, I get it. Of course. That's why you listened to my voice mail."

"Sarcasm doesn't become you, sweetie pie," Smith said severely.

"You have no shame, you know that? How would you like it if I listened to your—"

"Oh, pu-leeze, sugar. I have to know what's going on in your life and you have to know the same about mine. It's how to succeed in business."

"I would never listen to your private voice messages."

"That's why you need me as your partner, Ms. Holier Than Thou," She smirked. "Because I have no shame."

"Truer words have ne'er been spoken. I guess we should call Silvestri. Is there coffee?"

"Of course there's coffee," Smith said. "And bagels." She followed Wetzon into the kitchen and watched as Wetzon filled her mug. "Ummmm . . . I have an interesting suggestion."

"No doubt."

"Trust me on this, sugar."

Wetzon raised an eyebrow. "Let's hear it." After relative quiet, the phones all began ringing at once. Wetzon sat down at her desk and watched the blinking lights as Darlene fielded the calls.

Smith paid no attention. She was pacing the long room. "Listen to me. Micklynn said she had the proof. What do you think that means?"

"It means we'd better tell the police, because it gives someone a clear motive for murder."

"Look at it this way, sweetie pie. We have a dead client. But our consulting agreement—you did get her to sign one, didn't you?"

"She signed it, and it's in the file."

"Well, may I remind you that our contract says should the signee die, the agreement would continue until it's canceled in writing by the company that hired us. So we're still employed, technically, by Micklynn Devora—I mean, by her estate."

"Smith, that sounds a teeny bit like fraud to me, not to mention pure greed. Do you mind if I check it out with Bill Veeder? I believe he's Micklynn's lawyer."

Smith groaned. "I don't believe this."

Wetzon picked up the phone and called Veeder. She was put right through. Did Mrs. Copeland keep a list of priority people . . . ? And how frequently, Wetzon couldn't help wondering, were names added and subtracted?

"Hi." His voice was scratchy and deep, as if he'd had no sleep.

"How did it go?"

"Okay for now. They're going to keep her at Lenox Hill for a couple of days."

"I'm sorry."

"Sorry!" Smith gave a little shriek. "You must never use that word with any man."

Wetzon turned her back.

"It's not anything new," he said.

"Thank you for the beautiful flowers."

"What flowers?" Smith demanded.

"I'll call you tonight," he said.

"Okay. Bill, I need to ask you something about Micklynn's estate."

"I don't represent the estate."

"Oh, I thought—" Hadn't he told Silvestri there was a will?

"I represent the company."

"Then who was Micklynn's personal lawyer?"

"Your friend Arthur Margolies. Any more questions?"

She felt a kind of coldness creep into his response, but went on anyway. "Yes. What happens to The Groaning Board if one of the partners dies?"

He didn't answer right away.

"Bill?" That's right, Wetzon, she told herself, plunge right ahead.

"The company reverts to the living partner."

She hung up the phone and looked at Smith. "Well, that's an interesting twist."

"What is?"

"Arthur Margolies is Micklynn's personal lawyer."

"Fine, you can talk to him later." Single-minded Smith brushed Wetzon's words aside. "Now here's my thinking. We get paid until someone cancels our contract—"

"That's tenuous, Smith. Actually, that's *larcenous*."

"But if we find out who killed her and why, the estate will pay us, babycakes."

"Maybe."

"Absolutely. So what I think we should do is go up to The Groaning Board tonight and search for whatever it was she said she had."

"I need to talk to Arthur first."

"You have such a stubborn streak."

"Yes, especially when it comes to breaking the law."

"What exactly did Bill say?"

"He said in the case of one partner's death, the company reverts to the living partner."

"Lock, stock, and barrel? How truly fascinating." Smith's voice betrayed her thoughts.

"Dear partner, don't for one minute think we're going to renegotiate our deal."

Smith pressed her palm to where her heart ought to have been. "Babycakes, what do you think I am?" She batted her lashes at Wetzon. "I was just thinking what a terrific lawyer your lover is."

As Wetzon placed the call to Arthur Margolies, Darlene came up the stairs carrying Wetzon's flowers. She set the vases down on Wetzon's desk, then fished in her pockets for the message slips.

"Rosenkind Luwisher is merging Bob Walters' office into its other office in Wilmington," she told Wetzon. "Bob isn't going to be manager."

"But Bob has been managing the other office for only three months." The firm had transferred him from New York with all kinds of promises. "I hope he didn't sell his house in Connecticut."

"I think his wife stayed here because of the kids," Darlene said.

"I'll talk to him. Maybe they have something else in mind for him."

"I think they're going to let him swing slowly in the wind. He's too old. He's got to be in his late fifties."

"Yeah, boy, is that old," Wetzon groused to Smith after Darlene exited.

"Which is why, sweetie pie, we are very happy in our own business. Over-forties are unemployable on the Street and in most corporate environments." She cupped a rose and sniffed. "The flowers are gorgeous. I take it everything is going well?"

"Only moderately. Evelyn had another incident last night. She's in Lenox Hill for a few days." Wetzon picked up the phone and tapped in some numbers. When Arthur answered, she said, "Arthur Margolies, darling, this is Leslie Wetzon."

"Leslie, a pleasure. I hope all is well with you."

"It is. I have a quick question."

"Ask away."

"I'm not sure you know this, Arthur, because she was so secretive, but Micklynn hired me as a consultant."

Arthur gave a deep sigh. "It's a terrible tragedy. What were you consulting on, the IPO? She was dead set against it."

"No, not that. Mickey had a friend, Sheila Gelber, who was murdered about four months ago. Micklynn hired me to look into Sheila's death because she felt in some way responsible."

"Mickey felt responsible for the whole world, and I suppose it all got too much for her."

"I'd like to continue working on the case, Arthur. I believe Micklynn was murdered."

"Murdered. Leslie." He sounded shocked. "Oh, dear, this will change everything."

"I've come up with some really good information, Arthur. Will you okay my tracking down this lead?"

"I don't know, Leslie. Maybe we should let the insurance company handle it."

"She was insured?"

"I really don't feel comfortable saying anything right now, Leslie."

"Arthur, I swear to you you're going to hear any minute that she was murdered. What difference does it make if you tell me now what her insurance policy says?"

"I suppose you're right. . . . In case of suicide, there is no settlement. In case of violent death—that is, murder or accident—it is double indemnity. If Micklynn was murdered, her policy will pay one million dollars."

Wetzon let out a long exhale. "Which is precisely why you must let me investigate. The insurance company would rather it be suicide, isn't that so?"

"In case of suicide, they wouldn't have to pay off the policy. Leslie, you *will* tell the police about your information?"

She crossed all her fingers. God would forgive her this one time. "Of course, Arthur. You know me, old honest Leslie herself."

"You sound exactly like Carlos when he's dodging the truth."

"Not me, Arthur."

"Be careful."

"I will. By the way, who is Micklynn's beneficiary?"

"Leslie, you are pushing me beyond my limit." Gentle Arthur was sounding a little like Bill Veeder.

But determined, Wetzon pushed a little more. "I swear it, Arthur. Trust me." Oh, shit, now she'd said it.

Arthur sighed again. "Leslie—I would like you to promise me this information will go no further."

"I promise."

"Any income from Mickey's estate will be divided between two charities."

"That's it?"

"That's it," he said.

chapter   4 7

"I've spent my whole career with this firm," Bob Walters said. "I can't look for another job now. I'm fifty-eight years old. Who would hire me? I wouldn't."

"Hasn't Rosenkind said anything about another management position?"

"Not a word. They're telling me I'll have a desk in the regional office for a couple of months."

"And after that?"

"Who knows? They say nothing is available."

Wetzon knew very well something was available at Rosenkind. Word on the Street had it that they were looking to replace their manager in international. It was top secret because the man they'd brought in from Merrill six months before was still sitting there. But top secret on Wall Street never stayed that way for long. Brokers were terrible gossips. Word got around.

Bob Walters was a nice guy and they were going to let him hang there until he was humiliated enough to take retirement. His depression was palpable across the telephone wires. Although Smith would kill her if she ever found out, Wetzon was going to throw him a freebie. "Bob, there is something available that you'd be perfect for, and it's with your firm. I can't understand why they didn't offer it to you."

"Really?" He perked up immediately.

"International is looking to replace its manager."

"They never mentioned it." The amazement in his voice made Wetzon shudder. He was too naive by far. "Thank you for the tip."

"Go for it, Bob."

"How do you know Ellen's not there?" Wetzon asked. She'd gone home, changed into cat-burglar clothing: black leggings and a black long-sleeved cotton shirt, black cap on her head. She'd fed and walked Izz. Now she was sitting in Smith's living room while Smith addressed a letter to her son, who was doing summer stock in Ohio.

"She's staying with A.T. until . . ."

"Until the funeral?"

"No, until she gets her inheritance."

"What inheritance?"

"Ellen's the beneficiary of Mickey's will. A.T. told me."

"How nice for her."

Smith's lips formed a circle. "Oh."

" 'Oh' is right. If Ellen thought she was Mickey's beneficiary, she had a solid motive."

"It distresses me to hear that. She's applied to Princeton, Yale, and Harvard. I wrote letters of recommendation for her. The Tarot will tell us . . ." She began searching for her cards under her correspondence.

"Not now, please. I'd like to get this over with. And just for the record, I'm sure the cops have been over the place thoroughly. If there's a burglar-alarm system we can't chance it."

"We'll see." Smith put a stamp on the envelope. Pulling black leather gloves on her hands, she said, "Let's go."

"I've got a flashlight," Wetzon said. "How will we get in?"

"I have a few appropriate tools here." Smith picked up a black Saks Fifth Avenue shopping bag.

With the onset of evening, the heat had dissipated some. But the pavement still radiated with what it had absorbed for over a week. A rich sprinkling of stars filled the deep purple sky.

They walked the short distance to The Groaning Board, passing the crowded restaurants on Third and Second Avenues. It was ten o'clock on a weekday night. Didn't anyone have to be at work early the next day? Or were they all so young they had the energy to go without a night's sleep? Probably the latter.

The side streets, however, were almost totally residential and country quiet. The Groaning Board was shrouded in darkness, except for the lighted sign in the window that said: *"Due to Micklynn Devora's death, The Groaning Board will be closed until Monday, July 15th. Memorial contributions may be sent to CityMeals on Wheels or God's Love We Deliver."*

Ah, Wetzon thought, there were the two charities.

A metal grill and a padlock protected The Groaning Board entrance. On the door leading to Micklynn's duplex: no evidence of an alarm system.

"You be the lookout," Smith said. "I'll work on the outside door. We can always go downstairs afterward." She pawed through her Saks bag and came up with a crochet hook.

"You have to be kidding," Wetzon said.

"Shshsh. Anyone coming?"

"No." Although no one was on the street, who knew if someone was watching from one of the dark or curtained windows above them? Besides, Smith would soon find the crochet hook disappointing.

"Oops!"

"What, oops?" Wetzon swiveled to Smith. The door was open. "Did you do that with the hook? Nice going, partner." Wetzon reached into her shoulder bag and pulled on black gloves.

"I didn't do anything," Smith said. "It was open."

"Uh-oh. Someone must be up there."

Smith nudged her. "Go across the street and see if there's a light."

"Would a burglar be stupid enough to put on a light?" But Wetzon crossed the street and scoured the two upper floors of Micklynn's carriage house. Not a glimmer. She came back to Smith shaking her head.

"Let's do it, then." Without waiting for Wetzon, Smith pushed open the door and stepped aside. "Now go ahead of me with your light."

"So I can shield you, I suppose."

"That's not a bad idea, since I'm the one in our partnership who keeps her eye on the prize."

"Cracker Jack prizes." Wetzon pushed past Smith. "Close that door."

Smith closed the door. "The green stuff, sweetie pie. The big bucks. What life is really about."

"Life is with people, Smith."

"Oh, pu-leeze. Shall we bring on the violins?"

The stairs creaked under their feet. Wetzon whispered, "Hug the wall. That way if someone jumps out at us, we won't take a header down these stairs."

They paused when they got to the top of the stairs, where a big potted azalea drooped, begging for water. "You'll get nothing from me, death plant," Wetzon muttered, trying the door. It was locked, and what's more, it had yellow crime-scene tape sealing it. "Shit," she said.

"No problem. Stand aside, partner." Smith took a Chinese cleaver from the shopping bag and cut the tape, unsealing the door, and scarring it at the same time. "Kelsey Millhiser to the rescue." She began worrying the lock with a long, skinny knitting needle.

Wetzon lifted the doormat. No key there. "Kelsey Millhiser? Who's that?" She lifted the azalea pot. A small brass key lay in the tray under the pot. She handed it to Smith.

"You know. The Sue Grafton private eye."

"Kinsey Milhone, Smith."

"Whatever."

They stepped into the apartment and Wetzon moved her light around, keeping it close to the floor. At first she didn't notice anything different from her earlier visit. In the kitchen, however, she became aware of the faint scent of pine. The sink and countertops were all pristine.

It was when they moved on into the living room and Smith exclaimed, "What a great place!" that Wetzon began to realize how clean everything was. How orderly. No clutter. No magazines or newspapers. It could have been a showplace, not a home. And—she flashed her light over the sofa—no cat hair.

A short time later, upstairs, they found the bedrooms were also immaculate, nothing out of place.

"I had no idea," Smith said. "I always thought she was such a pig."

"She wasn't any too neat." Wetzon shone her light around the hallway. "Someone's cleaned everything up, but good. Trashing in reverse."

"Okay, where should we start?"

"Where would you hide something small?"

"In one of my shoes."

"Unlikely. Micklynn wore Birkenstocks. Do the drawers, and look inside the socks. I'll try the bed. She may have put it between the box spring and the mattress."

With surprising speed they went through everything thoroughly. "Nothing," Smith said, major disappointment in the set of her shoulders. "Is the phone working?"

Wetzon picked it up and got a dial tone. "It is. Why?"

"I want to see if Twoey's back from London." She reached for the phone.

"Not on your life. The police can check phone records."

"Who do you suppose she has on her speed dial?" Smith said.

"Speed dial, huh? Why not?"

Wetzon pressed #1 and listened to the automatic dialing. "Hello?" A.T. said. "Hello?" Wetzon hung up quietly. "A.T.," she told Smith. Pressing #2, she got no answer. Sheila Gelber? Possibly.

#3 was Arthur Margolies. #4 was Hem Barron's office. Hem Barron. Interesting. Were they still having an affair?

#5 was another answering machine. *You have reached Dr. Bowers' Animal Medical Clinic. Our hours are eight A.M. to six P.M., Monday through Friday, and nine to one on Saturday. If this is an emergency . . ."* The message continued, providing an emergency number, followed by the daytime phone number, which Wetzon jotted down.

"Are you going to tell me what you're doing?"

"Writing down the vet's number."

"I haven't seen a sign of a dog or cat, or even a goldfish," Smith said.

"Micklynn had a cat. It must have died recently, because she was so upset she wouldn't talk about it."

"Old-maid types do gravitate toward animals. I don't see what any of this has to do with anything."

Wetzon cradled the phone and trained the flashlight full into Smith's eyes. "Take that, bitch," she said. "For Izz and me and every animal lover in this world."

Smith covered her eyes. "It was a joke, for pity sakes. You think you're the only one with a sense of humor?"

"I beg your forgiveness," Wetzon said facetiously. "I think I'll pop in on Dr. Bowers on my way down tomorrow."

In the second bedroom, which looked as if Micklynn used it as a storeroom, were papers, recipes, bills, letters from happy clients, all in individual bins, all labeled.

Ellen's room was almost pathologically motel room neat and without the odds and ends girls collected that would have given it some kind of personality.

Wetzon shook her head. "I don't understand the anonymity. It's as if someone went through the whole place and cleaned out everything personal."

"Try the speed dial, sweetie, then we can leave."

There it was again. Speed dialing ranked with call waiting in Wetzon's mind as particularly narcissistic living improvements. Just as digital clocks that flashed the time kept children from learning how to tell time, and cash registers that told you what the change was kept people from learning how to make change, so with speed dialing phone numbers would also be forgotten.

As for call waiting, it was just plain rude. What was wrong with a nice old-fashioned busy signal?

The first response on Ellen's speed dial was loud music, then *"Yeah, man, you got Todd. Leave a message."*

"Todd Cameron," Wetzon said. "What's the matter?"

"I have this spooky feeling someone's moving around downstairs. Hurry up."

The next number was A.T.'s, and the last turned out to be Hem Barron's office. Not such a surprise.

"Isn't it odd," Wetzon said, "for a teenager not to have a lot of friends? Her speed dial should be full of girls' numbers, if not boys'."

"Why are you being so judgmental? Ellen is very like I was at her age."

"One, I'm not being judgmental. And two, maybe that's why you're drawn to her. Personally, I think she's manipulative."

"Sweetie . . ." In the darkness the hurt in Smith's voice seemed magnified. "Do you think I'm manipulative?"

"Of course." She grinned at Smith. "You always manipulate me to get me to do things you want me to do."

"For your own good."

"Really?"

"Humpf. I have only two words to say to you." Smith was chortling audibly.

"Oh, yeah?"

Smith leaned against the doorjamb and folded her arms. "Bill Veeder," she said. "Now let's get out of here."

"Smugness does not become you."

They went back down the stairs and now stood in the middle of the living room. "So what do we have?" Wetzon said.

"Nothing." Smith opened the doors of the armoire, then cocked her head. "Did you hear something?"

"No."

"Shush. I think it came from downstairs."

"Probably from the street."

"I guess." She shuffled through the contents of the armoire. "Micklynn really surprises me. She's not what I expected."

"What do you mean?" Wetzon checked the windowsills, peered through the slats of the blinds down to the street. It was very quiet.

"She was so neat and orderly. And such a yuppie after all."

"I told you, this is not indicative of who she was."

"And then there's that serious briefcase."

"What serious briefcase?"

"The one all the way back in the closet. Don't look at me like that, sugar. It was empty. Read my lips. E-m-p-t-y. Otherwise, I would have mentioned it. Where are you going?"

Wetzon rushed up the stairs. In Micklynn's bedroom, she threw open the closet door and crawled inside. Her hand touched an expanse of soft leather. She grabbed it and pulled it out just as Smith entered the room.

"See, I told you it was empty."

"You're right." Wetzon flashed the light on the saddle-leather case. "It's also not Micklynn's. Look."

Gold initials near the handle caught the light. SLG.

"Who the hell is that?" Smith asked.

"I don't know what the L stands for," Wetzon said, "but the S and G are Sheila Gelber."

chapter 48

"We should probably put it back where it was," Wetzon said.

"I think we should leave it here on the bed, sugar. It's proof Micklynn killed the Gelber woman."

"No, it's not. It's circumstantial. And who's to say it wasn't planted?" She thought for a minute. "The police have been through here already, because the tape was on the door. I bet someone meant for it to be found."

"They'll probably talk to us again, babycakes, so let's coordinate our stories."

"It's very simple," Wetzon said. "We were never here. I mean, I was never here after Micklynn died and you never saw her—alive—after your party."

Smith's smile was so feline Wetzon expected to see

her lick her paws. "That's not entirely true, sugar." She blew on her fingers and rubbed them under her collarbone. "I have to admit I was instrumental—A.T. and I, actually—in bringing Ellen and Mickey to their senses. We met downstairs, sort of a peace initiative, you know. Ellen is so smart. She saw the possibilities immediately. After all, Mickey was Ellen's only living relative. They needed each other. Mickey was so self-destructive and the business is . . . well . . . rather lucrative."

"Why do I think you're not talking about family values?"

"Because we're not, sweetie pie. We're talking about money. Of course, that's not what we said to Micklynn."

"Of course."

"It appeared that the major stumbling block in their relationship was that dreadful boy, Todd Cameron. And Ellen agreed she would stop seeing him. May I say there was a tearful reunion?"

"Well, we know how faithfully she kept to that, because we saw Todd coming from the pier as we were arriving. And Ellen admitted he was there."

"It was very indiscreet of her, but she's still a child. She doesn't understand adult thinking."

"Oh, please, Smith. She obviously understands money. But it's too bad, all of it."

Smith put the briefcase back on the floor of the closet and closed the door. "Too bad?"

"Never mind," Wetzon said. "I think we should get going."

They tiptoed down the stairs.

"Don't you want to take a quick look around at The Groaning Board kitchen?"

"What time is it? I promised Twoey I'd meet him . . ."

Wetzon flashed the light on her wrist. "It's almost eleven."

That's when the sound of something shattering came from the room below. They froze. Wetzon switched off the light.

"Damn," Smith whispered. Someone was moving around downstairs.

"Shshsh." They were trapped. Whoever it was down there was looking for something. "Another few minutes and he'll be up here."

"Can you believe it, a prowler," Smith whispered, outraged. "Call 911."

"*We're* prowlers, for godsakes, or have you forgotten?" Still, it wasn't a bad idea. Wetzon groped for and found the phone on the kitchen wall, called 911, and using a Spanglish accent, mumbled, "Dere's a prowler adda Groaning Board." She gave the address. "Come quick. Who I am? I'm coming out of restaurant wit my boyfrent." She hung up and grabbed Smith. "Come on."

"Shshsh. I want to see if he's still down there."

"Oh, please, Smith, come on. Before we get caught here. How will we explain?" She opened the door and started down the outside stairs just as sirens began to whine.

Smith threw on all the lights.

"Fuck!" a voice cursed below.

Wetzon ran, Smith right behind her. They were on the sidewalk when the cop car made the turn and came toward them. Putting her arm around Smith's waist, Wetzon said, "You are my own true love."

Smith giggled.

They crossed the street like slightly tipsy lovers and walked past the swirling lights, then stopped, obtrusively, to stare, as any innocent citizen of New York would. The Groaning Board was blazing with light. While Smith and Wetzon and others watched, the cops pounced on a figure attempting to sneak out of the shop. He was dressed not so differently from Smith and Wetzon, all in black, like a cat burglar.

This cat burglar, however, had a familiar face. It was Hem Barron.

chapter 49

Veterinary medicine was a good profession for a New
Yorker. The pet industry was booming.

Dr. Jennifer Bowers ran a busy animal medical clinic
in the heart of cat and dog country on the Upper East
Side on East Eightieth Street.

Wetzon arrived at 600 East Eightieth Street at eight-
thirty in the morning and gave her name to a skinny girl
whose jeans were carefully sliced with airholes in the
knees, the edges evenly frayed. The waiting room had a
gamey odor.

"Where is your pet?" The girl peered at Wetzon as if
she had a snake up her sleeve.

"At home. I need to ask Dr. Bowers a quick question,
so I'll pay for a visit." Wetzon handed the girl her busi-

ness card and took her seat next to a droopy golden retriever with a mangled ear. "Phoebe doesn't bite," her owner informed Wetzon and then went back to the monologue of reassurance she was murmuring into the animal's good ear.

Across from Wetzon, a man cuddled a wheezing Persian.

When a woman and a small boy in tears arrived carrying a whimpering dachshund with an apparent broken front paw, the whole waiting room erupted with human and animal suffering. The golden wet the floor.

Thus it was almost ten o'clock before Wetzon was shown into Jennifer Bowers' surgery. Dr. Bowers, an attractive, snub-nosed woman in her early thirties, had a nice tan and sun-streaked blond hair pulled back in a ponytail. The preppie look, as befitted female residents of the Upper East Side. A white lab coat semi-protected good-quality khakis. After a no-nonsense handshake, Dr. Bowers said, "What can I do for you, Ms. Wetzon?"

"My firm is looking into the death of Micklynn Devora."

"Yes, I read about it. I knew her, of course. You're aware of that or you wouldn't be here." She pointed to one of three dilapidated plastic chairs. "Have a seat."

Wetzon sat gingerly. The chair was lopsided and someone had taken a bite out of the seat. "You were on her speed dial. I understand she owned a cat. Jimmy."

"Yes, Jimmy. A pure Angora. A classic, with a royal personality."

"He died recently?"

"It was pretty awful." Dr. Bowers pulled out the drawer of a filing cabinet and riffled through it.

"What was?"

"Here," Dr. Bowers said, removing a folder. She opened it. "It was appalling." She sat down next to Wetzon. "I've never seen anything like it, and I've seen a lot, let me tell you."

"What happened to Jimmy?"

She smiled slightly. "Jimmy had the soul of an alley cat. He was a wanderer. He'd slip out a window at night and go off. I hate to think it was someone in the neighborhood, someone who knew Micklynn, but it had to have been."

Squirming in her rickety chair, Wetzon steeled herself for the rest. It was impossible not to think of Izz . . .

Dr. Bowers sighed. "Someone soaked Jimmy with gin and set him on fire. He died a horrible death."

Wetzon's morning coffee and orange juice threatened reflux. She was having trouble breathing. "Why do you think it was someone Micklynn knew?"

"Because whoever did it scooped up what was left of Jimmy and put him in a plastic bag with the empty gin bottle, then hooked it over Mickey's front door. Her niece found it and freaked out. Micklynn fell apart completely, and who could blame her?"

"Did anyone report it to the police?"

"I did. The cops walked around and talked to a few people, but nothing came of it, and Micklynn wouldn't cooperate. If you ask me, I think she knew who did it. The niece too. A friendship that had gone bad. Something like that."

"My God. The person who did that has to be sick and full of hate. Do you do autopsies on animals?"

"Sometimes. But really, Ms. Wetzon, I saw what was left of Jimmy. It wouldn't have told us much. And Mickey was devastated. An autopsy would have prolonged the agony and not allowed her to mourn."

Taking out her checkbook, Wetzon thanked Dr. Bowers for her time. "How much do I owe you?"

The doctor waved her off. "No charge," she said.

On First Avenue, Wetzon gulped great breaths of exhaust-filled air. What a horrible thing. First Jimmy, then Sheila. And last, Micklynn. What did it all mean? Was it possible that all three deaths were connected? What if Sheila had flipped out and killed Jimmy, and Micklynn killed Sheila for revenge? No. Not possible. Everything she'd learned about Sheila told Wetzon that Sheila was a caring person. She pushed the thought away.

Why had Todd Cameron tried to push Wetzon off Hem Barron's roof?

She began walking, then stopped. Something had come to her out of left field. What if someone was killing off the people around Ellen, to isolate her? But why?

And what was Hem, the cat burglar, searching for at The Groaning Board last night?

No doubt Bill Veeder was at the Nineteenth Precinct right now dealing with Hem's rap sheet. The thought tickled her. He'd left a message for Wetzon at eleven the night before, saying he was home, where was she?

Well, he hadn't really said it like that, but she'd enjoyed hearing it. He was so goddam sure of himself. She'd called him back at midnight and left a sultry, "Hi, talk to you tomorrow," with no explanation of where she'd been.

She chose to walk the thirty-one blocks to the office and by the time she turned on Forty-ninth Street, she was feeling much better, though the image of Jimmy hovered in her mind.

The office was wonderfully cool. "Good morning," Wetzon said.

Darlene looked up. "Good morning, Wetzon." She had an odd expression on her face. "Smith said you were to come up the minute you got here."

"Any messages?" She shivered suddenly and slipped on her jacket.

Without a word, Darlene handed her a packet of pink slips about an inch thick.

"Wow! What's going on? It's not even eleven o'clock. Did the market crash?" She flipped through the messages as she climbed the steps. Bill Veeder. Carlos. Laura Lee. Arthur. Bill again. Mort Hornberg. Louie. Bill Veeder. Nina Wayne. "My God," she muttered, truly puzzled.

Smith was on the phone when Wetzon walked in. She looked up, with obvious relief. "Hold on, sweetie, she just walked in." She put her hand over the mouthpiece. "It's Bill, sugar. He's called four times. He's just desolate about—"

"Did something happen to Evelyn?" She set her bag and briefcase on the floor behind her desk.

"No. Here take the goddam phone. It's the newspapers. You're acting like you haven't seen them."

"What newspapers? I've seen the *Journal* and the *Times.*"

Smith took her hand away from the mouthpiece and spoke into it. "She hasn't seen them yet. Here, talk to each other." She thrust the phone at Wetzon and reached for the stack of tabloids on her desk.

Perplexed, Wetzon took the phone. "Bill? What's wrong? Are you okay?" Then she thought, it's Silvestri. Something's happened to Silvestri. Panic began to creep into her bones.

"Leslie," Bill said. "I'm so sorry this happened." He sounded awful. ". . . but we'll deal with it together."

"Please," Wetzon said. "Did someone get hurt? Shot? Die? I'm sorry. Smith is flapping some papers at me . . . hold on . . ."

Smith was doing just that. "Read this," she insisted, sticking the *Daily News* under Wetzon's nose. She pointed to A. J. Benza's column. Wetzon focused and began to read. *"Just because—"* Her eyes shot ahead. "Oh, no."

"Leslie?"

She sat down at her desk; a wave of nausea swept over her. "Bill. I'll call you back." She began to read.

Just because your wife has been in an Alzheimer's fugue for eight years doesn't mean you can't go out and have some fun once in a while. Of course we hate to judge anyone over the temptations of a summer's day, but our spies spotted criminal defender Bill Veeder in Central Park the other day rolling around in the grass with the Legslie (get it?) blonde who danced up a storm in the *Combinations* revival eighteen months ago.

Wetzon hid her face in her hands. "Take it away," she said.

"There's more from my namesake in the *Post*," Smith said.

"Read it to me."

" *'Bashful (who are we kidding?) Billy Veeder, that very sexy, very married high-profile mouthpiece, has been quietly squiring around town a new lady who looks a lot like the diminutive former Broadway dancer we used to know before she struck it rich on Wall Street. Guesses anyone?'* "

"She didn't really say 'guesses anyone'?"

"She did." Although Smith's words and manner were solicitous, she seemed to be enjoying the drama altogether too much.

When her private line rang, Wetzon begged Smith to answer it, which Smith did, her eyes limpid. She handed the phone to Wetzon. "It's Bill."

"Bill . . ."

"I've got to be in court in an hour."

"I feel like a bimbo."

"I'm sorry. We can't let this make a difference. It's just something that happened. I want to see you tonight."

"I'd rather go home and hide."

"You can't do that."

"Oh, no?"

"I'll call you at home later."

"Sure," she said. She hung up the phone. "I didn't think this far ahead."

"It'll be okay. It'll blow over. You have to look at the whole picture."

"Yeah, I'm a cheap, trashy B movie."

"Do you have my shopping bag?"

"What shopping bag?"

"The one from last night."

"Jesus, Smith, don't you have it?"

Smith answered with a nervous smile and a shake of her head. "I can't find it. I thought I had it with me, but I didn't have it when I got home."

Wetzon started laughing. "Oh, God, life with you is a trip."

"Humpf," Smith said, running her fingers through her dark curls. "No one will ever know it was ours."

"Ours? Well, I dearly hope not. Did you take any messages for me? I take it you checked my voice mail, didn't you?"

Smith grinned. "Nothing important really. Oh, there was a call from your doctor. I wrote it down for you."

"My doctor? Oh, you mean Dr. Jennifer Bowers?"

"No, a . . . wait." She bent and dug around in her wastebasket.

"You threw one of my messages away with all of yours? You are absolutely outrageous. What am I going to do with you?" But she was laughing again and somehow Smith had driven away her distress, at least for a time.

"Here it is," Smith said triumphantly. "I told you he was a doctor. His name is Dr. Orson Furgason."

chapter 50

Wetzon folded the pink message slip into accordion pleats. "Dr. Orson Furgason is the headmaster of the Colton School, which our Ellen attends and where Sheila Gelber taught English."

"Why would he be calling you, sugar?"

"I spoke to him about Sheila Gelber and left my card. I sort of implied that we were working for their insurance company trying to avoid bad publicity or a lawsuit."

"Don't tell me he didn't ask for your credentials."

"I'm telling you. He never even asked me to verify the insurance company."

"Ha! I love these brilliant academics who always lord their degrees over you." Smith was silent for a moment, her eyes half closed. Then she said, "Who insures

Colton anyway? See if you can find out. Maybe I can do a little business development." Smith went into the kitchen and brought Wetzon a mug of coffee.

"Thanks, partner. How would you suggest I do that? I'm supposed to know the insurance company intimately. Anyway, the dear doctor was scared shitless about the reputation of his precious school, not to mention his job. He probably wants to know if Micklynn's death is going to connect to Sheila's, and therefore point to Colton."

"Bo-ring. Now, sweetie pie, try to be sophisticated and not let what happened today come between you and Bill. I love you both. You're good for each other. Anyone can see that."

"Then why do I feel like a bimbo?"

"You'll snap out of it. And by the way, sugar, you don't look like a bimbo."

"Thank you very much. But then, what does a bimbo really look like?"

"Darlene."

Wetzon giggled. "But she has no beau as far as I can see. Only that potbellied pig."

"Well, you're wrong there."

"Really? Have you seen him?"

Smith pursed her lips. "No, but I've heard them talking."

"You've heard them talking but you haven't seen them?"

"The telephone, sweetie, is an amazingly versatile instrument. Little recording devices can be attached—"

"Smith, really. You're spying on our employees. You listen to my voice mail. Please don't tell me any more. You are so goddam nosy."

"Oh, pu-leeze. One of us has to take the initiative. We'll be able to stop any potential problem before it arises. Tell me you don't love me for it." She said it with a shockingly ingenuous smile.

Despite herself, Wetzon's eyes teared. She cleared her throat. "Right now, I love you for being there for me." Checking her watch, she added, "And now it's time to make my daily call to Keith Pullman." She punched in his direct number.

Smith groaned. She pressed the intercom button. "Max, sweetie, are you there? Say you're there."

"Good morning, Smith. Good morning, Wetzon."

"Max, sugar, Wetzon and I want to order lunch. Two tunas, one on a toasted bagel, no mayo, one on white toast, lots of mayo." She looked over at Wetzon. "Okay?"

Wetzon nodded, listening as the number rang in her ear. "And rice pudding. A double order."

"Keith Pullman."

"Hi, Keith, this is Wetzon."

"Wetzon, Wetzon, what can I say? I can't talk to you now. Call me tomorrow right after the Close."

As Wetzon hung up, Smith's private line rang. "Xenia Smith here." She looked over at Wetzon. "She's all right. Aren't you, sugar?"

Wetzon shook her head.

"Here, talk to Twoey." She held the phone out to Wetzon, who came around her desk to Smith's.

"Hi, Twoey. I feel humiliated."

"Hold your head up, kiddo. You have a lot of people who love you."

"Thanks, Twoey." She handed the phone back to Smith, who made kissy sounds and hung up. "He's so nice," Wetzon said.

"Sometimes too nice—"

"Smith!"

"See, now don't you feel better?"

"Not really. I feel like shit."

"I was putting this off, sugar, but that woman detective, Mulcahy, called. Dick Tracy would like to talk to us later today. I said four-thirty would be okay."

"Oh, God, Smith, I can't. Not now. You do it. Tell him I had a conflict and that I'll call and schedule another time. I can't face him right now"—she waved her hand at the newspapers—"after this."

"It'd be better to get it over with. You've got to get him out of your system so that—" The intercom buzzed. "Max?"

"Mark for you, Smith. Carlos for Wetzon."

Grabbing her phone, Smith cooed, "Babycakes . . ."

God, Wetzon thought, she still treated her nineteen-year-old son as if he was ten. She blocked out Smith's voice and picked up the phone. "If I wasn't so goddam depressed, I would say, 'Hi, babycakes.' "

"Birdie, darling, I know. I know." His voice was so kind, so dear, so loving. She began to weep. "Oh, Birdie."

"Carlos, I'm in trouble."

"Now, you listen. Are you listening?"

"Yes." She sniffled into a tissue.

"Madam will put on her dancing shoes and Carlos will collect her at six-thirty at her humble abode. No excuses. Okay?"

"Okay." She dried her eyes after she hung up. When her private line rang, she reached for it without thinking. Heavy breathing. The breather was back again. She hissed into the phone, then followed Metzger's instructed routine, hang up, press star fifty-seven, hang up. As soon as she did, the phone rang again. "Yes?" she answered cautiously.

"Leslie," Bill Veeder said. He seemed surrounded by noise. "How are you doing?"

"Not great. Where are you?"

"At the Federal Building. Can we have dinner?"

"No. I'll call you at home later." She cradled the phone quickly, not giving him a chance to plead his case, which she knew very well was without foundation.

"Lunch," Darlene called cheerily, coming up the stairs with a brown paper shopping bag.

"That was fast," Smith said.

"I was going out for mine, so I picked up yours too."

"Such a dear, isn't she, Wetzon?"

"Oh, yes, absolutely," Wetzon said. She smoothed the accordion-pleated message with her palm and dialed the number Dr. Furgason had left. It was a 516 area code, which meant Long Island. East Hampton, no doubt, where the parents of Colton scholars congregated of a summer. A man's voice answered on the third ring.

"Dr. Furgason? This is Leslie Wetzon. Am I disturbing you at home?"

"Thank you for returning my call, Ms. Wetzon. The school is closed down for the next three weeks while we're being painted. Ms. Wetzon, I was wondering how your investigation was coming along, particularly in the light of Ms. Devora's rather shocking death. I want to be sure that the Colton School is not tainted by this affair in any way."

"Thus far, Dr. Furgason, I believe we are in the clear, although the police may want to talk with you—especially if they learn of the scene Ms. Devora made about Ellen Moore's losing the chance at Hopkins to Stacy Morgenstern."

After a rather long and peculiar pause, Dr. Furgason said, "I'm not following you, Ms. Wetzon."

"The anti-Semitic accusations . . . Dr. Furgason. You told me about the scene Micklynn Devora—"

"I'm sorry, Ms. Wetzon. I did tell you about it, but I must not have made myself clear. The woman involved in the regrettable incident, the woman who made the accusations, was not Ms. Devora."

"Then who—?"

"My understanding is that it was Ms. Devora's partner, a Ms. A. T. Barron."

chapter 51

A. T. Barron answered her phone on the first ring. "Ellen?" Her voice quavered.

"No, it's Leslie Wetzon. I wonder if I can come over and talk with you this afternoon."

"Really, Leslie . . ." The chill was on. "We have nothing to talk about."

"It will only take a few minutes. It's about Micklynn. How is three-thirty or four?"

"Oh, very well. Make it four."

"How is Ellen doing?"

"She's very upset. You and Micklynn were becoming thick as thieves, so I'm sure she must have told you. First Ellen's father, then her mother. Now Micklynn."

"It's very understandable. I'll see you at four."

The entrance to the block-long Beaux Arts building where A.T. lived was just off Riverside Drive in the Eighties. It had vaulting frescoed ceilings and a marble lobby that went clear through to the next block, interrupted only by a courtyard with three marble nymphs holding a politely gushing fountain.

In spite of the fact that the pre-World War I building had been designated a landmark and repairs were costly within the guidelines set by the Landmarks Commission, when an apartment came on the market, a rare event, it was the seller's bonanza. The rooms were palatial, with wood paneling, marble-manteled working fireplaces, yawning ceilings and gigantic bathrooms.

Landmark it might be, Wetzon thought, but the plumbing was old. How fragile the pipes and how often the leaks?

From Seventy-second Street to Ninety-sixth Street, Riverside Drive was a gracious winding road leading up to the westernmost part of the Upper West Side. Elegant town houses and apartment buildings looked out on Riverside Park, a rather eccentric boat basin at Seventy-ninth Street, and the Hudson River, across which could be seen the cliffs of New Jersey.

It was an expensive place to live, as well as hideously cold. In the winter, west winds whipped without mercy across the frigid Hudson, rattling and at times even breaking windows along the Drive with their ferocity. But just now the Drive was lyrical with greenery, and the Hudson was becalmed and flecked with white sails.

The sky was a serene blue and birds held conversations in the trees. On an arching lamppost a row of pigeons sat wing to wing as if waiting for the No. 5 bus down Riverside Drive, which never came, or came three at once, each on the other's tail. Wetzon knew from experience, because she'd lived on Riverside Drive when she first came to New York.

Bucolic was the word for the afternoon, for the area, but she'd come here to talk about murder.

Wetzon gave her name to A. T. Barron's doorman, a shriveled man with an oversized, almost musical-comedy mustache. In his dark blue uniform and peaked hat and white epaulets, the man looked like a musical-comedy New York cop. He buzzed up announcing her, then told her to take the appropriate bank of elevators to 8A.

A.T. stood in her open doorway talking to a tall woman, whose black hair was pulled tight into a bun. Huge glasses magnified her eyes. A grand Chanel purse swung from her shoulder. A.T. wore black, but since she rarely wore any other color, it was unlikely she was in mourning.

The tall woman, who was also in black, gave A.T. an affectionate hug as Wetzon emerged from the elevator. "Take care of yourself, dear." She fixed her sharp eyes on Wetzon.

"This is Leslie Wetzon, Enid," A.T. said. "Enid Nemy . . ."

Nemy and Wetzon shook hands. Nemy did interviews and character pieces for the *Times* and chic magazines. Had Nemy done a quick double take on Wetzon after hearing her name? Or was Wetzon's paranoia getting the best of her?

"Bye, Enid, dear. Thank you." A.T. held the door for Wetzon, then followed her inside and shut the door. "Anita," she called. "Ice teas." She looked at Wetzon. "Okay?"

"Fine."

When there was no response from Anita, A.T. said, "I'll get them. Go on into the living room." She waved her hand in no particular direction, opened a side door, and went off.

The foyer was a huge square; it ended in an arch leading to another huge square. Wetzon wandered forward and eventually found the living room full of plants, overstuffed sofas, fat easy chairs with ottomans. Persian rugs left more than enough of the elaborate inlaid parquet floor visible.

Wetzon had absolutely no idea what she was going to ask A.T., but she knew she needed to verify what Dr. Furgason had told her and she hoped to get an explanation.

The plants were profuse in clay pots and jardinieres; the azaleas were aflower, spicing the area with their deadly essence. She sat on one of the easy chairs as A.T. set a tray with two tall saucered glasses of iced tea on a book-laden Brancusi coffee table. The lemon slices were wrapped in cheesecloth.

A.T. handed Wetzon a napkin and one of the glasses. "Lemon?"

"Yes, please. You were expecting Ellen when I called. Did you hear from her?" Wetzon squeezed the lemon into the tea and dropped the remnant onto the saucer. When she sipped the tea, it was fragrant with mint and . . . something else, something pleasant.

"Yes. Not long after I spoke with you. She'd gone over to Colton to pick up some of her papers and talk with one of her teachers. She'll be home soon."

Oh, sure. "I suppose she'll stay on with you now that Micklynn's gone?"

"I'd love to have her. Ellen's like a daughter to me, and of course she's only sixteen. She has another year at Colton before college."

"It's costly supporting a child these days, and then there's college . . ."

"I'm sure Micklynn left enough for Ellen to be independent."

"Oh, I see."

"Do you? I suggest you tell me why you're here," A.T. said. She sat on the sofa like a coiled spring. She hadn't touched her tea.

"My partner has been telling me what a fine girl Ellen is and we wondered if she's going away to camp or summer school because . . . we may have a part-time job for her with us. That is, if she'd like to learn executive search."

"Well." A.T.'s expression turned from suspicious to moderately cool. "That's a nice thought. I'll ask her, of course, but I don't think she'll want to do it."

"Is she going to summer school?"

"No. She's brilliant, you know. She'd won a place at Johns Hopkins, but the teacher in charge of it chose someone less worthy than Ellen."

Wetzon set her glass down on the tray. She felt a little queasy. Maybe it was the vet's story about Jimmy. Maybe it was the gossip columns and the emotional upheaval. . . . Maybe it was everything, culminating in Micklynn's death. What was she doing here anyway?

"Are you all right, Leslie?" A.T. asked. "You've lost your color."

"I'm fine. It's the heat, I guess. What a shame Ellen isn't going to Johns Hopkins. How could that happen when she won the place?"

"You tell me. I have nothing against Jews, some of my best friends are Jewish, but, really, when the teacher, who is Jewish, chooses another child, who's also Jewish, over Ellen, don't you think that's questionable? We protested the decision."

"By *we*, you mean Micklynn?"

"Oh, no. Micklynn did nothing, absolutely nothing. Ellen was very hurt. I tried everything in my power to get the headmaster to see how suspect the decision was. But then, of course, the teacher happened to be one of Micklynn's friends."

"Oh, that's the woman who died. Sheila Gelber."

"Yes."

"Micklynn told me she wanted to go into a mail-order business with Sheila."

"That was one of Micklynn's many illusions. Or delusions, I should say. Our partnership contract would never have allowed it. Micklynn got crazy ideas when she was drinking, which was almost constant over the last two years."

"I wonder if you know that Micklynn hired me to try to find who killed Sheila Gelber."

The spring uncoiled. A.T. sprang from the sofa waving her arms. "See. See what I mean about delusional? I hope she didn't pay you out of our company funds?"

"She paid me with a personal check. I didn't think she was delusional. I think she was a very unhappy woman." Wetzon rose. "I won't keep you any longer. I hope you'll mention our offer to Ellen."

"I will," A.T. said warily.

As they moved back down the gallery toward the door, Wetzon said, "Your plants are very beautiful."

"Yes, they are, aren't they?"

"Didn't you tell me once that you couldn't grow anything? A black thumb is what you said."

A.T. smiled. "A black thumb. Yes, that's me. Can't grow even a cactus. The plants are Ellen's. She's a wonder."

Wetzon took the elevator to the lobby. Ellen had the wherewithal; A.T. had the same. If Ellen thought she'd inherit, she had motive. And the partnership agreement, as written, gave A.T. a superb motive for murder.

Minnie Wu was a callous bitch who was insanely jealous of every woman Hem looked at, and Minnie and Hem had a greenhouse full of azaleas. Hem wanted to do The Groaning Board IPO and Micklynn stood in his way.

Then there was still the inexplicable Todd Cameron.

She got out of the elevator and walked toward the lobby entrance, stopped short. Ellen was in a car in front of the building. As the girl started to get out, Wetzon did an about-face and fast-walked through the courtyard and out via the uptown entrance.

Once outside, she raced around the block to the other entrance in time to see Bill Veeder's black Mercedes make a turn onto the Drive and speed off.

chapter 52

"Birdie, darling, it's a question only you can answer. You're not the first person in the world who's gotten involved with a married man." He spun her around and two-stepped her out of the traffic. Carlos had taken Wetzon to Denim and Diamonds in the Lexington Hotel to dance Western, which meant two-step, couples, and line dancing, the latter a craze these days in New York.

"Not me, Carlos. Never. I always thought about the wife. *The wife*. Bill has a wife in name only."

"How *Back Street* of you, darling."

"See, you're not taking me seriously."

"*Au contraire*. It is definitely a most serious situation you've gotten yourself into."

She tilted her head. Was he twitting her? "You're being his advocate."

"No, I'm your advocate and I always will be."

"The newspapers make me sound like some kind of bimbo."

"I think they call girls like you Twinkies now." He ducked when she swatted him. "Get real, Dear Heart. No way could you ever impersonate either a bimbo or a Twinkie. You're a bit too long in the tooth."

"Thank you. I think."

"And what important, caring people in your life would pay attention to what those columns say?"

"You. Laura Lee."

"No. We read them because they're titillating; what is said in them is meaningless."

"In other words, I'm making a big deal over nothing?"

"No, darling. Not at all. It's your life. You have to decide how important he is to you and whether it's worth how you're feeling."

"Carlos, tell me honestly, what did you think of Silvestri?"

"Hmmm. What a question." He kissed her sweaty forehead and steered her over to the bar. "Bartender, two icy-cold Amstels," he said. When the bottles were produced, he put a five-dollar bill on the counter and opened both bottles, handing one to Wetzon.

"So?"

"So what?" He took an elephant swallow.

"Don't try to get out of it. Silvestri. What did you think? I need to know."

"Okay. I liked him 'cause he loved you."

"But?"

"Who said anything about a but?"

"I'm saying it, I guess. We misunderstood each other all the time. The relationship was such hard work. He was such hard work. We had very little in common. He never really was more than a transient in my life. He never wanted to be more."

"Okay. Okay. You've convinced me."

"I have a fuller relationship with Bill Veeder than I ever had with Silvestri."

"Ahhh, so. Look at it this way." Carlos crossed his eyes. "There is no such animal as a perfect relationship."

"You and Arthur."

"Close. But Arthur is a solid citizen. He's not dangerous. I miss that in my life—the high, the abandon . . . you know . . ." He winked the most lecherous of winks and rolled his hips at her. "You know . . . what you have with Billy Veeder."

"Outrageous. That's what you are."

"An' ole Billy, he's safe too. He ain't gonna ask you to marry him while the wife lives."

"So what are you saying? I should snap out of it?"

"I'm saying, Birdie darling, throw away your white plume and forget about that crap in the papers and do what makes you happy. Does Veeder make you happy? Think about it. You don't have to answer me."

"Yeah."

"It doesn't strike me that you're lonely, babes, and need some man to fulfill you."

"I'm not and I don't, but he does. Does that make sense?"

"Not especially, but that's all right. It doesn't have to make sense to me, just to you. Are you danced out?"

"Yup. Can we walk for a while?"

They strolled onto Lexington Avenue, sated, and headed west. It was on the tip of Wetzon's tongue to say something about Veeder and Ellen, when Carlos said, "Now that we've settled your life problem, tell me about Mickey. She was not exactly what you would call well adjusted and she had a major drinking problem. But suicide?"

"It wasn't suicide, Carlos. She was murdered."

"Birdie, darling, you have murder on the brain. Who would want to murder her?"

"Well, let's see. There's a regular lineup. Hem and A.T. because she refused to allow The Groaning Board to go public. Her cousin's kid, Ellen, because Ellen thought she might inherit. Ellen's boyfriend Todd because Micklynn hated him. For that matter, even Laura Lee and Bill Veeder have financial motives. And then there's Minnie Wu. She's just plain mean. She doesn't need a motive."

"But she did have one, Dear Heart. Although many moons have passed and water's gone under the bridge and gift horses have been looked in the mouth, Min bristles with grudges. She never forgave Mickey for her affair with Hem."

"Poor old Hem. The women just can't stay away from him. Do you mind if we walk up Fifth a way?"

"Where a way?"

"The Museum Tower. Do you mind?"

"Not at all. But don't think I'm going to leave you there just like that."

"Why not?"

"It's eleven o'clock, Birdie darling. What if he's not home. What if he's otherwise engaged?"

"Oh, God, Carlos. Do you think—?"

"I think nothing. We'll just stop and ask the concierge to ring him up. Then we'll see."

"Honestly, Carlos. I am forty years old."

"Don't argue with me, Birdie," he said sternly.

The Museum Tower stood an elegant understatement next door to and above MOMA, the Museum of Modern Art. It was arguably the most expensive multiple dwelling in the City.

The doorman tipped his hat and actually said, "Good evening, Ms. Wetzon." They passed through a revolving door and entered the sleekly modern lobby of natural wood, marble, black leather, and an expressionistic sculpture.

The concierge's desk was high and curved against the left wall. "Good evening, Ms. Wetzon," the concierge said. He was a tall man with the build and demeanor of an airline pilot . . . or an FBI agent.

They all know who I am, Wetzon thought, feeling her cheeks burn. "Would you ring Mr. Veeder, please, and tell him I'm here."

"Certainly." He looked at Carlos. "And you are—"

"I'm not here to see Mr. Veeder," Carlos replied. "I'm Ms. Wetzon's bodyguard."

"Carlos!"

The concierge didn't crack a smile. He picked up the phone and pressed a button. Everyone waited, including the elevator man, who was standing at the bank of elevators.

"Maybe he's not home," Wetzon said.

"Oh, Mr. Veeder," the concierge said. "Ms. Wetzon is here. Yes, sir." He looked at Carlos. "No, sir." He hung up the phone. "He said you're to come right up."

"Please tell him I'm with a friend and ask him if he would come down."

"I'll wait outside, Birdie," Carlos said.

"You can leave me now," she said, going outside with him. "I'll get a cab home."

"I don't think so." Carlos leaned against a car and folded his arms. "My, my," he said, eyes focused beyond her.

She saw Bill coming through the lobby, looking for her. The concierge pointed outside. Veeder wore cut-down, washed-out khakis, a white V-necked tee and loafers without socks.

"I hate men who go sockless in loafers," Wetzon said through her teeth.

"He's gorgeous," Carlos said.

"Yeah. Be still my heart." But it was all bravado. Her heart wasn't still; it bounced around like an adolescent's.

His skin was taut over his cheekbones, his beard a surprisingly ruddy stubble. When he caught sight of her, the tautness disappeared.

She looked at Carlos.

"He loves you," Carlos said in her ear. She gave him an elbow in the ribs. "Oof. What's that for?"

"Acting surprised."

"Leslie." Bill looked at Carlos and stopped.

"Bill, this is my friend Carlos." The two men shook hands.

"Will you come up for a drink?" Bill asked.

"Not tonight. I've interrupted your work and there's a little dog I'm responsible for. I just needed to see you to clear my head." She could feel Carlos grinning like a fool beside her. "Carlos, darling, Bill and I are going to walk to the corner and back."

"I'll be right here, kiddies."

They walked toward Fifth Avenue. "Leslie," he began, "I'm sorry. I was cavalier. I'm not handling this well."

"And I was naive. I didn't see the possible consequences. Don't you think forty is too old to be naive?" She was suddenly self-conscious in her leotard and short skirt, as if he hadn't seen her in less.

"No." The blue eyes blurred.

He's vulnerable, she thought. "Carlos took me line dancing tonight." She curtsied in front of St. Thomas Episcopal and he caught her shoulders.

"Stay with me," he said. "I'll take you home early in the morning."

She shook her head. "Not tonight."

"Tomorrow, then. I'm doing my summation in the morning, the case will go to the jury by noon. The Camerons are coming to the office at five tomorrow."

"I want to be there."

"Come at four-thirty." They turned and began walking back to Carlos. "Are we going to be okay?"

"I don't know." But when she looked at him, she knew. "I almost ran into you this afternoon," she said.

"This afternoon?"

"You were with Ellen."

"Ellen Moore?"

"I think that's the only Ellen we know in common."

"Leslie, I was in court all day. I haven't seen Ellen since that night Micklynn died."

The front door of Wetzon's building was unmanned and unlocked. She made a mental note to call the president of the co-op board and got on the elevator.

When she unlocked her door, there was no shriek, no bark, no sound of paw nails clicking on the floor. Odd. She turned on the light. "Izz?" No response. She went from room to room, turning on the lights, calling Izz. Oh, God, she thought. How can this be?

The buzz from the lobby intercom hardly pierced her panic. All she knew was that Izz was gone.

c h a p t e r   5 3

The persistent buzz from the lobby intercom finally got through to her. Heart thudding in her ears, Wetzon automatically pressed the respond button, screaming into the voice box, "Yes? Yes?"

Static greeted her, then what began to sound like a string of Spanish words: "Saytellhavmissdog."

"What? Rafael, please speak English."

"I speak English," he said, offended.

God, she thought, Izz is gone, stolen, kidnapped, and I have to worry about other people's feelings. "Say again. Slower."

"Your friend he say he take dog overnight, not to worry."

"My friend? My friend? What friend? How did he get in?" Oh, shit. Silvestri. Relief buckled her knees and she went down.

"The policeman," Rafael said. "Everything okay?"

"Okay," she told Rafael. She removed her finger from the button. "Not okay," she said to herself. How could Silvestri be so thoughtless? Anger surged through her like a fever, squeezed tears from her eyes. "No way," she said. "No way." He wasn't going to get away with this. Who cared that she wasn't thinking rationally? She didn't want to be rational.

Without bothering to turn out the lights, she grabbed her bag and left the apartment. It was when she was locking the door that she saw the note: a flimsy piece of scrap paper stuck to the door with Scotch tape. It said: *Les, the guys missed Izz. Will return her tomorrow.* Oh, yeah. I'll bet. He was probably losing, so he thought he'd bring Izz back to poker night and distract the other players.

She got on the elevator. How had she missed the note? She'd been too preoccupied by the events of the day. Also, she'd never told her doormen that Silvestri was not to be admitted. Hey, wait a minute, why was she taking the blame?

In the lobby, Rafael was solicitous. "I'm sorry, Ms. Wetzon."

"It's okay, Rafael. How would you know? Lieutenant Silvestri is not welcome here anymore."

"He had key."

"Not anymore," she repeated firmly. She was going down to Chelsea now to collect her dog and her key, but it was not Rafael's business.

It was almost midnight when the cab pulled up in front of Silvestri's brownstone. The poker players—Metzger, O'Melvany, and three others she didn't know—were coming down the steps a little too boisterous for a weekday night in a quiet neighborhood.

"Go once around the block," she told the driver. "Slowly."

When the taxi approached the brownstone again, the street was empty. She paid the driver and got out.

On the street, she suddenly felt permeable. She'd come to a strange neighborhood to do battle. She'd come without armor or weapon. Just her anger, which percolated like a hysterical coffeepot. She was woman. Did that mean her anger was hysterical?

"Fuck it." She climbed the steps, opened the door, and stuck her finger on the buzzer for 2R. She kept it there an extra-long time, then gave it one more jab.

"Yeah?"

"Bring Izz down here right now," she said.

"Come on up, Les." He pressed the button that released the inside door.

The sound of the buzzer covered her furious "No!" She waited a minute, then buzzed him again.

"Well, where the hell are you?" he demanded.

"I'm not coming up."

"What the hell do you want from me?"

"I want my dog and my keys." She banged her fist on the mailboxes. "You bring them down right now, Silvestri."

"Oh, no, dearie," a cigarette-coated voice shrilled. "That isn't going to do you a bit of good. These boys need honey, not horseradish."

Spinning around, Wetzon saw a mass of curly black hair surrounding a face of pronounced features, all enhanced by makeup. The ophthalmic eyes wore long fake lashes and phony green contacts. The Streisand nose had a diamond stud in one nostril. Thin lips were extended beyond their natural limits by crimson lipstick. The apparition smiled at Wetzon, showing a mass of horsey teeth, and extracted a key from her little gold-mesh purse. "Come on, dearie. Let's beard the lion." She burst into giggles. "Beard the lion." She poked Wetzon. "Get it, dearie?" What Wetzon got was the choking scent of Diamonds—Elizabeth Taylor's, that is.

Wetzon's smile was uncertain. "You live here?"

"Of course, I do." The apparition stuck out her hand, a rather large hand with long gold nails that matched the low-cut strapless sheath she wore with more assurance than Wetzon would have. "Patrice Buchanan, dearie, but I believe in a woman's right to choose. You must be Les."

"How do—"

"No questions, please." Patrice pushed the door open as Silvestri's voice came over the intercom.

"Les? Les? Goddammit . . ."

"If you keep this up, dearie, you'll wake the whole neighborhood," Patrice purred. "Les and I are coming up together. Pour the wine."

"I want him to come down," Wetzon insisted.

"Listen to Patrice, dearie. They like to think they're tough mothers, so we let them win the little ones." She nudged Wetzon through the door, then led her up the stairs.

Patrice wore gold ankle-strapped, high-heeled, open-toed platforms, sheer hose on her long, slim legs.

When they got to the second-floor landing, Patrice stretched her body in the gold sheath and adjusted her bosom. "Keep 'em horny is my motto, dearie," she whispered to Wetzon.

A jean-clad Silvestri stood like the wrath of God in the doorway of his apartment. Izz shrieked and scrambled over his feet, then took flight, aiming for Wetzon, who came around Patrice to catch Izz in midair. "I thought I lost you," Wetzon murmured, burying her face in the wriggling dog's fur.

"I left you a note and told your doorman to tell you."

"Missed both," Wetzon said.

"Come on in. Not you, Patrice."

"Silvestri, dearie, I'm crushed. You ought to be filled with gratitude."

"Oh, I am, I am." He handed Patrice a beer. "Good night."

Patrice took the beer and blew a kiss at him. "Remember what I said, dearie. Honey, not horseradish," she whispered to Wetzon. *"Ciao."* She started up another flight of stairs.

Silvestri's apartment looked as if he'd just moved in. And it smelled of stale cigarettes and beer. Cardboard boxes served as end tables. Plastic shopping bags hung from every doorknob. A card table held two brimming ashtrays, empty beer cans, half a salami sandwich, and the remnants of the last game. Around the table were five folding chairs. A lopsided, lumpy sofa sat against the long wall. No pictures on the walls, no tchotchkes, window shades instead of blinds.

"Do you want a beer?" he asked.

"What's going on with you, Silvestri?" He looked strange to her, familiar and yet not.

He went to the fridge, which was in a tiny kitchen, and took out two Beck's, opening one and handing it to her. "Sit down," he said. He opened his beer and took a long swallow.

Still holding Izz, Wetzon moved one of the folding chairs away from the card table and sat. The chair looked a whole lot safer than the sofa. Exhaustion began to creep in with her first sip of beer.

"You owe me an explanation, if only for what we had together. I think we started falling apart when Sheila Gelber was murdered."

He didn't sit. He shook a cigarette from a half-gone pack and lit it, took a deep, deep drag. "Yeah, I'm smoking again. It's a long story."

"I've got all night."

He walked over to his window and stared out. "Sheila called me twice before she died."

"I thought you said you hadn't spoken to her in—"

"I didn't take the calls, Les. I avoided her because she was the kind of woman who wouldn't let go. When we were together all those years ago, she'd hang on my breath. It was flattering in the beginning, but then it became impossible. When she called twice out of the blue like that, I thought she was trying to get back into my life. But what she was trying to do was get help. She turned to me and I failed her and I'm a cop."

"You couldn't have known."

"It was my job to know."

"But I thought you were working on the case. Why did you take a leave from the Department?"

"I didn't. I went undercover."

"Undercover? By being Bruce Willis' brother, the bartender, at Hem's parties? I don't get it."

"Hem Barron's fingerprints turned up in Sheila's apartment."

chapter   5 4

"How the hell? Boy, if Micklynn had known— How did Hem explain it?"

"He said he paid her a visit to talk about funding her mail-order business."

"The one she and Micklynn planned until A.T. killed it?"

"Supposedly."

"I guess his fingerprints were on file because he once worked for Lehman Brothers in mergers and acquisitions."

"Micklynn was Sheila's friend," Silvestri said, "so she probably made the introduction. Veeder wouldn't let Barron say anything further."

"Micklynn and Sheila had a falling-out. I think Sheila thought Micklynn was making those harassing phone calls."

"For chrissakes, how do you know so goddam much?"

"Silvestri, Micklynn hired me to look into Sheila's death."

"Goddammit, Les!"

"You can't yell at me anymore, Silvestri."

"Fuck that," he said, kicking a chair.

"Before you close your mind, you might consider that I know a lot more about these murders than you think. I can help."

He gave the chair another kick. "I don't know why I—"

"I know stuff you need to know, so shut up and listen," she said. "A. T. Barron gets The Groaning Board, lock, stock, and barrel. It's how their partnership agreement was written. And if Micklynn was murdered—"

"She was."

"Then Ellen Moore thinks she will inherit a lot of money. There was a double-indemnity clause in Micklynn's insurance policy. For death by violence, not self-inflicted. That may be why Ellen didn't think she committed suicide. Then again, Ellen may not know about the policy at all. You can check the policy with Arthur Margolies. Yes, Carlos' Arthur. But be sure not to mention me."

"Up to your old tricks, huh, Les?" She almost caught him in a smile, but it was gone in a minisecond.

"Micklynn wouldn't let Hem and A.T. bring The Groaning Board public. Without Micklynn, the company belongs to A.T. and she can do exactly what she wants, which is make a ton of money by going public and then getting out of the business." Wetzon took a swig of beer and gave Silvestri a hard look. "How did Micklynn die? Did she drown?"

He shook his head. "Poisoned. Same as Sheila."

"Do you know that Micklynn's cat Jimmy was doused with alcohol and set on fire shortly before Sheila was killed? Micklynn found what was left of him in a bag at her front door. Sheila had broken off their friendship and was behaving strangely. My premise is that Sheila thought Micklynn had something to do with the horrible phone calls. And I think Micklynn may have thought Sheila had something to do with Jimmy's death."

"Jesus. How the hell did you find out about the cat?"

"I'm a good detective, Silvestri, but because I don't work your way, you don't give me any respect."

He dropped to his knees in front of her. "See, I'm giving you respect."

She stuck out her foot to push him over, but he grabbed her ankle, and they stared at each other. Then he set her foot on the floor and got up and went back to his post at the window.

"A.T. made a scene at Ellen's school—the Colton School—because Sheila chose another girl over Ellen for a special summer program at Johns Hopkins. A lot of anti-Semitic language was bandied about. Did you know about that?"

He turned away from the window. "No. Metzger's people did the interviews at the school. There was no mention of anything like that."

"Ellen's boyfriend, Todd Cameron, is the one who tried to toss me off the roof at Hem and Minnie Wu's party."

"Why the fuck didn't you tell me the night it happened?"

"I didn't know until I found the cross from his earring caught in my . . . um . . . dress . . . later that night . . ."

He folded his arms as if he knew why she was fumbling. "Where is it? The earring."

"Um . . . Bill has it. Todd's father is Judge Cameron. Bill's going to talk to the family tom—" She looked at her watch. It was quarter to two. "Today, at five in his office."

"Anything else you haven't told me?"

"Did you know that Micklynn and Hem had an affair and Minnie beat her up pretty badly? And that Minnie also attacked Ellen after she caught Ellen with Hem at Smith's dinner party? Minnie almost strangled her."

"A nest of vipers, all of them."

"Everything is connected, yet nothing fits, does it?" She yawned, covering her mouth. Izz lay across her lap like a hot pillow. Silvestri's air conditioner groaned. Her mind was getting fuzzy. How was she going to tell him about Sheila's briefcase?

"I don't suppose you and your crazy partner organized a little break-in at The Groaning Board Monday night?"

The question caught her with her defenses down. She began to stutter. "I—uh—no—why? Why would you think that? There was a break-in? No kidding."

"Oh, yes."

"Right. I think I read about it. Hem was caught, wasn't he?"

"He swears he never got upstairs. But somebody did."

"Do you believe him? What was he looking for?"

"Business papers. Or so he says."

"Maybe love letters?"

"Maybe. What about you and Xenia?"

"What about us?"

"Why were you there?"

"Who says we were?"

"It was amateur night. A cleaver, crochet hooks, and a brick in a Saks shopping bag."

"A brick?" Smith hadn't mentioned a brick.

"A brick wrapped in Charivari tissue paper."

"Christ."

"And a receipt from Saks made out to Xenia Smith."

"Shit. I'll have to talk to her about that." She grinned at him. "It wasn't my idea."

"You're crazy. You know that? So much for the chain of evidence."

"There's a briefcase with Sheila's initials in the back of Micklynn's closet, Silvestri."

"You found the briefcase. I can't believe it. Our people went all over the place."

She shrugged. "It's there now. It could have been put there afterward. The place looked as if it had been cleaned by an obsessive-compulsive. Not Micklynn's style. When I was there last, it was a mess—papers, cookbooks, magazines, and dust balls, not to mention cat hair over everything."

"It was clean as a whistle when we went over it. I was there myself. Didn't even feel lived in."

"Someone made sure you wouldn't find anything. The briefcase was empty, by the way. If we could only find out why, we'd know who . . ." Her eyelids were getting heavy. "I've got to get home before I konk out."

"You could sleep here."

"Oh, sure."

"I'll take the couch."

"No way. I'll get a cab." She picked up Izz and walked to the door. He followed her down the stairs. "I'm sorry, Les," he said.

"So am I. You're not a domesticated animal. You try, but it doesn't work."

"I love you. There isn't anyone else."

"I know." She did know. Patrice was the wild-haired woman she'd

255

seen him with on the street. "And I love you. So we can be friends. We can't be lovers anymore. It hurts too much."

"Okay," he said. He was solemn and a shade quizzical. "We'll be friends."

A taxi came down the street, and he raised his hand. It stopped in front of the brownstone.

"You can have Izz for your poker games if you want." She shifted the sleeping dog to the crook of her left arm and thrust her hand out to him.

"Thanks, pal," he said. He pulled her to him and kissed her. It wasn't the kiss of a friend.

She got into the cab with Izz and gave the driver her address. Not until they rocketed past Columbus Circle and up Central Park West did she realize Silvestri hadn't returned her keys.

chapter 55

"The perfect meringue," Laura Lee said.

"What perfect meringue?"

"You're not listenin', darlin'. It was the most marvelous interview on the radio this mornin'." Very patiently she repeated, "Arthur Schwartz, the food critic, was discussin' the perfect meringue with Carol Walter. It was sublime."

"Who, pray tell, is Carol Walter?"

Laura Lee groaned. "Where have you been, Wetzon darlin'? Carol Walter is a world-class pastry chef and teacher."

"Laura Lee, darlin', all I know about pastry I learned at Zabar's."

"Then you don't deserve the bread I brought back for you from Pain Poilâne."

"You brought me bread from Paris?"

"Just the most famous bread in the world. A walnut loaf for you. Same for me, plus a sourdough *levain.*"

"How can I ever thank you?"

"Well, you can't and that's all there is to say."

"And how am I going to get this wonderful *pain?*"

"I take it you and the seductive Billy are still an item?"

"Sort of."

"I have a luncheon meeting up there with Hem and A.T. and your lover. I'll leave a bag of *pain* with himself."

"So," Wetzon said, "while the body is still warm, plans for the IPO forge ahead. I read the rumors about it in *Crain's* today."

"Hem's the fuel, darlin'. He's determined to get this done. My company is determined to be the lead underwriter. I made the intros, so I have to see it through, though I must admit I've lost my . . . taste for it. But not a word, since it's not official yet."

"How are you pricing it?"

"We're aimin' at eleven-fifty a share. That would make it attractively priced."

"How many shares?"

"Three million five hundred fifty thousand."

"I wonder if the company can make it without Micklynn."

"If you want to get down and dirty, Micklynn did everythin' she could possibly have done for that company, includin' gettin' herself killed. There was nothin' more she could have added to it even if she were still alive. Except if she were, we wouldn't be about to bring it public."

"So, as it stands now, a few people are going to get very rich."

"That's what it's about, darlin'."

Wetzon hung up. She looked over at her partner, who was holding the phone to her ear, her palm over the receiver. Smith seemed very preoccupied this morning. "It's always about money, isn't it, Smith?"

"Of course," Smith mouthed automatically.

Money, yes. Get cracking, kid, Wetzon told herself. She picked up the phone and called Keith Pullman. "Well, hello, there, Keith."

"Next Tuesday, Wetzon. I promise. Call me next Tuesday at three o'clock sharp."

She smacked down the phone. "Fuck you, Keith, and your call-me-next-whatever. One more time and you're history." A look of absolute horror swept across Smith's face. "And what's the matter with you?" she asked Smith.

Smith cradled the receiver very carefully. "She's giving phone sex."

"Who?" Wetzon was baffled.

"What are we going to do?"

"What does it have to do with us?"

"It has everything to do with us. She's using our phones to do it."

"Wait a minute, Smith, are we talking about Darlene?"

"Who else?"

"And you're *listening* to her do it? You're as bad as she is."

"She has to go."

"Maybe it's a misunderstanding, Smith. She'd be stupid to use our phone. We ought to have proof. If we fire her, she might sue us for wrongful termination."

"Okay. I'm going to buy a little recording device and get her on tape. We can't have someone like that working for us."

"I have to admit I've never liked her, but she's brought in a lot of money."

"Not lately, or haven't you noticed, sugar?"

"It's been slow."

"You're still making placements."

"Not in abundance. Still, I won't be unhappy to see her go, and that's being honest, Smith. There's always been something odd about her. But next time I want to be included in the hiring process."

To which Smith replied with her famous last words: "Of course, baby-cakes."

Having had only about three and a half hours of sleep the previous night, Wetzon was dragging by the time she arrived at Bill Veeder's office for the meeting with the Cameron family. She'd washed her face and redone her makeup before she left the office, but the heat and sleep deprivation were taking their toll.

Veeder, in spite of his optimistic prediction, was still in court.

"He's running a little late," Mrs. Copeland said. "He said you're to wait in his office. Would you like something cold to drink?"

"Iced tea, no sugar, lots of lemon." Wetzon walked down the hallway to Bill's office, thinking maybe she could catch a nap on his sofa.

The office was cool and serene. No papers were on the desk. She sat down on the sofa. The Hispanic man she'd seen before brought her a tall glass of iced tea and left. The sofa was very soft. Much as she'd like the nap, it wouldn't do if she was groggy during the meeting. She stood and walked to the window, looking down at Rockefeller Center. Every summer the skating rink became an outdoor café full of greenery and umbrellaed tables.

"Oh, excuse me," a voice said.

Wetzon turned. A small, gray-haired woman had come into the room. She was carrying several manila folders.

"I'm Carolyn, Mr. Veeder's secretary," the woman said.

Wetzon smiled. "I'm Leslie Wetzon." They had spoken on the phone but had never met. "I'm here for the Cameron meeting."

"It's so nice to finally meet you." Carolyn shook Wetzon's hand. "Bill's on his way. I just wanted to leave these papers for him. The Camerons haven't arrived yet." She set the folders on Veeder's desk and left the room.

Wetzon sat down on the sofa again and took a sip of tea. The glass was sweating profusely onto the coffee table. She wiped up the flood with her napkin. What a mess. She looked in her purse. Only a few tissues left. Maybe Bill had some in his desk. She got up and walked over to the desk. The folders Carolyn had left were in a neat pile. Staring at the folders, Wetzon told herself: Remember what you said to Smith.

But I'm here, she thought. No one will ever know I've taken a peek. The top folder was labeled: *The Groaning Board IPO.* Nothing new there. She moved it slightly with the tip of her finger so she could look at the label of the next folder. *Rubenstein,* it said. She opened it and saw that Bill had taken the recent case that had been in the news, the one of the husband who'd murdered his wife and her lover, another woman.

She clicked her tongue against her teeth. Keep your comments to yourself, she thought.

By moving the Rubenstein file a fraction she was able to see the label on the last folder. It said: *Barron-Moore.* She set the other folders aside and opened this one. A contract of some sort faced up at her. Her eyes flicked over it.

The aura in the office suddenly began to vibrate. She heard Bill's voice in the hall outside his office talking to Jonathon Nazario, his associate.

Quickly, she slapped the Barron-Moore file shut and set the others on top of it. When he came through the door, she was sitting on the sofa drinking her iced tea.

He looked so good in his dark blue pinstripe, crisp blue striped shirt. Just his presence gave her a rush, made her smile.

"Jury went out and came right back with an acquittal," he told her. He was jubilant. "We'll celebrate tonight—after we deal with this Cameron business." He removed a clean shirt from a closet shelf, took off his jacket, the gun and harness, his gold cuff links, and his shirt. She watched him unbutton the clean shirt and slip it on.

"Would you like me to do the buttons?"

"Why not?" He stood waiting for her in the middle of the room.

She did them extra slowly, starting at the bottom, taking her time, making sure her fingers brushed his skin. When she did the last one, he grabbed her hands. "You're a tease," he said.

"But I pay off."

"We'll see about that." He attached his cuff links, tucked his shirttails in, and slipped on his harness again, then his jacket. "I'll be right back with the Camerons. Are you ready?"

"Yup."

"I want you to sit over there next to my desk. Don't say anything unless I ask you."

"Don't say anything?"

"I know it's going to be hard," he said, "because you have so many opinions—"

"Enough. I won't say anything." Well, she would try not to say anything unless . . . Well, she would try.

After the door closed, she let herself think about what she'd seen in the manila folder marked *Barron-Moore*. A formal adoption agreement pertaining to the unborn child of Ellen Moore.

chapter 56

Tilghman Cameron was a thin, nervous woman with gold hoops in her lobes and graying blond hair. Her shoulders were a wire hanger for her peach linen dress. She was half a head taller than her husband, surrogate court judge Douglas Cameron. She winked at Wetzon.

The judge himself was carrying around at least twenty pounds more than he should. His hair, which he combed over his bald spot, was a shade too brown and a shade too long. The heels on his wing tips were a smidgen higher than normal.

"Toddie will be along in a minute," Tilghman said. Wetzon saw that the tic in Tilghman's eyelid was what had made Wetzon think Tilghman winked at her.

Toddie, Wetzon thought. He'll be along in a minute, she says, as if he was just parking the car.

Bill made the introductions, exchanging a barely discernible conspiratorial gesture—hand on the elbow—with the judge. What the hell was the subtext here?

Wetzon rose and shook hands, trying to dismiss the intense stare Douglas Cameron focused on her. She returned to her chair while Tilghman sat on the leather sofa and Douglas chose the other straight-backed chair.

"As Doug and I discussed over lunch the other day, we want to keep—" Bill sat down at his desk. He didn't look at Wetzon.

Lunch? Was that it? Why hadn't Bill said anything to her about his having had lunch with the judge? That would mean they had discussed the incident . . . and had come to some conclusion. So what was *this* meeting for?

The door opened and a sullen Todd Cameron sauntered in. Immediately, the atmosphere in the room changed, and Wetzon was not the only one who felt it.

Gaunt to the point of emaciation, Todd wore tight black jeans and a brocade vest. His right biceps showed a death's-head tattoo and, under it, a swastika. He wore a dangling cross earring in one lobe. A Band-Aid covered the other lobe.

"Sit here, Toddie." Tilghman Cameron patted the spot beside her on the sofa. "Toddie dear, this is Mr. Veeder and Ms. Wilson. Mr. Veeder had lunch with Daddy and they're going to tell us—"

"Shut up, Till," the judge said, slicing the air with his hand. "You see what you're doing? This is exactly why I wanted you here. Todd is not eight years old. Let's get to it, Bill. I've got to be up in Albany tonight."

Todd took a bent cigarette from a pocket in his vest and lit it. The sweet smell of pot blossomed.

Bill Veeder said mildly, "I'd prefer you didn't—"

The judge stood up and smacked the joint out of Todd's mouth.

"Oh, dear, oh dear, oh dear." Tilghman Cameron snatched the cigarette from her lap, where it had landed, still smoldering. She dropped it in an ashtray on the coffee table.

Todd's mocking laughter filled the room as the judge apologized to Bill Veeder and Wetzon.

"What happened to your ear, Todd?" Veeder asked.

"Poor Toddie was mugged," Tilghman said. "They tore off one of his earrings, right through his earlobe."

"Mugging," Wetzon muttered. "That's a good one."

"Tilghman," the most honorable judge said, "I'd like our son to answer the question. Todd? What do you have to say?"

Todd smirked.

"Is this it?" Bill held up the little gold cross. He came around to the front of his desk. "You have a voice, son. Speak for yourself."

"Why should I say anything? You're all talking for me."

Were she standing, the venom in Todd's voice would have made Wetzon step back. But it didn't faze Veeder.

"Toddie!" Tilghman Cameron stopped wringing her hands long enough to take the cross from Bill's hand. It was obviously a match to Todd's other earring. "It's yours, dear. See. Thank you for returning it, Mr. Veeder. Where did you get it?"

"From Ms. Wetzon."

"It was Ms. Wetzon who was mugged, Till." Judge Cameron lost what was left of his patience. "Our son here tried to throw Ms. Wetzon off a roof at the Barrons' anniversary party."

Todd churned to his feet, his fists clenched, face in Bill's. Bill did not move.

"Sit down, boy," his father said, getting up himself.

"Lies, all lies!" Tilghman cried, standing now too. "Toddie's a good boy. I won't let you slander my baby like that!"

"Go on, Bill," the judge said.

"We're not going to press charges, but let this be a warning—" Bill caught Todd's arm as his fist came at him and with a twist forced him grunting to his knees.

Todd shot Wetzon a look of such undisguised malevolence that she felt her hackles rise on the back of her neck.

"I mean it, son," Bill said. "Straighten out your act."

"Sure," Todd said, scrambling to his feet. He snatched the little cross from his mother's hand and left, slamming the door hard behind him.

Bill sat down at his desk. "I think you're going to have a problem, Doug."

"Don't I know it. I don't want to spend my declining years sitting in a courtroom having you defend my son for something he's done to get back at me."

"How could you, Douglas?" Tilghman said, dabbing her eyes with a tissue.

"You see how his mother is—"

"It's that girl's fault. He was always such a good boy."

"What girl?" Veeder asked.

"The one from school, the nice one. What's her name, Till?"

"Ellen Moore. She's not nice, Douglas. Since he's been with her, Toddie's been getting into trouble."

The judge heaved a sigh and put his arm around his wife. "Not true, Bill. Todd's been in and out of trouble for the last four years. I wish that girl had more influence on him. She's a nice kid, doesn't dress crazy, gets top grades in school. She'll get into one of the Ivy League schools while my son'll get his education at Rikers.

"I'm sorry you were there," Bill said, taking her key from her and unlocking her door. "That kid's an ugly piece of crap."

"From an obviously dysfunctional family."

"We're all from dysfunctional families, but we came through, didn't we?"

"Each in his own way. Watch out for the mad dog," Wetzon warned. She dropped her bag and briefcase and scooped up Izz, got a big wet smooch, set her down again. "Okay, okay, dinner." She went into the kitchen and filled Izz's bowl with dry food, then gave her fresh water. "Todd scared me," she admitted to Bill. "Micklynn once asked me if I believe in evil."

"Do you?" She watched him put her keys in his pocket. He knew what he was doing.

"Yes. It hasn't happened often, but sometimes when I meet someone, I've gotten a kind of atavistic feeling of revulsion as if for some ancient evil. Once felt it years ago in an apartment I looked at before I bought this one. I felt it in Sheila Gelber's apartment too." She sighed. "Micklynn felt it, but we all attributed her behavior to drinking. Do you believe in evil, Bill?"

"Some people are just plain bad, Leslie. They hurt people, they kill people, but they might not necessarily be evil. Then there are people who are truly evil but might not actually kill. Does that make sense to you?"

"You're saying that bad people are not necessarily evil. That evil finds its own level."

"Let's walk the pooch and get some dinner," he said, changing the subject.

"Okay. Go sit down but don't get too comfortable. I feel my appetite coming back. But first I want to scrub the last few hours off my face."

"You have some messages on your answering machine," he said, coming down the hall after her. He watched as she took off her makeup and washed her face. "You've got beautiful skin." He took the towel from her hands and patted her face dry.

"Go away," she said, "or we'll never get dinner."

From the living room, he called, "Do you want to hear your messages?"

"Sure."

"First message: Carlos." As she replaced her makeup, she heard the rhythms of Carlos' voice but not what he said. "He wants to know if you're okay and whether the big bad wolf hurt you."

"He didn't say that."

"No, but it's what he meant. Next message: Silvestri."

Uh-oh, she thought.

"Wants you to call him and not go off half-cocked. He says he'll work with you. What the hell does that mean?"

She touched her lips lightly with a pink glaze, then started down the hall. Silvestri was still talking. "It means investigating Micklynn's death." She heard the tape go "beep" as she came down the hallway toward the living room.

"Why are you still doing that?" Bill asked after a moment's hesitation.

"Because—"

The voice on the tape was grotesque, distorted. It surged from her answering machine like a poisonous cloud: *"It's me again, cunt. I know you're up there on the twelfth floor thinking about how I'm going to do you. It's getting closer now . . . any day . . . any day."*

chapter 57

Bill Veeder put ice into two glasses, poured a couple of fingers of his single-malt into each, then ordered burgers and fries from '21' around the corner. Just your everyday hundred-dollar burger and fries. Wetzon began to laugh; she laughed until the tears ran down her cheeks and the hiccoughs came. After all, it was only an obscene phone call. An obscene phone call that a murdered woman had also received.

"That goddam dirtbag," she sputtered between hiccoughs.

"You'll feel better if you eat something," he said, setting out the burgers.

"They look like burgers," she said.

"What did you expect?"

"Caviar, truffles, considering the cost."

"I want to know about Sheila Gelber's murder," Bill said. "And about how you got involved."

She began to talk, picking at her food. She talked until she was exhausted. He never interrupted her. When she looked down at her plate, there was no food left. Had she eaten all of it or had he? His eyes watched her intently.

She awakened, gasping for air. The room was dark. She was alone. She didn't remember getting undressed and going to bed. Rolling over, she saw the clock said 4:00. God, two nights in a row with almost no sleep. It began to come back to her, in chunks, fitfully. Don't get emotional, she told herself.

She switched on the light. Her suitcase was on a bench at the foot of the bed. She got up and pulled an oversized tee shirt from the bag. He'd helped her pack though she hardly remembered for the blind rage the phone message had incited.

Bill was sitting in front of the big window in his living room, Izz on his lap. He was staring into the night. He didn't hear her come in, but Izz did, stirring to let him know Wetzon was there.

"Couldn't sleep either, huh?" Wetzon said.

He held out his hand and she snuggled in next to him, and so they sat, all three of them, till the sky was streaked with pastels and the sun began to rise.

"Feels different in daylight," she said. Feels good, she thought, just like this.

"Always does." He gave her a weary smile.

"Thanks for last night. I overreacted, I think. It's been a long time since . . ."

"Since?"

"Since I went to pieces like that."

"You can't always be in control, Leslie. Sometimes you have to let go."

"I'll get myself back to my place later today."

"I don't think so. I want you here with me. Security is better here and I'll know where you are until we get this business straightened out."

"My God, the cassette. It's still in my apartment."

"No," he said. "It's here. I took it."

She wasn't in good shape. She'd dropped the phone twice, trying to make her call. Her hands vibrated as if her brain were sending some kind of garbled warning signal.

When she finally punched in the numbers and heard the ring, she almost hung up.

Then he answered, "Yeah?"

"Silvestri—"

"Jesus Christ, Les, it's five A.M."

"Silvestri, he called me." She was whispering into the phone in the bedroom, although with the shower on, Bill wouldn't be able to hear anyway.

"Speak up, goddammit," Silvestri said. "What the hell are you talking about?"

"Stop shouting at me." She hung up on him.

"Leslie?" Bill stood in the doorway in a short terry-cloth robe, diamonds of moisture in his hair, concern on his face.

"Nice shower?"

"Who were you calling?"

"Don't be angry."

"Why would I be angry?"

"I called Silvestri because he's working on Sheila Gelber's murder. I told you that Sheila got the same message on her machine before she died."

"Okay." He sat on the bed beside her. "What did Silvestri say?"

"He started yelling at me. So I hung up on him."

"Give me his number."

"You're going to call him?"

"Why not?" He took the phone from her and punched in the number she'd given him.

He held the receiver away from him and Wetzon heard Silvestri shout, "Goddammit, where the hell are you?"

"She's with me, Silvestri." Bill looked at Wetzon and smiled, stroked her hair back from her face. "She had a frightening message on her answering machine, like the one Sheila Gelber received before her death. No, she's fine. But this creep seems to know where she lives. I didn't want her staying there alone." He covered the mouthpiece and said to Wetzon, "He wants to come over."

"Okay."

"Come ahead. Museum Tower. Thirty-second floor." After replacing the receiver, he said, "Get dressed. I'll make some coffee."

A short time later while she was putting her hair up into its topknot, he came into the dressing room and gave her a mug of coffee. "I thought I'd cancel my appointments and we'd spend the day together," he said.

Wetzon was taken aback, covered her confusion by sipping the coffee. He would do that for her? "I don't want you to do that," she said. "I'm going to the office and get on with my life. I can't hide, and I don't want him to see he got to me."

"Him?"

She shrugged. "With those distorting gadgets, could be a her, I guess, but it feels like a him."

"Todd Cameron?"

"Seems as if it might be something he'd enjoy doing, but I don't think so. I've been getting these calls since April, in the office and at home. Artie Metzger—do you know him?—he was Silvestri's partner and Sheila Gelber's brother-in-law—told me how to report it and the phone company gets the info to him. All we know is that some came from a phone in Saks."

"Not exactly an isolated place."

"There's a piece I'm not seeing, Bill. Something I should know. . . ."

Silvestri's arrival was announced by their concierge, then signaled by Izz's shrieking leap at the door.

"You don't look too bad." He gave Wetzon the once-over, nodded at Bill Veeder.

"Thanks," she said drily.

"You have the tape?"

Bill handed Silvestri the cassette from Wetzon's answering machine.

Silvestri looked at the cassette, then dropped it into his pocket. "Let's go, Les."

"Go? Go where?"

"Wait a minute," Bill said.

"We're going to get some breakfast and then we're going to the lab. I want the guys to compare this with the other one."

"I'm going with you," Bill said.

"Forget it, Veeder."

"Hold on there, Silvestri."

Wetzon put her hand on Bill's arm. They were getting all pumped up on her. "It's okay, Bill. I'll call you when I get to the office. You're not going to keep me long, right, Silvestri?"

He looked down at Izz, who was trying to get his attention. "I'll take you to your office myself."

"Will you excuse us a minute, Silvestri?" Wetzon said.

"Take ten. Izz and I are going for her constitutional. Where's the leash?"

As she left the room to find the leash, she heard the two men talking. The leash was hanging from the closet door in the bedroom. When she came back to the living room, they stopped talking.

Silvestri picked up Izz and Wetzon hooked the leash to the collar. "Be right back," he said.

She closed the door behind him, then turned to Bill. "What were you two talking about?"

"You." Veeder fenced her in at the door. She breathed his scent. When he kissed her she tasted toothpaste and coffee.

"Mmmmmm."

"I don't think you should go anywhere alone."

"Right. How can anyone be anywhere alone in this City?"

"Call me when you get to the office. I'm going to stop by to see Evelyn around seven and I'll be home afterward. I was supposed to have dinner with Hem and Min, but I'll cancel . . . unless you feel up to coming along."

"Where?"

"Their place. They're having a few people over, Hem said, which means at least twenty-five, so it won't matter if I'm not there."

"It's not business?"

"Hell, no."

"Then maybe I'll go with you. I can come home, take care of Izz, put on my basic black . . . if my manservant packed it . . ."

He grinned at her. "He did."

She thought: Both Hem and Min have motives for Micklynn's death. Means and opportunity too. But how did Micklynn's death connect to Sheila?

In a coffee shop near the Police Academy, while Wetzon nibbled at her bagel with cream cheese, Silvestri had two eggs over easy, sausages, hash browns, and four slices of buttered toast.

"You okay?" he said, wiping up the egg yolk with his toast. "You're not eating."

"I'm okay, just not hungry."

"That'll be the day. Wrap this up for her," he told the waitress.

"Silvestri, I saw an agreement between Hem and Min Barron to adopt the child that Ellen Moore is carrying."

"Oh, yeah?" He was taking change out of his pocket.

"You're not surprised?"

"I'm listening. I'm not going to ask you how you know that. You're an unreconstructed snoop. I'm not going to tell you how to live your life . . ."

"But?"

"Who says there's a but?"

"There always is, Silvestri. Just say it right out."

"But don't confide in Veeder."

"He's a cop, Silvestri, just like you."

"Not like me, Les. Now he works for the other side."

The waitress handed her the foil-wrapped bagel and she slipped it into her briefcase while Silvestri paid the bill.

"Where are we going?" she asked.

"I want you to hear what we got from Sheila's tape and I want the lab guys to see if this"—he patted the pocket into which he'd dropped the cassette—"is the same voice."

At the Academy, Wetzon was given an ID badge, then they went up to the lab, where Silvestri introduced her and turned the tape over to Detective Montebello. "See if it's the same as the other one. I also want you to play what you got for her. Maybe she'll recognize the voice."

The lab looked like an old-fashioned recording studio. Montebello's thin, dark hair was in a low-slung ponytail. His eyes were intense behind horn-rimmed glasses, his irises black. He explained, "Once we know the process used to distort, we can undistort." He put the tape on the spool. "Ready?"

Wetzon nodded.

The tape began as she'd heard it on both Sheila's and her machines. Her fists clenched. At first the voice was drawn out like a whine, then it altered. The words made her shudder, but the voice was unmistakable. Wetzon had heard that voice only yesterday. And for that reason it was doubly shocking.

It was the voice of the Honorable Douglas Cameron.

chapter 58

"I can't figure Veeder. Why the hell did he let you in on the meeting? He made you a sitting duck."

"I insisted, Silvestri."

"Yeah, I'll bet. I can almost sympathize with the poor bastard." He stopped for the light on Forty-ninth Street, only half a block from Wetzon's office.

"I think I'm going to take offense."

He cocked an eyebrow at her. "Don't say anything to him about Judge Cameron. Leave it to us. If you tell Veeder, he's going to use it and it'll come back in our face."

"Silvestri, you're wrong about Bill."

"We'll see. I want to hear you promise me you won't say anything."

"Okay, I promise. You always think you know better—"

"I do."

"I'm getting out here . . ." Wetzon paused because his attention had gone to the woman making a call at the pay phone on the corner. Her skirt barely covered her ass. "That's our associate, Darlene Ford," she said. "Would you like to meet her?"

"Huh?"

"Forget it." She opened the door and got out. "It's been grand." Darlene was just standing there at the phone, not talking, then she hung up.

"Watch yourself, y'hear?" Silvestri called.

Wetzon slammed the door. Darlene was coming down the street, tottering on too high heels. She hadn't noticed Wetzon, who had tucked herself into the shallow doorway of Le Bon Café.

"Well, good morning, Darlene." Wetzon stepped out in front of Darlene.

"Oh, my goodness!" Darlene's hand flew to her bosom.

"Sorry I startled you. Are you usually in this early? It's only seven-thirty."

"I stayed in town last night."

"Oh. Doesn't your key work?"

"My key? You mean my key to the office? Ummm . . . why?"

"Because I saw you standing at the pay phone on the corner and wondered why you didn't just use the phone in the office."

"It sticks sometimes. My key."

"I'll get you a new one."

"You don't have to do that, Wetzon. If you give me yours, I'll get a new one made."

"Nonsense, you have more than enough to do." Wetzon picked up the fat roll of mail from their mat and tucked it under her arm. Unlocking the door, she stepped inside, dropping her key case back in her purse. She held out her palm to Darlene and smiled. "Hand it over. I want to make up a spare to leave with Bill anyway."

With obvious reluctance, Darlene produced her key and gave it to Wetzon. "Thank you," she said. "Do you want me to sort the mail?"

"I don't think so. By the way, I've noticed that our pace of placements has slowed down considerably."

"Well, nobody wants to go anywhere without a deal."

In that respect, Darlene was right. No one wanted to move without an upfront check, or hiring bonus, as the outside world called the cash payment a successful broker received if he made a move to another firm.

Wetzon said, "I have the distinct feeling that they're going to reinstate all the deals including upfront very soon now. So I think we should have a ton of candidates interviewed, primed, and ready to go when it happens."

She went upstairs, dumped the roll of mail on her desk, and made coffee. As she waited for the coffee to drip through, she opened the mail. Bills, newsletters, five checks, now that was nice. Each went into a category pile. The magazines too. She filled her mug, then steeled herself and listened to her voice mail.

The breather came through loud and clear, along with the sound of street traffic. Now, wasn't that interesting.

She called Bill Veeder, and was put right through. "I'm in the office," she reported.

"You okay?"

"Yes. I may have an answer to half of the problem, but I want to talk to Smith first because it's a business decision."

"I'm not following you."

"I don't mean to be abstruse. I'll explain later." After she replaced the receiver, she wondered why she hadn't told him what was on her mind. Damn Silvestri. If he was trying to unsettle her feelings about Bill, he'd succeeded.

Sighing, she picked up her private line to call Smith, and heard a crash downstairs. Setting the phone down, she walked over to the stairs and called, "You okay, Darlene?"

Darlene's swift reply practically cut Wetzon off. "Yes. Knocked my lamp off the table, but it's okay."

Back at her desk, Wetzon punched in Smith's number. It rang three times, then a man answered. "Xenia Smith's residence."

"Are you her butler now, Mr. Goldman Barnes II?"

"Hi, Wetzon. You never know who's going to be calling Xenie—Sandy Weill, Arthur Levitt, Donald Marron." Twoey named three moguls of the financial community. "I wouldn't want to compromise her."

Wetzon laughed. "I'd let you compromise me anytime, Twoey."

"See, I was just telling Xenie that you're the nicest person I know."

"I don't know if nice wins any prizes anymore, Twoey, but thank you. Where's my lady?"

"In the shower."

"I need to talk to her as soon as possible."

"I'll tell her. Is everything okay with—"

"Yes. It's not that, it's business." She cradled the phone and went over her messages. It was after eight; managers were in their offices and brokers were beginning to arrive at their desks.

An hour passed and Smith had not called. Wetzon tried again. Now there was no answer. I'll kill her, she thought. Smith figured what I had to say could wait on whatever she had on her agenda first. What was on her agenda anyway? Wetzon checked Smith's datebook. Time was blocked out between nine and eleven that morning, but Smith's scrawl was illegible. Damnation.

She shuffled through her suspect sheets, made a follow-up phone call to a manager about an interview the previous day.

"How did it go, Frank?"

"I think it went great. I want him. I don't know if he liked me, though. Find out what he thought."

"I'm sure he thinks you're great, Frank." Salesmen are all the same, Wetzon thought. And Wetzon was a salesman, no question. We want people to like us—hell, love us—so we're constantly trying to prove ourselves lovable. "I'll talk to Rich and get you some feedback."

When she got the broker on the phone, she asked, "So, Rich, what did you think of Frank?"

"He's never going to float my boat, Wetzon."

"Can you live with him and a check for half a mil?"

"I said he's never going to float my boat, Wetzon, not that I'm stupid enough to turn down half a mil."

"Fine, then, I'll let him know you want to go forward." So it went. She reported back to Frank that Rich *really* liked him. Everybody lying to each other. For money.

For love.

Silvestri was wrong about Bill. It was Silvestri who had an ulterior motive. He wanted to poison the well. That's right, Wetzon, you, my dear, are the well. But she felt certain that if her interests and one of Bill's client's interests were on a collision course, the Bill she'd come to know would opt out of the client relationship.

On the deck, the sun had about burned off the haze as Wetzon began her third cup of coffee. Where the hell was Smith? She leaned back in the deck chair.

"Wetzon?"

She jerked awake. Where was she? Jesus, on the deck. Sound asleep.

"Wetzon, excuse me." Max stood in the doorway. He looked sick.

"What's the matter, Max? Are you all right?" She got up and they went inside. The phones all seemed to be ringing at once. No one was answering them.

"No, yes. It's—" Max was incoherent.

"Smith? Has something happened to Smith?"

"No, Wetzon." He picked up the phone. "Smith and Wetzon, good morning. She'll have to call you back." Answered the next line the same way, and the next. When he finally replaced the phone he said to Wetzon, "I think you should come downstairs."

She followed Max down the stairs. Something wasn't right. She could feel it. "Max? Where's Darlene?"

"I don't know. It was like this when I got here."

Like this meant, the usual stack of suspect sheets atop Darlene's desk was not there, her knickknacks were gone. The filing drawer in her desk was open and empty. The top of Max's desk was similarly cleaned off.

"Well, well, well," Wetzon said, hands on her hips. "The worm has turned." And she'd done all her mischief that very morning right under Wetzon's nose.

The months of breather calls had been a campaign designed to upset and distract Wetzon, while Smith was already distracted by show business. They had been so easy.

"I don't get it," Max said. He grabbed the phone when it rang again. "Smith and Wetzon, good morning." Looking at Wetzon, he said, "She's right here." He handed Wetzon the phone. "It's Smith," he said.

"Well, it's about time. Where are you?"

"Listen to me, sweetie pie." Smith was breathless. "Are you alone?"

"No, I'm downstairs with Max."

"Go upstairs where we can talk privately."

"What's going on, Smith?"

"We have a problem. I know who Darlene's lover is."

"Do you really? May I hazard a guess? It couldn't possibly be Tom Keegen, could it?"

A deathly silence, then Smith said, each word dripping venom, "Don't tell me."

c h a p t e r   5 9

"That lying, cheating little bitch is not going to get away with it." Smith stood in the middle of the office bristling. She pointed a magenta fingernail at Wetzon. "And *you* should have suspected something was up."

"If we're looking to place blame here, I'm not the one who hired her and gave her a big cut and a fancy title."

"Now, ladies," Shirley Boley intervened, "recriminations are going to get us nowhere. Let's just give her a dose of her own medicine and hit her with a restraining order. Darlene stole papers that belong to Smith and Wetzon, and we have her signature on a noncompete contract, which means we can swear out a complaint against her and sue her for theft and breach of contract. We can effectively put her out of business. Temporarily."

"Perfect," Smith said. "I want her to suffer."

"What good will that do?" Wetzon said. "It's all revenge, and revenge takes energy and money. Let's just replace her and go forward."

"Taking her to court might make you feel better," Shirley said.

"It certainly will." Smith was adamant. "And now let's talk about Tom Keegen. I've about had it with him. Let's discuss what we can do to put *him* out of business."

"Forget it, Smith. The best revenge is making so goddam much money he's dying with envy."

"Sweetie, you may feel comfortable turning the other cheek, but not me."

"Ha! You'll have to kill him."

"That can be arranged, babycakes. You just watch me." She turned to their lawyer, an elegant woman with shoulder-length streaked blond hair. "Shirley, go do your worst. We're with you, aren't we, sweetie?"

"Put a goddam ad in the *Times*. Help wanted. No lying cheating bitch need apply," Wetzon said. "And please, Smith, let's move on."

"We'll put the ad in, but I'm not dropping this. Are we agreed?"

"I give up," Wetzon said. "Have it your way."

"Good," Smith said. "It's settled then."

They shook hands all around and Smith walked Shirley downstairs.

Wetzon immediately began to search through the mess of suspect sheets on her desk. Smith came through the door and watched her for a few moments. "What are you looking for, sugar?"

"Oh, thank God, here it is." Wetzon plucked a suspect sheet from the mound. "Benny Flaxman. Rivington Ellis is bringing him to New York for the full-court press. He's going to meet all the department heads—the head of retail, the head of domestic branches, managed money, syndicate, you name it. He and Gerry Brooker, the Rivington manager who's wooing him, get in tonight."

"From where?"

"Ashland, Oregon."

"I bet he wears white socks."

"You know, Ms. Turn-up-her-nose-at-the-provinces, I don't care if he wears clogs, and you won't either."

Smith smiled. "I take it he's big."

"He's a thousand-pound gorilla from Loeb Dawkins. Two and a half mil gross with a hundred fifty million in assets."

"You are absolutely in your prime, sweetie pie," Smith said, waxing eloquent. Then she grimaced. "Wait. He's not one of Darlene's, is he?"

"No, no, bless us. Max cold-called him. I've been having Max call into Washington and Oregon from that list we bought in January. We've been trying to get this trip set up for three months. Now it looks as if it's going to happen." Wetzon set the suspect sheet aside. "How did you find out about Darlene? Did the Tarot give her up?"

"Very funny, sugar. The Tarot did hint that we had a problem in our midst, but I wanted immediate gratification. I hired a private detective. I had to rush out to meet him this morning because he was catching an early Metroliner to DC, where he's doing some work for that dear Newt Gingrich."

"Please. If you'd called me back, I would have told you I practically caught her in the act."

"Stealing our suspect sheets?"

"No. Making the breather calls. From the pay phone on the corner. She was trying to spook me. And she succeeded. But she underestimated me. Being nervous doesn't make me stupid."

Smith brushed her hands together. "Well, that's that."

"Not really. When Bill took me home last night, we found a really horrible obscene call on my answering machine, and it was exactly the same as the one on Sheila Gelber's answering machine."

"Sheila again. I am so bored with her. Can't we forget about her?"

"No, we can't, because her killer killed Micklynn and Jimmy."

"Jimmy? Who's Jimmy?"

"Micklynn's cat."

"Oh, for pity sakes—"

"Bill moved me and Izz in with him at the Museum Tower for a couple of days."

"Sweetie, what a setup. You are so smart. I am taking some of the credit."

"Hey, Smith. Read my lips. Obscene, threatening phone calls. Very scary."

"Oh, you."

"Oh, me. Yes. Silvestri's checking my tape against Sheila's."

Smith rolled her eyes and sang, "Hello, two lovers . . ."

"Very funny. By the way, Max said he'd work full-time till we find someone to replace Darlene."

"Haven't I always said he was a sweetie? Let's order lunch."

They worked the phones side by side until four-thirty, when Smith rose, stretched languidly, and announced, "I've had it. We're going to Hem's for dinner—"

"I'll probably be there with Bill."

"Good. Close down at five. There's no point in killing ourselves."

"Okay. On your way out tell Max he can go, but he should lock up when he leaves. I'm just going to set up my book for tomorrow. I'm meeting Benny Flaxman for a drink late in the day to hear how it went. Wanna come?"

"You have surely lost your mind, sugar bun. Xenia Smith never, ever wants to meet broker and sit with pond scum on a Friday night in July when she can be in Westport. Well, really."

Smith blew her a kiss. "Night, sweetie. See you later."

"Good night, Wetzon," Max called a few minutes later.

"Lock up, Max."

"Okay."

The phone rang. "Go ahead, Max, I'll get it. Hello, Smith and Wetzon."

"Les? I'm on my way uptown. Where you gonna be in the next half hour?"

"At Bill's."

"I don't want to talk there," Silvestri said.

"Okay. Why don't you meet me in the sculpture garden at the Museum of Modern Art?"

When Wetzon left the office, she rechecked the locks, tweaking herself, sure, lock the barn . . .

The heat had subsided and a light breeze enveloped the City. A faint gust of cigar fumes wafted at her from across the street where a heavyset man leaned against the newsstand reading the *Post*. The headline said: MICKEY GETS MICKEY. It didn't take a brain surgeon to figure out that they meant Micklynn had been poisoned. Shuddering, Wetzon hurried her steps.

The sculpture garden of MOMA was serenity in stone, a place where one could transcend the hectic pace of the City. It was a canyon surrounded by glass and steel and concrete on three sides and the tops of old brownstones on the fourth.

Wetzon sat on a wire chair beside one of the rectangular pools and listened to her own breathing. Her mantra came drifting into her consciousness like an old friend. Yes, she thought. Welcome. She closed her eyes.

Someone pulled a chair over and sat down beside her. "You smell of cigarettes," Wetzon said. She opened her eyes. "It's peaceful here, isn't it?"

"Yeah." Silvestri was staring hard at Picasso's *Goat.*

"I love all the flowers. Hey, look at that."

"Look at what?" He swiveled his head around.

"That man over there near the doorway."

"What about him?"

"He was smoking a cigar across the street from my office a little while ago."

"Oh, he was, was he? Didn't know he was into art."

"You know him?"

Silvestri didn't answer, because he was off the bench like a shot. He cornered the man, then, as Wetzon watched incredulous, actually shook hands with him. What the hell was going on?

When Silvestri returned, she asked him.

"It's okay. He's an ex-cop. Veeder hired him to keep an eye on you."

"Keep an eye on me! That's insulting."

"No, it's not. He's worried about you and so am I."

"I'm fine, Silvestri. What did you want to see me about?"

"It's the same voice, Les. On both tapes."

"Judge Cameron?"

"He made a speech at a PBA dinner this past winter. It was recorded. When we got a voice match, I had a little chat with him."

"He didn't seem like a psychopath, Silvestri."

"They're never what they seem. And he may not be a murderer. He may just be an obscene caller. Or he may be none of the above."

"Whatever. One thing's for sure. He's not the breather who was calling me."

"Say again?"

"The breather turned out to be our associate. You know, the one whose ass you got hung up on this morning while she was making a phone call."

"She's the breather? How do you know?"

"She knew I was on to her and she flew the coop to our competition, taking a lot of our papers with her."

"I'm sorry, Les."

"We'll get through it, if only I can keep Smith from killing Tom Keegen."

"He's the competition your associate flew to, I take it."

"Yup."

"How long are you going to stay at Veeder's?"

"Don't know. Does it matter?"

"I just want to know where to reach you if I need you."

He hadn't answered her directly, but she gave him Veeder's phone number. "What exactly did the judge have to say about the tape?" she asked.

"He admitted it was his voice, but said he never made those calls. He was in Israel with his wife around the time Sheila got her call, and when you got the call last night he was in Albany having dinner with the Governor. Didn't know Sheila and only met you once, in Veeder's office. Had no idea of your existence before you made it into the tabloids."

"And you believed him."

"Yeah. He was pretty upset. He asked for a copy of the tape."

"A tape can be pieced together with words and phrases collected from other taped conversations, can't it?"

"It can. And if it was, the lab will be able to pick it up. The judge said he wanted someone to hear it and he'd call me."

"It's that horrible boy. Todd. He could have poisoned Sheila. And Micklynn. Micklynn hated him. And Jimmy. Are you going to arrest him?" Oddly enough, she felt the tension leave her body. It was a relief to know. She looked up at the sliver of the Museum Tower and counted up the floors.

Silvestri heaved an uncharacteristic sigh. "No."

"Why not?"

"Because Todd Cameron's in Lenox Hill Hospital on life support."

chapter 60

"What happened? Did he o.d.?" She heard her voice rise; several strollers looked over at her.

Silvestri put a restraining hand on her arm. "I just came from Lenox Hill. We don't know anything yet. Mulcahy's over at the apartment checking out Todd's room. That's where his mother found him."

"Is he going to make it?"

"They don't know. There's not a hell of a lot of brain activity."

"I feel sorry for the parents, but he did kill two people. He must have known you were getting close and after his father played the tape—"

"The judge never got to play the tape. Todd's girlfriend broke it off with him for some other guy." He stood up. "I gotta go. I just wanted you to know you can go home, because I don't think there'll be any more calls like that."

"Can I come along and watch?"

"Nope." He chucked her under the chin. "See ya."

"Wait a minute, Silvestri. What about Micklynn? Is it official now? I saw a headline in the *Post* on the way over."

"Yeah. Poison. Same as Sheila. The M.E.'s had a tough time with this because here in the City they almost never see plant poison as a cause and wouldn't think to look for it. Metzger and I kept pressing."

She watched him leave the garden, then tried to recapture the sense of peace she'd had when she'd sat down. But to no avail. It was gone. She rose and took a turn around the garden. As she passed Calder's *Black Widow,* she had the disturbing impression that the spider sculpture and the enormous shadow it cast were mocking her.

Izz was delighted to see her and even more delighted to be fed. While the dog slurped her meal, Wetzon checked in with Bill Veeder.

"You hired someone to bodyguard me," she said when he came on the line.

She'd caught him by surprise. "How did you find out?"

"Spotted him. I was in the sculpture garden getting an overview of the case from Silvestri and there he was. I knew I'd seen him before. Silvestri knew him too."

"Silvestri. He does manage to stay in touch."

"It was strictly business."

"Fine. What did he have to say about the obscene call?"

"All roads lead to Todd Cameron." Trying to keep her promise to Silvestri, she did not mention that the voice on the tape was Judge Cameron's.

"Jesus. I feel for Doug. Maybe I can help."

"I don't think you can right now. Todd seems to have tried to end his life. He's at Lenox Hill on life support. Ellen dumped him for someone else."

"I'll stop by the hospital on my way to Evelyn's. How do you feel about all this?"

"Relieved. I think I can move back to my place."

"Not yet, Leslie. I'm just getting used to having you with me. Don't make any decisions. We'll talk about it when I get home. You still up to going to Hem's?"

"Yes. I'm going to walk my pooch, then take a nap."

A half hour later she was lying up to her neck in luxury in Bill's huge marble bathtub, a bath pillow supporting her neck. Steam came from the water in scented clouds. The radio was playing jazz from the Newark station. Izz sprawled on one of the marble steps overlooking the tub, head dangling over the water. Every so often, she stuck her snout in the water and snuffled.

All the strains of the day floated from Wetzon. She draped the washcloth over her breasts and drifted off.

Izz's excited bark wakened her. Wetzon opened her eyes. The Maltese was dancing around on the slippery marble. The bath water had grown tepid.

"Leslie?"

"In here." She turned on the hot water.

"I don't want you to be upset about Huberman." He was coming closer. Izz was going crazy. Wetzon shut off the hot water.

"Who's Huberman?"

"The cigar-smoking asshole who let you make him." Bill stood in the doorway. He was in his shirtsleeves, no gun. Izz shrieked.

"Oh, what the hell," Wetzon said. "It seems to be the only thing you and Silvestri agree on. You can call him off now, though."

"We'll see. A little while longer can't hurt." He took off his cuff links and put them in his pocket. "I stopped by the hospital. The boy has less than a fifty-fifty shot. Doug asked me to defend him if he pulls through." He began to unbutton his shirt.

"What did you tell him?"

He came into the room and stood looking down at her. "You look very comfortable there."

"Come on in, the water's fine," she said, doing Lauren Bacall. She held out a dripping hand to him. "But first you have to answer my question."

At that moment, perhaps because she was tired of waiting for attention, Izz leaped off the ledge, straight up in the air, and, like a cannonball, landed in the tub with such a mighty splash that it almost, but not quite, obliterated Bill's "Yes."

chapter 61

"I'm appropriating your little friend here." Hem Barron
locked arms with Wetzon and took her away from Bill
Veeder.

She felt like that bratty kid Little Iodine, and had to
fight the urge to kick Hem hard in the shins, or somewhere more appropriate. But she was in Hem's home
with Bill Veeder and Hem was obviously a very good
client. Good manners won out. This time. Besides, there
were questions she wanted to ask Hem about Sheila
Gelber. The kick could come later.

Dinner was a Chinese buffet being prepared dish by
dish by Minnie Wu in the open kitchen. Min's short,
stubby body could hardly be seen over the huge woks

and steaming pots. Only her hands and the pot slamming let her guests know that she was doing the presentation.

"You'll just love Min's cooking," Hem said. He was wearing a navy double-breasted blazer, a striped shirt, and a red-and-blue ascot.

"At your own peril," Laura Lee said, vamping over. She held a bottle of beer in one hand and a carrot stick in the other. "Go for the veggies. Do not dip."

Hem gave a whinnying laugh, his attention down Laura Lee's cleavage. "Leslie, this is Laura Lee Day. She's a money manager in real life, not a comedienne."

Laura Lee rolled her eyes at Wetzon. "We've met, Hem darlin'. Why don't you get Wetzon a plate of plain old white rice so she'll be able to go to work tomorrow."

"Don't believe a word she says, Leslie. How about a plate for you, ducky?"

"Ducky?" Wetzon mouthed.

With a wicked smile, Laura Lee patted Hem's hand. "I'm just fine the way I am, Hem darlin'. Had to attend one of those borin' luncheons today." After Hem left them for the buffet table, Laura Lee said, "Believe me, darlin', stick to plain rice and steamed veggies. Otherwise, just drink. Min's food is toxic, like Min."

At the help-yourself bar, where a small, parched crowd had gathered, Wetzon chose a bottle of Amstel from the variety in the tub of ice. "Just what I need. Damn, here comes Hem with a full platter. What am I going to do?"

"Make mushy on the plate, darlin', then the minute you can, feed it to one of the plants upstairs and watch the poor green thing die a torturous death." In a theatrical whisper, Laura Lee added, "Compliments of the chef."

Out of the kitchen, hugging a huge bowl of rice, came the aforementioned chef herself. Minnie's eyes flicked around the assemblage, rested on Wetzon, hooded over. She set the bowl on the buffet table without so much as a friendly smile for her guests and returned to her pots.

"Here, Leslie, you'll love this." Hem handed her a platter. In his other hand he clutched two stemmed glasses and a bottle of red wine. "Now leave us alone, Laura Lee, so Leslie and I can get better acquainted. I know we're going to be buddies." He set the glasses and the bottle on the floor. When he saw she was still drinking beer, he filled only one glass.

Behind Hem's back Laura Lee stuck a finger in her open mouth, then waved goodbye to Wetzon.

"This is so nice, Hem," Wetzon said. She tried out Smith's technique of batting her eyelashes at him. It must have worked, because he leaned in to her, or rather, in to her breasts. They sat on a polished wooden bench and she, following Laura Lee's instructions, made mushy on her plate. "Someone told me . . . now who was it . . . that you and my friend Sheila Gelber were . . . in the getting-acquainted stage."

Hem almost dropped his glass. "Well, I . . . not really . . ."

Across the room Bill caught her eye. He was surrounded by several smart-looking, thin women in short linen shifts and fat pearls. Their slim arms were tanned, their legs glossy in sheer hose. Wetzon pursed her lips at him and he laughed. The women turned to look.

To Hem, Wetzon said, "Oh, dear, maybe I heard wrong. Was there *nothing* between you and Sheila?"

Hem watched her move the food around on her plate. "I thought I could help her out—you know—put her in business. It was Mickey's idea. She felt she'd gotten Sheila all excited about going into this gluten-free baking business, then A.T. put the kibosh on it. Micklynn was a decent person—" He stopped talking and jumped up, his attention on the open kitchen, where suddenly it had gotten very quiet.

Minnie Wu was standing still at the center island, ignoring the fire under her woks and pots. She rounded the island and bore down on Hem and Wetzon, murder in her eyes. Steam from the stove gave the illusion it was coming from her.

"Excuse me a minute," Hem told Wetzon hastily. "I see Min needs some help." He gave Wetzon a nervous smile, and went to head off the fire-breathing dragon.

Wetzon didn't hang around. She was beginning to think she shouldn't have come. She loathed these people. Neither A.T. nor Ellen was here. One would have thought Ellen and Min had made up their differences in the rowboat in Central Park, where the adoption of Ellen's unborn child must have been discussed. But Minnie nursed grudges, not children.

Sighing, Wetzon set her plate of food under the bench, pushing it well back with the heel of her shoe.

"You're not eating," Minnie Wu said. "Don't you like my cooking?"

Wetzon stood up. "It's not that."

"Oh, I see, maybe it's my husband you like." Min's matte black eyes wouldn't let Wetzon go. "Women who like my husband live to regret it."

"Oh, please, cut the melodrama. Strange as it may seem, I am not at all interested in your husband. Why don't you tell him to stay away from *me?*"

"Min, sweetie, so nice!" Smith grabbed Minnie's hand, which was raised to give Wetzon a mighty slap, and pumped it enthusiastically, sending Wetzon an urgent get-out-of-here message.

The bitch ought to attack her libidinous husband, Wetzon thought. Simmering, she moved across the room toward Bill. Laura Lee caught up with her.

"Laura Lee, look at these women. There's not a soft line among them. They all look . . . well . . . varnished."

"It's okay to eat dessert," Laura Lee said. "A.T. and Ellen made it." She handed Wetzon a cup.

"What's this?"

"Rice pudding. Seems just-your-Bill gave A.T. a special request for you. Oh, dear, I forgot the spoon."

" 'S all right. I'll be rude." Wetzon dipped the tip of her finger in the rice pudding and tasted it. Not bad. "Listen, Laura Lee, Minnie Wu is certifiable. This is the last time I'm going to come anywhere near her. Or Hem, for that matter."

They drifted over to Bill, who was talking to two horsey-looking women with manes of sun-streaked hair. He didn't see Wetzon and Laura Lee stop behind him.

"When will you be up?" one woman asked. "We're going on the first, if I can tear Alfred away from his precious office."

"Evelyn leaves tomorrow, and I'll come up around the fifteenth."

"Well, we'll all be waiting for you. Everyone says the real fun on the Vineyard doesn't start till Bill Veeder favors us with the last two weeks of the summer."

It was unlikely that Wetzon gasped, but she must have made some small painful sound, for Laura Lee touched her hand, relieving her of the cup of rice pudding before she dropped it. Or threw it. And Bill Veeder, turning, looked stunned.

Wetzon pulled away from Laura Lee. She wanted to leave, hide.

"Leslie." He came after her. "Wait. Let me explain." He cornered her near the staircase, but she broke away from him and ran up the stairs to the roof. He followed her. "Leslie, please."

The air was spongy with humidity. She stopped at the parapet, sensed him come up behind her. "When were you going to tell me?" she said.

He put his hands on her shoulders; she twisted away. "I would have told you. I was waiting for the right time."

"Oh, really? When would be the right time? The day before you left? 'Oh, Leslie, by the way, I always spend August with my wife on the Vineyard. See ya in the fall.' "

"I've made arrangements for you to come up."

"Without asking me?" She was so outraged, she turned to face him. "How civilized. Your mistress is your houseguest?"

"I thought maybe the inn . . ." He reached for her again.

She pushed him away, hard. "You just don't get it, Bill. You're making me into a chippie or Twinkie or whatever they're called now. I can't live with it. I want to go home now, please."

For the first time since she'd known him, Wetzon saw Bill was totally flustered. "Leslie, I love you. I would never— I'm sorry. This is very important to me and I seem to be fucking up right and left."

"Maybe it's because you're thinking of me as *this*. I'm *Leslie*."

He stared down at her. "Let me make my rounds and I'll get us out of here. Come with me."

"I'll wait here, thanks. The air is less noxious." She watched him go down the stairs.

"A toast to you, Leslie Wetzon!"

A.T. came out of the greenhouse in a pother of pot. "So the great unattainable Bill Veeder has met his match." She held out her cigarette. "Want a toke?"

"No, thanks. Booze is my drug of choice."

A.T. shrugged. "I've been smoking pot since I was a kid. With the kind of father I had, it was all I could do. I'm sorry I eavesdropped, but you trapped me up here sneaking a little smoke."

"I thought you weren't here tonight."

"Oh, I'm here, all right. I made the desserts. Or rather, Ellen and I did."

"Where is Ellen?"

"She had a date."

"Did you know that Todd Cameron tried to kill himself?"

"Oh, dear." A.T. took a long inhale, squeezing the smoke into her lungs, then let her breath out. "That will really upset Ellen."

"Maybe she already knows."

"I don't think so. It's bad enough that Micklynn delivers a blow from the grave, so to speak, since they haven't released her body yet."

"I don't understand." The pungent fumes of marijuana were seeping into Wetzon's blood.

"Her will, Leslie. Micklynn cut Ellen out of her will completely. Gave everything to Meals on Wheels and God's Love We Deliver."

"What will Ellen do?"

"As far as money is concerned, I have more than enough. I'll take care of her. It's the slap in the face that really hurt her."

"Leslie . . ." Bill stood at the foot of the stairs.

"Good night, A.T."

A.T. took another long inhale. She gave Wetzon a cynical smile. "Good luck," she said.

The ride uptown was uncomfortable for both of them.

"I'm sorry," he said. "Talk to me."

"I keep forgetting you have another life. You make me forget it. Then I turn out to be just the other woman."

When they got to his apartment, he said, "All right. What do you want to do? I don't want to make you unhappy."

"Good. Let's keep it that way." She strode to the elevator. He followed her and they rode up in silence, standing well apart. She refused to make eye contact. Persuasion is what he did for a living.

When Bill unlocked the door, Izz gave them her usual effusive greeting, then stopped, sensing something was not quite right. She looked up at Wetzon.

"Get your leash. We're going home." Wetzon went into the bedroom and began throwing things into her suitcase.

"Leslie, it's late. We're both upset. Let's wait until tomorrow. Please."

The peculiar catch in his voice made her stop. She turned and stared at him. He looked miserable. Be strong, she told herself. "I need to work this out on my turf. It's so complicated. What do all your friends think when they see me with you? Will you say, 'This is my friend Leslie Wetzon'? The whole world seems to know we're lovers."

"Evelyn's family has owned a place on the Vineyard for a long time. It's something we've been doing for twenty summers."

"And you planned to bring me into that? Oh, Bill, you want everything, don't you?"

"If everything means my career, you, yes. Short of my having a commitment to Evelyn, I don't care about anything else."

She studied his face for a long time. And when he put his arms around her, she didn't resist.

The dream—and she knew it was a dream—was terrifying. She was dressed in leotard and leggings, standing in front of a harvest table so laden with food that its center dipped. Minnie Wu and Hem Barron, Micklynn, a vivid blue, more dead than alive, Ellen, Bill in his blue pinstripe, Todd Cameron with tubes coming out of him, held up on either side by his parents. All there. Jonathon, Bill's associate, passing out the plates. "Taste this, taste this," they were chanting. Someone held her and force-fed her. "No! No!" she cried. She couldn't breathe.

She awoke struggling, a weight pressing her chest; she was strangling, choking . . . She tried to say, *Help me,* but couldn't get the words out.

Bill stirred beside her.

She groaned . . . sick . . . have to get out of here . . . get air. She swung her feet to the floor. Stood. Her legs buckled. Falling . . . protect face . . . floor coming up at her. Hold on, she thought, hold on. But she couldn't.

Somewhere far away a dog barked.

Someone was lifting her. A distorted voice said, "Leslie, hold on to me. Let me help you."

She came to shivering, retching, on the bathroom floor, hugging the cold porcelain bowl. Bill held her head. Horrible retching, again and again. She didn't have the strength to push him away. Didn't care how she smelled or looked. She wanted to die, was dying. Tears ran down her cheeks and she retched again, afraid, shaking so she could almost hear bones rattling.

He washed her face with a warm cloth, wiping her mouth. "Go away," she mumbled, teeth chattering. "Let me die."

Holding her shoulders, he put a glass to her lips. "Rinse," he said. "Go on. I've got you."

Good thing too, because the room was spinning black clouds and she was shaking with cold. Eyes closing . . . limbs collapsing.

Kind oblivion.

"Something she ate," Bill said in a low voice. "It was pretty bad all night long. She kept throwing up and passing out."

"How long has it been since the last?"

"About three hours. Look at her. She's white as the pillowcase."

She opened her eyes a fraction and felt Izz creep over and cuddle against her. Bill stood near the doorway in khakis and a V-necked tee shirt. His face was haggard. The man with him wore a business suit. He was younger, curly brown hair. Izz licked her cheek.

"Well, maybe she's gotten rid of it." The man approached the bed. "Let's have a look at her. Well, hello," he said. "You're awake." To Bill: "Go make some tea."

"I think I should stay—"

"Beat it, buddy." The brown-haired man waited till Bill left the room, then said to Wetzon, "I'm Steve Levy. I'm a doctor, a friend of Bill's. Bill called me about an hour ago. He was pretty worried. How are you feeling?"

"Don't know. Hot." Cotton mouth. She tried to move. Couldn't. Trapped by blankets. Couldn't lift anything.

"No wonder. Let's get some of these blankets off. Bill said you had chills." When he peeled back the covers, she saw she was wearing a man's blue cashmere sweater. Dr. Levy's hand touched her brow. "No fever." He took her pulse, nodded, prodded her belly with knowledgeable hands. "Okay here. Can you sit up? I'll help you." Propping the pillows up behind her, he raised her into a sitting position, then reached into his inside pocket for his stethoscope. "Lean forward." He laid the cold knob under the sweater and listened. "Breathe. Again." He eased her back against the pillows and drew one of the blankets over her. "You'll be okay. Take it easy for a few days."

"Poison," she said. She wondered what she looked like, tried to pat her hair. It was in a braid which she didn't remember doing.

"Probably something toxic you ate. And you're dehydrated. That's why you're so weak. Drink a lot of fluids."

There was a knock on the door. "May I?" Bill stood in the doorway holding a mug on a small tray. The tail of a tea bag hung from the mug.

"Club soda, ginger ale, clear soup. Later soda biscuit, dry toast. Go light. Call me if you have another attack, but I think you're through the worst." The doctor's hand brushed her cheek. He looked over at Bill. "See that she drinks a lot of fluids."

While Bill walked him to the door, Wetzon closed her eyes again. She was helpless, so weak she couldn't lift her head.

"Well," Bill said, "you're starting to get some color—"

"I didn't know you wanted me to stay that much." When he looked puzzled, she added, "Bad joke. I've been poisoned."

A shadow crossed his face. "You think I poisoned you?"

She hesitated, studying him. "No. It had to be the rice pudding. It was all I ate. I didn't have enough of it to kill me, just enough to make me really sick."

"What rice pudding?"

"Someone . . . God, it was Laura Lee . . . gave me a cup of rice pudding last night, said you'd ordered it for me."

"I didn't."

"Laura Lee forgot the spoon, so I dipped my finger in and tasted it. Bill, did you tell anyone I love rice pudding?"

"I don't remember. Maybe. Hem . . ." He sat down on the bed facing her.

"I'm so thirsty." She reached a shaky hand for the mug of tea.

"Here, wait. I'll do it." He held it for her. "Just sip."

"What time is it?"

"Seven-thirty."

"I've got to get dressed. . . ."

"Steve said you're to take it easy for a few days. That means you stay here where I can keep an eye on you."

"But the office—"

"We'll get Xenia on the phone. She'll cover for you."

Sure, Wetzon thought. And make me pay for a lifetime. "Bill, really, I've got to go in. Benny Flaxman—he's a broker. He's come all the way from Oregon and is spending the day at Rivington Ellis and I'm meeting him for a drink afterward."

"Oh no you're not. Why can't Xenia handle it?" He held the mug for her again and waited till she swallowed.

"You don't know Smith. She hates brokers, thinks they're pond scum." The thought of Smith sitting down to a drink with Benny Flaxman was so funny, a weak laugh came. She clutched her ribs. "God, I'm sore."

"Small wonder. You heaved your guts out all night."

"And you held my head and cleaned me up." She touched his face. "And braided my hair."

He caught her hand, kissed her fingers.

"Okay," she said, surrendering. Lying back, she closed her eyes. She was wasted. "I'm buying us time. I couldn't leave now even if I wanted to."

For a good part of the morning she drifted in and out of sleep, waking once when Bill told her he was taking Izz and going over to his office to pick up some work. She had a long drink of water and slept again. Waking at last, she thought: Benny Flaxman. She had to call Smith. It was after eleven.

She reached for the phone, dragged it to the bed, almost knocking over the pitcher of water and the glass.

"Babycakes! How are you feeling now?" Smith demanded after Wetzon had listened to Max read off her messages. Only Silvestri needed answering.

"Hollowed out. Benny Flaxman—"

"Already done, sweetie. Bill called me—he's such a dear. He told me you wanted to come in because of someone named Benny. Well I'm meeting him for a drink this afternoon."

"Where's he staying? I'll be better later. I'll take him for the drink."

"The Michelangelo. You might be better, but Bill told me the doctor said you're to take it easy for a few days. That means I'm in charge, sugar, and I will suffer through a drink with one of your sleazebags."

"Where will you take him?"

"The Four Seasons, where else? I also talked to Gerry Brooker at Rivington Ellis. They're pulling out all the stops for our Benny, and if all goes well, they're prepared to up the deal."

"You done good, partner." Wetzon felt a twinge of disappointment. Sometimes she wanted to be irreplaceable, and it was a shock to find life went on without her. "How is everything in the office?"

"Oh, Max and I are working like an efficient machine, aren't we, Max, sweetie? Don't you worry about a thing. I'll call you and fill you in on everything."

"Thanks."

"By the way, did you know that Bob Walters is now manager at Rosenkind Luwisher's international office?"

"No. How nice for him. He called and told us?"

"It was in the *Wall Street Letter*."

Wetzon sighed. "I deserved a thank-you for that."

"I hope you're not saying what I think you're saying."

"I felt sorry for him, Smith. They were going to let him hang and the job was right there in his own firm."

"I don't know what I'm going to do with you. Okay, forget it, this time, but I don't want to ever hear you got softhearted again."

"You're so good to me."

"You must be feeling better, because you're starting to make jokes. Well, I'm going back to work. Just one more thing, sugar?"

"Yes?"

"Be gracious and let Bill take care of you."

"I'm always gracious. Did he tell you I was poisoned?"

"Poisoned? Is that what they're calling stomach flu these days? Really, sweetie, you're so dramatic. We'll talk about it when you're feeling better." Smith hung up before Wetzon could sputter a word.

Damn Smith, Wetzon thought. She never took Wetzon seriously, and at this moment, Wetzon needed someone to take her very seriously. She poured herself a glass of water and drank it down. Physically, she was feeling better. She debated whether to call Silvestri, then decided to call Laura Lee first.

"Poor baby," Laura Lee said. "It was the upset, hearin' Bill make summer plans that didn't include you."

"That upset me, but his plans did include me. He was going to have me come up and hang out at an inn. Be on call, so to speak."

"I take back all the nice things I said about him. Men are such shmucks."

Wetzon laughed, holding her ribs. "What would your parents say to hear you corrupted like this?"

"They'd say it was comin' from hangin' around with Jews and that New York had ruined me."

"I think what made me sick—"

"After all my warnin's you ate one of Min's concoctions?"

"No, it was the rice pudding."

"The rice puddin'? I gave that to you myself."

"Who told you to give it to me?"

"Min did. She said Bill had asked A.T. to make it specially for you."

"He says he didn't. I only had a taste of it. What happened to the rest of it?"

"I took it away from you and set it down somewhere. I don't remember. I probably tossed it."

A few minutes later Wetzon was explaining where she was and why to Silvestri. She left nothing out.

"Who made the pudding?" he asked.

"A.T. and Ellen made the desserts."

"Veeder ordered it for you?"

"Bill says he didn't. And I believe him."

"I'd rather you weren't at his place, Les."

"He saved my life, Silvestri. I have no doubt of that. I'll be here another day or so, then I'll go home. How is Todd Cameron?"

"Holding on by a hair."

"Did you find a suicide note?"

"No. Don't think we will, although we're still looking."

"You don't think he's a suicide?"

"The doorman says a man brought Todd home reeling drunk and semiconscious early yesterday morning. A man in a blue pinstriped suit."

chapter   6 3

She went back and forth in her mind about how to ask Bill where he was yesterday morning. It couldn't have been Bill. Yet she could only remember he said he had meetings all day and then was going to see Evelyn.

It behooved Silvestri to instill doubt in her mind about Bill Veeder. God, it was *Gaslight* doubled. Silvestri was trying to make her doubt her own judgment. But then perhaps she was so infatuated with Bill Veeder, her judgment was impaired. No, it was Silvestri manipulating her, and she wasn't going to let him do it.

She awoke to the smell of buttered toast. It lured her out of bed. She wrapped herself in Bill's terry robe and made her unsteady way to the kitchen. "Hungry," she said. The clock on the oven read 1:00.

"You're better," he said, scanning her face. He sat her in a chair and set two slices of toast on a plate in front of her. "You gave me a bad scare, babe."

"Gave myself a bad scare, boyo."

He watched her eat, then said, "Silvestri called me."

"About what?"

"You. Wants me to keep you away from The Groaning Board group until they catch the murderer."

"He has some nerve. The group, and not you?"

Bill seemed surprised. "Why me?"

"Silvestri told me that a man in a blue pinstripe brought Todd Cameron home semiconscious yesterday." She looked at the crumbs on her plate. "I guess every third man in New York City wears a blue pinstripe."

Speaking in measured tones, he said, "Do you want me to account for myself, Sergeant Wetzon?"

"If you don't mind."

"Why should I mind? I was in the office all day. Spoke to you, spoke to clients, went to see Evelyn. If you're okay, I'm going to stop in again tonight. I'll order up steamed chicken and soup for your dinner."

"I thought Evelyn left for the Vineyard."

"She's leaving tomorrow morning."

"I think I'll get dressed and maybe take a walk around the block."

"I'd rather you didn't go out by yourself. I don't want you to have a relapse. Steve said to keep you home the rest of the week."

She held up her hands. "Okay, Big Daddy." Bill might have told her his whereabouts, but that didn't mean he was where he said he was. So, she wondered, could he be the man in the blue pinstripe?

Gaslight.

By midafternoon, she felt strong enough to shower. She put on leggings and a cropped top and guided her creaky bones through simple ballet exercises. Afterward, she called Smith to make sure the drink with Benny Flaxman was still on. It most certainly was.

At five o'clock Bill was home again, this time with the Care package from '21,' and stood over Wetzon while she picked at her food; he fed Izz, walked Izz, went back to the office.

Wetzon lay on the sofa dozing. The phone rang. Bill's answering machine picked up on the fifth ring.

"Wetzon!" Smith's voice shrieked across the tape. "I know you're there. Pick up."

Groaning, Wetzon plucked up the receiver. Damn. Had something gone wrong with Benny Flaxman? She said, "You're supposed to be having a drink with Benny."

"I *am* having a drink with Benny. In fact, we've almost finished with our lovely drink, and Benny and I are coming over to see you on his way back to his hotel."

"Oh no you're not. I'm not dressed and I have no makeup on."

"Trust me, sweetie pie. Benny just told me something utterly fascinating and you have to hear it from his own mouth."

"Smith, for godsakes, I look like hell."

"Who cares, sugar? Benny knows we're pros and that you've been sick. I told him you had a touch of ptomaine, so he understands. He's eager to meet you. We'll be there in ten minutes."

"Oh, fuck," Wetzon told Izz as she slammed down the phone. She ran a comb through her hair with trembling hands and pulled it up tight in a topknot, mascaraed her lashes. What had gotten into Smith? She dusted blush over her paleness and touched her lips with gloss.

True to Smith's word, not ten minutes passed before the concierge announced, "Ms. Smith and Mr. Flaxman."

"Ask them to come up, please."

Benny Flaxman had a jowly face and a receding hairline. His nose was red and his eyes watered. "Big Apple allergies," he explained, blowing his nose. " 'S why I went to college in Oregon." He strolled around the apartment, gaping at the view. Izz came out from behind the sofa and followed him, sniffing at his shoes.

"The poor dear is suffering so, sugar." Smith gave Wetzon a protracted wink behind Benny's back.

"Boy, am I impressed, Wetzon. You girls must be really successful." Benny was built like a series of bagels, a small one for his neck, a bigger one for his chest, a fat one for his middle.

"How could you think otherwise, Benny?" Wetzon said. "Didn't we girls get you to New York?"

"Let's sit down," Smith ordered, steering Benny to a club chair.

"Benny only has a minute or so before he gets to have dinner with a few of the Rivington Ellis honchos, right, Benny sweetie?"

"Yeah, what a day, let me tell you, Wetzon."

"All has gone well?"

"Yeah. I'm real impressed. Their technology is a knockout. State of the art. I met a couple of analysts—"

"Tell Wetzon where you live in Oregon, sugar." Smith batted her lashes at him.

"Ashland," Wetzon said, watching Benny melt when he looked at Smith.

"No. I work in Ashland, but actually I live in Medford."

"Medford . . ." Wetzon frowned. "Medford."

"I told dear Benny"—Smith was speaking very slowly, enunciating with her lips, as if Wetzon were deaf—"how impressed we were with a high school girl we interviewed for our intern position. A girl who used to live in Medford, Oregon."

Medford . . . of course . . . "Ellen Moore," Wetzon said.

"Yes." Smith beamed at her and patted Benny's arm. "Benny told me all about the tragedy. Go on, Benny, tell Wetzon. I could never do the story justice."

"Well, I don't know. I hate telling stories out of school. . . . I don't want to hurt the kid."

"You told me, Benny. Tell her."

"Okay, I guess. You girls aren't going to let it get out of this room, right?"

"Right," Wetzon said.

"Positively," Smith said.

"Listen, she's just a kid, but in Medford we called her Baby Death."

chapter 64

Wetzon looked at Smith with horror. "How did she get that name?"

"Let Benny finish," Smith snapped. She pointed to Benny. "Go on with your story."

Benny grinned. "You remind me of my wife, Smith."

Smith scowled.

Benny's grin faded. "Okay. It's because everyone around her dies. First, her father dies when she's ten or so."

"I thought he had cancer," Wetzon said.

"Yeah. They confirmed that when they exhumed his body."

"Exhumed his body," Wetzon murmured. She felt a little dizzy.

"Anyway, her mother dies a few years later. Course, Viv Moore liked her hooch, so when she fell down the cellar stairs and cracked her head open, no one was real surprised. Then it turned out that maybe she was pushed. Baby Death admitted it was an accident when her mother tried to hit her, claimed Viv was abusing her. They took it to trial and got a hung jury. Twice. Third time, called it involuntary manslaughter. She served a few months in one of those juvenile detention places. The boyfriend got five years."

"Wow," Wetzon said. "Did you say 'the boyfriend'?"

"Yeah. She said he set up the whole thing."

"Tell about the old lady," Smith prompted.

"Yeah, old Mrs. Applegate, the neighbor, took the kid in afterward. The old lady had a bad heart and the kid was supposed to help her out around the house. Maybe eight or nine months, the old lady's heart gives out. Boy, let me tell you, everyone was relieved when the kid left town and came East. Figure in New York everyone's like Ellen Moore. Maybe you should hire an exorcist when she goes to work for you. Haw, haw."

"God," Wetzon said.

"Seriously, there are people who give off this kind of energy," Benny said. "I read about it once."

"Well, I'm not sure we should hire her. What do you think, Wetzon?" Smith ground her eyes into Wetzon.

"I don't think so, especially since we have at least two other really outstanding candidates."

Smith made a big show of checking her watch. "Oh, my, Benny, look at the time. You'd better get going, sugar." She took his arm and wrestled him out of his chair, steering him toward the door. "It was so grand spending time with you. And by the way, Wetzon and I feel certain by accepting the Rivington Ellis offer you're going to just fly through the next tier into portfolio management. You'll have so much support, plus an advertising budget; it will leave you plenty of opportunity to bring in new business."

"Thank you, Smith. Hope you'll feel better, Wetzon. I'll think it all through on the way home tomorrow. You can be sure of that."

Smith rushed him out the door, closed it and leaned against it. "That brilliant, beautiful child is a serial killer."

"We don't know that for sure, but . . . I'm calling Silvestri." Wetzon picked up the phone and punched in Silvestri's number. "I thought it was A.T. A.T. is in danger."

"Oh, my God. We should call her and warn her."

A man answered. "Silvestri's line."

"Is he there? It's important."

"No, but I can take a message."

"How about Mulcahy?"

"Not here."

"Okay, page Silvestri, please. Tell him Leslie Wetzon needs him to call her right away." She gave the cop Veeder's number. She hung up. Damn. She stood stock-still for a moment, then went into the bedroom, returned with her shoulder bag.

Smith's hand was on the phone.

"What are you doing?" Wetzon said.

"We have to warn A.T."

"We can't. If we do, we'll alert Baby Death. Besides, A.T. won't believe us. She'll protect Ellen with her dying breath."

"So what do we do?"

Wetzon took Smith's arm. "Let's go," she said.

chapter 65

Riverside Drive was still bathed in bright sunlight, but the shadows cast by the apartment houses were lengthening. The foliage on the trees in Riverside Park was so lush and dense one could hardly see into the park.

"Pay the driver." Smith opened the door to the cab and stepped out. "All I have is plastic."

"So what else is new?" Wetzon gave the driver eight dollars and joined Smith on the sidewalk in front of A.T.'s building. Two small boys were sauntering up the street, one had a catcher's mask over his face; the other, dragging a bat, was talking on a cell phone. Wetzon moved out of their way. Her legs were still a little rubbery. She took a deep breath. "Okay, let's go."

But Smith was already speaking to the doorman.

"Wait." When Smith paused, Wetzon took her aside out of the doorman's hearing. "Use your name. A.T. could be pissed at me because I told Silvestri she was responsible for the rice pudding."

Smith told the doorman, "Ms. Smith to see Ms. Barron."

"And the other lady?" the doorman asked.

Smith stared at Wetzon through slitted eyes.

"Ms. Marple," Wetzon said.

When the doorman stepped into a cubbyhole to ring up A.T., Smith said, "Very amusing."

"I try. I do try." Wetzon looked outside. Too soon for Silvestri, but damned if her bodyguard, Huberman, wasn't standing across the street puffing on a cigar. The sight was oddly reassuring.

The doorman returned. "You can go right up. 8A."

A.T.'s welcoming smile for Smith disappeared instantly when she saw Wetzon. "You!" She shook a finger at Wetzon. "You told that cop I poisoned you with the goddam pudding. The police were here for hours. They just left." She ran nervous fingers through the disheveled frizz on her head, something she'd clearly been doing for a while, because with that hair and her sharp pale features, she had the aspect of a creature of the wild.

"Where's Ellen?" Smith asked, getting right to the point.

"Ellen?"

"Yes, A.T., this is very important," Wetzon said.

"You don't know how helpless this all makes me feel."

Smith took A.T. by the shoulders and gave her a small shake. "Ellen, A.T., for pity sakes, where is she?"

Stunned by Smith's manhandling, A.T. stammered, "She went . . . to the hospital to see Todd."

"Oh, no," Wetzon groaned. "She's going to put him out of his misery."

"What's going on?" A.T. demanded. "No one tells me anything. It's like Daddy all over again: 'Alice, you don't have to know.' "

"A.T.," Smith screamed. "Your daddy's been dead for ten years. Get a goddam *life!*"

"Let's get out of here." Wetzon tugged at Smith.

"Wait," A.T. screamed. "Tell me what this is about. You've got to leave Ellen alone. She's been through so much—"

But Smith and Wetzon were running down the hall. Smith pressed the down button again and again. They watched A.T. come toward them. Where was the elevator?

"Please—" A.T. said.

"Who told you I like rice pudding?" Wetzon asked.

"You mentioned it when we first met, then Bill asked me to make some up for you."

"Where is the goddam elevator?" Smith screamed, punching the button with her fist.

"Bill called and asked you to make the pudding?"

"Well, not directly. He had his associate, Jonathon, do it. Please tell me where you're going."

The elevator arrived and they got on. Smith said, "Go back inside, A.T., and take a Valium."

Out on the street, Wetzon said as they looked for a taxi, "Jonathon is Ellen's new boyfriend."

Not a cab in sight, wouldn't you know? Only Huberman leaning against a tree smoking his cigar.

Wetzon waved frantically to him. "Put out that bloody cigar and come with us."

Taken by surprise, he dropped the cigar and crossed the street.

"Who's this?" Smith's lip curled, registering his thick chest and cheap suit.

"My bodyguard," Wetzon said. "We're going to Lenox Hill Hospital, Huberman, to try to stop a killing. Let's combine forces. Can you get us over there?"

He said in a surprising basso voice, "Let me handle this." He charged ahead of them to West End Avenue and instantly flagged down a cab.

Smith and Wetzon got in the back and Huberman sat in front with the driver, a man with a turban.

"Lenox Hill Hospital," Huberman said. "Make it fast." He shifted his attention to the backseat. "What's all this about?"

"I don't think that's any of—" Smith began.

"Shut up, Smith. A sixteen-year-old killer named Ellen Moore is going to pull the plug on her boyfriend. We're trying to stop it."

chapter 66

They raced into the lobby of the hospital and then were stopped short by the crowds. It was visiting hours and a steady stream of people came in from the street carrying flowers, books, suitcases.

Smith forced her way to the information desk. "Todd Cameron," she said to a kind-faced black woman.

"402," the woman said, without consulting her computer screen. How odd, Wetzon thought. She knows the room without checking.

"You girls leave this to me." Huberman's face was florid. Sweat dripped as if someone had poured a bucket of water over him. "I'll take the stairs. The elevators in this place are a mess."

Wetzon lost sight of him immediately, but hell, he seemed to know what he was doing.

"I'm sorry," the woman at the desk said. "Only the family is allowed up. His sister is with him now. She just went up."

"His sister?" Wetzon said. "Todd has no sister."

"Oh, dear me."

"Don't 'oh, dear me,' lady," Smith said severely. "Call hospital security at once. We are Todd's aunts. We just flew in from California and his dear mother is expecting us."

"There's really nothing to worry about," the information woman said, somewhat agitated. She picked up the phone. "Security, please." To Smith she said, "Now don't you worry, dear. There's a policeman right outside his door."

"How long is this going to take?" someone yelled. An impatient line had formed behind them.

"We've been waiting a half hour," complained another voice.

"Liar," Smith sneered.

"Okay, okay." The woman behind the desk was growing more and more distressed. She hung up the phone. "Go on up," she told Smith.

Hordes of people stood in front of the elevators, and when one arrived and emptied, everyone rushed on at once. And, of course, it was a local and stopped at every floor. People pushed off, staff pushed on. Wetzon said, "Good thing Huberman took the stairs."

Even before the elevator doors opened on the fourth floor, they heard the thumping sound of footsteps. They were immediately gathered into the turmoil, buzzers going off, nurses and doctors running from all directions.

"We're too late," Wetzon told Smith. She felt faint. "Go see. You can make it faster than I can right now. I'll wait here."

Wetzon watched Smith go off down the hall. She leaned against the wall, her knees quavering. She was never going to make it. She'd been running on adrenaline; now it had caught up with her.

A candy machine stood near the bank of elevators. Chocolate. She groped in her purse for some change.

Smith came rushing back. She was wearing a white coat with a hospital ID tag clinging to the lapel. "Somebody pulled his plug."

"Is he dead?"

"They're trying to resuscitate him."

"Where was the cop?"

"The cop stepped away to pee."

"Did you see Huberman?"

"No. He probably went to the wrong floor."

"Why are you wearing that coat?"

"It looks rather nice on me, doesn't it?" Smith pulled a stethoscope from the pocket and hung it around her neck.

"Jesus, Smith. You'd better give the costume back to Dr. S. Grover."

"Who's that?"

"That's the ID pinned to the coat."

"Oh, for pity sakes. What you should be doing instead of criticizing me is seeing if Ellen's still around. Don't these serial murderers usually lurk in the crowd to watch what happens?"

"Sometimes, I guess." Wetzon was clutching the candy machine like a lover. One day, she thought, she would have to bail Smith out of jail for one of her crazy stunts.

"What's the matter with you?"

"I feel a little light-headed."

"Well, don't just stand there hugging that machine. Get a candy bar." She threw those last words over her shoulder, then took off to continue her impersonation of Dr. S. Grover.

Wetzon's head began to throb. Silvestri was right. She shouldn't try to do cop work. At least not when she was feeling so rotten. Where the hell had Huberman gotten to? She put coins into the machine and punched the button for Hershey. The bar slid right out. She propped herself up in the small space between the machine and the doors leading to the east wing, which was the opposite direction from where Todd Cameron lay dead or dying, and tore the paper off the candy bar. She took a big bite.

Out of the corner of her eye she saw a door on the other side of the elevator bank edge open. Someone peered out. Wetzon flattened herself against the vending machine.

Ellen Moore, wearing a scarf over her hair and dark glasses, stepped out of the ladies' room and headed for the door marked EXIT. She opened the door and slipped through.

chapter 67

"Oh no you don't," Wetzon said. "You are not going to get away with this."

Two nurses went by, giving her only a casual look.

If only, Wetzon thought, she had one of those dreadful phones. She took another huge bite of the chocolate and headed for the EXIT door through which Ellen had just gone. She pulled it open and followed her.

"Get help!" a woman cried. "There's a man down here having a heart attack."

The staircase was well lit, and while it wasn't the best means of travel, it was certainly faster than the elevators. Nurses and attendants used it more often than visitors, which was lucky for Huberman. He was sprawled on the landing, gasping for breath, his color gray. Near his hand was a cell phone. Wetzon moved out of the way as a nurse ran past her up the stairs.

"My God, Huberman!" To the nurse kneeling beside him, Wetzon said, "His name is Huberman." He groaned. Beady sweat oozed down his face.

"Hold on, Mr. Huberman," the nurse said. "You're in the best place to have a heart attack."

Wetzon straightened. "Did a girl come down the steps a minute or so ago?"

"Yes," the nurse replied. "She didn't even stop when I asked her to go back and get help." A door opened above them and two orderlies came down the stairs with a stretcher. "Oh, good," the nurse said.

Wetzon watched them go, then picked up Huberman's cell phone and called Silvestri. "This is Leslie Wetzon again. Is he there?"

"Silvestri said if you called I should find out where the hell you are."

"Sounds just like him. Tell him I'm at Lenox Hill Hospital. Ellen Moore just pulled the plug on Todd Cameron and she's at least two floors below me right now. I'm going after her. Over and out." She slipped the phone in her bag and headed down the stairs.

She stopped on the second floor. Just below her, she could hear the sound of body mass meeting door, rattling the panic bar, punching, thump, thump. The door to the street was either stuck or locked.

Wetzon came down the last flight of stairs, fighting her weak knees. Ellen was in a frenzy, crying, beating on the door with her fists, kicking it.

"Do you want me to help you?" Wetzon said calmly. She sat on the steps.

With an odd, mechanical motion, Ellen stopped beating on the door. She turned and focused wide, babydoll eyes on Wetzon. "I was just taking a shortcut to the street."

"After putting your boyfriend where he can't get in your way?"

"Todd's not my boyfriend."

"Then why are you here?"

"His parents asked me to come."

"Did they really? I thought his mother didn't like you."

"They're really dreadful people." Ellen made a clucking sound. "Poor Todd. I always try to do the right thing for everyone, but they don't listen."

"Excuse me? You poisoned Sheila Gelber and Micklynn, not to mention Todd. You destroyed Micklynn's cat. And you say you always try to do the right thing?"

"It's very simple," Ellen said, turning back to the door. "I don't expect you to understand."

"Try me."

"Micklynn did it to herself. She was a drunk, like Mama. I was just helping Mama down the stairs. It wasn't my fault she fell. She was abusing me and anyway, Sam did it."

"Sam, your boyfriend in Medford?"

Ellen nodded.

"And you helped Micklynn over the side of Hem's boat?"

"Todd did that."

"Right. Was the old lady in Medford who took you in a drunk too?"

"Mrs. Applegate? No. She thought I was going to take care of her, wait on her. Who did she think I was?"

"How come she died?"

"She was old." Ellen gave Wetzon a hurt look. "You said you'd help me." Her fists beat on the door.

"What's going on down there?" someone called down the stairwell.

"Door's locked," Wetzon called back.

"Can't be. Give it a good push and stop all that racket."

Wetzon could feel the chocolate taking hold, finally. "Okay, I'll help you." She got up and came forward, leaned on the bar of the door. "Push on three. One, two, three."

The door didn't give.

"Awr," Ellen screamed, fists pounding the door. Her fists left a bloody imprint on the door.

"Tell me about Sheila Gelber. Push now."

The girl was panting, giving off a fetid animal odor. "She had articles from the Medford paper that said I spent four months in jail for involuntary manslaughter."

"Sheila was going to tell?"

"She was a very wicked person. She wanted to punish me. But I didn't do it. Todd did it."

"Todd ground up the azalea and put it in the corn muffins Micklynn was baking?"

"He was too dumb to do that. It was my idea. Todd did Jimmy."

"And Micklynn?"

"I hate drunks."

"She found out about you too."

"She had all this money. She didn't need it. I did. Why aren't you pushing?"

This time the push blew the door open and the force of it carried them both to the ground. People immediately surrounded them. As a man came forward to help, Ellen scrambled up, holding her arm, which was hanging at a strange angle. She forced her way through the crowd and began to run.

"Ellen, don't," Wetzon shouted, accepting the helping hand. "You'll never get away . . ." Nevergetaway, nevergetaway, music swirling in her head . . . around around . . . She was going to faint.

"Are you all right, miss?"

Bubble lights on a cop car, voices, people . . . slow motion. Stopped.

Ellen had run headlong into a woman with a shopping cart. The cart tipped over; Ellen staggered, went down. She picked herself up, progress slowed briefly, but now she was heading for Park Avenue. Wetzon went after her on wet-noodle legs.

"Les!"

Was that Silvestri? Sounded like him. Hooray for the cellular phone.

Ellen stopped suddenly, looking uptown. She swayed, began to move again. A tall man came into view. He was sprinting down Park Avenue toward them. Blue pinstripes.

Jeté passé. Wetzon poised in position. The jump threw her forward. Contact! Her grip so intense, she forced them both to the sidewalk.

Ellen's forehead hit the cement with a dull smack.

"What the hell? Leslie, what are you doing?" Bill crouched over her, staring into her face. His blue pinstripe was wrinkled. He tried to peel her hands away from Ellen but she held on. "Not *Gaslight,*" she said. "Not *Gaslight.*"

Then she let go. Mulcahy and another detective led a dazed Ellen Moore away.

"Get out of the way, Veeder," Silvestri said, bending over her. "You okay, Les?"

Veeder ignored him. He gave Wetzon his hand and she sat up.

"Who the hell knows?" Wetzon rubbed her bruised elbows. "Where were you, Silvestri? Do I have to do everything myself?"

epilogue

September

The opening reception at the Rodman Gallery on West Broadway was crowded with well-wishers. Louie's paintings, great slashes of color, were mounted and lit beautifully. Half were already marked with the blue sold dot.

A radiant Louie Armstrong wore black silk pants and a fitted quilted vest, her red hair natural and bohemian, as befitting an artist.

Pam Rodman said, "The response has been wonderful. We already know the *Times* is good. *Vanity Fair* wants to do a photo session."

Louie shook hands with Bill Veeder while Wetzon hovered, holding her breath for a comment. "Nice bones," Louie said, studying Bill's face. She smiled at Nina Wayne, the forensic anthropologist and Louie's lover. "Or have I stolen your line?"

"I think we've met before," Nina said, shaking Bill's hand.

"We have. We discussed the possibility of your consulting on a case a few years ago."

Bill Veeder knew enough people here tonight to make it seem as if he was there on his own invitation. Wetzon watched him work the room. He stopped to talk to Arthur Margolies, and Carlos joined them.

Champagne flowed, but not into Wetzon's glass; she didn't like it and it didn't like her. She stood in front of the painting Louie had given her, which Wetzon had loaned to the show. Its vivid emotion had stirred something Wetzon had buried deep. It still did. For others as well, it seemed. "Isn't it fabulous?" a white-haired man said. "Too bad it's been sold."

"Methinks I've seen this beauty before," Carlos said, planting a kiss on Wetzon's nose.

"Me or the painting?"

"What painting?" He took her hand. "Come vit me."

"Vere are you taking me?"

"Don't always be asking questions, Birdie. Just say, for once, 'Yes, darling, whatever you say, darling.' "

She scrunched up her face to show what an effort it was. "Yes, darling, whatever you say, darling."

"Now, Dear Heart." Carlos put his arm on her shoulders. "Tell us how it's going."

"How do I look?"

"Let's see, is ripe the word?"

"Ripe?"

"Well, you're floating around with this sappy Mona Lisa smile and a kind of pregnant sheen."

"Pregnant? I don't think so."

"A mere figure of speech, my darling. Covers the stars in your eyes. So what is it? Tell Uncle Carlos."

"Uncle Carlos," she said, "I'm crazy in love. It's scary, like letting go without a safety net."

"Aw, Birdie mine." He hugged her. "I'd say, be careful, but I'm afraid it's too late."

"Too late for what?" Bill Veeder asked. His hand touched Wetzon's.

Carlos patted her topknot. "If you hurt my Birdie, big boy, you'll have to answer to me."

"Carlos!" Wetzon felt a mortified flush rise from the throat.

"And a host of others, it seems," Bill said with good humor. "Is it all right if I take Leslie away now and feed her?"

"Why don't you ask Leslie?" Wetzon snapped. She gave Carlos a sharp nudge with the toe of her shoe. "She's reached a terrifying age and can make mature decisions for herself."

Carlos caught her and whispered in her ear. "Not if she thinks with her—"

"Where are we?" Bill was full of surprises. He'd taken her to a small pizzeria-type restaurant in the section of the City known as Little Italy. He'd been greeted by the owner, as more friend than client.

"Lombardi's," Bill said. "The best pizza in New York is made here."

"Better than John's?"

"Yes. How about pizza with fresh clams? Their specialty."

"This makes me so happy. I thought at first that you didn't like food."

"Why would you think that?"

"No food in your fridge."

"I missed you. The Vineyard was—"

"I couldn't." He'd sent her tickets and she'd gotten in the cab and ridden as far as Fifth Avenue. Then she'd told the driver to turn around and take her home.

"For a while there you thought I might be the killer. *Gaslight,* you said."

She smiled. "It was the blue pinstripe. Todd's doorman said a man in a blue pinstripe had brought him home. Seems ridiculous now, but things happened between us so fast. I didn't trust it. It seemed too slick."

"I think you meant *Suspicion,* not *Gaslight.*"

"Cary Grant may or may not be trying to kill his wife."

"That's *Suspicion.* In *Gaslight,* it's Charles Boyer."

"Oh, dear, I much prefer Cary Grant to Charles Boyer."

"I'm going to defend Ellen Moore," he said.

"I'm sorry."

"She's entitled to a defense. That's my job."

"And A.T. will foot the bill. I guess Ellen's entitled, but she's a monster. She killed five people and has no remorse. You're going to plead insanity?"

"She isn't sane."

"What about the baby?"

"What baby?" He was probably a great poker player, because he didn't give anything away.

"Wasn't there an adoption agreement between Ellen and Hem and Min?"

"Now how would you know that?"

"Um . . ." She separated her knife and fork, moved them from one side to the other.

"Remind me never to leave you alone in my office."

She grinned at him. "My guess is there was no baby. Ellen is pathological. She lies. Am I right?"

"Attorney-client privilege."

"Did you ever read a book called *The People of the Lie* by a psychiatrist named Scott Peck?"

"No."

"You ought to. You'll find your client there."

"Thank you for the advice."

She squinted at him. Was he making fun of her?

A sudden, decidedly unpleasant thought came to her. "You're going to call me to testify."

"Yes." Flat out, there it was. "I have to."

She threw up her hands. "Hey, what the hell. What did you do about Jonathon?"

"I fired him. His behavior was unprofessional and inappropriate; his judgment was atrocious. Of course, he's not the first man to be besotted by a woman."

She raised her beer to him. "I'll drink to that."

He reached across the table, held her chin for a moment. "Your friends . . ." He paused.

"My friends?"

"Margolies and Carlos, and the two . . . lesbians. They've all warned me in no uncertain terms that I'll be dog meat if I hurt you."

"I love my friends."

"I would never hurt you. I'm in love with you."

"You're married." She held up her hand. "Don't say it. My friends know me." She thought, *If you don't take risks because you're afraid of*

320

getting hurt, what kind of life do you have, after all? Can you say at the end of it, I've lived fully? She'd always been a risk taker, albeit a timid one.

Who risks starvation and security to become a dancer? Who leaves dancing to open a business in a profession totally unfamiliar to her with a partner she hardly knows? Who ends a relationship with a solid citizen like Alton Pinkus, who wants to marry her?

As for Silvestri, their entire relationship had been fraught with risk, and she'd gotten hurt.

But she wouldn't rewrite anything so far. Basically she loved her life, for better, for worse.

So, was Bill Veeder, the married man, a risk? Oh, yes. Should she play it safe and walk away because she might get hurt? Never. She would take the risk. She was forty years old and the rest of her life was ahead of her. Whatever it held for her would be a surprise. That's the way she wanted it.

"Leslie?"

"Bill?"

"Tell me."

"Gender games are not my style, Bill Veeder. I never went to singles bars, never did a share on Fire Island or in East Hampton. My friends . . . they know. They're afraid for me. I want you. It's a constant. Maybe this is what happens to forty-year-old spinsters whose hormones are percolating."

"Leslie, I don't give a damn about hormones, or spinsters, or how old you are. If I were free I would marry you. As I'm not, I want you in my life any way you'll have me."

"Marriage never interested me. I don't want to be anybody's mother. I've never felt maternal. However we can do it, I want you in my life."

"Then it's a deal," he said gravely. "Let's shake on it."

Lordy, lordy, she thought, but she gave him her hand. "It's a deal," she said.